Quality Focused | Custom Art Glass | Guaranteed Products

I0524975

Providing the Highest Quality
Raw Materials for Glass Artists
Around the World

For More Information
on Borro Glass Studio visit:
www.borroglass.com

A Borosillicate Product Manufacturer

THE
GUARDIAN
ANGEL
OF DEATH

JOHN DERHAK

MOOSE HARBOR BOOKS
IN THE HEART OF THE LOST KINGDOM

THE GUARDIAN ANGEL OF DEATH

"The best deception is the one we ourselves believe in, and that is always the sort of deception that saves our lives." Alan Furst

For Mary Augusta
Oh mother of mine,

& Uncle Del

who once upon a time, many, many years ago, convinced a very young boy that he played third base for the Brooklyn Dodgers.

This book is

moe.

APPROVED.For

moe.

INFORMATION
PLEASE SEE:

moe.org

When the Ghost Becomes the Haunted
Porter Gibson 'Digit'
Journal Entry
24 December 1932

A man came to me one day—walked right out of the past. We talked for some time, and spoke of many things. If not for his eyes I would have been surprised when, from the blue, he mentioned to me how heavy the weight is that he carries now of a secret. It was given to him unexpectedly—suddenly—with no recourse but to listen.

"When one divulges their past they transfer to you the guilt and shame of a thousand sleepless nights and move on the journey," he said. "It's yours, then and there, to hold. The pain is transferred to you without time limits. Such are the ironies of life that the ghost becomes the haunted."

He went on to say that he now knows what Robinson Crusoe dreamt as he lay down night after night—the day to be freed from the solitude of captivity. For Crusoe did not want to be castaway on that isle any more than he wanted to be held captive by a secret.

All but for a chance meeting.

Now I stand upon a shore.

Look upon a restless sea.

I wonder, watch, and wait—where and how and when—I will be set free.

1932, Early Fall

Prelude to a Storm

The man leaned back in his armchair slowly, nervously. A revolver, the barrel of which could have housed Lou Gehrig's baseball bat, was inches from his face. So close, the odor of its oily residue filled his head. He could pretty near lick the damned thing. That option was not on the table, however—he wasn't holding the gun. That would be one of the two men who had crept into his front parlor—somehow—where just moments before, he sat alone reading the newspaper; taking sips from a glass of Scotch whisky and gently puffing a cigar. They had come into the house, without warning or invitation, under the cover of darkness and an approaching storm. Opened and shut the parlor door without notice. He had lowered the paper to take a sip of whisky and they, and the gun, were there. Fear, sudden and complete, rushed through him. The paper slipped out of his hands. The cigar fell from between his lips, bounced off his lap, and onto the floor. He wavered on the brink. In all certainty, he was fit to shit himself. The great Houdini could not have conjured such magic so dramatically to such an end.

Ah, the end.

The evening was late. The radio had signed off and he had been minutes from bed. The headlines in the paper had been of little interest to him. A depression was on and a fella named Roosevelt was running for President. Another man, Brann, a Maine Democrat, had just won the governor's seat. That bode well for the fella named Roosevelt. In a matter of weeks, he'd find out if it was true, the old adage, "As Maine goes, so goes the nation." The Association Against the Prohibition Amendment had held a rally in Bangor Tuesday. Roosevelt had pledged to end the social experiment. Yet, politics and the economy didn't matter to the man in the chair. His interest had been drawn to a pair of stories on page three. The two men shot dead in a Cape Cod warehouse in August were related to illegal smuggling, one story had read. The other story had been closer to home—the waning coverage of a local fisherman whose body had floated in on Moose Harbor. The blow to the head must have resulted in the fall overboard, the coroner had determined, rendering him unconscious, which resulted in the fisherman's drowning. But what caused the blow to the head?

He had been so engrossed with the latter story, he had not heard a thing except the sound of distant thunder and the wind, which, he now realized, had betrayed him. It had rattled and rocked the old house,

5

muting the sound of their entry. He glanced from one man to the other and back at the gun barrel. The two before him were in long, dark overcoats, and stared menacingly from under dark fedoras. The scene was eerie and frightening, and another wave of fear rushed at him.

Never one to ponder the fates, he did now. Thinking of the years he'd spent at sea, fishing and lobstering, the catch and the haul. Sweat and toil went hand-in-hand with the brush of death that confronts a man daily when he sets out on a thirty-foot trawler to challenge the elements and harvest the sea of its life. He thought of that—life—the life he had made for himself and his wife Mildred, and the family they had raised. There, on the eastern frontier of Maine, on the shores of Bean's Point, in the Lost Kingdom of Moose Harbor. How fortunes here had risen and fallen with the rest of the country, if not the world, these past four years. The lobster catch had gone bust, but he had found a way to survive. He had always found a way to survive.

The shorter of the two men had walked up to him where he sat. The pistol was in his hand. He was sure the shorter man was going to pull the trigger without explanation. But then the taller one, who stood inside the parlor door, said, "I think you know why we're here, so I'll get to the point and we'll be off. Tell me, who have you been talking to?" He spoke softly, perhaps not wishing to disturb the other occupants in the house, all of whom were sleeping—or, more likely, to create an unnerving effect when he spoke. He had an accent; it was distinct and leant itself well to intimidation.

"Huh?" the man answered, utterly confused. "Who? About what?"

"I'll be more specific," the tall man said more forcefully. "Who did you speak with about your trip to Hyannis?"

The man in the chair thought about it for a moment, and then shook his head, "I don't know what you mean," he answered, barely above a whisper. "I've never set foot in Hyannis." He knew they wouldn't believe him anyway, but stalling meant surviving, he reasoned.

Survival, he had learned, and life, were a struggle. He had watched a man go under once, out to sea, while fishing. Though he had lunged to save him, the icy water sucked the man in when he fell, entangled, within his own nets. The man was his grandfather and namesake, Minard, and he never came up. There was no time to say goodbye.

That was the first time he had seen someone die—but not the last. He had survived six grisly months in France over the spring and summer of 1918. Serving with the 26th, named the Yankee division because all the boys were from New England. The Yankees were sent to a remote hamlet, the Village of Seicheprey, to await orders. Nothing he had ever seen, heard of, or trained for could prepare him for what happened there that April day. How the German Stormtroopers had descended on them, like winged demons, from the cover of *Foret de Mort Homme*—the Dead Man's Forest—took them all off guard. When they struck, the Stormtroopers, he was with some boys from Connecticut, visiting a distant cousin, a fellow who shared the same last name as him, Severance. Anarchy and disarray erupted with the first shots. A friend of his from Moose Harbor, who was serving with him, shouted out the warning. It was enough for those who heard him to find cover, but not enough to save himself. Flamethrowing Huns immolated men to his left and to his right. The battle—the fight—was a brawl really, to the death. Fierce hand-to-hand combat up and down the narrow lanes and into the village square seemed to linger for hours. It was as though they were standing and fighting in the center of the Coliseum of ancient Rome, he imagined, not in the middle of some village in rural France, unknown to the world but forever branded into the body and soul of each and every man that made it out alive. There were no spectators in this coliseum, either. The villagers had fled in fear for their lives or burrowed deeply into their cellars in terror. They, the Yankees, were farmers and factory workers fighting battle-hardened gladiators. So desperate was the fight to survive, the cooks and the regiment's marching band joined the rumble. He watched one cook deflect bayonet thrusts with a skillet in one hand and hack two German soldiers to death with his meat cleaver in the other. Minutes later, he saw a Stormtrooper get brained with a tuba. The fight was a sad, tragic affair. Yet, when the day was done, somehow, he had survived.

The tall man, who had studied him for the past minute, sighed. "I don't believe you, but I would not expect anything less from you." The man was a Scot. Minard had met up with a regiment from the Highlands on his way to France. This one's eyes were as dark as his features. His brows were thick and wide and as heavy as the moustache that narrowed to the corners of his mouth. His square jaw was covered by a day's, perhaps two days', growth. The other man's face was covered by a heavy growth too. They had traveled a distance without stopping, like hunters, he reasoned, to find him. But why? For what? These were hard men accustomed to leaving death in their wake, much like the Stormtroopers

7

at Seicheprey.

When he had made his way back home after the war, he thought all of that was behind him, the brutality of men—of humanity and its base predatory core—until now. The quiet safety of Moose Harbor was no more. There was the house fire which claimed the life of one of his mates. That left him unsure. He knew it was certain when they found his other mate drowned. An accident, they claimed, the risk a seafaring man takes, but Minard was wiser.

He found no solace that his children were mostly grown. They and Mildred were upstairs sleeping. If he shouted out or made a move in desperation, it would cost them their lives. Yet, he wanted to hold his wife one last time, look into her eyes, breathe in her essence, and say goodbye. He wanted to tell his children to make good with their lives, and above all, be happy. Minard knew, like his grandfather, there would be no time. All he could do was stare helplessly at the revolver in his face, make no sound, and hope none of them, his family, came downstairs.

"Do you know who I am?" the tall Scot asked.

Minard shook his head again, but said, without thinking, "One of the bad guys."

The Scot smiled. "That is relative to whose side one is on," he answered. "Or if one believes there are any sides at all."

"Who are you, then?" asked Minard.

"I am a messenger," the tall man replied, "and I have a message for you to deliver."

With those words, the man with the revolver lowered the pistol from Minard's face, then turned and stepped beside the tall Scot. Minard eased slightly in his chair. His bowels quaked. Beads of sweat, which had formed on his forehead and temples in those tense moments with the gun in his face, released, sliding down his face.

"Do you think you can deliver a message?" the Scot asked him.

"Yes," Minard said, and relaxed. He reached for his glass, and said, "May I?" The Scot nodded.

"It's an important message," the Scot said, "for the people you run for."

Minard swallowed some whisky, and welcomed its burn. Somehow, he had survived, again, the brutality of men. When they left he would finish the bottle. "What do you want me to say to them?" he asked, and placed the tumbler down.

"It's not so much what I want to say to them, but the statement I wish

8

to make to them," he replied.

"What might that statement be?" Minard asked, befuddled.

"Mr. Smith," the tall Scot addressed his companion. "Please convey to the man the statement we wish to send."

Minard looked at Mr. Smith, who stood to the right of the Scot, but Minard became momentarily distracted by a sudden burst of wind that struck the house, and a loud thunderclap that followed immediately. The vibration rattled the windows and made the house timber creak and settle. In the distraction, he did not notice Mr. Smith raise his hand. Only when the lightning bolt struck and the second thunderclap exploded overhead did Minard notice Mr. Smith had his revolver aimed at him. He fired it as the thunder rolled—before Minard could react. The bullet struck him above his right eye and exited through the back of his skull into the fabric of the chair.

The paralytic grasp of his physical being was as instantaneous as the torturous pain. Slumped to the back and left corner of the chair, Minard felt the intense burn of the bullet's trajectory through his head. White hot needles, millions, singed the nerve endings of his brain along its path. He wanted to scream in agony as the scalding ice pick sensation penetrated his skull and streamed through his body. But he could not move, motion, or scream.

His attention shifted from the pain and was drawn to the two men, where, for the first time, he noticed an inky, dark aura that seemed to envelope them. More alarmingly, even darker shadowy figures stood, or hovered actually, by them. Mr. Smith began to walk toward him, unencumbered by the darkness bound to his essence. Minard's first reaction was to jump at him, but as much as he willed himself to move, he could not. Mr. Smith placed the revolver in Minard's limp hand. Unexpectedly, one of the dark figures moved away from Mr. Smith's side and came closer to Minard. Eyes, set deep within its head, which Minard had not noticed before, began to smolder and glow like embers. The thing peered at him closely and sniffed several times. It appeared to smile, or at least Minard thought so at first, by the even darker, oily pitch of its mouth, which reeked of rot and waste. But then the thing's mouth continued to spread and open wider, forming a gaping hole, a dark, rancid pit, as though it was preparing to devour *him*. Minard distinctly heard a guttural, primordial growl bellow up from deep within the cavity, followed by another, and then several more. He was defenseless against the thing, and was struck by fear when realizing, in all probability, that he was looking into the abyss of Hell itself, and he was seconds from being swallowed and cast into it.

But something happened. The air pressure around him shifted abruptly. The burn in his head began to recede, along with the pain. His thoughts drifted away from the hideous thing before him, and with it, all fear. In his mind's eye, his wife and children appeared, surrounding him, then his late parents, his siblings, his friends, and finally his grandfather. He saw his friend, too, the one who saved him in France. All of them crowded in around him. At the vision, the dark presence paused. Disappointed, angrily, its mouth closed slowly. Across the room a light flickered in midair, and from its center a vaporous purple haze began to sift through. It began to expand and billow and brighten. Mr. Smith turned and walked to the tall Scot, nodding, oblivious to the inky shadows and dark aura around them, and the increasing purple haze that spilled out and filled the room. The eyes of the thing in front of Minard dimmed, though. *It* could see the haze, and quickly it rushed to Mr. Smith's side, rejoining its host, finding its place among the other tarred demons.

The winged thing came from the ether, bursting into the room like a goddess affixed to the prow of a fleeting clipper ship. It was bathed in a radiant light, a violet hue, which filled the room with a warm glow. The thing wielded a scythe, too, that was starlit yet translucent. The gaze that fell upon Minard was one of angelic beauty, feminine and powerful. In her eyes he saw all there was and all he ever knew, but so much more. Through her eyes, he was sure, was immortal wisdom. "I am Markéta," she said, and then she swiped through some of the shadow figures with her scythe, leaving a swath of glistening amber stardust in its wake. That, and the inhuman squeal of the damned.

The winged thing reached Minard and took his hand. At the touch, a brilliant flash of violet burst through the room. The tall Scot and Mr. Smith could neither see Markéta nor the glow of purple haze that filled the parlor. The dark figures that clung to them, that she had not scythed, cowered at the flash and her presence, but the men, as men often do, remained indifferent to the light. What passed their eyes, a flash of lightning with a violet hue, went unnoticed.

"This is the end, then?" asked Minard, finally able to speak.

"No, old friend," Markéta answered.

Minard stood in spirit with the winged thing. Released from his body, he understood—became *aware*—as though he was and always had been—as though he had always known Markéta; who smiled, and then swung the blade of her scythe again, slicing open the fabric of time and space. Stars rippled and wobbled through matter. Purple light flowed out and a mass of energy, calm and peaceful, enveloped Minard. He drew on that energy, and that from within his very soul, and went with Markéta into the bliss.

The tall Scot and Mr. Smith went to the door. Quietly, they left the parlor without looking back at the body of Minard Severance. "Well stated," was all the Scot said to Mr. Smith, who acknowledged the remark with a nod as the pair left the house, fading into the night, like the roll of distant thunder.

Another Message

Ambrose stood beside a short row of file cabinets in a narrow office. The top drawer of one was open, which gave him just enough room to maneuver between that and his desk. He was, to say the least, crammed. Only a large window facing the street offered comfort. That gave the small room some illusion of depth. Often, he found himself gazing out it, as he was now, watching daylight fade and shadows fall across the old mountain beyond. The phone buzzed on his desk. He slammed the drawer shut and picked up the receiver. "This is Ambrose Hughes."

"Ambrose?" a voice spoke curtly.

"Yes, Mr. Crowe?"

"Come here. And bring the apothecary's file with you." The line went dead.

Ambrose turned and pulled the file, then walked the short distance down the hall and entered a spacious office. Across the room, Mr. Crowe sat with his hands clasped together on the center of his desk. A younger man than he, Thompson Crowe was not yet forty. He was thin and of medium height. His hair was light and receding in a widow's peak, below which, a set of dark, sunken eyes was already etched—the irony did not elude Ambrose—with *crow's* feet. Specks of gray had sprouted on his temples and the side of his head, too. With his hair slicked back it reminded Ambrose of greased straw. The overall appearance was that of an aged wolf, ten years older than he was. In contrast, though he was thirty-nine, Ambrose looked the part of a man ten years younger. He had come to work for the previous Mr. Crowe, Thompson's father, Wendell, by chance. Ambrose wanted out of the city, Boston, upon his return from Ireland following the war. Wendell, who knew Ambrose's father, reached out and hired him on as an assistant and confidante. After the accident, Ambrose reluctantly stayed on. For Thompson was overbearing and difficult on his best days.

At the moment, Thompson seemed lost in thought. With his hands folded together, he looked as though he were lost in prayer. Pious, actually, Ambrose thought, but improbable, unless he were praying for more foreclosures. For piety he was without. "The file, sir," Ambrose said. He approached the desk with the file extended.

"Leo's fallen behind on his note once again," he said.

"His dwelling?" asked Ambrose.

Thompson nodded. "I think he's fucking with me. But because he knows Sterling and knew old Jonah, I will give him till the end of the month."

"The Huxley accounts are very important, Mr. Crowe." He paused, then added, "Your father would have approved."

That seemed to register approval with Thompson, for he gave a quick nod. "I have another message from her, Ambrose, for that friend of yours to pass on." He handed him a sheet folded in half, vertically. Ambrose laid the file on the desk and took the sheet.

"When, Mr. Crowe?" he asked.

"Radio later this evening." He checked the clock on the wall. "Actually, 10 o'clock."

"Yes, sir," Ambrose answered. He took the sheet and tucked it in the breast pocket of his suit coat.

"Wait for confirmation of receipt, and do let me know tomorrow morning." He smiled, or maybe grimaced. Ambrose had lost the ability to tell the difference. Since Wendell's death, he was never that sure.

"I'll have the reply waiting for you in the morning, Mr. Crowe."

"Good, good, Ambrose," he said with a wave of his hand. "And dispose of it, per usual. You know what to do."

Ambrose nodded, and then left the office. Shutting the door behind him gently, he walked back to his office. The sheet of paper was open in his hand. A couple of lines. Cryptic and in code. In his head, he deciphered it in seconds. He had, after all, taught Wendell the code, who in turn had taught his son. Oddly, Thompson had never acknowledged that, and Ambrose wondered if Wendell had ever told him who he had learned the code from.

Or if he simply saw Ambrose as an automaton, one of Čapek's robots, programmed to function as factotum and radio operator. He reread the cipher and shook his head. More trouble of the kind he had left behind in the war.

He busied himself filing away the last of the foreclosure notices. Outside, the sky had darkened. When he had finished, he left for some time—took a meal at the Silent Woman Tavern, went to a show at the Bijou, and then returned to the office. By then, he heard the first rolls of thunder. Far enough away he thought he imagined it at first, but then he saw a flash of lightning, and then another. A storm, he thought, how strange for this time of year. But these were strange times.

Throughout the evening, the message came back to him. He couldn't stop thinking of what he had read, and worried for his friend in Boston, his counterpart. The radio transmissions were under constant surveillance by the Feds, he knew that for certain, but also, he feared, by the gangsters. He had warned him that the danger was very real, to be careful and cautious. His friend's only reply was, "God is on my side." Someone somewhere had to take notice. People were dying here. At 10 o'clock he sent the message via the radio, and then, with the strike of a match, disposed of the paper.

Chatham

Static, chatter, and then more static, more chatter—Pendleton had a headache. He rubbed his temples, adjusted the headset. The night lingered, no end in sight, like a stretch of rail on the high prairie. Six messages intercepted in the past seven hours. Each message was international commercial plain text, four in English, two in French. He usually averaged three or four an hour. The long-range receiver was on, the recorder was on. He played with the shortwave, adjusting the knobs; the needles floated on the dial. This puzzled him. Rum-row was never this quiet.

He was expecting at least one more transmission. Two days ago, he had an intercept at 46ºN 56ºW. He began to monitor the frequency. Yesterday another intercept, but at 45ºN 59ºW. A ship—departed St. Pierre et Miquelon and passed Sydney. It was heading down the Nova Scotia coast. He forwarded the ciphers, per usual, but there was nothing else on that frequency tonight.

He made himself comfortable. Lit a cigarette, sipped tea from a coffee cup. His back was against the wall, literally. The chair leaned into the wall panel. His hands were folded behind his head. His feet were propped on his desk. Maybe things were winding down, maybe this was really over. He thought of Kinsale, the war days in Ireland, his friends—the priest, the radioman, and the rebel—and the irony of how war could make life-long friends. He had been at this job since '23. The operation began at the RCA ship station in Chatham, the old Marconi place, where he worked, about three years after he arrived from New Brunswick. They found him walking by the Post Office Block in town—recruited out of the blue. Well, a man did, one Friday afternoon:

"Solomon, from the Times Radio in New York," he introduced himself, extending his hand.

Yes? Do I know you? Pendleton thought, shaking it weakly.

"You're the radioman for RCA's international circuits?" he asked.

Confused, he nodded, yes, one of them. "How did you know?"

"Why, you're our radioman—for the Times."

"I'm everyone's radioman."

"You're very good. We've been admiring your work."

"What do you want?"

"Ostensibly, you'll operate radio for the New York to London commercial circuit," he told him.

Ostensibly?—he hadn't heard that since the war—Wait! "That's what I do, what RCA hired me to do, what they pay me to do."

"International circuits are our primary intercept targets."

"Whoa! ... Intercept? ... Targets?"

"You'll be paid in cash."

"I could be deported."

"You will be naturalized within two weeks."

"I could get fired."

"Or promoted."

"How much cash?"

"How does $35 sound?"

"A month? Wow!"

"No, per week."

"How can I turn it down?"

"You can't."

"That's definitive."

"It is, yes."

"How do I know it will work?"

"I am the wise one."

"Solomon."

"Yes."

That was, vaguely, in his mind's eye, how it began. Monitor illegal radio traffic. Use RCA circuits. Conduct radio intercept. Prepare and mail the transcripts to Mr. W. Reynolds, Liberty Insurance, Bond Building, Washington, D.C.

It lasted a year, and they moved him out of RCA. Solomon visited him as before—unexpectedly. This time he appeared beside him as he walked out of the Orpheum in Chatham:

"You've performed admirably. We're making good progress."

Pendleton nodded appreciatively.

"We've come to a decision about you."

"I'm out."

"Yes."

"Just like that."

"No. Give RCA a proper notice."

"What?"

"Tell them it is government work."

"So, I'm in?"

"Am I not being clear enough?"

"Yes."

"We've established offices near the Marconi Station. You'll be right at home."

Pendleton liked his office. He liked the space, the view. He liked the Cape—warmer than Fredericton—up in the woods of New Brunswick. He liked living by the ocean. He wasn't meant for the forest. He wondered how long they would keep the office operating. Would RCA hire him again? There was a depression on now. Lines of people in every direction hoping for a day's work, let alone a job. He had learned a trade but felt vulnerable regardless. Didn't like it—had learned long ago in the navy about vulnerability—cover your ass—but they never said what to do when they put so much money in your hands it left your backside open and your ass exposed.

He could feel a draft now, and looked at the window. "Damn," he said, and got up and shut it, and then sat back down. Tapped a pencil. Sipped cool tea. Lit another cigarette. That's when the static broke, a signal, not commercial. Was that Nova Scotia checking in? No, a different frequency. He copied the information, encrypted and indecipherable. A ship? A shore station? No, an exchange at 44ºN 68ºW—the same coordinates from a few weeks back. Maine again. Could it be? Even though he already knew the answer, more out of habit, he grabbed a nautical chart from the bookshelf and ran his fingers to the location to be sure. "Moose Harbor?"

He wondered if he should wait for confirmation, or alert New York directly. He glanced at his watch. "Better wait," he mumbled.

The Visibility of the Dock

The visibility of the dock extending into Moose Harbor was limited, which lent itself well to the smuggling operation that had evolved there. A thick stand of cedar, pine and maple trees obstructed the dock from a broad meadow that bordered a distant county road. Harbor side, the dock was on the southern edge of a cove bordered by a natural granite wall, raked up and tossed there ten-thousand years before. A well-kept lawn, which rolled up to a large mansion, abutted the granite wall. The dock was wide enough and sturdy enough for a vehicle to drive on. It extended far enough that a schooner or trawler could dock there even at low tide. That had occurred on more than one occasion over the past decade. Boats arrived at all hours, loaded with whisky, rum, scotch, gin, beer and champagne. The cargo was loaded onto waiting trucks and cars that drove off into the night, off to cities and towns near and far, or stored in a small building near the dock until so.

The dock, then, offered privacy to conduct affairs rendered illegal by the 18th Amendment, commonly referred to as the Volstead Act: to satisfy an unquenchable thirst that Americans had for alcohol and profit directly from it—tax free—by the illegal importation, distribution, and sale of booze and beer.

The limited visibility of the dock was an asset for the two men who stood on it that morning, men who had profited greatly from the Volstead Act. They were alone, with the exception of the cormorants and gulls around them. The taller man watched one cormorant dive. The man next to him smoked a cigar anxiously, and looked about as though to reassure himself that they were indeed alone. Only the car the taller man had arrived in, and the occupant behind the wheel, were there. When he was satisfied, he asked, "Well?"

"It's done," the taller one replied. His accent was thick, Scottish.

"And?"

"He didn't have much to say, but then neither did the others. But I believe this one knew more than he said."

"How do you know?"

"It was in his eyes. When the end is nigh, the eyes of a man are worth a thousand words—if you take the time to look, you'll see much and learn more."

"*What?*" he pulled the cigar from his mouth. "Am I to understand you conducted your line of questioning by staring at him?"

"You're a sarcastic bastard, you know."

"Yes, I am. It's served me well through the years, living in this festering boondock."

"At the very least we saved him from himself … we saved him from his future … he will say nothing to no one that could jeopardize his friends and family in the years ahead. His secrets went with him."

"What the fuck are you talking about?" the man snapped, and drew on his cigar.

"Would you like to find out for yourself?"

He shook his head. "No," he said. "I understand."

"Good," the taller man said. "Because I'm beginning to think that you don't understand—understand how important it is to find *all* the men responsible for stealing from Mr. Walker, but even more so, how important it is to find the leak and plug the hole permanently. I found the thief, and I've a man on his way to Edinburgh as we speak. I'll send another to Shanghai if I have to, to find the one who told him. Do you know why?"

He clenched the cigar tightly between his teeth and shook his head no.

"Because this will *never* happen again."

"I've done my part."

"Have you? I know you're a wiseass and a sneaky bastard, and I sure as shit haven't plugged that hole, not with the people you've sent my way, and I've been backtracking for weeks now."

"I passed on what little information I had," he defended himself. "Hell, I had no knowledge of a warehouse, let alone where it was or what the fuck was going on with it."

"What about the radio?"

"The *radio?*" he replied, genuinely perplexed.

"We picked up a shore-to-shore from around here to Boston passing news about a certain fisherman who drowned. We've tracked the location there. It will be dealt with."

"What has that to do with me?"

"You must deal with it here."

He stoked his cigar until the end glowed red, clenched it tighter, and said, "I don't know about any radio, but if the news came from here, I'll find it."

"If it came out of here, you'd better find it," the tall man said.

"I've put everything on the line for this operation, and held up my end," he snapped. "We've processed millions and come clean each and every time. It's my ass on the line, not yours. So if I do get wind of any damned radio bull I'll let you know."

The tall man breathed deeply, holding his anger, and said, "You can come down off the cross now. I'll return for the next shipment and finish the job."

"You can greet him here, and whoever else is with him, and jump 'em. He's asked a friend to help."

"What friend?" he interrupted.

"Ask Mr. Walker. I've already run it by him."

The tall man glared angrily at the words.

"I'll arrange a drop. Another accident—steer the boat back out to the harbor to sink—something like that—*be* creative. Just no blood this time." He paused. Puffed casually on the cigar for a moment, then added, "I gutted a dozen haddock down here after a fishing trip last summer, and have had a bear of a time rinsing the blood off the dock. It stains, you know."

"Listen, you fuck—understand I'll be talking to Mr. Walker about *everything.* You have the rest of the properties *sold* by the end of next month and the money ready. I want to be done with this."

He nodded slowly and ash fell from the cigar to the lapel of his coat. The taller man did not see him nod. He had turned and walked to the car. As he brushed the ash off his coat, he noticed the driver, though. His eyes were set upon him, at once, wolfish, diabolical and deranged. The end of next month could not come soon enough. For then, he would be rid of these bastards forever.

The Equitable Building

A man in a dark suit and overcoat lumbered down Broadway, lost in thought. A gust of wind struck him broadside as he passed an alley. His fedora went airborne but he snatched it at arm's length and dropped it back on his head. The sidewalk was crowded even for a Monday morning. Clerks and secretaries rushed by in each direction. Horns blared from passing cabs. Newsies shouted out headlines, but he didn't hear what they said, only the sound they were making. A thin man, unshaven and worn—a bum—draped with a sign board that read, *Jesus is the Road to Salvation, Visit The Reverend John Chapman's Shelter, Exfoliating Salvation to Soothe the Soul Since 1924,* stood near the curb. As he passed him the man held out a coffee can, and asked, "Donation for the Reverend John Chapman's Shelter, sir?" The bum's eyes were glossy and gray as the sky above. He paused and dropped a coin in the can. It bounced and rolled. Monday was a slow day for alms. "Thank you, sir," the bum said, and the man acknowledged the gesture with a nod, and continued walking. Further down the block he came to a stop, looked up at where he was, in front of the Equitable Building, and walked to the entrance. A doorman was there, as he was each morning, and greeted him cheerfully, as he did each morning. "Morning, Mr. Redfern," he said, holding the door.

"Morning, Seymour," he replied. "A pleasant day."

"Looks like rain, today, I think, Mr. Redfern."

"Yes," he replied. "I should have brought the umbrella."

Seymour looked confused at the remark.

"I meant a pleasant day to *you*, Seymour," Mr. Redfern added with a smile, and went to the elevator and stepped in.

"Thirty-four, please, Whit," he said to the elevator operator.

"I know, Mr. Redfern," he replied. "I may be old, but I'm not daft." He smiled, and then added, "Just don't ask the wife."

They laughed, and the elevator began to launch.

"How's the insurance game, sir?" Whit asked.

"We're still ahead in the game, Whit," he replied. "Doing better than the Giants."

"So I heard," Whit said. "It's gonna be a long season."

"It will be, if they don't learn to tackle."

The elevator came to a stop and the doors parted. "Have a good week, sir," said Whit. Mr. Redfern, with a tip of his hat, stepped out. The door shut behind him. He walked the length of the corridor until he stood

19

before a door. A brass plaque beside it read, *Mutual Insurance, Inc.* He knocked twice, turned the door knob and entered.

"Hello, Mr. Redfern." A slim woman, about fifty or so, her auburn hair pulled back tight in a bun, offered a smile. The room, the largest of a suite of three, smelled of coffee and burnt tobacco. No wonder. An ashtray on her desk was filled with cigarette butts, filters upright and listing like medieval headstones. There was one lit, balanced on the tray's rim, the smoke rising and drifting toward a window ajar. She sipped at coffee, with a fleeting glance at a single folder on her desk. A curl of hair, turning white but salty, had slipped out of the bun and hung 'round her right temple. Mostly, he noticed the rings under her eyes. He wondered if she'd slept at all. "Coffee? I just made a fresh pot."

"Need I ask good morning, or good evening, Mrs. Banks? Or how was your weekend?"

She glanced out the window. A cloud, the color of lead, hung over Broadway. The sky was like twilight. "What time is it?" she said.

Mr. Redfern smiled. "A long weekend?" he asked.

"A typical weekend, for the most part, Fred," she replied.

"For the most part, Lillian?" he said, taking off his coat and hat, and placing it on a rack in the corner.

"Could I get your coffee?" she asked.

"I can manage, thank you," he said. "I'd rather hear more about your weekend."

"Yes. We picked up a signal from a shore station near Montauk. The operator's talking to five ships off of Long Island. Decryption should be here some time mid-morning. Another signal picked up two boats somewhere due east of Newark. A schooner, we calculate, is sitting twelve miles from the tip of Cape Cod."

"Probably that fellow, Captain Williams, again," Redfern interrupted.

"Probably," she agreed. She took a sip of coffee. Lifted her cigarette and puffed. Then rested her elbow on the desk and held the cigarette between her fingers, away from her face. "You'll like this—reports from St. Pierre et Miquelon are Henri Moraze has loaded three more schooners with enough Scotch whisky to fill an Olympic swimming pool."

"That's a lot of Cutty Sark, even for that Frenchman."

"The manifest says they're going south, to the Bahamas."

"My guess is south all right—right to Boston," he said, "Or right here to New York."

"Well, we'll know soon enough. They embarked yesterday." She placed the cigarette to her lips, and inhaled deeply. Tapping the ash, she exhaled, took another drag, and then crushed the butt hard in the tray. "Apparently, the French do not observe the Lord's day when it comes to whiskey."

"Or profits," he added.

"We also received a cable from our man in Nova Scotia—the Canadians don't like him, by the way. I've heard discreetly that ..."

"Ah, ah, ah," he scolded her. "Discretion is advised, Lillian, or I could say I don't really like him, either." He smiled at her. "Too Protestant, a missionary type—he tends to interpret information rather than convey it. Clouds the message."

"Well, yes. That's what they've said. Today, he reported a sloop passed the Yarmouth lighthouse Saturday afternoon," she said. "It was registered out of Digby."

"A sloop?" He rolled his eyes and went for the coffee. "He was probably sailing home."

"It's all in the folder in your office. Copies ready to go to Section." Her eyes glanced at the folder on her desk then back at Redfern, "Except for this intercept from Maine." She picked up the folder.

"Another?" he said, solemnly. She handed it to him, nodded. "We're too close, Lillian."

He reluctantly took it, opened it, and shook his head.

"A signal from a shore station, near 44 degrees north and 68 degrees west," she said.

"Moose Harbor," he read the transcript.

"Yes," she said, "up by that mountain, way up the coast, on the way to Governor Roosevelt's summer house."

"So we're sure about this? It's been confirmed?" He stared at the transcript.

"Oh yeah, we're sure. He took it right above the eyeball. Chatham confirmed it."

"Shit. Things are heating up, up there."

"Shall I inform the Commander?"

He rubbed his chin for a moment. His thoughts drifted. He was about to nod yes, but instead said, "Not just yet, Lillian. I have a better idea."

"What are you thinking?"

"Oh, my friend from college days might be able to help. He's from up that way, plus I think he might be a good fit for us. I've been meaning to meet with him since the accident. I'll ask him to lunch."

"You mean ...?"

"Yes, Lillian," he interrupted, "Porter Gibson."

Lunch at McBride's

The morning after, the day after, a week down and over a month gone by—time passed like an iceberg in black water. Porter sighed and looked out from the labyrinth of his mind. Focused on the present. In the cab where he sat and the lunch he was to have with an old friend. Finally, a job offer, something different than baseball and the dead-end where his writing was taking him. He had to get there first, though, to McBride's Restaurant. The mid-afternoon traffic was as heavy as the rain falling. The sky had turned a darker shade of gray that morning. By noon, the rooftops were bound in fog and a front had hit. The driver cussed out at a man who stepped off the curb to snake his way through the stalled traffic. It allowed another cab to cut him off and take his parking spot. Finally, the cab jerked forward to the end of street and pulled to a stop.

"We're here," the cabbie said, "right over there," he pointed to his left. A few storefronts away, a green awning lettered with the name, "McBride's," hung over a set of tall doors.

Rain pelted the cab windows hard. Porter eyed the distance. "Can you get any closer?" he asked.

"How intimate do you wanna get?" the cabbie replied.

Porter handed him the fare with a smile. "Keep the change," he said and stepped from the cab into a downpour. He held his hat on his head, leaped over a puddle onto the crowded sidewalk, and jogged through the raindrops. Under the awning he stomped his feet and shook the rain off before he entered. McBride's was a modest affair, and always busy. Before Prohibition, it was noted for the colorful banter of a barman named Seamus O'Dale, who happily doled out advice he never used to blind drunks that were stoned deaf. It made for good theater. Nowadays, McBride's was known for good food at cheap prices. Today was no exception. A waiter brushed past Porter as he scanned the crowd in search of his friend. His eyes went along high-backed booths that lined the walls and down a row of tables in the center isle of the restaurant, searching.

"Porter!" he heard the familiar voice and saw a man stand from a booth in the rear.

"Redfern," Porter waved and approached him. "It's been too long."

The men shook hands and slid into opposite sides of the booth. Before Porter was out of his coat, a waiter stood at the table. "Good afternoon, gentlemen." He presented the menus.

Redfern looked at him, then Porter, and said, "I know what I want. Coffee, corned beef sandwich with a side of fried potatoes, please."

"I'll have what he's having," Porter said, and watched the waiter hurry away.

"It *has* been too long, Porter," Redfern smiled. "I've been meaning to get a hold of you for some time, to check in on you."

"I'm okay," Porter said.

"How are you holding up?"

"I'm fine, Red." Porter hadn't come here to talk about Scoop, but he knew it was inevitable. "It's been a long season, okay? I'm glad it's over because I was done with it." He lowered his eyes and noticed a couple books on the table. One, a copy of his latest work, *The Deferential Continuum,* and the other was Herbert Yardley's, *The American Black Chamber.*

Porter pointed at Yardley's book. "He's made a mess of things, hasn't he?"

Redfern nodded. "He's really made a mess of the business."

"They said when Henry Stimson found out the Cipher Bureau could tell him what they were saying in the Vatican, he canned Yardley—him and his whole spying operation. 'Gentlemen do not read each other's mail,' Stimson is quoted as saying. If that is true, I'm not sure we've ever had a Secretary of State that numb! That much of a pilgrim!"

"Don't be naïve, Porter," Redfern replied. "Stimson's been around the block. He's a Yale man, Skull and Bones type, one of the good old boys. They like to maneuver outside of government—do business out of sight, out of mind—position themselves and then bring the army in to clean up the mess they make. Believe me—they make a mess of things wherever they go. If Yardley had been spying on Moscow say, instead of the Vatican ... who knows?" He shrugged.

"Well, now they've published foreign editions, too—in German, Russian, Japanese—where all those fine gentlemen live."

"I hear Stalin reads it on the shitter," Red joked.

"It's not *that* long of a read," Porter laughed.

23

"Speaking of books," Red pointed at the table. "How is yours doing?"

"My publisher, Brown, said it's left him parched."

"It's political history and theory, but it's not that dry?"

"I think he was talking about the well."

"Oh, sales," said Red. "That will come. Have him sell it as a textbook."

"He, or they, thinks it's too Red—Red. They can't get it out of committee, let alone agree on how to sell it."

"It's not about the class struggle, for the love of God."

"You're telling me?"

"I am," he smiled. "I mean, I know you know it's not about the class struggle, but the history of the structure of our society, and why—when people are given a chance to control their destiny—they still continue to defer to their 'betters,' as you say, to make decisions for them—decisions against their own interests. The lower sorts, the middling sorts, and the better sorts—the way of the English—the mind set of class—everyone has their place. We can't seem to shake it and think for ourselves in a way that would benefit one and all."

"Shit, you really did read the book, Red," he said. "Just throw in a few farmers, free-thinkers, merchants, missionaries, ranchers, lawyers, bankers, con men, bullies, whiskey and whores, a dash of gullibility, a gallon of stupidity, a whole lot of arrogance, and you got yourself the America experience."

"You forgot to mention the wolves and jackals."

"But I mentioned the lawyers and bankers, Red."

Red laughed. "Good to see you still have a sense of humor, Porter."

"I feel it's all I've got going for me these days," he said. "Otherwise, I get too riled up."

"Come on, you have baseball, and you have your books. That's something." Porter flicked him the bird. "Oh, and your modest innovation, there, too," he grinned, "to sign language."

Porter lowered his finger. "It's been a rough stretch, Red, that's all. Go ahead and say it. You know it's not just about my book."

"Porter. It was an accident. Stop blaming yourself."

"I miss the little shit."

"We all do."

"It's haunting me, though," Porter hesitated, had a thought to tell him how much it really was. Instead, he just said, "If you only knew."

"Ah, Porter, I didn't ask you here to dwell on what happened. But I will offer you this piece of advice—take as much time as you need."

"For a lawyer, you're a very wise man, Red," Porter said, "as wise as Solomon."

Red acknowledged the word with a hint of a smile and slight nod, and continued, "Porter, *you* were always the wiser one. But for things like this, when accidents happen, I just know, if you don't take as much time as needed to heal, it will haunt you in many ways, for a long, long time."

"Thank you, Red."

"You are very welcome, my friend," he replied. "Maybe a trip is in order. It might help to get out of town."

"I'll find out soon enough. I'm going to Boston next week on business."

"That'll be good for you. Is the club sending you up there? Or is your book taking you on the road after all?" he asked.

"Yeah!" Porter smirked. "I suppose the book *is* taking me somewhere. I am off to Beantown to meet with my publisher. He wants to remind me once again that Boston is as far as that book is going."

"Oh, Porter! Give him time."

"Ah, he's not a bad egg. He's got us tickets for the Braves inaugural football game Sunday. Ironically, they're playing the Dodgers."

"Ha! The Giants are going up there to play them next," he smiled. "I had a passing thought of going to the game, but don't have the time."

"Timing is everything. I tried to postpone the meeting for a few weeks to bookend it with a trip up to Maine."

"Now, that's just what you need."

"It is, and it will be good for me. The club is sending me to Bangor to meet with a prospect—gives me a chance to go visit my sister and niece in Portland on my way north. After, I'll head back home, down east. I've haven't seen my aunt and uncle for a while."

"It will be nice to rest and relax."

"I'm afraid I won't be resting too much. I have a friend who needs my help. He just wrote me to come up. I wired him I had to go to Boston next week, but could do it in a few weeks, after Bangor."

"Anything serious?"

"No, I don't think so. He's a fisherman. Going out on a mackerel run, or something like that—shorthanded, lost some crew, he said."

"Lost some crew! How? If you don't mind me asking."

Porter shrugged. "He didn't elaborate, Red—mentioned it, that's all, in the letter."

"Of course," Red said. "I didn't mean to pry, it's just, well—I didn't know you knew how to fish like that, commercially."

"Ha! I steer the boat," Porter grinned. "All I do is point it at Moose Harbor and go—don't stop until we pass the islands and are way out to sea."

"Moose Harbor."

"Yes, under the old mountain by the sea," Porter smiled.

"Good. The old mountain, I wanted to make sure. One of the reasons I asked you to lunch. The reason I brought in Yardley's Book. Up where you're from. The job I mentioned. They're all related." Porter looked confused, but Redfern continued, "You know and I know, you can't play baseball forever but you'll stay connected to the game in some way. That and your books," he pointed at *The Deferential Continuum*. "You'll always have a book in you. I think baseball and writing are very good and interesting diversions."

"*Diversions?*" Porter asked. He was now genuinely befuddled.

"Yes, from any attention you may receive for the work you will be doing while you travel."

"What!—What the hell kind of work do you *do*, Red?"

"Gentlemen," the waiter interrupted, balancing a platter in hand, "two coffees, two corned beef sandwiches and two fried potatoes." He placed it all before them, and added, "*Bon appétit!*" and rushed off.

Redfern looked Porter directly in the eyes, leaned forward and answered in a low voice, "Some things we learned from Yardley."

Coincidence or Connection?

Redfern stepped from McBride's onto the sidewalk. The rain had let up. Behind him, Porter disappeared amidst busy foot traffic. Ahead of him, he eyed low clouds rolling down Seventh Avenue over and between the high buildings. The walk back to the Equitable Building from McBride's was only fifteen minutes. He decided to chance another downpour, and tucked the books he had brought under his arm and paced himself. His thoughts went to Porter. It was good to see him, but not to see the heaviness in the man's heart and sadness in his eyes. Redfern felt for him. The accident was suffocating him, would not let him breath, heavy as the clouds above. Time is what Porter needed, but Redfern did not have time to spare. The last intercept was an indication. And now in Boston—more disturbing news had arrived yesterday. Chatham had reported a murder. Possibly connected somehow to whatever was going on down east in Maine. Of all places, Moose Harbor, in the middle of nowhere but at the center of all things. Time to heal would have to wait. He would hate himself later. He needed Porter now. He was going there. The opportunity was there—be it a coincidence or a connection. Porter had a good friend who fished. He was short crew. He asked for Porter's help—all the way from New York City to Moose Harbor—there was no one else to help? How could he be shorthanded in a fishing village with a depression on? With so many people desperate for work everywhere? Unless ... call it a hunch. That gut feeling Redfern likened to standing on the doorstep of probability. He was standing there now—had to knock. No matter how bad it made him feel.

Redfern entered the Equitable Building. Up in the office, he found Lillian at the window, arms crossed, staring out into the ether. "How did the lunch go, Fred?" She turned to him.

"It went well, Lillian," he answered.

"He showed interest, then?"

He nodded. "Yes, he's interested, but ..."

A second passed. She let him drift, then asked, "But *what?*"

"I told him to think about it. He said he needed to, anyway, but wants to talk more."

"That's par for the course, Fred. You always say, 'One step our way is a step in our direction,' right?"

"It is, Lillian, and it's true."

"You don't seem too positive."

"Porter's my friend. I don't want to manipulate him—*use* him." He held the books up. "I want to work *with* him. I feel guilty, but we really need his help."

"Oh, I see."

"I wanted to get right to it. That's why I brought the books, but he wasn't ready for it. He's still carrying a load. I should have known, Lillian."

"Stop it Fred," she said. "You're offering him a way to move forward, do something different. It will clear his head."

He went to a nearby shelf and placed the books down. "We agreed to meet again."

"Shall I block off a time for you?"

"Thanks, but there's no time to block yet. He's out of town for about a week."

"You have the meeting with Reynolds coming up, in Washington."

"I haven't forgotten. He'll be back from Boston before I leave for Washington."

"Speaking of Boston," she walked back to her desk, "about what happened there." She sat down, lit a cigarette, and then handed him a file. "We have an update."

Redfern opened the file. "Dear God!" he whispered.

"A priest," she said. "The recipient of the intercept—it's been confirmed."

Redfern closed the file visibly disturbed. "Speak with our man. Tell him to go to Boston."

"Why Fred?"

"The bastards have no boundaries."

"What's going on?"

"Call it a hunch, Lillian, but I think our friend may need a guardian angel."

A Seamless Wall of Darkness

Porter exited the bookshop and looked into the night. Daylight had succumbed to darkness hours ago. He had lost time again. But how? After his lunch with Redfern he had gone over to the train station to purchase his tickets for the trip to Boston. After that, he remembered going to Newberry's where he bought a new tie. Maybe he could dazzle Brown and his people. The next thing he remembered was stopping at Augusta's Bookshop, only a few blocks from his office. Inside, he proceeded to lose himself for a spell. Finally, he bought a copy of Remarque's, *The Road Back,* for the train ride north. A morally bankrupt society and the war culture it spawns was probably not the best choice for his current state of mind. Nevertheless, he would force himself to read it. He needed distraction wherever it came from.

On the sidewalk, he trudged along. Redfern's offer churned in his head. That was a welcome distraction. One of a handful over the last week—he had received letters from his sister in Portland and his best friend back home up on Moose Harbor. She needed to talk; he wanted his help. Then, out of the blue, yesterday afternoon, he received an invitation to lunch with his old friend from college to talk about a job. Maybe his guardian angel—or even God—was listening to his *thoughts!* Because he had surely given up on praying for a break he so desperately needed.

28

Something to support himself in the offseason and then, after he was done playing baseball.

Could he teach? Yeah, he could—that's what most historians did. They sure as hell just don't write for a living, let alone play catcher for a professional baseball club. He had given it a shot once, teaching in the offseason, but he tanked. That was after graduate school. He had already spent a semester engrossed in the New York City socialist-anarchist movement, well, its poontang. By then, he had even developed *the* bird, what he liked to call the working man's shaft. That aside, what really changed his mind about a lot of things was due to baseball. His travels throughout the cities in the National League had made him *aware* that things were not what they were. City-to-city, what was written in the newspapers and what was said on the radio was not what he had seen and heard with his own eyes and ears. That was his conversion. What passed as history was a tool, he realized—a sharp, blunt instrument—a noble lie. There was no manifest destiny. Disadvantage, however, was manifest, and all that went along with its manufacture, propagation, and maintenance. Try *explaining* that to someone like, say, Reginald St. Germain Woolsley, the head of the history department. The man was deaf as a haddock and had the visual acumen of a star-nosed mole.

The teaching gig fizzled after one semester. Right about the time Reginald handed him his walking papers. He didn't need it anyway. At that point, he had convinced himself he was a *writer*—a guy who could earn enough to float by just *writing.* Imagine that—such a grand delusion! After finishing his first book, *The Urban Diaspora,* his confidence was such that he took a space to write, the top floor of an empty storefront. That space became his refuge—not only an ideal place to write at, but a place to hide. It was in a quiet neighborhood, which he liked. There was a speako around the block where the barmaid knew his name, which he liked even more. The walls of the room, like the building's façade, were brick lined. He liked that, too. It reminded him of the family shop back home. That familiarity helped him concentrate, or so he had convinced himself. He had convinced himself of such a farfetched notion because of a book he had written in that space—*Escape From Industrial Time,* which had put some good coin in his pocket for a while. On the other hand, his latest book, *The Theory of the Deferential Continuum,* was sitting cold on the press. Cold enough to convince him of just how delusional he was. That maybe it was time to look for another line of work. If Redfern only knew how much he needed it. He was going to Boston to get the brush-off from his publisher. He was sure of it. Brown was a decent enough fellow to do it in person.

On the other hand, Redfern's offer filled him with as much hope as doubt. And much of that doubt was related to his sanity. For he was certain he was in the midst of a functional breakdown. Since the accident, his sleep was frequented by ghoulish nightmares and his days were filled with episodes of some imaginary catastrophe or impending doom. Or, like today, he would lose track of time. Gaps in his day happened all too often. He would find himself at a coffee counter one moment, then walking through a park the next wondering where he was going and how he had arrived there. In these moments he had experienced a sensation, inexplicably, that someone or something was approaching him or was around him. He couldn't shake it. It was not without irony he had told Redfern he was haunted, he had meant it.

Porter went past a narrow alley. In stride, he gave a casual glance that way. He thought he saw a thick curl of fog snaking along toward him. Suddenly, it stood on end, swaying like a cobra in a trance, captive to the music of its charmer. Only this fog had a pale, violet hue to it and, to the best of his recollection, he had never seen fog sway. Two steps past the alley entrance the imagery registered in his head. He stopped short—felt the hair on the back of his neck and arms stand on end—and went back. The fog he *saw* had been no more than a half-dozen steps down the alley and no more than four or five seconds had passed. Now, there was nothing but scattered trash cans and the silhouette of a drunk listing in the corner, belching loudly and pissing against the wall.

He quickened his pace, slightly shaken. The next street was his, where his office was located. But when he turned onto it, he passed seamlessly into a wall of darkness. Around him, the air pressure compressed sharply, felt it in his head and sinuses. There was no sound. Not a single streetlamp was illuminated. Not a single soul on the street. No traffic or anything at all. Was he even in the right place? Abruptly, the silence broke with a murmur. It popped his ears. He heard a voice, nearby, mumble something. And another, even closer, mumbled a reply. No one was there. He was completely alone. Then, three or four people mumbled over each other, chitchat no louder than a cocktail party. The banter increased, grew louder and reverberated into thousands of people roaring in anticipation. A sound not unfamiliar to him—he heard it each time he stepped to the plate at Ebbets Field on any given summer day. But this was an autumn evening in a lonely

Village neighborhood. Fear welled up from deep within his loins to form a dry ball in his throat. His imagination ran wild—was that another wisp of fog rising? A faint hue of violet beginning to glimmer? There, just ahead, near—was that his building? Something approaching? He swallowed hard, lowered his head, and began to walk toward his office nonetheless. As he did so, with the first step, the crowd noise hushed and faded out completely. As he walked, each lamp he passed lit up as if on cue. He dared not lift his head until he stood before his door. When he did, all the lamps were on and a few people were walking along the street. All was *normal.*

He went inside and rushed upstairs to his office space, rummaged his bottom desk drawer for the bottle he kept there. Scotch never went down so easy and smooth. Porter stepped slowly to his office window and scanned the narrow street below, searching for any sign of his sanity. People strolled casually under streetlamps and cast long shadows into the night. Yet there was not enough light for him to see what he was looking for. There were too many shadows, and in one of them, he was certain, someone stood. Waiting for him, his next move. Either that or he was truly haunted.

A Harbor View

"A writer, you say, Finlay?" Smithy stood at the office window, looking out on Boston Harbor. Ships passed in either direction before him. In the distance, a fog horn blared dully. Though the sky was pale and gray, the view across the harbor was clear. There, a fleet of rum chasers was docked. He counted seventeen ships. More than a habit, it was a principal reason for the office's location.

"Aye, Smithy," he replied. Finlay sat in a leather-backed chair at an oak paneled desk. But for a revolver and, the newspaper next to it, the desktop was barren. "From what we are told, he's the kind who involves himself in the affairs of others."

"Very much a meddler," Smithy grinned broadly. When he did, his thick, dark eyebrows clenched together and his expression changed—into something wolfish, hungry, eager. "That kind of writer is he?"

Finlay nodded, "and very much a problem. So New York has informed us. If he were to become involved now, our man fears he would interfere in the investigation we are presently conducting or worse—it might place the whole operation at risk," he pointed straight ahead. His office door opened to an outer room. There, a sofa and a set of armchairs were to one side. In one chair, a large man with a large round head sat rigid, his back to the office. Opposite, in the corner, a shortwave radio was stacked on a side table. There, a man sat attentively with a headset on, listening intently. Above him, an oversized nautical map was tacked to the wall, a detail from Long Island to Cape Cod north to the Maritimes and Newfoundland.

"His is an inquisitive mind, then?" asked Smithy.

"Make no mistake, he's a canny one."

"Is he vulnerable?"

"Aye, to our benefit, though," Finlay said. "Word is he recently suffered a trauma. The grief is such he can't go on."

"How sad."

"We must show resolve in relieving him of his guilt, but in a way that explains itself."

"Accidents happen, everyday, terrible accidents."

"It would be best by his own hand. I'm told he is high profile."

"In what way?"

He flipped the newspaper on the desk. Bold, block letters spread across the top under the paper's banner. *Tragedy At Ebbets Field*, read the headline. "That's our man," Finlay said pointing at a picture beneath the headline.

"We are going down to New York?"

"*We* are not going anywhere," Finlay smiled. "*We* must not be seen together just now because of what happened."

"I see."

"I hope so. That sloppy play with the priest was not well received." He said it loudly, enough to be heard in the outer room.

"It was not me who acted," he replied, defensively.

"You may recall that I was there," said Finlay. "I'm reminding *you* of that folly as a word of caution."

He grinned another wolfish grin. "I'll go pack a bag."

"No need to. Our man was followed to Grand Central this morning. He boarded for Boston." Finlay handed him the newspaper. "Go to South Station. Find him, follow him, relieve him of his guilt."

A Fine Line

"There's a fine line between light and darkness," she said. "It's the place where all human mythology breaks down."

"The end of the line or the end is nigh?" Porter asked. He had yet to get a name out of her, but she was talking a good game. Better than the one he had been to that afternoon, a 14-0 loss for the Braves—their inaugural game. He had declined an offer for dinner with his publisher—said he was beat—and retreated to Fran's alone, a speako he and Scoop had frequented when the team was in Boston. There was a stool with his name on it at the end of the bar, but when he walked in, he found her sitting on the stool—alone. A stacked blonde with no drink in front of her—who was she waiting for? *Him?* Such luck, but the thought crossed his mind—the way she looked him in the eye and beckoned for him to come sit. It was not much, but not much was just enough for him. If so, the art of seduction had never been this fun, or interesting.

"No, not the end or even near it, a beginning," she replied, "a place of infinite profundity."

"Infinite profundity, huh?" said Porter. "Okay, count me in. I'm up for the challenge. But what about good and evil? Are the distinctions just as fine?"

"The necessity of evil came about as a juxtaposition for good," she answered him, as though she had answered the question a thousand times before. "The practice of evil, and its distinction from good, well, that's a whole other realm—neither for the weak of heart, nor the meek."

"The weak and the meek?" asked Porter.

"Precisely!" she replied. "The will of men and women, their souls, are prey to evil." She paused. A crooked, mischievous smile spread across her face. "Amazing thing, this whole realm of evil, how susceptible they are to the fall."

"*They?*" Porter asked, intrigued. "The fall?"

"Humanity," she answered. "How *easily* they submit themselves to darkness over light."

She was pulling him in slowly, had been anyway, for the past half hour. She was picking up speed now. To what end? He wondered. Such talk of humanity as a distinct species from herself had him guessing not only where she was from, but where she was leading him.

"Whenever I visit, I find myself looking into the souls of the fallen—how darkness came upon them—for what end? Are people truly blind to the choices they make? You see, for most—the weak and the meek—when a soul inhabits the realm of flesh and blood, it's as though the blind are making their way through a city. Men and women are not conscious of the universe or what its power has in store for them. They act without

33

consequence."

"You speak, my dear, as one who knows," said Porter.

"I do," she replied.

"I think I'm smitten," said Porter, the hot blood pulsing through his veins at the thought of intellectual *and* carnal energy, "by you and your philosophy."

"It is not mine—my philosophy," she said, "But one I share whenever I must, when the time comes."

"Then I must thank you for sharing it with me." She smiled at him. "For, it is profound." Porter looked upon her face—one of angelic beauty. A face of innocence, of a child, and—he wasn't sure—but on some level—immortal wisdom. Yet, a familiarity there, too—he was certain he had seen her—that face—before.

"You must excuse me," she said, standing up.

"Where are you going?" asked Porter, taken aback. He wanted more.

"The time has come," was all she said, and turned, walked slowly away toward the exit.

Porter watched her move the length of the bar. The gentle movement of her hips swaying side to side with each stride, seductive and alluring, pulled at him. He became intent upon her, willing her to look back his way—to play mouse to her cat—he was prepared to do so, anything, he thought, to have her. That he must—get to know her on every level.

"Stop!" he thought, and she *did,* paused at the end of the bar. She *is* coming back, he giggled to himself. Oh, to plucketh the bird again. Seconds passed, time froze, until, like a sloth, she moved slowly, and began to turn, in Porter's direction, but not fully. Instead, she reached up with her hand and, with near imperceptibility, like a magician, waved her palm and fingers over the back of a man's head who was sitting at the corner of the bar. Sparks crackled and snapped from her fingertips—kinetic energy, he thought—his hair fluttered and stood on end along the back of his head. Porter became engrossed by her actions—as much by the imperceptible caress of the man's scalp as his impervious response to it. The thread-like blue and yellow and auburn flashes continued, even as time returned, sped up to normal, as she dropped her hand, and then walked out the door. Porter, frustrated and confounded, perplexed and awed, stared at the space vacated by her, wondering how and why. She never looked back.

In the void she created, Porter noticed the sparks crackling and popping still, and the man at the corner of the bar remained oblivious to it all. In fact, nobody appeared to respond to the woman's actions, including the bartender, who placed a tumbler of Irish whiskey down in front of the man. The glass, half-filled, was placed next to a broad-rimmed fedora. As he lifted his glass to his lips, the man looked directly at Porter. He flashed a wolfish, diabolical grin, and sipped his whiskey. Lowering the glass, he placed his other hand into his breast pocket and began to draw something out slowly. Behind him, a thin man in a bulky overcoat, wearing an oversized hat, stepped through the door where, seconds before, *she* had stood. He was lightly freckled with a boyish face, except for the scar, an inch or so long, above his left eyebrow. There was also the intensity in his eyes, a look of determination and urgency. Porter's gaze went back to the man at the bar, who smiled now like a deranged, crazy bastard. A gun! The prick was pulling a gun from his breast pocket. Porter froze. Was this a robbery? Then, with the nonchalance of a man checking the time on his wrist watch, the man who had just entered the speako drew a revolver from his inner coat pocket and, point blank, fired one bullet into the back of the deranged, crazy bastard's skull, which fragmented instantly, forcefully thrusting the body forward. The gun blast was deafening, and sent the crowded speakeasy into a fit of terror. Screaming and shouting and general pandemonium filled the room. Patrons ducked, a few went to the floor hard, rolling in sawdust. Porter, for the life of him, he did not know why, made eye contact with the gunman, locking on his gaze. For a split second, he expected a bullet between his eyes for his stupidity. In that moment of crisis, Porter was certain of two things. He would never forget the man—the angular jaw, the freckles, his scar—and the intensity in his eyes, which bored into his soul. In those split seconds, when he was certain his life hung in the balance, Porter sat motionless, mesmerized and transfixed by the act of violence this man had perpetrated before him and the entire bar. Not only was his memory branded with the shock of coldblooded murder, but he would never forget what happened next, when the dead man, blood and brain and skull fragments splattered everywhere, finally stopped twitching. The sparks that had been crackling from the back of his head since *she* had brushed her hand against it erupted like a volcanic flame from the point of the bullet's entry. Blue and green flames shot upward until, in the final seconds before it extinguished itself, a black molten mass, oily and tar-like, exited the wound, formed into a shadowy creature above him, and lunged downward. The monstrous thing simply dissipated into the man.

"Get outta here!" the barman shouted at him. It roused him from the trance he was in. The gunman was gone. Porter slid his ass from the barstool, holding the bar tightly for leverage, while he balanced himself on the floor. The experience had made him dizzy, and he found himself moving clumsily toward the back of the room, finding his way through the kitchen, and stumbling out the back door into an alley.

The alleyway reeked of rot and piss. Sirens wailed, their distance closing rapidly. A bum was propped up against the opposite wall, passed out. A rat jumped at his feet and disappeared into heaps of nearby rubbish. Porter's senses were overwhelmed by what he had seen. He knew he had to move or he would never leave this town. Glancing to the street, motorcars and pedestrians rushed by.

There he spied her. On the opposite sidewalk, staring directly at him, was the mysterious woman who, moments before, had piqued his intellectual curiosity, touched his being to the core. He hailed out to her, caught that mischievous smile forming at the edges of her mouth, when a trolley car lumbered by between them. Porter began to run toward her. He needed to know. He needed answers to the sight he had just witnessed. What she had done? How she was a part of it? Who the hell she was? Or, as the possibility entered his head, *what* she was?

At the alley's edge, he slowed, panting in excitement and anticipation. The first squad car had arrived, and another was pulling up. He moved to the sidewalk, into the flow of pedestrian traffic casually, and went behind the gawkers who were gathering near the entrance of the speako. Porter stepped into the street, timing his crossing. The trolley car rolled by, its bells clanging as it approached the intersection. There she stood, her mouth formed into a wider smile, looking directly at him, still. He heard the word clearly, loudly, a command. "Run!" The odd thing was, in retrospect, the sound came not from a nearby pedestrian or out of the crowd, but from within. He was sure of it. Something, a voice not his own, inside his head, shouted for him to run. But he slowed to a stop. Behind her, the gunman stood, staring right at him, boring a hole through him with his eyes.

The car came up on Porter rapidly, too fast for either him or the driver to react. Her hand reached out, or so Porter thought, for him, even though it was too far to grasp. As her hand thrust toward Porter, a bolt of light flashed past him, a violet hue. The vehicle screeched sideways, spinning around him, coming to an abrupt halt with only a nudge to his hip. The driver, stunned, his eyes bugging out as much as Porter's heart bulged in his chest, went slack-jawed. The man stared, unable to comprehend what had just happened, but even more so by what he now looked upon. Centered on the front end of his car, on the edge of the hood, indented slightly, smoldering and glowing red hot, was the print of a hand, delicate and feminine. The expression on the man's face drew Porter to the hand print immediately. He stared uncomprehendingly himself, watching the red glow evaporate, and leaving the print scorched into the surface.

It was enough for Porter to explain how the car had swung around him in an improbable, near one-hundred-eighty-degree turn, let alone the hand print seared, embedded like a fossil, into the hood of the car. But reason eluded him completely at how the woman—in the split second Porter looked away from her, to the car about to strike him, and then back again—had surely vanished into thin air.

A Man of Vengeance

He saw what he saw. There was no doubt about it. In the war, they had trained him to observe and remember. Every nuance, in any environment, he absorbed. It had saved his life more than once. But what he had just witnessed defied reason. The car had spun one hundred eighty degrees around him when it should have flattened him into jelly. Done the work the corpse inside was set to do—a public execution. There was nothing left of the stiff at the bar in Fran's, now. Only a mystery and a poorly-attended funeral for the bastard, who was presently in a freefall to hell. From his own experience, most people were too shocked or stunned or scared shitless to remember much when a gun popped off in a public place, especially in a small speako like Fran's. They went into survival mode, not witness mode. It was messy, nevertheless. More than the blood and bone, he knew there was a chance someone could finger him.

He had no choice. He had to act. He had followed him this far. The man was going to shoot the man sitting at the end of the bar, in an old navy blue suit. To make matters worse, the bastard he saved saw him. When every other drunk and whore in Fran's was ducking for cover and sucking sawdust, this one sat there gawking at him—the ballplayer—the one in the crazy, freak accident a month before.

He left quickly, went outside, stood in the shadows across the street, waited and watched the alleyway beside Fran's. That was the way out for *him*. Even when the sirens grew louder and all the *witnesses* were stampeding out of the joint like rats out of a burning barn. He stood there. People ran past him without notice, brushing sawdust off their tailored suits and dresses. He waited as the sirens closed in. Sure enough, the ballplayer came out of the alley and, incredibly, walked blindly into traffic. He was sure he saw a flash, a powder light—a bright violet—as he blinked. Then nothing but the ballplayer standing there—on the other side of the car—its front end smoldering.

At that moment, he realized, there was something to this. The ballplayer now intrigued him. It was no longer just a job. He needed to know more about him, and would. Somehow, a connection was made. More than he could explain. It had happened to him that Easter week in '16, in Dublin. Something similar, an unseen intervention saved his ass. The scar was there to remind him every day.

He took a step back, blended into the shadows, as police cars rapidly filed in and around Fran's. The sirens blared loudly amidst the hysteria. Yet, the ballplayer did not take notice, of the insanity or him, and slowly walked off. From a distance, he fell in behind him, all the way back to his hotel. He followed him into the lobby, discreetly scanned the crowded room, and made for a bank of phones in the corner. From there he looked around. He was safe, the ballplayer, for now.

His thoughts drifted to his friend Terence. Why had no one watched *his* back? Where was *his* guardian angel? He then thought of himself, what he had just done, what he was, or had now become—a man of vengeance.

Redfern Throws a Pitch

"Holy shit, Porter!" Redfern blurted out and looked around. He didn't want to draw attention. They were sitting in a dark corner at Jack and Charlie's, a speako over on West 52nd Street, for a good reason—to remain unnoticed. "It's unimaginable!" Redfern sat there stunned at what he had heard from him for the past twenty minutes. Up to that point, he had only managed to utter, "Unbelievable" or "That's inconceivable," while Porter told him what had happened at the speako in Boston. "It was in the papers here—some kind of gangland killing—but they always like to sensationalize violence."

"It was sensational all right—sensationally gruesome," Porter said, "the whole thing. It happened out of nowhere. I can't even piece it together now. It feels like some kind of trance. One moment I was talking with a beautiful woman, who suddenly got up and left, then a guy walked in, and next thing I know a gun went off." In truth, he was still unsure what he *witnessed* or what he thought he *saw*—that ghoulish thing—the gunman—he'll never forget the scar—or how he pulled himself out of the speako or how he made it across the street. But for *her*—somehow—he kept thinking. It all had something to do with *her*. Whoever she was she was part of it. "I got caught in a riot once, Red—you know which one—and I saw what the swing of a billy club can do to a man's jaw. That's pretty bad, but it's not in the same league as what a bullet can do to a man's head when fired from the same distance." Porter shook his head. "Now look at me. I can't stop blathering."

"You're dealing with the shock of it all. It's normal."

"Normal!?" Porter exclaimed, his voice rising. "The last month and a half feels like I've been standing center stage in the Theatre of the Macabre. Nothing is normal, Red."

"That's not what I meant," Redfern said.

"Look around," Porter continued. "You think this is normal? A drink amongst friends is illegal—has been for over a decade. This is criminal behavior. We're nothing but a couple of outlaws."

Redfern sighed, "I can't argue with that." He lifted the Scotch in front of him. Porter nodded and did the same, except all Redfern saw was his giant hands hover around his lips. A glass was in there somewhere, in the center, but he saw no trace of it until Porter tipped his hand and swallowed.

"Sorry, I didn't mean to jump on you, Red."

"You have a point, Porter," Redfern replied, "the hypocrisy of it all—me sitting here with you at Jack and Charlie's. Hell, I'm charged to intercept the smuggling of the stuff. We do our jobs. We've learned a lot. We've even gotten creative, but the Volstead Act was and has been a farce—impossible to enforce. The estimate is that over thirty-thousand speakeasies are in this city alone. I have to pretend I don't know any of them exist." Redfern shook his head. "If we closed them, what's left of the economy in this city would collapse. That's the thing with illegal trade. There's a design to it—a singular purpose—to only benefit the few. The collective 'we' cut ourselves out of billions of dollars of customs revenue, and have since spent half that making a feeble attempt to enforce the Act."

"You can beat yourself all you want, but you're my kind of copper," said Porter.

"Ha!" said Redfern. "Let me be specific—enforcer I'm not—was never my role in this debacle, thankfully."

"What exactly is your role in this debacle, Red? Because I've been wondering ever since you dropped Yardley's name last week."

"I only told you enough for a reason—to feel you out—your interest," replied Redfern. "As for me, I head a team that monitors radio transmissions over the Atlantic."

"You eavesdrop on people? Like Yardley?"

"It's busy work, but yes," he shrugged.

"You are a nosy son-of-a-bitch?"

"We monitor, then sift through the transmissions, make determinations, prioritize and forward information and findings to other bureaus, agencies and departments. My staff is small but able."

"Now you sound like a dull bureaucrat, Red."

"I've become one, Porter—at least forced to process the information I receive like one." He smiled weakly. "There is a certain detachment one must have, otherwise, the information—all that data—would consume me and everyone on the team."

"And where do I fit in this *data*, Red?"

"It's not so much where you fit into the data, Porter, but the amount of data emanating out of where you're from. I've been asked to look into it."

"That's no secret," interrupted Porter. He thought of his best friend, Jeffah, who had turned to running the minute the ink dried on the Prohibition law. "Every able-bodied fisherman with a set of balls has carried a cargo of booze." Redfern nodded. "And you know what they say about fishermen up in Maine, Red? Every one of them has a set of balls. That's what makes them men."

"It also makes them as criminal as we are, Porter," Redfern said, and lifted his glass. "We know there are runners all along the Maine coast, coming down from the Maritimes and St. Pierre. But what differentiates us, and most of them, from what's happening up in your home town is the degree of violence associated with the activity, and the people who profit from it."

"You're losing me, Red. You're talking as if a bunch of gangsters have moved in on Moose Harbor."

"I don't want to alarm you, especially after what you just went through, but they have, Porter," he replied, and fell silent.

Whether for effect or not, Porter wasn't certain, but he was struck by a sudden fear for his friend's life, and the lives of others.

Moments passed. Porter sipped his Scotch, as did Redfern. And then Redfern leaned forward and said, "Now that I have your attention, this is what I can share with you, which is another way of saying, this is what you need to know. Above all, I speak in confidence."

Porter nodded, "I understand."

"My man in Chatham has pinpointed onshore radio transmissions, very troubling ones, coming out of your home town. One pertains to a couple of fatal accidents, the other to a suicide. The victims were able-bodied fishermen with a set of balls. Not good."

"No, it's not good," answered Porter. "Was that recently?" Redfern nodded. Porter raised an eyebrow. He'd read nothing of any deaths in the letter he had received from Jeffah, only that he needed his help. Then again, Jeff had said he needed a swing man that he could trust, but didn't say what happened to the other swing man he'd been trusting. He braced himself when he asked, "Do I know them?"

"Do you?" replied Redfern, "a Minard Severance, a Howard Bailey, or a Lawrence Philpot? They're out of Bean's Point."

Porter shook his head, no. "Bean's Point is on Moose Harbor, but that's the next town over from where I grew up, Downeast Way," he said, relieved it had nothing to do with Jeffah. "Is Bean's Point the place where you received the transmissions from?"

"No, it isn't," said Redfern. "The transmissions are coming from your home town, where or from whom, we don't know."

"Where are they going to? If you don't mind me asking."

"Fair enough, Porter," replied Redfern. "They're going to Boston."

"Boston, huh?" said Porter. "What a *coincidence*."

"A very strange one."

"But didn't you say the deaths were accidents and a suicide? You sure it wasn't just that, Red?"

"The deaths were referenced in transmissions before their deaths were made public, Porter. So to answer your question, sadly, it wasn't *just* that."

"I see what you mean."

"Do you know what I mean, Porter?" he asked pointedly. "Do you know people in the trade?"

"I have good friends who cast their nets in those waters, Red, that I'll tell you. And some of them are crazy bastards, I'll tell you that, too. They may shoot at you over their lobster pots, but they aim to miss, and warn you off. But I can't believe any of them are mixed up in killing off locals. Their kids all go to the same schools, and on Sunday most of them go to the same church."

"I wouldn't expect you to tell me who they are, Porter. In fact, I can respect that, but there's a bad apple up there. There's no doubt about it."

"You are asking me to find the bad apple, the person?"

"That would be nice, but no."

"What then?"

"The lay of the land, maybe—make an assessment of what's going on in town. We're looking for context concerning Philpot, Bailey, and Severance. Who are the people connected to them? Chances are, that will lead us to where we need to be."

"Wait a second—this is a job for the revenue agents, not me."

"My assistant said the same thing. We talked about that very subject. But then I thought of you. I recalled that you were from this place. So I said to her, I wanted to speak with you first—ask you. Take a different approach. I then spoke to my man about it, the one I report to, and he agreed."

"Have an inside man give you the lay of the land?" Porter sniggered. "You're a piece of work, Red."

"I know I am, and I apologize. But, honestly, I couldn't unload on you."

"No, but you let me unload about Scoop, and just now about Boston."

"That's different and far outside and away from this—you know that."

"Dammit!" Porter rubbed his forehead.

"I had to feel you out."

"About what? If I'd be willing?"

"No, Porter," he replied. "If you'd be *able*—able to do it—able to see the playing field and make the right call. You're the ballplayer, the catcher. That's how you think. That's what *The Differential Continuum* is about—a level playing field."

Porter took a calming breath, and sipped his Scotch. "I appreciate that, Red. Nevertheless, I'm not sure if you have the right man for the job," he said. "If I'm even as *able* as you say or think I am. For God's sake, I'm an amateur, and these are my people."

"Ha, ha!" Redfern laughed. "Believe me, we need amateurs like you in this kind of business, Porter."

"Thanks—I think," he replied. "But I'm telling you this as a friend, Red—I'm not one to double-cross *any* of my friends."

"That's why I'm asking you, Porter, and not sending in the likes of Izzy and Moe, or the Coast Guard. I think you'll be more effective," Redfern said. "But more to the point, and I want you to consider this—the way the story goes with these bastards, whoever is connected to Philpot, Bailey and Severance, is in line to go. There may be double dealings going on, or they may be cleaning house. But the next person in line might just be one of your friends."

Porter's only concern was for Jeffah. If anything, by doing this, he could warn him, and maybe find out what Red wanted to know. "You are a bastard, Red, you always were." Porter downed his Scotch. "But that's what I always liked about you."

Redfern nodded his approval. "Please stop by my office next Monday, around eleven," he said. "Is that time okay? It's best we get underway and I know the afternoon is booked."

"Monday at eleven is fine," Porter said.

"Good." He handed him a slip of paper. "That's the address. I won't be there. I have to go to Washington tomorrow and will not return until sometime next week. But that's all right. You'll be dealing with my assistant, Mrs. Banks, anyway, from here on out. She will fill you in on procedure, provide you with sufficient funds, contact information, credentials, etcetera, etcetera," he said. "Thanks for agreeing to do this, Porter. There's a future in it for you if you want one," he paused. "One more thing—be sure to knock twice, and loudly, before you enter the office. You don't want to be mistaken for a pigeon."

Mr. Digit is Born

Porter knocked twice, very hard, on the office door, as instructed. Rather than enter, he stood there, hesitant, on the 34th floor of the Equitable Building, staring at the brass plaque that read, Mutual Insurance, Inc. Whether Red was bullshitting him or not, after he informed him of Mrs. Banks's proclivity to shoot first and ask questions later, he thought it best to wait for someone to shout, "Enter," before going in.

Instead, the door opened and he was greeted by a woman in her fifties—maybe—bookish, a librarian, and attractive. Wisps of grey and auburn hair fell out of a tight bun from the top of her head. A cigarette dangled from her painted lips. She eyed him cautiously, studied him. All the while, she raised her hand, planted the cigarette gracefully in the V between her middle and index fingers, and removed it. Blowing smoke away from Porter, she smiled, and then said, "Hello."

"Mrs. Banks?" Porter asked.

"Yes," she smiled. "Please, come in, Mr. Gibson. I've been expecting you."

"Hope I'm not too late. Red told me around eleven o'clock."

"No, not at all," she answered. "Actually, it's an honor to meet you, Mr. Gibson. Not only have I seen you play out at Ebbets Field, I've read your work. Mr. Redfern was right to bring you in."

"Thank you, Mrs. Banks. As for how right Mr. Redfern is about bringing me in, considering I don't even know what he's really brought me in to, well, time will tell, I suppose."

"They're always modest in the beginning," she said to herself with a laugh, "too predictable."

"What's that, Mrs. Banks?" asked Porter.

"You're no different," she answered him. "Mr. Redfern likes the modest ones. He says they're prone to honesty."

"Redfern's a very good bullshitter, Mrs. Banks. Knows how to throw the bushwa, that one, but I suppose you know that, too," Porter smiled.

Mrs. Banks placed the cigarette to her lips and took a drag. Removing it as gracefully as before, and with the same studied gaze, she said, "You and I are going to get along splendidly, Mr. Gibson."

"Please, call me Porter," he grinned.

"Lillian," she answered, and extended her hand. Porter shook it. "Have a seat at the desk, Porter. We have a few things to go over." And they did, for the better part of two hours. Years later, he would look back with fondness at the conversation. She was affable and intellectual. Alas, a weakness he always had in women. But at that time, it was much more than that. What he carried with him out of that office was the one thing he would always be remembered by: the code name she'd devised. "In this game," she said, "we all need an element of discretion and incognito. Henceforth, Porter, I dub you, Mr. Digit."

Porter laughed so hard he nearly fell from his chair, and then realized she had touched his core.

"True," she said. "Keep it to yourself, if you dare. But I can certainly understand if you run with it. As my father often said to my mother, 'You wear it well.'" Mrs. Banks flashed a big smile.

"I think it's bigger than both of us, Lillian," he said.

"Whenever you communicate with this office, use the monikers, yours and ours, I gave you, and all will be copacetic," she said.

Porter said he understood—said he got it.

When she was finished, she lit another cigarette, sat back in the chair, gave him the same once-over as before, examining from head to toe and back. By then, she had gone through a half pack. The ceiling was obscured by smoke. Studying him, looking into his eyes, she inhaled with a sense of satisfaction. "Can you come back on Friday?" asked Lillian, "At say, one o'clock?"

Porter nodded.

"I'll have your credentials ready, funds, and some forms to sign. We can finish up this orientation then—and answer any questions you may have on protocol and procedure."

"It's been a pleasure," Porter said, shaking her hand. He was standing when there were two loud raps on the door.

"Ah, my one o'clock is a little early," Lillian smiled. She walked Porter to the door and opened it. An older man, tall and lanky, well into his seventies, stood there smiling. "Please come in, Nick," she said. "Porter and I were just finishing up."

"I did not interrupt?" Nick said, apologetically, and entered the room. He had an accent, barely. Somewhere from the middle of Europe, but Porter wasn't sure where.

"No, no," she said. "Nick, this is Porter Gibson—Porter, this is Nick—gentleman."

They shook hands and exchanged greetings.

"Wait—you're the writer?" he asked. "Yes?"

Porter nodded slowly.

"I read your work, *Industrial Time,*" he said. "It's very good. I like the way you think."

Porter's eyes widened.

"The machine will either liberate us or enslave us all," Nick continued. "It's not the intention of the machine to do either—you have to wonder—but the intention of the ghosts in it, as they say, and who or what put them there. Will we ever learn? That is our conundrum."

"All the ghosts," Porter mumbled, "Such ... *possibilities* ... To be forever haunted—or not."

"Ha! A poet, too," Nick smiled. "Fancy that, Lillian."

Porter noticed Lillian. She was smiling, but still holding the door, so he said his goodbyes. As he walked out, he placed the thin, angular face, the high cheekbones, the narrow chin. Yet, it was the intensity of his sunken eyes, that's what struck him. He had heard about his eyes before. They were as light as he had heard, but he wasn't expecting *colors*. One was more blue than gray, and the other more gray than blue. At least that is how he described it later on, when he would tell people about the chance meeting he had that day. Or was it chance? With Redfern he never knew. *Things* just happened—would happen—in a most unexpected way. Like today—the very first time he met him, the most brilliant mind he'd ever meet, Nikola Tesla.

Hallowe'en, 1932

The Lay of the Land

The train station for Downeast Way was a modest affair. The concourse was no larger than a lobby of a small bank or an oversized front room with lofty ceilings. To one side, a pair of ticket windows fronted an office area. A small number of wooden benches were along the side walls. Opposite the office, a windowed façade opened onto a platform where the train pulled in and rolled out. The station was large enough to handle the increased flow of summer traffic to the region, but not large enough to go unnoticed or unseen in. That is, if one was in the business of going unnoticed and unseen. Therefore, after surveying the station, the man kept his distance. His approach was from the end of a narrow winding street, more an alley but for the few shop fronts along it, that came out opposite the station.

He had set out north when the call came, to the eastern frontier of Maine. The distance was great, but no matter. He pushed hard and arrived early in anticipation, wanted to know the lay of the land. He met an old friend, who had made his way there after the war. He had given up on the city life, his friend had told him, and found himself in the middle of nowhere, but at the center of all things.

It was the friend who filled him in on the growing legend of the ballplayer. This was his hometown—he who had *invented* the great symbol of the age with a mere flick of the middle finger. Amazing. There was much more about him that he wanted to know, but what he wanted to know most was how he had survived the car impact: The flash—and then the car spun around him, its front end left smoldering, but him left without a scratch. How?

The trains arrived four times a day: mid-morning, early afternoon, early evening, and midnight. He had come to survey the crowds amidst the arrivals and departures for three days. Saw nothing amongst the ordinary, but trouble was coming. That he was sure of. There was a car with Massachusetts plates. He watched for it, but he had seen enough to know that wolves hunt from all directions.

Tonight, on the third night, instead of a wolf, he spied the ballplayer—the prey—walk out of the train station. There was another man, a friend by the greeting, who met him, but that was it. There was no one else around. The two strolled off, joking and laughing, down the street. He followed them from afar, until, at the edge of town, they walked up to a small caravan hitched to a motorcar. He waited there for some time, watching, observing, and then he was gone.

Borrowed Time

"You're living on borrowed time," the gypsy woman said softly. There was an air of caution in her voice, all the more accentuated by her distinct accent, some kind of English, but kind of something else.

"Borrowed from whom?" replied Porter casually.

"That's what took you here," she continued, evading his question. "It's part of your journey."

"My journey?" said Porter, confused. "What took me here was my buddy Jeffah, and I'm still not sure why. Told me I *had* to come here and *he* wouldn't tell me why."

"You will," she answered, reassuring him. They were sitting at a round table in the back of a small caravan. The lighting was dim even though rows of candles flickered on the surrounding shelves. He'd been sitting there for fifteen minutes or so, his hands in hers, listening to the story of his life as told by Madam Luna. Not that being reassured by her was discomforting. Porter hadn't expected her to say she was a gypsy woman. An itinerate. That she stopped in town after town for a few days or weeks at a time, reading the fortunes of rubes and rednecks up and down the coast. The lettering on the side of the wagon said it all—*Fortunes Lost and Found, Read and Told, by the All-Knowing, All-Seeing Madam Luna.*

"How do you know that?" responded Porter. "What is your game, anyway?" He was getting testy and impatient with being there. The train had dropped him in town a short while ago and he had not yet made the rounds or said the proper hellos to his aunt and uncle.

"I have a third eye," she answered him coolly.

"So do I," replied Porter. "It's not all-seeing, but it does have a great sense of direction, especially in the *heat* of the night." That finally got a smile out of her.

From the first look at her, Porter thought she was a hot ticket, with her dark blue, penetrating eyes. When he and his life-long pal showed up, she simply studied them for a minute and said, "Well, I can't do both of you." That prompted the two of them to giggle like school boys. "At least not at the same time," she added, innocently. Then Jeff commented, "Thanks, but I'm a married man and father of three."

"No, no, no!" the woman snapped at them. "Men are so predictably dull. Always—it's about *them*. Did either of you take notice of the sign on the wagon?" She shook her finger at them. "I *do* know what you're

50

thinking!" She was feisty, which got Porter's attention right away.

"I was just kidding, Miss Luna," replied Jeff, defensively.

"Learn to think with your other head," she scolded him.

"I didn't mean anything by it," added Jeff.

"Men never do." She pounced on him. "Yet they squander every opportunity to make the world right." Then her demeanor changed. Smiling pleasantly, she added, "I was talking about reading your auras. One cannot do both simultaneously. Too taxing and diluting." She eyed Porter. "It is you I need to speak with, anyway." She grabbed his arm with a gentle tug. "Your friend must leave. He has done as I asked."

"Just as well," mumbled Jeff, relieved. Porter stared at him, confused. He'd played along with him, but this was too much. "I imagine the missus must be wondering where the heck I'm at. I'll meet you back at the house." He bounded off the back of the caravan and slipped away before Porter could say a thing. At thirty-five, Jeff had the energy of five boys in a playground. Porter woke up each morning and his knees were stiff and ached. Years of catching can do that, through high school, college, and pro ball. A lot of catchers his age limped. Had a scar or two across their knees or hands and arms. Not Porter. He still had game in him, and could compete with any of the twenty-year-olds. What got his goat was Jeff and why *he* couldn't keep up with *him* anymore.

"You pick your friends well," Madam Luna smiled. "He's a good man, but should quit while he's ahead."

"Quit what?" Porter asked, unsure of what she meant. "Because I'd say he just did."

"No." She cleared her throat and thought for a moment. "In England, where my father's from, when a man sets out on a career path he finds himself situated, more likely than not, for life. Here, one refers to their situation as a job. It can be a temporary station or quite permanent. For your friend, I see a boat. He goes to sea. Trades in cargo."

"Shoot, that's just a lucky guess," said Porter, bluntly. "Anyone can tell he's a fisherman. The guy smells like a fucking mackerel. Half the town does."

She smiled, and said, "Madam Luna does not guess as you insinuate." Porter was about to excuse himself and go catch up with Jeff. He was tired and felt foolish being there. Besides, he had long ago made it a habit to avoid anyone who spoke of themselves in the third person—particularly when there are only two people in the room. "It's not fishing that I see, anyway," she ventured. "That's not the cargo. That's not what he's on to. You know what this is about, too. And you're the only one who can stop him." She paused and closed her eyes. "Which is one of the reasons why you're here ... sent here." He had to admit, she'd just piqued his curiosity. "It's for his own good. The odd thing is, he's ignoring his own intuition, too. He knows he's crossed the line one too many times. There's real danger afoot. Lives in the balance. Betrayal at hand."

"Lady, you said you needed to see me," said Porter. "Was this to tell me about my buddy Jeffah? That his ship's run aground?"

"No, and you may call me Viola," she said, except it sounded like 'Fee-ola' to Porter, the way she pronounced it.

"Fine!" he replied. "How'd you do, Viola. My name's ..."

"Shush!" she interrupted him. "I don't want to know *your* name. It's better that way when I'm reading the energy off you."

Porter studied her long and hard without saying a thing. Jeff was right. She was quite the cat. Attractive. Buxom. Dark complexion, dark hair, yet those blue eyes. High cheekbones that sculpted her face like the image of a Roman siren. Jeffah had told him, besides her good looks, she was a mysterious woman who had come through town late last spring. A gypsy who read fortunes. One morning, the sight of a caravan appeared atop a hill at the edge of town. There it stayed for the better part of two weeks. In that time, a slow, awkward parade of the curious and curious-minded made their way to the wagon. Jeff had visited her the night a heavy fog rolled in, her last night in town. He'd found himself confused after the visit. She'd told him all the good things he expected about his wife and family. That he'd remembered. But what struck him initially was what she'd told him when he'd entered the wagon. "Ah, you've finally come," as though she had expected him. She had eased him into the caravan—treated him as an old friend. They shared a glass of something called slivovice or slivovitza—a clear, fiery liquid that ignited your throat and lungs and tasted of toxic plums. He took more than one shot—it'd be rude not to. There was laughter, too. He felt like he did when Porter was around—able to open up and be himself. Not the serious man that the trade was turning on—the one that the runners and shadowy money men depended on to make it happen. Most of all was how she'd left it. "Your fate is tied to another," she had said. "A man. Lanky, strong, athletic, yet sensitive and observant. He works with his hands, head, and his heart. So much a part of you, like a brother, but not related by blood. You must bring him to me." That was the last thing he'd recalled with the gypsy woman. When he found himself in the cabin of his trawler, the sun shining brightly through the port holes, he thought it had been a dream. He stepped out on the deck and looked around. Up on the hill, the caravan was gone as though it had never been. Church bells pealed loudly, calling in the flock, as it did each Sunday morning. The funny thing was that Jeff had wandered up to see the gypsy right after dinner on Friday night. Somehow he'd lost thirty-six hours. More importantly, no one had missed him for thirty-six hours. His wife asked him how the catch was when he went home, as though they'd talked about it. He never spoke of the gypsy woman, what she said, or the time lapse to anyone. No one but Porter. Then today, the gypsy woman's caravan reappeared on the side of the hill, as though she knew he was coming. That's why he had convinced Porter to go—hell, dragged him here from the train station. Everything that had happened to Jeff had been bottled up for months. He didn't care if Porter believed him or not. He couldn't spend another day wondering about the spell the gypsy woman had put him under.

That's what Jeff had told Porter. She was the real deal and more. There and then, looking at her across from him, Porter could not argue the point. That she should arrive the same day as he was odd. He wasn't even sure the exact day he was arriving in Downeast Way until after he had seen his sister, Gracie.

"Viola, you say?" asked Porter, after a minute had passed without her speaking.

"Yes," she answered. "That's right."

"I thought you gypsy women were supposed to be old crones and have names like Natasha or Katrina or Olga. Something with a Bohemian or Hungarian flair or ring to it?"

"Ha!" she laughed lightly. "Well, if it helps, my real name is Fialová—Viola in English—and I'm from Moravia, right between those two places, from a city named Brno."

"Well, I was only saying—I didn't mean to pry."

"Yes, you did," she said. "Could I offer you a tea, or perhaps a drink? Scotch I believe."

Porter scratched his head. "You do know a way to a man's heart, Viola. I haven't had a decent Scotch in a while. There's a Prohibition going on here—Federal offense—highly illegal." He looked at her and smiled slyly. "Make mine a double, please."

"You've read too many books," she said while pouring him the drink. "And I can see by your aura that you've read considerably. You could teach, but you chose not to. You do write. It's the writing that's in you. It's how you express your anger over what's gone wrong. The injustice." She handed him the Scotch, and held up one of her own. *"Na zdravi!"* She tapped the table with the bottom of her glass, raised it swiftly and met Porter in the eye. Before he blinked, she had downed it in one gulp.

"Where are you taking me, Viola?" asked Porter. He was impressed. The woman was starting to get inside his head. He looked at her, hoping to pick up any hint of deception. For the first time, he wanted to make sure he wasn't being had. That Jeff hadn't set him up for a laugh.

"Come, sit down at the table. Lay your hands flat, palms up." That's when she'd clasped each hand with one of her own. "Ah, such large hands, too. Callused, rough. You work with your hands. You catch objects."

"Only what's within my reach, Viola." Porter said it with a smile and stared into her eyes. She returned the gaze. Later, when he recalled this moment, this was the part that had always confused him. He'd asked himself a thousand times throughout the years. Was he hypnotized? The longer he stared, the further he fell into the well of her soul. He always wanted to say it was him falling into her, but when he came through the other side, it was she who had passed through him. That's what it felt like. Because that was the moment she held his hands tightly and said, prophetically, *"You're living on borrowed time."*

"Borrowed from whom?" was what Porter had replied, coolly and aloof.

His casual tone did not fool her. Even after he had made her smile with the off-the-wall 'third eye' comment, Madam Luna did not ease her grip. She smiled kindly, but continued. "You have an old soul; restless and wise. Too much really for one lifetime. Yes. You have already lived many lives. You'll stand and fight against the hypocrisy, but you must keep moving. You know instinctively. If you don't, she'll catch you as she has before."

"With my pants down?" Porter said, smiling. "It wouldn't be the first time."

"So you know her?"

"Know who?"

"The Angel of Death."

"Never met her. I thought you meant Emma Goldman."

"She's around you."

"Emma?" Porter said, playfully. "I haven't seen her since they sent her old, chubby ass back to Russia."

"You know who I'm talking about," she said. "The Angel of Death. She wants you—*you* know."

"Viola, if she's anywhere near inviting as you are, then I'm a dead man."

"What was your name?" she asked, knowing full well before she had told him the contrary.

"Herbert Hoover," he said, loudly, with a look around the wagon. "I currently live in Washington, D.C."

"You're endowed with a sense of humor, too," she said. She squeezed his hands, and then rubbed the centers of his palms gently, with her thumbs.

"I've been told that, among other things," replied Porter, feeling flush and slightly disoriented.

"I think you could make me laugh all night," she said. "But it's time I know your name. Think."

"I thought you were averse to such things," said Porter, concerned all of a sudden.

"With you, you're an exception to the rule. You've always been an exception," she responded. "She's there. The Angel. Hovering. I want to know why she's after you, or following you. That's why I need your name now."

"If she's close by, I'd rather not say my name out loud," said Porter. "Might not be the best move at the moment. I'm not in any hurry to cash it in—to meet her or it or whatever."

"There's no hurry, love. We have all night." She smiled coyly.

"I was hoping you'd say that."

"I know," she said. "Remember? I have a third eye."

"You are perceptive," said Porter, "but lest you forget, so do I. Remember?"

"It's hidden within you."

"Blind and mute, actually, but the boy's as deft as Helen Keller about finding his way around." Porter laughed. It was all he could do. He'd only had a couple of sips of his Scotch, but his head was light and he suddenly felt giddy.

"More than that," she ignored the double entendre, staying focused, "and you know it." She paused to grip his hands securely, as though to prevent a fall she knew would come otherwise. "Such was the fate of your young friend," she said sadly, solemnly. She felt the give, as he tugged and nearly tumbled from the seat.

"What the!!!" Porter gasped.

"Shush," she said soothingly. "It's okay. He's all right. Leave him be. What matters now is before you." Again she paused, staring into his eyes as if caressing him in her arms. "You know to trust your instincts or she'd have caught up to you again. One does not easily elude time. There are people who are plucked from the garden as they peak and bloom. There are those who grow like weeds, choking the vitality of the flowers around them. Others wilt, and overstay their welcome, but cling to life long past the autumn frost and into winter. That's just the way it is. Then, I would argue, there are the few who find out on their own or with the aid of generations, and manage to put themselves in the way of things. People like you ..." She trailed off, hesitated, and then seemed to concentrate hard for a moment, searching for the correct word, before releasing the name, "... Porter. They rise to greatness."

That was the moment of truth for Porter. It was too much. Stunned, he released her hands, as though an electrical charge had passed through him. In fact, he realized, it had. His hands and arms tingled. She had bored her way into his mind. He knew he'd met the real deal.

She reached for his hands and gripped them tightly. "People who find their way to the front of things, who lead, must beware. For the Angel is relentless. She's always there, hovering and waiting."

"I only know one thing right now," he said. His mouth was dry and he swallowed hard. "And so do you."

"Yes." She released her grip and leaned back and reached for the Scotch. With a nod, she topped off Porter's glass and poured herself another. "It's time to blow out those candles..." She smiled that knowing smile at him. Porter sat frozen—stunned, really—as she extinguished the flames, one candle at a time, and then quietly led him into the sweet warmth of the darkness.

The Packard

The Turnpike Road wound its way along the central Maine coast until it reached the Waldo-Hancock Bridge. Considered an engineering marvel, the newly completed bridge shaved hours of driving for motorists going down east or to the Maritimes. Before, motorists veered north, followed the road all the way up to Brewer. Only there could they cross the

Penobscot River to Bangor, and steer south or southeast to their destinations. Or motorists and pedestrians could take a ferry across Penobscot Bay, share it with sheep, swine, oxen or cattle, pick up the Turnpike Road on the other side and continue east, back on the winding road, through small towns and villages near and along the coast. The road became treacherous there, too, in places, because coastal Maine becomes rugged. Low mountains rise a thousand to fifteen hundred feet high along the Eastern Frontier. They could beat the best cars; more than one had gone through a curve or off a cliff. Filling stations became irregular the further east one traveled. A turn into a village for petrol meant a drive down a dirt road, over cattle crossings, past horse drawn carts, with no guarantee of a filling station at the end. Yet the roads were traversed. Down east had its allies. Governor Roosevelt summered just over the border in New Brunswick at Campobello. The Rockefellers, Morgans, Van Camps, and the like, had turned Mount Dessert Island into a summer retreat for the Gilded Class, and then turned it into a National Park, Acadia, to preserve *the* wilderness.

Hardy had been informed, on the first trip he had made, how difficult the journey would be. The ride took a full day from Boston, sometimes longer. But he never was bothered by the length of the trip. The business pushed him. He was paid well and time was of no consequence to him. The first few trips, he had gone alone, quietly leaving town when he finished and quietly returning when the time came. Introduced himself as Mr. Walker's representative that first day he arrived—to a banker and businessman he had been instructed to contact. He enjoyed the silence of the long rides. It gave him time to think. But that didn't last—couldn't— once the unfortunate accidents began to accumulate at sea and on land— pirating in the Gulf of Maine and holdups along the Turnpike Road. On one ship, a cook had been shot—in the back! Hardy had known it would be only a matter of time before it started, and when it did it would necessitate escorts. Usually he took just one, but today necessitated two. He looked at them in the front seat of the car. Mr. Walker sent him there regularly to collect the residue of whisky money. Booze flowed down from the north— Canada or the Island of St. Pierre—and a sizeable chunk of Mr. Walker's flow went through the small hamlet he now approached. How foolish Americans were, he thought. A land mass, a country this large, regulates the social habits of the citizenry because they don't have the will to regulate it themselves, and end up a bunch of drunks. Peaceful habits, mostly, gone bad. He long ago concluded that Prohibition was a mockery, enacted by narrow-minded rubes, but it had made his employer, and many men like him, millions. No one but fools abided, and made every other man a criminal and every other woman a whore.

The car, a Packard, approached the crest of a steep incline. Hardy leaned forward from the back seat and spoke to the driver. "Be careful here on out, Mr. Calvin, on your descent. It's gonna be steep and winding for a time, until we near town." Mr. Calvin nodded.

"It's fine country, Hardy," said the man next to Mr. Calvin, "Peaceful."

"Aye, Murton," he replied. "Fine country, I'll grant you that. But peaceful?" He shook his head.

"It reminds me of home some."

"You went home. You had a job to do there. You did it. You earned some points. What peace did you find there?"

"I meant I see a lot of the Highlands here."

"We're not on holiday, Murton. There's business to attend to."

"It's got me thinking, that's all," Murton said.

'Well, there's much to think about, Murton."

"I know our business here."

"Do you?"

"Yes," Murton replied, and said no more. But he did think—about what lay ahead, what he was, and what he knew. When every man's for himself, then every man becomes an outlaw.

Mr. Hardy looked out the window. The Packard was picking up speed. "Easy does it, Mr. Calvin. The road is *very* treacherous ahead."

Riddles of a Gypsy

"I'll see you again, Porter." He was laying on the edge of the bed, facing her, staring into her eyes—another shade of blue in the morning light, bright and shiny. "You're thinking, no," she added, "How is that possible? But even I don't know. It's more of a feeling."

"No, Viola," he shook his head, "I'm thinking, how soon? And when?"

She smiled. "That's not how men think."

"That's the problem. They generally don't."

"Sometimes, I think, all but a game." She squeezed his cock. "Like that!" He leaned in close, kissed her forehead and cheeks, and then leaned back.

"They're barbarians, men. More ape than man."

"Including you?"

"Yes. Especially me." He smiled slightly.

"Ha!" she said, and reached to the window sill. A pack of cigarettes was there. She pulled one and lit it. Took a long drag and then handed it to Porter, who causally took a draw. "Men move on. Women move forward. That's what I was told by my mother—her causal explanation for the accident of my life."

"Your father?" He leaned back and exhaled.

"Yes, a British businessman."

"After Gypsies, was he?" Porter joked.

"No. The things they need to make guns with," she answered. "They did that well in Brno. The foundries."

"I hear they still do."

"Yes," she nodded. "They still do. But now they make the guns there, too—the Zbrojovka, for all the armies everywhere—the Communists, the Socialists, the Monarchists."

"You talk like he was into more things than business?"

"It was no accident he was there. That I'll grant you," she nodded. "Even then, before the war, the old landed power was decayed. The peasants had turned from the field to the factories. That's where the new power was, the power of the machine—foundries, factories, plants. Everyone wanted guns. They got them, and then—ka-boom! War."

"You're very observant, my dear," he said. "Because it's going that way again, it's going to happen again."

"Again?" She feigned a laugh. "You don't know the old way of thinking. The feudal world. The nobility—the counts and barons and bishops—against the peasants and their counterparts, the workers. No, it never ended, Porter. Neither side surrendered. The war continues in its way. In the shadows."

He thought for a moment, reflecting, and then said, "A shadow. I think so, Viola. It's here, too, over this country, over this town. Prohibition and depression." He inhaled the cigarette again, and handed it to her. "Desperation is everywhere, like a long shadow."

"Yes. Where reason falters, chaos follows." She took a long drag, and slowly released the smoke, only to pull it back through her nostrils before blowing it out, up toward the window. "Life becomes a series of continuous accidents. That is the times, the world, in which we live."

"This is no accident," he said. "I had my doubts, but you made me a believer."

"I don't know how I found this place, or why. I grant you that. When I came through last spring, dragging the caravan, I stopped."

"And you met Jeffah?"

"The man who brought you here? Your friend? Yes. He spoke of his life, and he mentioned his best friend in Brooklyn. That was all I needed to hear."

"Wait! You mean you knew about me?" Porter asked, stunned. "Is this a confession?"

"No. My mother had family in Brooklyn. For me, it was a connection, a sign, why I was here."

Porter fidgeted, confused, maybe angered or felt had. He felt hosed, and sat up and placed his bare feet on the cool floor.

"That was all he told me." She took one last drag on the cigarette and crushed it on the sill, talking to his back. "You just told me you're a believer." Her voice rose, but then, pausing, she spoke softly, innocently, "Now you all but say I am a liar?"

Porter stared blankly. "No," he said. "It just sounded too much of a coincidence."

"Relax, then," she said. "It was not *a* coincidence, but a *meaningful* coincidence. I'd found the reason I had stopped. I knew. That's when I told him to bring you to me, and we spoke no more of it."

"She had family there, you said, your mother?"

"Yes. Important people, you could say."

"Really? Important gypsies?"

"My mother, nor I, are of the Romani blood—we're not really gypsies. It is a *cover* for me. But I *do* have a gift, and it's easier in this country to *be* a gypsy for my gift to be accepted as genuine."

"What? Are your people in Brooklyn real gypsies? Did *they* up and move?" He glanced back at her. He couldn't stop himself. "Or your mother—did she up and move to Maine, maybe? Is *that* how you got here?"

"No." Her eyes narrowed. "*She* up and died." Pausing, she let the arrow strike, and then added, "*That's* how I got here."

The sting of the remark buried Porter's head in the palms of his hands. "I'm sorry, Viola," he whispered. "I'm such a jackass."

"There is much about me you may not like, and even more you may never know. The wandering, the cavorting, fortunes found and lost—with strangers no less, too many, but I don't lie to people. I do not even mislead them. For most, I hold back fear and darkness that they have and hold—carry with them like a tumor. I wish for them to release it. It's much to ask wherever I go. That I know. My time is short. I stop and park for a day, a week. The ones who come to me do so freely. They seek answers. I do all I can to provide them."

"I said I'm sorry." He stood, searching for his clothes.

"Very well," she said.

Moments passed in silence before Porter could speak, "I have to go. I need to wire a friend."

She watched him dress, and encouraged him, "Yes. It is important you do. Today's the day."

Porter finished dressing, unsure of how to respond. He felt lost. He felt doubt. Was about to wish her well, to say goodbye, but she suddenly gasped for a breath, and began to speak urgently, "Everything you've been through in the past months will come to a head today. The reasons you're here, and there are many, will come at you at once. There is love, there is family, and there is relief—penance is fulfilled." Porter reached for her. He opened his mouth, but she placed her finger across his lips. " ... But there is more. There is also harm, great harm. It's coming this way." A tear welled up in her eye. "I fear her—I fear the Angel ..." She exhaled slowly. The tear released, and she breathed deeply. "She has and will show herself in many ways. Look and *listen*. Hear that word."

Their eyes met. Porter stared into her, searching for an answer. He grasped her hands, held them tightly. Finally, he whispered, "So many riddles. I ... I don't want it to end this way, Viola."

"I know," she replied, "And it won't ... I *will* see you again." She leaned forward, embraced him, and then kissed his lips and cheeks.

The Deferential Continuum

The telegram sat atop stacks of file folders and papers arrayed on the desk. Lillian crushed a cigarette out in the ashtray that was on center, and blew the last of the smoke from her lungs gently. The small cloud moved slowly toward the open window, being drawn, less than pushed, by the pull of air from without. She was tempted to open the window further, to allow the lingering haze of smoke to be sucked out completely before Redfern arrived, but pigeons cooed on the ledge. Since the screen had launched in a late summer thunderstorm, she'd been reluctant to open the window too wide. On one occasion a bird had flew in, and she'd spent the better part of an hour attempting to grab the thing as it flailed and flapped haplessly against the window glass and walls. Finally the drama had ended in rage and terror for woman and bird, respectively, when she pulled a .38 from her purse, took aim and fired. The hole was still there, and the bullet, too, lodged in the upper part of the wall, to the right of the window jamb above the door. Fortunately for the bird, she hadn't gone skeet shooting in years and missed. Frustrated, she had taken aim again, just when Mr. Redfern opened the door, walked in, and the bird flew out. "Morning, Lillian," he had said, cheerfully, and then added, "Scavenging for breakfast?" She had lowered the gun and asked for a raise. He had laughed, but complied. She now glanced at the bullet hole. Thought about opening the window further, but only grumbled. On the other hand, she could just stop smoking for a minute to let the room clear. After all, the cigarette pack on her desk was empty. Juxtaposed, the tray was heaped with ash and filled with butts rimmed with red lipstick. Light smoke continued to rise from it like a steamy cauldron. With a sigh, she pulled a fresh pack from her purse, lit another, and went for coffee.

The familiar jingle of keys at the door was followed by two knocks, and then it opened.

"Afternoon, Mrs. Banks," said Redfern. He stepped in and shut the door behind him. Through the haze of smoke, he spied the stacks on the desk, but mostly the ashtray, overflowing and smoldering. "It's beginning to cloud up outside, too," he smiled. "Rain, I believe, no later than tomorrow." He glanced at the window. "You might want to leave the roost and venture out while you can. While you're gone, I'll open the window a tad further, but could you leave the gun? Just in case?"

"You're funny, Fred," she said. "How was your lunch with Reynolds?"

"Predictable. He's on his way back to D.C." He placed his hat and coat on the corner rack, and then went back and opened the door again.

"Funding?"

"We're still afloat. He believes if Hoover wins, and he's confident he will, we'll all be farting through silk for a while." His head dropped and his eyes moved around as though he were looking for something on the floor.

"And the work?"

"It's only a matter of time."

"Old man Volstead is fit to retire, I know. But what about us? Our kind?"

"Not everyone shares Secretary Stimson's view." He stopped, then picked up the waste can and propped it against the door. "Then again, we could always write a book, like Yardley did."

"Ha!" she laughed, and returned to her desk. "I'm not the one you should be talking to about writing a book."

"So you've been reading our friend's new book?"

"Yes, finally, I have," she said.

"And?"

"I think Porter's on to something."

"You mean common sense."

"Yes, that's his whole point, right? Porter's all Thomas Paine, not Karl Marx—yet by observing our country's profound lack of common sense, he's been labeled a Communist because of it."

"He *was* front and center at the Washington Square riot."

"Protesting the war with Goldman and her crowd didn't help things, Fred, I know that. But anyone who protested the war was labeled a Communist or Socialist or Anarchist."

"True, and Porter distanced himself from them very quickly after that debacle. He found his own autonomous symbol of protest right in his pocket." He flicked Lillian the finger and held it there for a moment. "He introduced this as a hearty 'Fuck you' to the man. That's what he told me. Somehow he got a couple hundred protestors, on his signal, to raise their middle fingers at a wall of coppers running at them, billy clubs swinging, and shout, 'Fuck off,' simultaneously. That's the stuff of legend."

"Well, the finger flicker flies once again," she smiled. "Your tourist dropped you a line, Fred."

"A postcard, Lillian?"

"No, a telegram," she pointed at the desk. "Mr. Digit sends his greetings."

"He's arrived, then?"

"Safe and sound, and in the company of friends, family, and a gypsy," she said.

"Should I even bother to ask?"

"I think we should *defer* to his better judgment," she said. "There's one other thing, Fred, that's been on my mind."

"Yes, Lillian?"

"I'm starting to have reservations."

"I've had mine, too." Redfern still wondered if he *had* done the right thing, involving Porter, asking him as he did, but also sending him in blind. It was futile to second-guess now. "But then, he's not alone—have you heard from his guardian angel?"

She nodded. "Saint Malachi arrived two days ago. There's been no other occurrence since that close call."

Redfern nodded, "Porter's in good hands." He then placed his hands under the window sill. "Ready? Let's clear the air."

"Yes," she said, and held down or covered the files and papers on the desk with her hands, arms, and head. Mr. Redfern slid the window all the way up. In one thrust, like the suction of a mighty vacuum, the room cleared of smoke.

Lunch at Leo's Drugstore

"Well, it is what she said, Jeffah," Porter explained. "I'm not making it up." The two men were sitting at the lunch counter of Leo's Drugstore, nursing coffee and eating fish and fried potatoes. "Look! You're the one who brought me there. You're asking me what happened. What she said. I'm telling you what she said."

"Yeah, but you never showed up last night. What were you—out all night, Porter?" he asked.

"I got distracted. In all the excitement, I forgot about the time. It was very late before she was done with me."

Jeff rolled his eyes. "Okay, this ain't fifth grade and we're not sitting in Mrs. Kimball's class. That I understand. I don't need to hear every last sordid detail of your visit with the gypsy woman, either. That exotic beauty I was so kind to introduce you to."

"What do you want me to say, Jeffah? That I gave her the finger?" Porter's voice rose sharply above the noontime hubbub when he mentioned the finger. Jeff laughed out loud.

"That's all I need to know, Valentino," said Jeff, and let out a low whistle. "You're a son-of-a-bitch, you know that?"

Porter thought about it for a moment and heaved a sigh. "I thought you wanted to know what she *said?*"

"I heard you," replied Jeff. "I'm not deaf and dumb. She said you were being followed by the Angel of Death. Did she happen to mention if it was *the* Angel or *an* Angel of Death?"

"I didn't know you were an authority, nor that there was more than one," Porter answered.

"Oh, there's more than one. In these times, it's about the only job they're hiring for," Jeff said with a laugh.

"She didn't say actually, whether it was *the* Angel or *an* Angel." Porter thought about the question. "But she did say that it was a she."

"The Angel of Death is a woman?" said Jeff. He sounded indignant. "Can't be—why would a woman go around killing everybody?"

"I don't know. Maybe she's just meant for me. Maybe she's *my* Angel of Death. Maybe she was assigned to me the moment I was propelled from my mother's womb."

"Porter, you think too much about too many things."

"First of all, you're the one who opened up the discussion. Seeing as you did, and for once it's interesting, think about it for a minute or two." He hesitated, and then added a little louder, "Or doesn't anybody think anymore?"

"Shush—damn you Porter," said Jeff. "At least let me finish my lunch."

"I'm asking you to think about what you just asked me," Porter said, insisting. "If you believe in all that heaven and hell stuff, then that means you have to believe in all those angels and demons—right?" Jeff nodded his head and stuffed a chunk of haddock into his mouth. "It's in the manual, whether it's the one King James wrote, the Pope wrote, Abraham wrote, or Mohammed wrote. Now, the Almighty, in all His magnanimity and omnipotence, even He came to recognize, early on in the game of running the universe, that He couldn't manage all these souls. There's simply too many of us. So, He made angels to help Him guard over all these souls. To keep them from being harvested by demons set forth by the fallen one."

"Considering the times, I'd say He didn't make enough angels to cover the spread," said Jeff.

"No denying that," replied Porter. "Which brings me back to the Angel of Death, and her pursuit of me, and my whole damned point."

"Which is what? Because I have no idea where you're going with this."

"Course you do," said Porter. "What if my guardian angel is also *my* Angel of Death? What if it's the same for everyone?"

"You mean the one sent to guard over us is also sent to kill us?" Jeff pondered.

"Yes," Porter replied.

"Sounds like marriage to me," Jeff said.

"Ha! It is what you make of it. There's a balance to everything and there's always retribution—one way or the other, it will catch up with you, as sure as the Angel of Death will someday. If not on this side, then on the other."

Jeff glanced around and noticed more than one ear bending hard in their direction. "Here we go," he thought. "The rumor mill is beginning to turn." He took a sip of coffee and mumbled, "Not so loud, Porter. There's something to be said for keeping 'em guessing."

Porter turned his head slightly. Heads receded smoothly into the booths that lined the wall and tilted casually away along the lunch counter. "Probably a good thing to hear," he said a little louder. "Each and every one of us that comes onto this plane of existence is assigned a guardian angel. That's what we're told, according to the manuals."

"I'm not sure they would agree with you," said Jeff.

"Agree with what?"

"Your vision of heaven and hell sounds like some kind of bureau," said Jeff.

"I've often wondered," Porter mused, "given all the rules and regulations in the manuals."

"You wouldn't think the difference between right and wrong could be that hard to master."

"No you wouldn't, but I've come to realize over the years that there's a fine line between free will and what someone can get away with."

"Ha!" Jeff laughed. "That's because free will is just that—free!"

"You're inspiring me, Jeffah," said Porter. "If the choices between right and wrong were free, all those hucksters running the show and hawking the manuals would be shit out of luck and have to find a real job like the rest of us. In all the cities I've been through during this depression, I haven't seen one minister or preacher out on the street looking for work, let alone miss a meal. I find it funny how the business of saving people from themselves has become so damn profitable for such few people. But no, we're centuries away from putting those hucksters out on the street. Especially now that they have the radio. No more old-time camp meetings to spread the *word*. It's freed the bastards up to mass communicate and say anything to anyone as *gospel*. Hide behind their religion—in the name of God—wanting to convert everyone. Into what? I ask. Into the type of thinking that took the country into Prohibition? Into the Depression that's on? Into the kind of people who go around burning crosses and beating and lynching Papists, Jews, queers, or Negroes if they so much as blink an eye? Have you heard what happened up in Milo? It's Klan central up there—in the middle of the Woods of Maine. They're lily-white yet still find reasons to hate."

"Hey, settle down will ya," replied Jeff. "You got a whole lot of rage built up in you, Porter," said Jeff. "It's scary how you get so pissed off at times."

"I can't help myself," he said, and lowered his voice. "There's a little bit of the Klan in a lot of people, Jeffah. I see it everywhere I go and it's tough to swallow. And this Depression only makes it worse. On top of that, our leaders, so called betters, are out of touch, dammit. We have a President in office who keeps telling us everything is fine and prosperity is right around the corner. Meanwhile, entire families are out on the street. In Cincinnati, Chicago, St. Louis, Philadelphia, Pittsburgh, New York, and Boston—every damn city we play in—hell, it's happening here! I suppose if something is wrong long enough, it gives the superficial appearance of being right. People tend to accept it as fact. Think about that. Thomas Paine said something pretty close to it a hundred and fifty years ago—he called it '*Common Sense*'—and even after all these years, we're still suffering from an overwhelming lack thereof."

"I think I know what you're saying," Jeff said, "sort of."

"I hope so," replied Porter. "I hope you all are," he spoke up a little louder. "Because all I'm really asking, what I really want to know is, where are all the guardian angels hiding? Where have they gone?"

Porter quieted. Jeff hesitated for a moment, then said, "Maybe there's just too many souls to manage. Maybe we've gone too far."

"You might be right," Porter said. "Could be that there is too many of us now. Hell, just consider the cat. One female can procreate over four hundred thousand cats in seven years. Now, *that's* a lot of souls."

"Yeah, but—hey," Jeff stopped, confused. "Cats don't have souls."

"I can say emphatically that they *do*," Porter winked. "Because that gypsy woman's one helluva pussy, and believe me, she's got plenty of soul."

"You ol' horn dog, you! I knew it! You son-of-a-gun!" laughed Jeff, giddy with anticipation. "What was *it* like?"

"What do you mean—what was *it* like?" asked Porter, grinning. "You're talking like you actually think there's a difference from one to the other."

"Well, there is, you know," Jeff countered.

"Ha! *Mon ami*—'all cats are gray in the dark!'" said Porter. "Or have you been married *that* long?"

"Don't bring my Catherine into it!" groaned Jeff. "God—do you ever stop bullshitting, Porter?"

"I was trying to have a serious conversation with you about the meaning of life and death," Porter defended himself, "and all you want to know is if I got laid last night."

"Shush ... not so *loud*," Jeff implored. "You'll have the whole damned town talking, and I'll have to explain to Catherine how I don't know a friggin' thing ... again!"

"That shouldn't be too difficult, Jeffah."

"If you're trying to piss me off, it's working."

Porter nodded. "Speaking of which, I gotta take one." He twisted and slipped off the stool. As he walked toward the rear of the drugstore, a man in a long, black coat passed him. Porter was drawn to the white collar fixed snugly around his neck. He nodded and smiled at him, but the priest did not notice. His eyes were fixed ahead.

"Good afternoon, Jeff," the priest waved, and went to him.

Jeffah's Confessor

"Father Durrell—good to see you," replied Jeff, standing and shaking his hand.

"Sit, sit, my boy, please," he said. He noticed Porter's place setting, the half-finished meal and half-filled coffee mug, and asked, "Am I interrupting?"

"No, no, Father," answered Jeff. "That's my friend's—you must have just passed him."

"Oh, that tall fellow," he said, throwing his thumb over his shoulder, toward the back of the drugstore.

"We were just talking about religion, matter of fact," said Jeff, who noticed Porter walking back their way.

"All good, I venture to say?" asked Father Durrell.

"Somewhat, Father," answered Porter. "We were reflecting on the growing influence of religion over the radio waves, for one thing."

"I see," Father Durrell said, thoughtfully.

"Father, this is my good friend, Porter Gibson," said Jeff. "He's in town visiting."

"Ah, yes. Jeff has mentioned your name to me on more than one occasion." He grasped his hand and smiled. "Pleasure to meet you, Porter."

Porter shook his hand, entirely engulfing it in his. "The pleasure's all mine, sir." He returned the smile.

"You must have been discussing Father Coughlin," Father Durrell said, with a shake of his head. "The radio is no place for the pulpit."

"And the pulpit's no place for the radio," answered Porter. "I couldn't agree more."

"Ah, yes," said Father Durrell, sounding confused. He turned to Jeff, "Will I see you at the Gaelic Hall tonight, Jeffrey? The Hallowe'en gala always has a good showing."

"I'm not a hundred percent certain what we're doing," answered Jeff. "Catherine mentioned a Hallowe'en Social at Central Hall, too. I always leave it to her," he smiled.

"Of course—family comes first," he said. "But I do hope to see you, nevertheless. If not tonight, then surely before the end of the week," he winked.

"Surely," Jeff responded. "Perhaps after Mass tomorrow."

"It's a blessing to know you, Jeffrey Grant," he said. "I don't believe I could have eased the suffering these past few years without your continuing charity." He bowed slightly, winked, and smiled broadly. Not sure how to respond, Jeff blushed, and Porter laughed. "Well, I must be off. My cook and housekeeper, Miss Giroux, is returning this afternoon from an extended stay at her sister's in Auburn. I must tidy up the rectory, and I have several more stops before I hear confessions this afternoon. See you tomorrow if not tonight, then, Jeffrey," he said, and extended his hand.

"Father," Jeff nodded, and shook his hand. "Always good to see you."

Father Durrell acknowledged the gesture, and then addressed Porter, "Young man, it was nice to meet you," and extended his hand to him.

"And you, Father," said Porter, shaking it firmly.

"Keep an eye on that Father Coughlin, Porter, and his ilk," Father Durrell said, and added, "The love of Jesus is not for sale."

"His, Father Coughlin's, evidently is," replied Porter.

"And therein lies the problem, my son," said Father Durrell. "Beware of the man who offers his religion for sale. The path to spiritual enlightenment has no price."

"You mean John actually wrote, 'Make not my Father's house a house of merchandise' for a reason?"

"Ha! 2:16—that's very good, young man," replied Father Durrell, "And impressive. After, 'Thou shalt not kill,' and 'Thou shalt not steal,' perhaps the most summarily ignored verse in the entire Bible." He patted Porter's shoulder, and nodded good-bye to both men. Porter and Jeff watched him, his long coat flowing, address a few people as he moved through the lunch tables, before he walked out the door.

"I think I'm fit to be converted," Porter laughed.

"I think he has your number, Porter," said Jeff.

"Could be, but he seems rather fond of you," Porter said.

"We've bonded, so to speak," said Jeff.

"I never knew you to be so rooted in the faith, Jeffah," said Porter. Pausing, he spoke quietly from the corner of his mouth, "For a man who runs the rum," then laughed out loud.

"Dammit, Porter, shush up," Jeff said, and looked side-to-side, "Be serious for once. Cripes, you never know who might be *listening*."

"Shit, Jeffah, even the local priest knows what you're doing," laughed Porter. "I imagine by now the Bishop does, too."

"You know what he meant?" asked Jeff, flustered.

"Well, it wasn't like you were buddying up to him. He was buddying up to you," replied Porter. "He wasn't looking for you to come by with a hunk of mackerel or something. What else *could* it be?"

"You never *do* stop thinking," said Jeff. "Do you?"

"I was reasoning why a priest was buddying up to you, that's all," said Porter.

"I'm a goddamned likeable guy for starters," snapped Jeff. "Secondly, he's a priest. Priests and pastors are known to do that—mingle with their flock. Not all of them are hucksters!"

"Hey—I was just wondering about your chum. He seems like a nice guy—and surely intelligent—even if he does likes you," said Porter.

"You're wearing me out, and it's only been what—not even a full day," said Jeff, lowering his face into his hands.

"You got nothing to worry about," said Porter. "You have your buddy, Father Durrell on your side."

"Can you just be serious for a second, Porter?" said Jeff. "I don't think religion is bad. Come Sunday, I make a showing with Catherine and the kids—more often than not. The woman never gave up her religion when I married her—you know that—and it didn't matter that much to me which church I went to. She's never shoved it down my throat, either, but families go to church together, so I go with my family."

"Religion's not a bad thing," said Porter. "It's the hucksters and carnies selling it for a profit I have issues with."

"You have issues with everything," said Jeff.

"Point taken, but that doesn't answer the central tenet of the supposition?" said Porter.

"Ask anyone around me and they'd ask the same thing I'm about to ask you—what the *hell* are you talking about?"

"The priest—how the heck did he become your buddy?" replied Porter.

"I figured you'd figured it out by now—like everything else," said Jeff.

"I have," Porter grinned. "But I want to hear it from you."

"Dear Lord, Porter!" Jeff sighed. "Okay—I know the man on friendly terms since he arrived here from Auburn a few years ago. That's all. He's not a bad egg."

"From Auburn to Saint Patrick's? He must have fucked up pretty good," said Porter.

"What do you mean?"

"People don't volunteer for this place. You don't actually think the Church is that interested in helping people out in hard times, do you? They're interested in numbers—that's where churches get their *support*, as in, funds. In Auburn, they have numbers—the town's all French Canadian Catholics. In Downeast Way they don't have numbers, other than what there is up on Celtic Hill and a few Acadians from Nova Scotia and New Brunswick."

"This may come as a shock, but you're losing me," said Jeff.

"For a priest to be reassigned from Auburn to Saint Patrick's—well— he was buried for something."

"It's a wonder you don't get in a row wherever you go," Jeff said.

"You'd be surprised."

"I don't think I would."

"But I am right about Father Durrell?"

"Yes, Sherlock, the man likes his Irish whiskey. I give him a couple bottles every week or so."

"Funny, isn't it?" asked Porter.

"What now?"

"Why they call you guys rum runners when it's whiskey and Scotch that's run."

Jeff rolled his eyes.

"Well, that's what everyone drinks," Porter defended himself, "including most priests."

Jeff sighed, and then lifted a large piece of haddock to his mouth, stuffed it all in, chewed and swallowed hard.

"But priests don't get demoted for drinking, do they?" asked Porter.

"No, Porter, I don't think they do."

"If anything, there are not enough parishes like Saint Patrick's to go around."

"No, I don't believe there are," he agreed.

"Well?"

"Do I really have to say it?" asked Jeff.

"I think you do," answered Porter,

"I'm not one to gossip. Besides, I like the priest."

"I like him, too."

Jeff took a breath, looked to his right and left, then spoke in a whisper. "There's some who'd say he's a little too close to his housekeeper."

"The Miss Giroux mentioned," Porter whispered back.

"Yes, the one and the same."

"It sounds like a long story."

"And a very boring one."

"Indeed, but are you going to tell me, anyway?"

"Now who's acting like a fifth grader?"

"Ha! Ha!" Porter laughed out loud.

"Well, if it isn't Porter Gibson," a voice rose behind them, at once haughty and condescending. Porter turned slowly. Jeff remained still, which struck Porter as odd, until he noticed that the hair on the back of his neck, hands, and arms stood on edge.

"That voice," Porter said. "Tom Crowe? Or are you still calling yourself T.C.?"

"It has, and always will be, Thompson," he answered sternly. "Has the class struggle addled your senses?" A young boy, near teenaged, was at his side. The resemblance was unmistakable. "Hmm? Are you on the lam, rousing the proletariat, drifting through town—or maybe all of the above?"

"What brings you down from the mountain, Tom?" asked Porter, yawning. "Misery or business? Or is misery your business? Not like you to walk among the lower sorts, unless you're after something from them. Seems out of place."

"See, son," Thompson responded. "I told you that he could still hit one if he had to."

"So I shouldn't let his .227 batting average last year fool me, Father?" the boy asked. He had a squeaky voice, and the kid said it with a feigned innocence which, Porter noticed, made Jeff's fists clench.

"That's right, son. His problems at the plate are far greater than his inability to make contact with the ball—it's the people in his way who should fear for their lives," he cackled, which made the boy laugh.

"That's uncalled for!" Jeffah snapped, as he began to swing the counter stool. Porter caught him by the arm, twisting the stool back slowly. He met Jeffah's eyes, and with the slightest movement, Porter shook his head as if to say, "Not now."

"This must be your spawn, Tom," said Porter, coolly.

"It's Thompson, and yes, he is my son, Porter," he replied. "His name is Jacob, and I'll have you show some respect!" he added sternly.

"Respect?" Porter laughed at him. "How about I give you a *penny* for your thoughts instead?" He winked. "I'd have bet the farm that you'd never mate." Thompson gasped and his eyes narrowed. The vein in his right temple suddenly bulged. "Good thing I didn't, because, from what I hear it's one of the last in town you haven't foreclosed on." A few oohs and ahs, snickers and giggles, rose from the booths and counter.

"Maybe you should have asked a *gypsy* to read your fortune, Porter," Thompson responded coldly. "Then maybe Lady Luck would be on your side from time to time. Then maybe, just maybe, you'd know what the future would bring, and you'd really know what's good for you. Come, Jacob. We must not waste our time here further." He said it with as much authority as disdain. It caught Porter off-guard. He wondered how he knew anything about Viola or if it was simply a lucky guess. No, he knew. Porter never liked being surprised, particularly not by the likes of Tom Crowe. Before he could take another swipe at him, the two walked out of the drugstore. The boy slammed the door hard behind them. In its wake, a sudden, awkward pause followed among the patrons. Nobody knew what to say.

"Well? What's everyone gone lockjaw over?" Porter shouted out and looked around. "I got rid of him, didn't I?" There were a few bursts of laughter and relief, and the lunchtime crowd started up their conversations again.

An old man came limping out of a back office. He walked slowly on the inside of the counter until he stood before Jeff and Porter. Resting his hands on the counter, he leaned forward. "Sorry, Leo," Porter muttered apologetically. "I didn't mean to make a scene."

"Nonsense," Leo replied, barely audible, breaking a half-grin. "You actually made my day," he whispered. "Your money's no good here today, boys. This one's on me."

"Guess I'll be havin' dessert after all," Jeff quipped. "You got any chocolate Foy Joy bars?"

"Have two," said Leo, "and enjoy." He smiled and limped away, waving to a customer.

"Thanks, Porter," a man spoke up from a booth behind them.

"You're a good egg, Porter," someone else added from the far end of the counter.

"You should run for mayor, Porter," a woman shouted. "You'd have my vote."

"Thank you, everyone," Porter blushed. "I didn't mean for my grudge with Tom Crowe to spill out like that."

"Porter, there's nothing for you to apologize about or fret about." A gray-haired woman moved into view from the corner booth. "It's hard to believe that you and Tom are from the same town, let alone the same class."

"You always were my favorite teacher, Mrs. Parker," said Porter kindly. "But I never want to be in the same class with Thompson Bradford Crowe as long as I live."

"You never shall, my dear boy." She smiled at his wit.

"That's very kind of you," he added.

"Porter, as long as I've known you, and that's some time, you've been in a class by yourself," she spoke loudly for all to hear, moving from the booth toward them. "It's refreshing to see someone stand up to that bully. He's changed so much since his father died. Sadly, not for the better, I believe."

"Thank you," Porter replied, glancing at Jeff and back at Mrs. Parker.

"But you, Porter, you've changed, too. You're not the bright little boy who always knew what to say and when to say it. Who always stood for what he believed in. Who, if he wasn't holding a book in his hands, he was swinging a baseball bat or throwing a baseball with his friends," she reminisced pleasantly. "You're a man now. Just as bright and eager and still playing baseball. It makes me think that, with everything you've done and everywhere you've been, it's so much, it's as though you're living on

74

borrowed time." She smiled thoughtfully, standing before them. Porter smiled back, struck by the Fates, again, wondering what the hell was going on and if, indeed, this whole existence was borrowed time. "Yet, here you are with your childhood friend. Visiting us once again, speaking your mind, and standing up for what you believe in. That which everyone in this room believes in, I might add. Right over wrong. Well, I must be off. Good to see you, dear." She patted his hand and, smiling again, she fixed a scarf around her head, buttoned up her long coat, and departed.

Porter stared absent-mindedly at the space Mrs. Parker had occupied moments before, and then turned to his lunch. His mind was suddenly churning, his thoughts percolating—gypsies, Viola, his Guardian Angel or Angel of Death. And there was his young friend, Scoop Comeau—ever haunting, ever present—how did Viola know about that? Was he really on *borrowed time*? Was it supposed to have been him, not Scoop? Jeffah was speaking but he heard nothing. Porter pushed the plate away, stood, and began to drift toward the door. "Jeffah, I'll catch up with you later."

"But we have a meeting with Sterling," replied Jeff, following him.

"I haven't forgotten," he answered him, stepping outside.

"Wait 'til you meet his secretary," Jeff said, raising his brows.

Porter smiled and said, "Mrs. Parker got me thinking. I have to take care of something now before I run out of time."

"What's that?"

"I gotta see Uncle Stu and then Aunt Effie. Time I checked in. I have to ask him something about the family business."

"Wait! You actually thinkin' about moving back to town?" he asked, surprised.

"Nah, not me. My sister."

"No shit? Gracie's coming back to the Lost Kingdom?"

"It's one of the reasons I'm here, besides seeing the gypsy woman."

"Hey, what about me?"

"What about you?" he grinned.

"Right—*thanks*. I'll meet you in front of the Silent Woman Tavern at four-thirty—*o'clock!*"

Jeff stood in the cool breeze and watched Porter take several long strides. "Tell Uncle Stu I said, 'Hi,'" he shouted, but Porter had disappeared around the corner. Jeff looked at the clock on the Queen's Chapel steeple. Four hours to kill before meeting Sterling to discuss that night's rendezvous, his last, he'd told himself. "Maybe I'll have the pumpkin pie instead," he thought, and went back inside.

Behind Closed Doors

"He's back in town, Sterling, and I don't like it! He insulted me and he insulted my son in front of *those* people at Leo's Drug just minutes ago!" Thompson Crowe fumed in a third floor office of the old Custom House. A middle-aged man sat quietly across from him, puffing a Corona, listening to the tirade. Sterling Huxley was a patient man. Though, at that moment, he was more interested in enjoying his cigar in peace rather than listen to Thompson wail like a wounded mink snared in his own trap. The man had walked in unannounced, past his secretary, Abigail Michaud, and began his caustic rant. "The indignation of him to address me as such—'*Tom!*'he called me, like we were old chums, like I was some errand 'coon boy," he snarled. "I want him out of town. I never want to see him again. The world would be a better place without him!" At that remark, he looked long and hard into Sterling's eyes. "I hear that life here on the frontier can be very dangerous. Prone to *tragic* accidents."

"Are you done, Thompson?" asked Sterling, calmly. The outbursts were nothing new, Sterling realized, with a person like Thompson. The man was too attached to himself, and it didn't take much to set him off. Sterling's late father, Jonah, had taught him early on to never wear his emotions on his sleeve, especially when it came to business. And it was all business. He supposed that Jonah had learned that from his father, Colonel Josiah Huxley, the hero of the Battle of Fredericksburg, who established the family business of textiles and real estate. Or maybe it was simply common sense. Wherever it came from, Sterling appreciated the advice he'd received from his father, Jonah, and grateful for the close relationship he had had.

On the other hand, Thompson's relationship with his father, Wendell, was, in the best of times, strained. In fact, Thompson had showed little interest in the bank until after his father's death. The old man, Wendell, had been found one morning at the bottom of his stairwell, his neck askew and twisted. The accident occurred shortly after the market crashed, which led many in town to speculate whether he tripped, was pushed, or simply jumped. After Wendell landed belly up, Thompson assumed control of the family bank, The Crowe Trust.

That's when the relationship between the Huxleys and Thompson began. Sterling and Jonah called on Thompson to meet about a certain business that they had conducted secretly with Wendell for years.

"There are certain truths best left unseen, overlooked, or ignored," Jonah had told the younger Crowe on that fateful day. "This bank, that is, your father, and Huxley Industries, that is, Sterling and myself, have conducted business for years. One venture of recent years has proved remunerative for each party involved." At this remark, old Jonah had lowered his voice, which made Thompson lean in close. "It was your father's wish," Jonah lied, "that if anything should happen to him before your thirty-fifth birthday, I should be the one charged with sitting down with you for this talk. Your father deliberately chose not to bring you to the table to protect you, which is why what I'm about to speak of shall not be discussed outside of this room—ever!" Jonah had said emphatically. Sterling had been watching Thompson closely, as his father had instructed him before the three met, to measure any reactions during the conversation. At that moment, Sterling would never forget, how the pupils of Thompson's eyes contracted to the size of buckshot, eager with anticipation, as menacing as a bird of prey about to dive. When Jonah finished explaining the details of the business, Sterling knew they were dealing with a true predator, erratic and volatile. Sterling's instincts proved true. On any occasion, Thompson would wander into his office unannounced to vent his frustration over a deal gone wrong, a foreclosure missed, or, much like today, his inability to deal with a man like Porter, who, Sterling realized, bowed to no one, yet posed no threat to them.

"Thompson," Sterling finally broke the silence. "If I told you once, I must have told you a hundred times," he sighed. "Do not let your emotions get the best of you. Need I say, especially with a man like Porter Gibson."

"Are you actually implying that I am a lesser man than he?" Thompson reacted with incredulity.

"No!" Sterling snapped. "Porter has virtually nothing to do with the community anymore—nothing but periodic visits to see his friends and Aunt and Uncle. He has nothing to do with you or me. And we do not need to ever draw attention to ourselves."

"But, you see, he does, Sterling," Thompson replied sharply. "He's with your man, Jeff Grant. That he would show up now, of all days, I find that more than a coincidence. They're up to something, the two of them, and they tried to bait me, to reveal myself."

Sterling should have rolled his eyes at the comment. Yes, Porter was here to help his friend, Jeff Grant, because Jeff Grant asked him to come and help him. But that's not what caused the confrontation. Within minutes of Thompson's encounter with Porter, he had received a phone call from the drugstore and was thoroughly informed of what had happened. Most notably, that it was he, Thompson, and his boy Jacob, who had initiated the exchange and provoked Porter. That prior to that Porter and Jeff had been talking and joking over lunch about some gypsy woman, minding themselves. So Sterling simply said, "I don't agree with you, Thompson. Jeff Grant has far too much at stake to try and pull a fast one on me. Besides that, he doesn't know of your involvement with the *enterprise*, or your father before you, for that matter. My advice to you is to let it go." Even as Sterling spoke these words, he could tell by Thompson's expression that he'd never let it go. The animosity that Thompson held for Porter was too deep and too visceral. Porter had bettered him once upon a time—right to the bone and into the heart of the matter. That was one time too many for Thompson, and he could not, nor would not, ever let it go.

"Mark my words, Sterling," said Thompson. "The man's a nuisance and a menace."

"Let it go, Thompson!"

"I'd say that, at the very least, Grant's a limited asset, and with Porter in town, a liability."

"Nothing of the sort, Thompson," Sterling responded.

"He can be easily replaced by another fishmonger. God knows there are enough of them wandering around the wharves and docks with nothing to do," he said disdainfully. "You'd think they'd find some work for Christ's sake."

It was pointless to continue, thought Sterling. His father had always told him such. At some point, you begin to wonder how many people will take your advice when they ask for it. Then you realize that people end up doing what they want anyway. And your advice to them becomes a liability. So you reach the point where it's best not to even interfere, to merely smile or shrug, make no commitment. That's easier and less time-consuming. Yet Thompson was a necessary liability—or he had been, because now it was all but over. The only person who seemingly did not know that their business arrangement was ending was Thompson. Sterling had quietly moved funds, some into the Harrington's Bank, but most into the banks of his silent partners in New York. "Grant's my responsibility, Thompson," he said sternly. "Not yours. Everything will be fine. Porter will be gone by tomorrow or the next day. He never stays around long. He's outgrown this place. It's too confining for him. Let me remind you, we need to keep focused on the business at hand."

"Very well, Sterling," sighed Thompson. "We shall see. I don't agree with you, but I've always respected you and your late father, so I will defer to your judgment."

"Is the deposit ready? That bastard Hardy should be here any time."

"Yes, but what about the other properties? You mentioned a dozen, but I have only ten listed."

"The partners know we have two properties to go. Hardy should, too."

"I can only hope," Thompson mumbled.

"Now you must excuse me," said Sterling. "There's much to do between now and tomorrow."

"Yes, there is," Thompson nodded, then stood up and shook Sterling's hand briskly. "Much to do!" He smiled weakly and left.

Sterling watched Thompson leave and wondered just how much the little prick could do, or would do.

Uncle Stu

"Honestly, Uncle Stu," said Porter, "how in the name of holy Jesus did you hear about me and Tom Crowe over at Leo's Drug?" Porter was standing in the back room of his family's shop, Ye Olde Books and Artifacts.

"What can I say, Porter?" Stuart Gibson shrugged his shoulders. "It's a small town."

"But it couldn't have been more than fifteen minutes ago!" exclaimed Porter. "It's mathematically impossible. It defies the law of physics. I just can't believe it."

"Settle down boy," Uncle Stu said. "It's no big deal." Porter shook his head in disbelief again, still unsure. "Were you there? That's it!" He seemed relieved. "Why didn't you say hi?"

"I could ask you the same thing, couldn't I?" Uncle Stu asked him. "How long have you been in town this time? Your telegram said you were arriving yesterday."

Porter knew he'd walked into it. If Uncle Stu knew about Leo's Drug, the old bugger had probably been tracking his every movement since he arrived in town. "Uncle Stu, I didn't get here until late last night. Jeffah picked me up off the train and had to bring me to meet someone. I couldn't get out of it. I was gonna come by after, but didn't want to barge in on you and Aunt Effie when it got that late."

"Whoa, Porter, you know damn well that our door is open to you twenty-four hours a day, with or without notice. You're family. I promised your father and mother, God rest their souls, that you'd always have a home in Downeast Way as long as myself or Aunt Effie was kicking." Uncle Stu was firm, but sincere. "You're not a kid anymore, but I do mean it. It is your home."

"Thank you, Uncle Stu," said Porter. "I meant no disrespect. You and Aunt Effie are in my thoughts. I rolled out of bed, grabbed a bite to eat, and came here to see you."

"Ah, I didn't mean to ride you, Porter," replied Uncle Stu, thoughtfully. "You're a son to me. You're my brother's boy and every time I see you, you look more like Andrew than he did." He smiled and gave Porter a pat on his shoulder. "Besides, I also want you to know that you still have a stake in the family business. Your parents' house is there, waiting to be opened up and aired out." Porter was about to say something, but Uncle Stu placed a finger to his lips. "I know you have baseball, and your writing is starting to gain an audience."

"That's nice of you to say that, Uncle Stu, but I can't see my books gaining that much of an audience," Porter remarked, "Not outside of academic circles. Hell, inside of academic circles, all they do is argue about them."

"Nonsense, my boy," Uncle Stu smiled. "We have a stack out on the front table. We've sold quite a few."

"You're selling *The Theory of the Deferential Continuum* here?" said Porter, astonished.

"Of course," said Uncle Stu. "Why wouldn't we? We're all very proud. In fact, I'd appreciate if you'd sign a few copies. I get requests you know, all the time."

"Really?"

"Why, yes. Just fifteen minutes ago, Mrs. Parker came in to pick up a copy of your new book," he smiled and winked.

"Ah, it was Mrs. Parker," Porter laughed. "Sure, I'll sign a few."

"Good, they're out front. Follow me." He picked a pen from his desk, which he handed to Porter, and led him out to the main floor of the shop. There were stacks of books laid out on tables and lined up on shelves.

Assorted paintings, antique maps, and old documents from the Civil War and Revolutionary War were framed and displayed along the brick-faced walls. The newspapers, magazines, postcards and stationery were up front. There was also a small section of toys, ranging from stuffed animals, dolls, boats, trucks, trains and soldiers, to balls, puzzles, globes, games and children's books.

"You still have the toy section?" Porter laughed.

"Heaven's, yes!" Uncle Stu replied. "It was your idea, Porter. How bored you and your sister were to come into the store as children. You told your father that we needed to sell toys and games, too, so children would want to come to the store."

"Yes," Porter responded, fondly. "I remember the look on my father's face. He thought I was crazy, and laughed about it."

"Until he thought about it," said Uncle Stu. "Until we both talked about it. Not only did the toys bring the children in the shop with their parents, it brought their parents in with their children, which right away increased the amount of customers coming into the store. Over time, we came to realize that those children grow up, and they still come by, but now with *their* children. Whether they're local or seasonal, they still come in and visit and shop. And it's all because of you."

"That's nice of you to say that, Uncle Stu, but I was a dumb kid. It was mostly Gracie's idea, not mine. She knew how to make the old man jump."

"You're too modest, my boy," said Uncle Stu, "and need I remind you that your father jumped for both of you." The old man paused when a large, jovial woman approached them, carrying a book in one hand and holding the hand of a young boy with her other.

"Stuart Gibson," she burst out excitedly. "Did you hear—Rudy Vallée mentioned the Lost Kingdom on his radio show the other day? Remember how much he loved to play at the Bijou in his early days?" She looked over his shoulder at Porter. "Oh, excuse me. You never mentioned you were expecting a celebrity in town, Stuart." She smiled and waved at Porter.

"Oh, Mrs. Harrington," blushed Porter. "It's good to see you."

"And you, too, Porter," she replied.

"Mother," the young boy interrupted. "May I go to look at the train in the window?"

"Yes, Oliver," she replied. "But first say hello to Mr. Porter Gibson."

"Hello, sir," Oliver said, and extended his hand.

"Nice to see you, Oliver," said Porter, and shook his hand. "You were a little fella the last time we met," he added. "What are you gonna be for Hallowe'en?"

"I'm gonna be a baseball player." Oliver's eyes lit at the realization. "Say! You're the baseball player my brother told me about, aren't you?"

"Well, yes, I play baseball."

"Are you in town for long?" Oliver asked.

Porter smiled, and said, "Unfortunately, I'm only here for a few days on business. Was up in Bangor checking on a ballplayer we scouted in the Industrial League over the summer. Thought I'd swing by and say my hellos before going back to Brooklyn and report in."

"Well, Jenny," said Uncle Stu. "I'm glad you and Oliver dropped by. You got more out of Porter in two minutes than I have since he arrived."

"Come on, Uncle Stu," pleaded Porter. "I was getting to it."

"Sure you were, my dear," comforted Mrs. Harrington. She turned to her son. "Oliver—run along," and the boy ran off to the window. She then turned to the old man. "Stuart—don't you pick on your nephew." She wagged her index finger, chastising him playfully.

"I wouldn't think of it," he shrugged. "Not in front of the customers, anyway."

"Let alone friends," she added with a smile.

"Especially," Uncle Stu responded.

"Very well, then," she said. "I must be running, but before I go, Porter, would you be a dear and sign a copy of your book for me?" It was the book she was holding, which surprised Porter.

"Yes, ma'am," Porter replied with a glance at Uncle Stu. "My pleasure." He reached for his pen, but she had already pulled one from her purse and held it for him. "Tell me, how's James doing these days?" Porter asked, taking her pen. "Still throwing the ball around?"

"Oh, that's very kind of you to remember. He's up to Bangor on business, but I will tell him the next time I see him, his old teammate asked about him."

"He was a good second baseman, Mrs. Harrington. One of the best here in town and at Dartmouth. He handled himself well on and off the field."

"And he still does," added Uncle Stu. "He's engaged to Enid Huxley, you know?"

"That's exciting news. Sterling and Flo are smart to bring a banker into the family," Porter remarked. "You must be very happy, Mrs. Harrington."

"Oh, I am," she nodded, but seemed at odds with the smile she made. "James has been so overwhelmed by the hard times, we're hoping that Enid will be just what the doctor ordered. She's such a *mindful* girl." Porter wasn't sure what Mrs. Harrington meant. So he simply returned a smile, blew gently on the open page to dry the ink, and handed her the book and pen.

"Be sure to tell James I said 'Hi,' and congratulations. Enid's a fine catch," he lied. Knowing Enid as he did, it gave him a fleeting thought about James' prospects. Enid was the oldest of the three sisters. Politically, for the Huxleys, she had to go first. What he remembered about Enid was her temper. She liked to have her way. James was easy-going and somewhat adventurous. If his family business had not been banking, he would have had a good time playing ball, or maybe even gone to New York and fit in nicely with the crowd there. The poor bastard was stuck.

"Thank you, Porter," she said. "I certainly will. Bye for now, and thanks again for signing the book."

"I'm flattered, Mrs. Harrington," he said with a nod. "You're too kind."

"Thank you, Jenny," Uncle Stu said. "I can take you at the front register."

Porter watched the two amble off, chatting about Rudy Vallée or some other radio show. He walked to the stack of books, and found himself looking about the shop. There were a dozen people milling around. In the front window, Oliver stood next to two children, the three hypnotized, watching toy skeletons bounce in the window. Not a bad crowd, he thought, for an early Monday afternoon. The prospect of running the store, to carry on the family business, had tempted him. Porter wasn't one to turn his back on family, but he hadn't seen everything he was supposed to see yet. There was no way he could come back to the Lost Kingdom to live and die until he had. Besides, help was on the way. His sister, Gracie, and her daughter, Caroline, were coming back to Downeast Way. That was one of the things he'd dropped by to talk over with his Uncle Stu. *One* of the reasons he had come *home*. He stood over the table of books, his books, pulled the cap off the pen, and began to sign them; all the while thinking about his sister.

If Not For Del 'Scoop' Comeau

Gracie was coming back to Downeast Way, rudderless and with a duckling. She needed to come back. Her husband, Bernie, had gone out west looking

83

for work. That was two summers ago, without a word. Porter knew he was never coming back because of a chance meeting with him. The team was in St. Louis for a three-game series with the Cardinals, when he'd seen Bernie walk into the back room of a drug store where the speako was, with a platinum blonde on his arm. Porter and his teammate, Dodger third baseman, Del 'Scoop' Comeau, had been informed of the medicinal cures available at McInerney's Drug Store by one of their old teammates, Stumpy Levon, who was now playing with the Cards. The three of them went there to take the cure after a particularly grueling twelve-inning game that saw, among other things, a rare unassisted triple play by Scoop in the bottom of the ninth. 'T'was bittersweet in the end. Stumpy put the game away himself, in the bottom of the twelfth, with a sacrifice fly to right. The temperature on the field that afternoon was a hundred and five degrees. The St. Louis air was stifling, humid and hazy, with little or no breeze off the river. Usually, the Mississippi was good for a slight push of wind but, that day, the air was dead. Porter remembered that well because he had caught all twelve innings. Sweated like a boar, too, and went two-for-five in the eight hole with a run scored and an RBI, and they still lost 5-4. The only good thing about it was Stumpy. The little prick was going to carry the tab for beating them and dragging Porter out of the hotel. This was Scoop's first trip to St. Louis and he wanted make sure the kid had a good time.

Porter kind of felt responsible for Scoop. He'd 'discovered' him in an industrial league in Central Maine, playing for a ball club out of Bangor—the same club he'd just visited that week. Scoop had wandered south from Nova Scotia. Took the ferry one day from his home town of Yarmouth over to Bar Harbor. His intention was to hitch a ride to Bangor and take the train down to Portland. He'd heard the ball club there was looking for a solid corner man. The first car that came upon Scoop was a '25 Chrysler Touring Phaeton. The driver, O.W. Tanner, happened to be the owner of the Bangor Black Bears, the *pride* of Central Maine baseball. He saw this square-jawed kid with no whiskers standing on the road side with his thumb stuck out a mile. He liked what he saw—a baseball bat and glove over his shoulder, a ball cap on his head, and a gunny sack at his feet. The look on his face said it all. That's what struck O.W. The kid was hungry. Eager to play. Which was why O.W. pulled over and picked him up. The two of them talked baseball the whole ride up to Bangor. "My name's Del Comeau," the kid said. "Thanks for the lift." O.W. smiled. He liked the enthusiasm. "Going up to Bangor to catch the train. I hear Portland's looking for a corner man. Well, here I am." O.W. laughed out loud, which caused the kid to crack a broad smile. The next afternoon, Del was suited up and playing third for the Black Bears. He had five chances and made them all. One was a diving backhanded stab down the line that saved two runs and the game. A scorching one-hopper that he fielded cleanly on the grass in shallow left. He stood up calmly, fired a bullet across the diamond, and bagged the runner by a step. That's when they started calling him Scoop. Though he could have easily been called The Rifleman with the arm he had. At the plate, the kid smacked a double in his first at bat, which drove in two runs. O.W. knew he had the real deal.

It wasn't too long after that when Porter received a letter from his old roommate at Dartmouth, O.W., about this kid playing third. If Otis Washington Tanner was for this kid, then Porter knew the organization had to check him out. Whenever there was a prospect in Maine, Porter would always ask O.W. if he'd heard or seen so-and-so. It was O.W.'s father, Milton, who'd put the call in to Wilbert Robinson, the old Brooklyn manager, on Porter's behalf, back in 1916. Porter never forgot the Tanners and the Tanners never took advantage of Porter's position in the organization. When Porter broke his finger in a play at the plate in late August that year, the club sent him to Maine to check out Scoop. The kid was everything and more. Enough that Porter convinced the team to invite him to try out the following year. Delbert Comeau made the team. He hit a respectable .288 that year, with 12 dingers and 58 RBIs. His performance solidified his place in the lineup for years to come. It also solidified Porter's role as a scout in the years to come.

Meeting that kid was meant to be. Porter was sure of it. From the first time they met, he connected with him. Porter took care of him wherever they went. He made it a habit to always show the kid around town, where the good restaurants were, and where they could find an ice-cold pint of beer.

That particular day in St. Louis, with Stumpy Levon at their beck and call, the three of them made their way to McInerney's, the most frequented drug store in the neighborhood surrounding Sportsman's Park. And there was a good reason. The back room served ice-cold beer and Irish whiskey. Maybe it was the way it was supposed to be. How the Fates always seemed to deliver and pony up. Porter hadn't seen Stumpy for a while and, for some reason, he got to talking about his sister. How bad he felt for her up there in Portland with his niece, the two of them alone to fend for themselves since Bernie lit off west to find work the summer before last. He didn't say he had been sending money when he could, but he did mention that Gracie was sure Bernie had been killed in some accident—left on the side of the road to die or something else frightfully hideous or despicable. Porter had just finished telling Stumpy that the only thing despicable that had happened to Bernie was Bernie. He'd just finished saying to Stumpy and Del that he had only ever met him once, but if he ever saw him again he'd give him a licking, when, out of the blue, the son-of-a-bitch walked into the bar with a big-chested platinum blonde on his arm. He was dressed in a striped zoot suit, with a broad-rimmed, beige-colored fedora on his head and white two-tone bucks on his small feet.

Bernie had gone out west all right, as far as St. Louis, where he was working a book—doing quite well for himself betting on baseball. The reason he'd left Portland, Porter would shortly find out, was because the book he was running there had gone bust—collectors were after him. They'd have killed him, and maybe even harmed Gracie and the girl. At least that was what he was pleading to Porter between the repeated blows being leveled on him by the grizzly-sized paws that were Porter's hands. What Porter didn't see in his blind rage was Bernie's man Friday, a German guy named Big Karl. Porter had lunged across the room in a fit and tackled Bernie the moment he realized it was him. Bernie didn't stand a chance. So quick was Porter's assault that he only had time to shout, "No! Wait! Let me explain!" before the first punch split his lip and the second smashed his right cheekbone. Big Karl, who preceded Bernie wherever he went, was at the bar when Porter made his move. The goon rushed Porter from behind. Bernie had only come to McInerney's that day to have a couple of drinks on the house and collect a bet from the old man, Devon. Bernie always liked to have Big Karl walk in ahead of him for a kind of theatrical effect. That, and the ugly bastard scared the shit out of everyone and cleared a path. Bernie would wait a few seconds to make his entrance, usually with a big-chested blonde, looking tough and acting dapper.

All of this theater was missed by Porter when he charged Bernie. "You fucking weasel!" he shouted at Bernie as he raised his hand to strike him again. The blonde was screaming. Big Karl was on top of him. He'd pulled a sawed-off bat from his coat, his preferred method of destruction, raising the club, readying to split Porter's head open with a single blow. The bar fell silent in macabre anticipation of the strike. When it came, the beer glass kerplunked like it had been fired out of a cannon at a brick wall from fifteen paces without breaking. Everyone heard it. Everyone in the backroom of that mundungus-reeking bar except Big Karl, that is. He didn't have a chance to hear it. It was *his* head that the mug struck, putting a dent in it the size of a walnut. Ten months later, when Big Karl finally gained consciousness, and that term must be applied loosely, he found himself staring blankly at the ceiling of an old monastery, long ago converted to a sanitarium. The first thing he focused on was the odd sensation that a piece of metal or something was embedded in the back of his skull. How it got there or how he arrived in that bed and place was beyond him. The ward smelled of antiseptic and rubbing alcohol. People were chatting and mumbling non-sensically all around him. He couldn't understand a word they said. When a large woman in white appeared at his bedside smiling, he smiled back. She said something to him, but he couldn't understand, except for the name Karl. Who was Karl? he thought. Was he lost? If so, how would *he* know where he was, for he didn't even know who *he* was.

Such would be the permanent effect on the goon, Big Karl, from the force of the heavy glass stein that Del 'Scoop' Comeau had fired at his melon from across the room in McInerney's that one mid-summer evening. Just before Big Karl was about to stove in Porter's skull, Scoop had grabbed Porter's mug—Scoop's was near full—and fired a strike with such precision and force that Big Karl would never know who he was ever again. And the world was a better place for it.

Though a major setback for Big Karl's career, it proved to be a greater blow to Bernie's. The news of the goon's demise was met with great applause in most circles, particularly at the speakos and blind pigs in and around Sportsman's Park. Scoop and Porter were looked upon as liberators. Stumpy, the grand ambassador, would play out his days in St. Louis and never pay a dime for a drink again. Neither did Porter or Del whenever the Dodgers were in town. Bernie went through a period of recovery and depression, having been exposed in those stark, brief minutes as weak, worthless, and a fraud. Having lost his goon, and pride, he retreated to the south side of Chicago. There, he ran a small-time book around Comiskey Park, knowing he'd never run into Porter again, as long as Porter stayed in the National League. Porter, for his part, never told anyone in Downeast Way except Jeffah about that fateful meeting with Bernie in McInerney's. He did take the eight hundred and sixty-two dollars Bernie offered to him as Bernie lay busted and bleeding out of his nose, lips, and mouth. Porter promptly wired the money to Gracie with a telegram stating that he was not coming back, signed Bernie.

That was then.

Gracie had somehow persevered, raising Caroline and working part-time as a librarian. She liked being around books. When Porter had seen her a few days before, he'd convinced Gracie that she should move back to Downeast Way with Caroline, into the old house. Porter told her he would talk to Uncle Stu about putting her to work at the bookshop. Her coming back and helping with the family business was natural. "I'm never gonna be able to do it, Gracie," he'd explained to her. "I gotta stay on the move. Uncle Stu and Aunt Effie would want nothing more than for one of the family to take over the business. These past years have been tough on everyone. First, cousin Joe in the war, then Mom and Dad to the flu. There's been a hole in their lives as big as the hole in ours. We can never plug it, but being around them would fill it up a little. I'm going through Downeast Way on the way back from Bangor, and I'd be happy to bring it up with him. Believe me, after everything that's happened between you and them and Bernie and all the rest it doesn't amount to much. It's time you went home. All those misunderstandings are lost. Think about it. It would be good for Caroline, too, having family around. I'll be at the Bangor House for the next few days. Send me word there if you want me to speak to Uncle Stu."

Gracie didn't have to think about it long. She told Porter the next morning before he caught the train north that she wanted to go back to the Lost Kingdom and help with the bookshop. When she left twelve years before to go to college, she never imagined it would take her so long to get back. But after she graduated from college in Boston, she landed a job in Portland right away at the Foreside Library. She was happy to be in the city, experiencing freedoms she never had or knew in Downeast Way—movies, theater, museums, lectures, book clubs. It gave her a degree of independence that was not expected from someone of her class, let alone gender. Gracie was much like Porter in that respect. She wanted to see and experience things. Go places, keep on the move. There was a gypsy spirit in her. Too much, she thought, for a librarian. All that shifted the night she met Bernie. Nothing she'd read had prepared her for the experience.

Not when it came. The grand build-up. The dance. The talking. The moods. The anticipation. The experience in total of falling in love. The first time it happens, you're not quite sure how it was meant to be. When Gracie fell for Bernard Pruitt, she simply assumed that was how it was supposed to be. She took a gamble with a gambler and lost the bet and her innocence. The marriage was a civil affair, literally and figuratively. A justice of the peace swore them in and the relationship soon evolved into a peaceful coexistence. The kind that often accompanies the missionary boredom of love, especially after the first baby arrives. That was the position that Gracie found herself in the day that Bernie said he could not find work in Portland. "The high tariffs the president and his congress passed on exports has exported the depression worldwide," he'd explained with an air of authority. "The Old Port's shutting down, the mills and plants are cutting shifts or cutting wages or flat out closing. They say California's the place to go and find work so a man can support his family."

"We can go back to my home town," she'd responded. "I know there's work there and a place to live." Though the civil ceremony had never set well with her family, she hadn't wanted to burden them with the cost of a traditional wedding. Porter had met Bernie once, in Boston, when Gracie brought him to a Braves-Dodgers game. He couldn't make the marriage ceremony because of baseball, though he did send his blessings and a few dollars. Aunt Effie and Uncle Stu had taken the train to Portland that day to give her away to a total stranger. They took the bride and groom to dinner before setting out on the evening train back north.

"I know that we could go up there," Bernie reasoned, "but that small town is no place for a man like me." There were two things that Gracie didn't know about Bernie at that time. The first being that Bernie was a bookie who had migrated north to work out of the Kite Track between Old Orchard Beach and Scarborough. The second being he'd come up on the short end of a long shot in the fourth race two days before. He was being hunted by a pack of jackals and Portland was growing smaller with each passing day. The day he had explained to Gracie the wonderful opportunities waiting for him and her and the girl out in California, he had barely escaped a pair of thugs. He left the next morning with no intention of ever returning. "I'll write soon," he lied, pecking her cheek and walking out the door. Those were the last words Gracie ever heard him speak. She naïvely clung to them until the day she received the wire and money. If it wasn't for Caroline, she would have thrown herself into the harbor. Oh, the shame and stupidity and pain that unrequited trust breeds! A wound deep and hollow it cleaves! A scar that will not fade! When Porter arrived and offered her and Caroline a way out—hope—for the first time in years, she looked forward to returning to the Eastern Frontier. Caroline needed a place *she* could call her own. And Gracie needed peace of mind. The Lost Kingdom would be that place, a place to call home. Porter knew that he could never make Gracie whole again, knowing what he knew. She'd never know the truth about Bernie, not from him. But he wasn't going to leave his younger sister alone in the city to raise his niece. And he sure wasn't about to settle in Portland, nor bring them to Brooklyn. He'd never stop worrying about them. He simply traveled too much. In the high stakes game of the depression, baseball was more than a game. He couldn't give that up. It was income. Nor could he give up his writing and research. There was also Red, and his friends from Washington, with their offer. The logical place for his sister was back home working alongside their Uncle. As he stood there staring at the people in the bookshop, Porter sensed that the business had survived the bad times for a good reason. That said a lot. It would be here for a while. Maybe, some far-off day, Porter would join them. Maybe that was why he was here today. To set the record straight. That, deep down, Porter was a family man, at least in a mindful way. The notion filled his head while watching the customers enter and leave, or chat and laugh with his uncle. His attention was drawn to Mrs. Harrington and Oliver, who waved good-bye to him as they left the shop.

Maybe, someday, he thought.

You Old Bastard

"You know, I always liked Mrs. Harrington," Porter said to Uncle Stu. The old man had made his way back after cashing out three other customers and taking an order from another. "And that Oliver—he's all grown up."

"That boy came late in life to Jenny and Gardner. He's very special."

"And such a well-mannered kid," Porter added, struck by the thought of Tom Crowe's son, the contrast.

"It doesn't surprise me. Mrs. Harrington is a nice person herself," Uncle Stu replied. "And she's well read, too, Porter. She stops by at least one day a week to pick something up. History, fiction, poetry, nature. If you ran into her in a few days, she'd be ready to take you to task on that book of yours."

"I'm sure she would," replied Porter. "James is the same way. Never figured he'd end up back here. Thought for sure he'd escape this small town. Thought he'd be more like ..." Porter stopped too late.

"... like you?" Uncle Stu finished his sentence. "One never really leaves, Porter, you know that. Not the Lost Kingdom. At times, the intervals may be longer, but sooner or later we all find our way back."

"If it's into the open arms of Enid Huxley, thank you not. I'd as soon stick my ass in a badger's hole and fart. I'm sure I'd get the same greeting each night when I came home."

"Oh, Porter!" Uncle Stu laughed. "James will have his hands full. I'll give you that. But there's a spark there between them. It's not like either family needs the money."

"Maybe it's an arrangement?"

"It's not an arrangement. What are you thinking? That the depression's pushed us back that far? No. The Huxleys are well off and so are the Harringtons. There must be something between Enid and James that you or I cannot see or feel."

"Funny thing how you never see or feel the sting of a mosquito until she's sucked your blood dry. And then the itch sets in and drives you insane."

"I'd say your sting is pretty harsh today, my boy," said Uncle Stu, knowingly. "It's not you who's marrying Enid. What do you care, really? You knew her growing up. You don't know what she's like now. She comes from a good family, though I have my reservations about the direction Sterling's taken some of his business these days. We had a connection with the Huxleys once upon a time. Jonah, Sterling's father, helped your father and me open this business."

"I know, Uncle Stu," said Porter, easing up. "Truth is, I'm just a little worked up today. Got a lot on my mind."

"That's quite obvious, Porter." He paused, making eye contact with him. "Well, put your cards down, nephew. Let me see your hand." Uncle Stu gave a caring, warm smile.

"It's about Gracie and Caroline."

"Did something happen?" Uncle Stu's eyes widened. "Are they all right? Why didn't you say so?"

"Yes and no," answered Porter. "Bernie ran off. She's been making it on her own, at least making it work. But she's hit the wall. I stopped in to visit her on my way up to Bangor. Believe me, it's in her eyes."

"Oh my," said Uncle Stu with a low whistle. "That foolish, stubborn girl." He thought for a moment. "How long ago did he leave?"

"Two summers back."

"Holy shit!" the old man said, flabbergasted. "We had no idea. Never a mention in her letters."

"She's not a quitter," Porter replied. "And you know how she feels."

"Doesn't want to be a burden." Uncle Stu took a deep breath and gave a heartfelt tsk-tsk. "So what I'm seeing on those cards you laid out for me, Porter, is I'm finally going to have some help around here. That one of you two have come to your damn senses." He looked into Porter's eyes and smiled broadly. "Your Aunt Effie is going to cry when I tell her the news."

"I may now, you old bastard." Porter wiped the sides of his eyes. His gigantic palms nearly enveloped his entire head. "God, I love you."

"Now see. That didn't take *too* long, did it?" he smiled. "I'm gonna wire Gracie and ask her if she'd be willing to help an old man in his labors."

The Crowe Trust

Thompson Crowe sat at his desk in his office, agitated and distracted, thinking of his son. After he met with Sterling, he rushed over to the depot to deliver Jacob to Penny, his wife and the boy's mother. They were taking the train to Portsmouth. From there, Penny was off to her mother's in Boston for the week, and he, the boy, to return to the academy in Exeter. The suspension was over, but if the boy found trouble again, and he seemed to thrive on it, that would be the end for him at Phillips Exeter. As Jacob boarded the train, Thompson warned him sternly the consequences for expulsion would be dire. He would be sent to Norfolk, to the military academy there. The boy smiled back, embraced his father as though giving a heartfelt good-bye. It was a show for all who could see but not hear, including his mother, who, oblivious, looked down from a nearby cabin window, aglow and touched by the scene. "Don't worry, Father," he whispered, "I'll never get caught again." He released him, and Thompson stepped back. The boy flashed a smile that unnerved him. Mocking, devious, cunning—but something else, too; fleeting, but it was there. Jacob jumped on the train just as it moved. Thompson watched it slowly gain speed and pull from the station. He stood there alone, on the platform, despite the chill in the air. He noticed the time on the depot clock. His appointment was in less than an hour. He turned on his heel, took a few steps, but stopped abruptly when the word formed in his head. It struck him, actually, very hard. "Wicked," he thought, and then wondered, if push came to shove, where *he* would land.

The Crowe Trust was a short walk from the depot. He entered the building, saw his man, Ambrose, who opened his office door for him and followed him in. "Yes, Ambrose?" he asked.

"That woman was here, sir," he said, "the one who works for Huxley."

"Anything important?"

"No, sir," he replied. "She did not say, or would not. There was no message. I informed her you would return soon for an appointment, but she left without another word."

"Interesting," Thompson said. "She's running out of time and she knows it. Very well, Ambrose, let me know when the goon arrives."

"Yes, sir," he answered. "Oh, and your newspaper's on the desk."

Ambrose left Thompson to his thoughts. Crowe opened the newspaper and studied it, pushing his son's insidious smile out of his head. There was a list of public auctions—the hammer price—on several of his properties—and he began to calculate the revenue he derived from the collective disposal. There was no profit in holding property, only in financing it or selling it off. Finally, the sale of Lawrence Philpot's, up at Duck's Head Pond, had gone through. "A simple matter of cleaning house," he thought. "They think I don't know what's going on."

His eyes moved to another headline: "Fisherman's Death Ruled A Suicide, Stuns Community," it read. His eyes narrowed as he read the details. "This has got to stop," he mumbled.

The image of Porter entered his mind, and his lip began to curl. There would be no besting Thompson Crowe this visit, or any other, ever again, by that Communist bastard.

The motor of a truck distracted him. He could hear it winding its way up the street. The motor paused, followed by a downshift, and the grinding of gears. An accident waiting to happen. Accidents do happen—all the time, people did themselves in, they lived troubled lives. Just like Porter—he's had a trying year. The man's been despondent since the accident. He blames himself, as he should. It was, after all, his fault entirely.

He settled back in his chair and grinned. A familiar grin, one his son had grown accustomed to.

A *Penny* For Your Thoughts

The train pulled from the station, slowly, haltingly. Penny Crowe stared vacantly at her son across from her. She could not tell if he was brooding or angry or simply indifferent. Then again, she never could with Jacob. There was a time when she thought he was inward and lonely, but now she was unsure, beginning to wonder—*what?* When Thompson had been speaking with him on the platform earlier, she had smiled dutifully and waited for Jacob to board. Thompson had seemed jolted by something Jacob said to him, but he'd recovered immediately as the boy climbed onto the train. He had looked up at her, caught her gaze through the window, nodded sternly, turned and left. Jacob pulled a book from his knapsack and began to read. Something by someone named Aleister Crowley. She turned away. The train was halfway through town. Her thoughts wandered—*nice to go visit in Boston—the city—my family—the theater— bookshops—writers—Porter*. The bastard was in town. Again.

And there he was.

Walking on the street approaching the tracks, as the train was picking up speed, was Porter Gibson. Impulsively, she pressed her palm against the window and thought of the day they met. She couldn't get him out of her head. What came next. A lurid, animalistic, coupling. A deep sigh. Eternal twilight. And nothing more. An abrupt ending.

That book—*The Urban Diaspora.* A radical argument for the redistribution of wealth—not of property, but intellect—the notion of sharing experience and knowledge—open source all of it from grade school forward—usher in a new era of enlightenment—lead by example—classes side-by-side—in the same neighborhood—'There is a tide in the affairs of men'—no matter the draft or ballast, all boats rise when it comes in. It was Porter's first work, and it was a bunch of idealistic drivel and bullshit.

She had only just met Thompson. He flirted—true—he had made an advance on her. His family had money and property. He *rowed* at Harvard.

Porter was baseball, the game of the hoi-polloi, and from a family of shopkeepers.

Gracie, his sister, was her roommate that sophomore year at Radcliffe. She introduced her to Porter, in town promoting his book. Dragged her to a reading in Cambridge. Thompson wanted Gracie, she thought. That's why he came around sniffing like a dog in heat.

But that rejection led to her.

She made her choice.

Her hand slid down from the window. Her gaze fell upon the boy. He was staring at her. "Father doesn't like that man, Mr. Gibson."

"Yes, Jacob, I know."

"Why do *you?*" he asked, with a tone of feigned innocence.

She raised her hand up, steadied it, about to backhand him across the face. "*Mother?*" he asked in the same inquisitive, exaggerated innocent tone.

A knock at the cabin door interrupted her, and the door slid open. "Good day, Mrs. Crowe," said the conductor. "Tickets, please," he added with a tip of his hat, and with a nod, "Jacob."

"Hello, Mr. Donnelly," she said, and lowered her hand into her purse and searched. "They're in here somewhere," she fidgeted. Her mind racing, anxious, flustered. "There they are." She produced two tickets. With much effort, she smiled, and passed them to him.

Jacob waved hello to the man, lifted his book, and continued reading.

A Shattered Compass

Porter left the bookshop in good spirits and with a sense of relief. As he walked up the street, the afternoon coastal express passed, gaining speed. With a little luck he would be on it tomorrow or the day after, he thought, making his way south. Report in and tell Redfern what he wanted to hear. He didn't like this business—being Redfern's *man*. It had made him uneasy. It made him feel like a snitch.

At least the weight of speaking with Uncle Stu about Gracie and Caroline was over with. It had worried him, troubled him. Even though it was the family business, he and Gracie had left it behind. Was it pride, then, which had made the subject hard to speak of? Or was it deeper? Fond as he was of his Uncle Stu and Aunt Effie, there was always an initial awkward first moment or two when Porter returned *home*, whenever he came back to the Lost Kingdom to see them. The transition, he called it. He had to ease in.

Why?

Maybe it was small town life. Maybe what scared Porter the most was that, one day, he would be stuck there. That he was expected to take over the family business. The thought of sitting in the bookshop day after day, week after week, month after month, year after hot-damned year, decade after ball-busting decade; going to church, attending the Masonic Lodge, having your life sucked dry—it petrified him—sent waves of anxiety through him. The whole idea of domestication, any kind, suffocated him. When he got picked up by the Brooklyn Baseball Club after he graduated, professional baseball opened the door of possibilities for him. He breathed freely, entered Columbia the following autumn to pursue a doctorate in history. Little did he know how that would change the course of his life. What it would lead to—the consequence thereof—a period of enlightenment, radicalism, love and love lost; freedom, liberation, adventure. What would seem on the front side going in, as he approached the opening, a mysterious labyrinth, on the back side was nothing more than a well-worn path to knowledge. Joining the war protests in New York City and flirting with anarchism, socialism and communism had changed him. No, actually, he smiled at the thought; the protests were real—the country was dragged into war by and for the Captains of Industry and Banksters to profit and plunder—but the "*isms*" were not. It took him a while to see that, distracted as he was by anarchist-socialist-communist poontang. In fact, he was lucky that the only lasting thing he conceived in those days was the *draw*—his little innovation on an age-old symbolic gesture. How the simple act of flicking the middle finger up and out rapidly, like pulling a pistol from a holster—while shouting out a hearty "fuck you" to the man—how that became the personification of him. That followed him wherever he went, all through the years of baseball, after completing his doctorate. It followed him back to Downeast Way whenever he came home, even though the concept of what home was and meant had changed so much since he first left, all those years before.

Yes, maybe *that* was it. When his parents died, victims to the equivalent of a modern plague—the Spanish Influenza that ravaged the planet in the post-war years—his compass was shattered. It's not that he didn't have any time for them before. He was simply finding his way in the world. He never looked at them as objects passing through time, or thought of time eventually encompassing them so violently that they confronted their own mortality. Sure, we all meet our maker, our own personal Angel of Death. But the house at number 57 Davis Street was not supposed to be vacant for some years to come. That was his refuge, Gracie's refuge—their North Star—the comfort of home and hearth, mom and pop, bouncing grandchildren on their lap. But when your compass shatters, it's all the more difficult to find your way. You lose your direction easily, your bearings become disoriented. The bread crumbs you left behind years before to find your way back to where you began, to where you belong, have dissolved. When your parents die, you're left alone to stand on the front lines of mortality. They're not there in the front anymore to absorb the blows of our ancestors. No, they leave to join them, eventually, as it must *be.* That day, when it arrives, and you find yourself standing there on the front, with the line of mortality drawn, is one of the loneliest days of your life. Porter never thought of it until that day arrived, when his father and mother, Andrew and Victoria, fell in succession, crossed over the line. He was not at home, but on the road in Philadelphia, when word reached him. Maybe it was for that reason, how he missed the tragedy, did not witness it—arrived after the burial—that he never mourned with the others, or felt like he'd said a proper goodbye. They were always supposed to be there, up on the hill on Davis Street, whenever he came home.

Maybe that was why he found it so damned awkward to come back. It wasn't so much to say hello, but the nerve to say a proper goodbye.

Celtic Hill

The Packard had been parked several spaces down and across the street from the old church for only a short time. The car had rolled to a stop under the shadow of a two-story building that had once been a feed store, but now served as the Gaelic Hall for the town's Irish community. In the car, three serious-looking men in broad-rimmed fedoras sat sullenly. Around them, a light fog began to crawl along the street. They had followed another car from town, a late model Dodge, which was now parked up ahead of them, across from a church. They had tailed the car from Crowe's Trust as it first headed northeast, but then, reversing direction, went south along the Shore Road that led to Bean's Point. That's when the Dodge took a sharp right, unexpectedly; and reversed direction again, up Celtic Hill, a twisting, narrow side road that eventually wound its way back into town.

Celtic Hill took its name from the immigrants who found their way to the Lost Kingdom and settled there in the 1850s. The road to the crest of the hill followed one of the ridges beneath Mount Agamenticus, and snaked its way through a neighborhood of assorted older, modest, two-story houses—sided with whitewashed and worn, weathered clapboards— and occupied by large families that crowded them. The Packard kept at a good distance from the Dodge, to avert attention. Nevertheless, as the cars drove past in succession, yards filled with playing children and barking, playful dogs, who stopped to gawk at the autos, a rarity on the hill. Leveling off near the top of the hill, the road narrowed further, slipping under a canopy of tall maple and oak trees. At the upper end, the neighborhood gave way to several abandoned brick warehouses, one of which had been converted into a Franco-American social club, and another that now served as the Gaelic Hall. Across the street, set off the road, was an old church, Saint Patrick's. A gravel driveway surrounded the church like a horseshoe. A rectory was to its left, on the other side of the driveway. Around back and adjacent to the right side of the church was a cemetery. Unadorned headstones listed, spread out in uneven rows that marked the passage of time for the working classes of the Lost Kingdom of Moose Harbor. There was an old saying in the neighborhood, which reflected the eerie, dark mood of the place: *Beware that when the road comes to meet ye atop Celtic Hill, do not tarry ere ye bones will come to rest.* It was, therefore, no coincidence that the man sitting in the front seat of the Packard, on the passenger side, uttered darkly, "I believe the vaults of Edinburgh only have chilled my spirits more, Hardy. But the sight of those stones, the look of that yard, and the fog rolling over 'em, this place is as close to that as I've seen."

"It's the devil's day, Murton, playing with your brain," replied Hardy. "Don't let the fumes of this papal enclave choke your sanity." Hardy glanced at Mr. Calvin, the driver, half expecting a reaction. Instead, Calvin sat like a man of stone—a boulder in size with the disposition of a gargoyle. He had red hair, a round, lightly-freckled face, with a pale complexion and dark, penetrating eyes. The man rarely spoke, and that was only in response to being spoken to directly. Hardy had never seen Mr. Calvin joke in the decade he'd known him—never swore, nor drank. He studied the Old Testament diligently and wallowed in its violence. He inflicted the wrath of God with the personal satisfaction and fervor of a Methodist with a hard-on. On one occasion only had Hardy seen Mr. Calvin approach the countenance of contentment. That was the evening he snapped the neck of a priest in South Boston with his left hand. A Father Kelly had asked quite boldly for them to state their business. Mr. Calvin replied courteously, "If you insist." Before Father Kelly could respond in any way to the remark, bat an eye or before Hardy could speak or respond, Hardy had detected a slight motion from Mr. Calvin, then the priest, in succession. The sound of a walnut cracking followed and Father Kelly clumped to the floor. Hardy did not even ask why. He did, however, notice the slightest nuance of peace pass over Mr. Calvin's face—pleasure, really—in slaying the devil.

On this day, because of the business they had to attend to, Hardy had requested the assistance of Mr. Calvin, though reluctantly. He would have preferred Mr. Smith, who also had accompanied them the evening they'd visited Father Kelly. Mr. Smith had a dry wit that Hardy appreciated. Regrettably, Mr. Smith had been too bold or too sloppy in the week after Father Kelly's expiration, a period of vulnerability for them all. He had followed a mark one evening into an Irish establishment in Boston. He did not heed the warning to keep his distance. Why? The plan was to make it look like a suicide or accident, not a public execution, which, as it turned out, it was. His. Smith had paid dearly, with a bullet through his skull, in a back room speako named Fran's.

Mr. Smith's demise had left Hardy with few choices but Mr. Calvin. The only reason he'd accompanied Mr. Smith and he on the fateful visit to Father Kelly was because Murton was in Edinburgh at the time. Then, as now, Mr. Calvin would factor heavily in the evening's reconciliation of business. He always did. Mr. Calvin was a presence, a force—intensely so. From the backseat of the Packard, Hardy could sense the unfathomable rage brimming in the very being of Mr. Calvin while sitting in front of a Catholic church. His gloved hands gripped the steering wheel at ten and two. Clenching, then relaxing, tighter and tighter, but never letting go, as though he waited for the chance to snap Father Kelly's neck again.

"I'm just saying it's spooky, Hardy," Murton continued. "The place's crawling with a bunch of ghosts."

"I never knew you to be afraid of anything, Murton," said Hardy. "Is the business getting too much for ye?"

"I fear no man, Hardy," replied Murton, "even Mr. Calvin here, whom I readily acknowledge could crush me like a beetle." He gave a nod toward Mr. Calvin, who did not respond nor move. "No, 'tis not man I fear at all—so don't tempt me. But a ghost? I followed that skate Burke into Bell's Wynd in Edinburgh—and I've seen things that no man had a right, or could explain, Hardy."

"In this business, we do not have to explain ourselves, Murton," said Hardy.

"I'm not so sure, Hardy. In our business, as in any business, a time of reckoning will come. It may be trite. It may be eternal. But I know now it will come as sure as the dead who walk the desolate, hidden alleyways of our great city."

"Murton," said Hardy.

"Yes, Hardy," replied Murton.

"Shut up, man."

Murton fell into silence. Minutes passed slowly. Men and women entered and departed the church. A woman and a young girl passed the car and could be heard chatting about a train ride from Auburn. They crossed the street in front of the Packard. The woman glanced at the men indifferently, but the girl stared until Mr. Calvin scowled at her and she jumped in fright. They disappeared around the back of the rectory, where the lights turned on shortly after. Hardy took note. Minutes went by, when suddenly the front door of the church opened forcefully, but silently, and a lone figure ran directly to the old Dodge, turned it over and spun out. Thirty seconds later, a man in black robes, a priest, stood at the door, glancing around the empty churchyard. He looked over at the Packard, or in that direction, then up and down the street. Satisfied there was no one about, he shut the door. Mr. Calvin started the car and put it in gear. "Wait!" Hardy spoke up, "Just a moment." The priest emerged from the back of the church, walking slowly, lost in thought. As he crossed the driveway, he paused and continued on. The priest appeared to look inside the car, though all he could really see was three shadowy figures. "Thank you, Mr. Calvin," said Hardy. "Forget the Dodge. It's a small town. Take me to the banker. We will plug this hole later."

Incident at the Graveyard

Porter wandered, lost in thought, before he realized where he was—in the midst of the Glebe. One of the oldest sections of town, Glebe Lane, cobbled and claustrophobic, wound off of Market Square, and meandered aimlessly between rows of brick front buildings. The lane was narrow, at different intervals not much wider than an alley, and inclined. The land rose up from the sea, and to walk on Glebe Lane from Market Square, one walked uphill. Perhaps its location on the higher ground was the reason the earliest settlers of the Lost Kingdom had set aside the land for the glebe, the church property. Here, the first church, Queen's Chapel, was erected in 1634. Though greatly expanded, its original frame and floor boards, hewed from local timber, had stood the test of time. Porter had made his way through the lane until he found himself before the church. As he raised his head slowly, following the steeple to the heavens, the tower clock struck a solitary gong—two-thirty. Rows of carefully tended gravestones, dating back three centuries, separated the church from the lane where Porter stood. A walkway of crushed stone connected the lane to the church steps, dividing the graveyard in half. A wrought iron fence enclosed the entire yard. He reached out and touched the gatepost. Icy, a chill surged through him, engulfed him. He could see his breath and shuddered, at which point he released the gatepost, and the chill lifted as quickly as it overcame him. Porter wondered why he was there, or what had drawn him there. And then he knew. What troubled him was how he arrived there, other than the last few steps that brought him to where he stood. He couldn't remember. He'd left the bookshop a short time after one, by his estimate. The church was no more than a ten or fifteen minute walk. As deep as Porter was in thought, it seemed close to impossible that he could have lost over an hour of time. Again.

Focusing, getting his bearings, it was then that Porter noticed he was not alone. Across the cemetery, opposite him, a woman stood staring at him—how did he know her? Familiar, he thought, in a distant way. She was dressed in a dark, charcoal suit. Her hair flowed out from under a black, brimless pillbox hat, golden locks curled and bouncy, radiant and shiny, down to her shoulders over a pronounced bosom. That got Porter's attention—the hair and the rack. Her shoulders were broad, almost padded-like, he would recollect later. Right then, she stared with an inquisitive look on her face that he found captivating.

"Hello, over there!" Porter finally called out after a moment or two of her looking at him. "Do I know you?" There was a pause before she tilted her head slightly, smiled warmly, and responded with a single nod. "I'm sorry, I can't place you, nor recall your name," he said, and pushed at the iron gate, in anticipation of getting a closer look. The gate latch stuck and he walked right into it, with a loud clang and involuntary grunt. Porter half expected to hear a laugh but, instead, he distinctly heard the name, "Josefa," carry across the yard. The voice was light, lyrical, feminine. As Porter looked up, the gate latch jarred free, at the moment the church doors swung open unexpectedly. His eyes shot up the gravel walkway, up the broad, smooth granite steps, into the dark foyer of the church. There was no illumination from the interior, no sound, no one there at all. How could that be? How could the doors open on their own? With heavy oaken panels and wrought iron fixtures? Not enough of a wind to blow a match out?

Panning the churchyard, then the headstones, Porter was overcome by another chill. His breath turned to frost in the air. This time, though, he could feel a presence, and as he looked around for an answer, it gave him second thoughts. Porter had met a cemetery caretaker once, up in Dover-Foxcroft. He was there recruiting a pitcher, Clarence Blethen, for the Robins. The caretaker was a little jumpy, had a nervous energy about him. Town folk said he wasn't quite there—had tended the graves for too long. That got the best of Porter's curiosity, made him wonder just what that meant. The man, who went by the name of Graves—*ha!*—had a small cottage and work shed adjacent to the cemetery grounds. The house and shed were at the top of a hill, which offered a view of the entire expanse of the cemetery. Winding paths crossed back and sloped away through carefully tended headstones, monuments, and tombs. A few maple and birch trees, scattered around the hill, stood as tall sentinels, their expansive roots cradling the dead in their eternal slumber. He told Porter, Mr. Graves did, that most nights, from his back porch, the hill was prone to activity. Hallucinations, his father used to call it. His grandfather did, too, as did his grandfather's father. Being from a long line of caretakers, it was no wonder that the Graveses had the reputation of being a bit jolted, if not batty, the older they got and the longer they lived in the house up on the hill.

Porter was in the *tea* room of the Blethen House, the hotel that Clarence's family owned—the grand, old hotel of the Maine woods—when he met the present day Mr. Graves. "I can see the spirits dance through the headstones," he claimed when Porter asked him if he'd ever noticed anything strange at work, "if that's what you mean." That's not the response Porter had expected. In fact, given the reputation that preceded Graves, Porter had only meant to play along while he waited to meet Clarence. Instead, he found himself intrigued. More importantly, Porter wanted to know what *he* meant. "Sometimes there'll be small balls of light, sometimes bigger ones, bouncing around. Other times you might see a shadow or two around the trees. On more than one night a month, right up by the tomb of old Judge Hale, I got to say he'll appear and the others with him. My grandfather called them foggy soldiers." This is what people came to expect from Graves. To some, when they first met him, he was a man who could pull the chain better than the best of them. The townies were more tolerant of one of their own, and only called him nuts behind his back. "Occupational hazard," he had said to Porter, "the insults. But none of the sons-a-bitches who run their mouth have ever come out to my house at the cemetery to spend the night." Where another person may have pondered how fast and loose the marbles were spinning in Graves's head, Porter was more impressed with how he did it. He had to ask him how he could sit there, night after night, from his porch or kitchen window, and watch the dead walk around the backyard? Graves merely shrugged it off. "It's part of the job. I get paid to plant 'em. What they do after that I can't say." He said it nonchalantly, with such calm that Porter was taken aback when he added, "Besides, they don't come in, if that's what you mean. At most, they just march two by two right in and out of Judge Hale's tomb like he was having a party inside."

As Porter stood there, staring into the foyer of the Queen's Chapel, he half expected a march of souls—each and everyone planted in the churchyard—to come, two abreast, out the door. His mind raced. What if his parents walked out? Would they even know him? Would he have the courage to say—something? Anything? His heart pounded. His mouth dried in anticipation. Too much, really, was in his head. He tried to remember how he arrived there again, but couldn't. Thoughts of the gypsy woman then flashed through his head, and what she had said. Was he under a spell? Like Jeffah had claimed *he* was? Porter looked all around again, and wondered where the big blonde in the suit had gone. "The Angel," he blubbered out loud, "… Of Death?" and swallowed hard. Straining his eyes, he looked into the dark entranceway of the church. "Is that you?" Complete silence. Then, in one seamless motion, he received his reply. It was unsettling enough when he touched the gate and felt its icy grip again—bad enough when the cold wave swallowed him up again. But when the church doors released, shut gently and latched, he was desperate to run, but could not move. Not until he stepped back forcefully—and that with as much effort as walking through a snowdrift—released the gate, and made his way onto Glebe Lane, could he move freely. Not until the clock suddenly chimed three times did he think to walk away, to leave the Queen's Chapel behind, which he did. Another gap in time had occurred. It was her, too, he was certain. How many times had she shown herself to him—how many ways—from Scoop sliding headfirst into home plate to that speako in Boston? He did not want to think of it now. Picking up his pace without looking back, he rushed off to make one more stop before meeting up with Jeffah.

Sacrament of Penance

Father Remy Durrell trudged back to the rectory wearily. The world around him was collapsing. He was sure of it. Doom and misery weighed upon him heavily. He needed advice—direction—he needed a confidante. The desperation the hard times had released was unending. Every day, a good portion of his flock trudged as wearily as he, in and out of the old church. The parish had had its share of hard times over the years. Composed of Irish and French-Canadian immigrants and their descendants, the congregation had never flourished. The founding of Saint Patrick's some eighty years before was in response to the influx of Irish who had found a welcome port to weigh anchor and begin a new life. The church was commissioned by the diocese in Portland to fulfill a need of the growing, though impoverished, Catholic community. In the best of times, the parish was barely able to support itself. The past three years, as Father Durrell duly chronicled to the diocese, were particularly acute. Day after day, week after week, month after month, Father Durrell had heard the confessions of the parishioners. Prayers of contrition were meted out—six Our Fathers, four Hail Marys for one; ten Our Fathers, five Hail Marys for another. The whole totality of his life had been reduced to the mind-numbing daily ritual of absolving the sins of his parishioners in the name of the Father, the Son and the Holy Ghost. Husbands beating wives, wives batting husbands, fathers and mothers beating children, children stealing their daily bread, and begging forgiveness from a God they did not know. Acts of adultery and fornication—coveting thy neighbor's wife—of alcohol-induced rage and vulgarity, the hurt and pain of the poor—he had heard it all, or so he thought, until today.

He had long ago abandoned the prospect of advancement. That was about the same time he lost his faith, he reckoned. Around the same time, the diocese found a hole to drop him in—in part, to bury his misdeeds and sins before he became too much of an embarrassment for them—in part, to punish him. If there was a purgatory on earth, they'd found it. The Parish of Saint Patrick's was more than a dead end. It was the bottom half of where the bottom bottoms out. It was a place—and there were many like places scattered over the planet—where prayers were not answered or even heard by Him.

Such thoughts crossed his mind often. In fact, given all the years he had spent in the priesthood—including the too many years he had laughed himself silly over a bottle of Scotch—not on one occasion had a single prayer ever been answered for a single soul. Not one prayer granted! Father Durrell was thoroughly and totally convinced that the meek would inherit the earth. Heaven did not want them and hell had no use for them. "Christ, now that I think of it, they already have," he had laughed himself silly on another occasion over another bottle of Scotch.

Father Durrell did thank God for one thing. Miss Giroux, his housekeeper, who had followed him into exile from Auburn. She came and went when needed, and never asked anything in return. Was this the meaning of love or His way of testing him further? Miss Giroux came into his life by chance, which, in time, only reaffirmed his conviction of the futility of prayer. She answered the ad he'd placed the week after his previous housekeeper, his mother's oldest sister, Aunt Marie, had passed away. Aunt Marie was the last of his mother's generation. His Aunt Teresa and Aunt Jean, matronly widows who had served the church, their God, and their nephew, had predeceased his Aunt Marie. There was no older relative to call upon to keep the rectory and, quite frankly, if there was he would have been hard pressed to recruit them. Even the parishioners joked that going to work for Father Durrell was akin to the kiss of death. The diocese granted him permission to hire. Several days went by without a response to the ad. A week had come and gone without as much as a knock on the door. At the end of the Sunday morning sermon, he mentioned the availability of the position, and he could have sworn he had heard a snicker or two from the pews. Not until Tuesday of the following week, in the early evening after hearing confessions, did he hear a faint knock at the front door of the rectory. That was the day Miss Giroux arrived. She was from neighboring Littlefield Corner near the Danville Junction—her father had worked the Grand Trunk Railroad there until he keeled over and died one morning, shoveling coal. That was eleven years before. In the years after her father's death, Miss Giroux swept floors and dusted houses, and then entered the mills. She had recently left a mill in Dover, New Hampshire. Her sister needed help in caring for her ailing mother. In Auburn, the shoe factory was hiring, her sister had told her, but a neighbor mentioned the opening at Saint Louis Parish to keep house at the rectory. Whether or not Miss Giroux would have applied for the position if she knew of Father Durrell's luck with housekeepers is for conjecture. As the sole applicant, Father Durrell eagerly welcomed the sight of Miss Giroux, offering her the position that very evening. That was the beginning. How *it* came to be—how, in one moment, his life was transformed by an enchantment he thought he would never know. Why, by what providence? Her plain features, long, dark hair, sparkling eyes, shy demeanor brought him a sense of calm and fulfillment he'd never known in the priesthood. At her appointment, Miss Giroux was twenty-six, he, thirty-seven. A year into it, her mother died peacefully in her sleep. That was the first morning Miss Giroux woke up sick, stricken by a nausea she could not explain. The waves of nausea would repeat most mornings for the better part of three months.

Word of an indiscretion concerning a young housekeeper at Saint Louis Parish in Auburn soon reached Bishop Murray in Portland. An ambitious man, the Most Reverend John G. Murray had been appointed Bishop at forty-eight. There would be no such embarrassments for the Church during his tenure. Bishop Murray's agenda was grand. So ambitious, he was in the early stage of expanding the Church and its influence throughout the state, and nearly bankrupting the diocese in the process. For his fiduciary incompetence, the Church would reward the Most Reverend Murray with the Archbishopric of Saint Paul. Father Durrell, however, who was summoned to Portland, was rewarded for his indiscretions with a transfer to a remote parish. He never returned to Auburn. The train left Portland for Augusta the very same day he had met with the Bishop. There he was met by a motor car that transported him to the coast, to a small town nestled under an old mountain by the sea. Amazingly, his meager possessions were awaiting him at the parish rectory of Saint Patrick's. That was 1925, and Father Durrell had not left the Lost Kingdom of Moose Harbor since.

God had also given him another break, he reasoned. That was for having Jeffrey Grant as a member of his parish, without whom he would have had to face the unrelenting hell he had landed in sober. A crooked, uneven smile cracked his face. He wondered now if the power of prayer could save him—Jeffrey Grant. Today's confessions had not differed much from any other day, except for the last one. The banal assortment of drunks and whores and liars arrived in succession as they usually did, droning on, asking forgiveness for the same sins they continued to commit day in and day out. His last charge had changed everything. He had just glanced at his watch, prepared to leave, when he heard the soft footfalls approach the confessional. A straggler, he thought, and sighed impatiently.

"Father, forgive me, for I have sinned," the voice said in a smoky whisper. "It's been months since my last confession."

"Shit," Father Durrell had wanted to say out loud. The last thing he wanted to hear was an unabridged autobiography of the damned. His stomach was growling and he needed a drink. But, like an automaton, he answered, "Yes, my child, go on."

"I'm party to murder," the voice whispered with a desperate intensity. "I'm sure of it."

"Indeed!" Father Durrell responded, nearly exclaiming, "Holy shit!" instead. He swallowed hard. His mouth dried. A swell of morbid anticipation rose within him.

"I fear for my life and the lives of others," the voice continued, unwavering, "for the blood that has been spilled and will spill again tonight."

"Dear God, my child," he responded, "do not do this."

"It is not I who has or will pull the trigger, Father," the voice steeled against any emotion.

The priest strained to hear the confessor, man or woman, attempting to place a face with the barely audible voice he heard. That was the moment, he would think later, that he should have stood, pulled back the curtain.

"Yet, I feel I have, nonetheless, just as sure as Jeff Grant will have a bullet through his brain before the dawn." There was a pause. Father Durrell was sure he heard a hard swallow from the other side of the partition, and then, "I am guilty for my sins."

Father Durrell found himself speechless, stunned and shocked. Moment after moment passed in silence as he tried to speak. His mouth went completely dry now at the drop of Jeffrey's name. Unable to talk, he could move. When the realization came to him, he jumped up, stepped from the compartment, and pulled the curtain aside. There was no one there. Spinning about, he looked all around. The old church was empty—eerily silent. He rushed to the entrance hall, pushed the door open, and glanced around the churchyard. Wisps of fog had gathered there, but that was all. There were several motor cars along the street. One larger sedan caught his attention briefly, near the Gaelic Hall. He could make out three men in fedoras sitting there, waiting to go inside. An urge to question them, if they'd seen anyone leave the church, subsided at the thought of the evening's Hallowe'en party at the hall. There was little time to be walking around the neighborhood. He was to give a brief opening invocation at the beginning of the festivities very soon.

Confused and uncertain how to proceed or what to do, Father Durrell walked through the church slowly, to the sacristy in the rear. "I should contact the sheriff," he said aloud. "But my vows? If the Bishop found out this transgression could not be buried." He hung his vestments distractedly. "I should tell Jeffrey Grant," he thought. "How could I explain a member of the parish was out to kill him?" His confusion grew. "If I contact the sheriff, then I would compromise Jeffrey—his position. But if I don't contact the sheriff, he could wind up dead." A grave weight fell upon him as he pondered the options. Then he thought, "What if this was a cruel prank?" Further, he thought, "Who could do such a thing? If I do tell Liam McO'Fayle, I could get Jeffrey in a world of trouble—he could go to jail—and then where would I get my Scotch?"

He pushed open the back door, went down the steps, lost in contemplation. Walking toward the rectory, he looked up at a sprawling, ancient oak tree that filled the backyard. He stopped, studying its gnarled, leafless branches, following its trunk with his eyes, downward. The mulch at its base needed a fresh layer, he noticed, as much as he needed a drink. Shutting his eyes, concentrating, he futilely attempted to place a face with the voice which had whispered penance through the lattice work in the dark, but could not get beyond the determination of whether he'd heard the confession of a man or woman. "Oh, dear God, what am I to do?"

As he crossed the gravel walkway, his attention shifted to the large sedan on the street again. Oddly, the three men were still sitting in the car and had not entered the Gaelic Hall. Maybe his confessor *was* one of the three? "Of course," he thought. Any inclination to approach the car was dashed when it started up and quickly sped away. "I'm such a fool. One of them is carrying a heavy load."

He wondered if Miss Giroux had returned from Auburn with Lucille or if she'd left the girl at her aunt's house. The company was dearly missed, the girl with her father's eyes and her mother's smile. It was good, he thought, how the woman and the child moved inconspicuously between Auburn and Downeast Way. The diocese had let them be. He wondered if he should confide in Miss Giroux. Cecilia was levelheaded—would know what to do—she always did. Not that he made a habit of directly sharing confessions with her. That was between him and God. The burden of confessor was heavy at times, though. The skeletal remains people threw in the closet were immense—too much for one man to carry. When the need for him to vent did arise, he'd learned to broach the subject gently. The conversation generally began, and evolved, along the lines of where want and ignorance intersected, desperation flourished. "Where desperation flourishes, so do the vulgar, the violent, the superstitious and the damned." His grandmother had told him that at a young age and Miss Giroux had heard him speak those words often. Then he would give her an example to illustrate his concerns, using a particularly troublesome confession that weighed heavy upon him. She would never interrupt him nor offer advice unless or until he asked for it. More often than not, she would simply listen until he worked out, expressing in words, what was in his head—forcing himself to absolve unrepentant sinners. Now that he thought of it, he had not absolved the person of their sins in the confessional. He never had the opportunity. The person fled at the admission of guilt before he completed the sacrament of penance and gave absolution. "I am free to contact whomever," he said positively, aloud, "without incurring the Bishop's wrath. This is splendid, Cecilia!" he thanked Miss Giroux, who, by the very thought of her, had lifted a great weight off his shoulders again. "But whom shall I contact first?" he asked himself, approaching the back steps to the rectory, "Jeffrey or Liam or both?" Confusion muddled his head once again. "Oh, I do hope Miss Giroux has returned."

Aunt Effie's Warning

Porter skipped up the walkway, jumped the steps, and knocked on the front door. An older woman with a round face and gentle smile opened the door immediately. Her hair, mostly gray with a few strands of auburn, was pulled back in a bun. Her eyes, bright hazel, lit up at the sight of Porter when she opened the door. A large, black dog the size of a Shetland pony stood beside her. The dog's tail wagged excitedly, and it cried out happily.

"Hello, Aunt Effie," he said, embracing her. "Hello, Mr. Perkins," he added, bowing to the dog and rubbing his head and belly. "How's my big pooch doing?" The dog barked once and jumped up on Porter's chest, then dropped to all fours, dancing side-to-side on his front paws. "I've missed you, too, old friend," Porter added, scratching the dog's head and neck.

"You'd better get that done with, Porter," Aunt Effie said. "Soon as I mentioned your name in front of him, he went in a tizzy."

"He's my special buddy, you know," said Porter.

"He knew you'd be here soon," said Aunt Effie. "I told him that your uncle called, said you'd dropped by the shop." Her smile grew. "Oh, I am so happy to see you. Come on in, my dear boy."

"It's good to be home," Porter replied, entering the house and shutting the door. He pet Mr. Perkins again in a futile attempt to calm the massive pooch down. "He's what—twelve years old now?

"Yes—and still bouncing around like a puppy," Aunt Effie replied.

"My God!" Porter inhaled. "Baked bread." He shut his eyes and breathed deeply. "I forgot how close I am to heaven whenever I walk into this house."

That made her smile wider. "I've got a couple of fresh loaves cooling down in the kitchen," she said, "and a jar of raspberry preserves with your name on it."

"You still pickin' the berries from the bushes up on the side of the mountain?" he asked, with a nod toward Mount Agamenticus.

"I'm not that old that I can't make your Uncle Stu drive me up to Uriel's Ledge in the Ford," she answered.

"And I'm still too young to be thinking of you and Uncle Stu parking up on Uriel's Ledge in the Ford," he winked, and they both laughed.

The three made their way to the kitchen. Mr. Perkins continued to nudge his nozzle between Porter's giant hand and hip. Aunt Effie put the kettle on and Porter made himself comfortable in a chair at the table near the big bay window. His eyes wandered out to the yard. The few birch trees scattered around the yard were bare, but the grass was still green. On the harbor, there was a light fog, but it did not obscure the sight of fishing boats and trawlers bobbing slowly in the water. On the distant edge of the harbor, he counted the four islands—Frenchman's, Clapp, Goat and Popham—the latter an uninhabitable mass of granite, shrubs, and stunted cedar. He recalled how he and Jeffah, along with his cousin Joe, had explored all the islands in their youth. Many a summer day was spent taking a lunch and rowing a dory out to the islands. Searching endlessly for a chest of gold said to be buried there centuries before by the most feared and dreaded pirate ever to sail these waters—One-Eyed Red Beard. Nothing ever came of it but a little adventure and a lot of fun—or an occasional bout of poison ivy if they explored Popham too closely; the island was covered in it. They had come to know the islands well in those years, learned all the places to hide. The thought of what lay ahead this evening struck Porter with irony. He and Jeffah, bound for another adventure, drew a half smile on his face and a hard swallow in his throat.

"That's a mischievous smile, Porter, if I've ever seen one," said Aunt Effie, placing two tea cups down on the table while balancing a loaf of bread and a jar of preserves on a cutting board. "Something tells me you're in town for more than a visit." She sat and began slicing effortlessly. Soon there was a short stack of soft, warm bread on the table between them. "Now, what is it? Don't keep this old woman waiting any longer—what's your business this time?"

"Oh, Aunt Effie! I was just looking out at the islands and thinking about the times that me and Jeffah and Joe would go out there," Porter replied. "Seems like another lifetime now."

"Hmm," Aunt Effie said inquisitively. "You should know more than anyone, Porter, 'We lead many lives in this one lifetime alone. Make sure ...'"

"'... none of them lead to a lifetime of regret,'" Porter finished the sentence. "I haven't forgotten what Dad told me."

"Andrew was a brilliant man, Porter. He's dearly missed."

"I miss him dearly—all of them—him and Mom and Joe. The house and my life have been empty without them," he nodded in the direction of the window across the yard.

"Well, the house won't be empty much longer," she said cheerfully, "and that void will fade away."

"I know."

"So you won't have any excuses not to visit more often."

"I'm sure I'll be able to think of some," he smiled, which made Aunt Effie giggle. "But I will make every effort."

"Just so you know, Porter, a lot of folks around here would love to see you come home when you're finished with baseball," she said, lifting her teacup and sipping.

"There will be a day I come back—that I promise you," Porter answered her. "This is where I want to take the big sleep. Granted, I'm not in any hurry, but I want to lay these bones here with my family." Porter quieted, looked out on the harbor, studying it, and then spread preserves over a slice of bread.

"Madam Luna get the best of you last night, nephew?"

"How in the hell?" Porter froze. A piece of bread dangled from his mouth.

"Relax," she waved him off. "Catherine called."

"How many people did she call, for God's sake?" he asked, pulling the piece of bread away.

"I think only me, this morning, looking for you."

"Jeffah put me up to it," he replied, defensively.

"Relax, I said," she smiled. "I'm not after you. You're a grown man, for one thing, and from those books you've been writing, just as smart as your father. You want to see a gypsy woman, you can—anytime you want."

Porter blushed. "Thank you, Aunt Effie."

Effie burst out laughing. "She must have had something important to say."

"She did."

"She's got you thinking?"

"Too much, really," Porter said, stuffing the rest of the jammed bread slice into his mouth, chewing slowly. His thoughts drifted to Madam Luna—Viola—then jumped to the graveyard—the angelic, buxom blonde he saw there—and quickly shifted to the night ahead—the warning leveled by her—Viola. He took a sip of tea and swallowed. "She had a lot to say," Porter searched for words. "But it was more the way she said it that got me wondering. Does that sound crazy, Aunt Effie?"

"It would be easy to say peanuts on the whole thing, Porter. Most would," she replied thoughtfully. "I don't know why, but I just don't. I told your Uncle Stu the same thing this morning. Whether or not you believe in such a thing as fortunes told—you have to consider this—she makes a living making people think."

"She's pretty good at it."

"Madam Luna's not a stranger to this town—came here last spring, too. I suspect she's here now because the town was good to her and she was good for it."

"A gypsy woman? She'd have been hung as a witch—or thrown off of Parson's Drop like Howlin' Minnie—not that long ago. Good for the town? How could she be?"

"You said yourself she's pretty good."

"Yes, she is."

"It seems obvious to me, Porter. She's able to convey to people something their preachers and priests can't—their fortune," Aunt Effie said.

"What do you mean, Aunt Effie?"

"I believe she gives them hope."

He eyed her quizzically. "You're pretty sharp for an old lady."

"There something you want to tell me, nephew?" she asked. Porter fell silent. Mr. Perkins snuggled tighter around his legs. "I thought so. Maybe it's just as well. Be careful. That's what I'll tell you. The town's been hit by the hard times. Good men believe there's easy money to be made on these shores and out on that harbor. They think that because the Lost Kingdom is so far away from everything that the world's passed us by or forgotten us. Nothing could be further from the truth."

The Unpromised Land

Destiny is a funny thing. A delicate balance between fate and chance. That's what Scoop Comeau told Porter the first time they'd met. All Porter had asked him was why he thought he'd make a good ballplayer. "Baseball's my destiny," he proclaimed. Too profound a thing to say for a kid his age was what Porter had thought at the time, especially one from a backwater seaport like Yarmouth, Nova Scotia—out on the fringe of the continent. Porter had always found that people, generally, who lived on the fringe were busier surviving than thinking. Much like the small pond he'd left behind. The ground he treads upon now? That had puzzled him often—how he *had* found the time to think—or really how his father and mother, his Uncle Stu and Aunt Effie, had found the time to think. For they're the ones who had pushed the lot of them, taught them how to think and ask questions.

"What's your old man do?" Porter had then asked Scoop. "Pounds nails," Scoop had replied. "A carpenter. He made me this bat—s'unbreakable—this is my second summer with it."

Porter wanted to ask him where he went to school, but he looked like he was a teenager—barely shaved—if at all.

"If your last name is Comeau or Robicheau or whatever—if you can claim yourself as part of the Acadian heritage of Nova Scotia, then you got Micmac blood in you—square jaw, no whiskers, an' pure athlete!" said Scoop eagerly.

From the first time Porter had met him, Scoop had been ready to play, displaying a confidence in body and soul beyond his years. "The kid's got a big set of balls, Porter," O.W. had told him. "Not to be confused with a big head. Kid's got no ego whatsoever. He's got game."

When Porter asked Scoop the next question, it was as though a spark erupted into a flame. All the more amazing because Scoop was on deck and he had no idea who Porter was or that he was there scouting him. Porter was standing on the other side of the fence. He had asked the first question, nonchalantly, before the game, as though Porter was just another fan passing by. The kid had given him the respect and courtesy of a straight answer, profound as it was. Porter had walked away, feigning disinterest. Now it was the bottom of the eighth inning, with runners at second and third, with two out. The Black Bears were down 4-3, and Porter had one more thing to ask. "Psst, hey, kid," he said. "What happens if you lose your balance?"

Scoop smiled that smile of his, as wide as a slice of watermelon, and giggled, "You either cast your fate to the wind, as most people do, or you land on your feet and fulfill your destiny." He promptly went to bat and lined the first pitch into the left-center gap for a bases-clearing double. "I ain't going back to pound nails," the kid told Porter after the game. "That's not my destiny."

Pounding nails, Porter thought. Pounding nails on the head. "You could always pound nails," he heard a voice say.

"Porter?" shouted Jeffah. "You in there?"

"What?" Porter answered, trying to focus.

"I said you could always pound nails—you listening?" Jeffah said. "This depression isn't gonna last forever, and I've been really thinking about becoming a landlubber. Maybe if you moved back, we could start a business together—pound nails."

Porter smiled, not so much at Jeffah, but *for* Jeffah, for being his friend, for bringing him back. Not that he'd gone anywhere, but another gap had occurred. The last thing he'd remembered was sitting with Aunt Effie and Mr. Perkins, looking out on the harbor, talking old times. Then, Porter said his good-byes and promised to return for supper. He'd walked out the door, and old Delbert Comeau was before him, casting his fate to the wind like fly fishing on a breezy day. They began to stroll together, side-by-side, reminiscing about that first time—or so Porter imagined—until he found himself in stride with Jeffah.

The gypsy woman, he thought. What kind of spell *am* I under?

"I think you should pound nails regardless of what I do, if that's what you want to do, Jeffah," Porter answered. "You know if I come back here I'd be attached to the bookshop. Besides that, I can't stay in one place too long—don't know how anymore—as it is. I'm sure as hell not gonna make a promise to you I can't keep."

"I figured as much," Jeffah sighed. "Thought I'd run it by you, just the same. Catherine's the one that suggested it."

"She's looking out for you as much as me. You gotta like that. I tell you, Jeffah, if I had a Catherine in my life, I'd happily pound nails for her."

"I'm thinking I will, Porter. I'm thinking this fella Roosevelt is gonna win the election and he's gonna turn back Prohibition," Jeffah said. "The lobster's all but gone, and I don't know if I can go back to catching mackerel full-time."

"You're damn straight Roosevelt's gonna win," said Porter. "He's gonna roll out the barrels and make an honest man out of you once again—whether you pound nails, cast a net—whatever."

Jeff grinned. "It's been a good run, and I've been lucky." He paused, started to speak, then hesitated, his mood shifting, then said, "I haven't said anything about this, but, a few weeks back they found Minard Severance with a bullet in his head—right in his den, right over in Bean's Point. He was a fisherman, and he was known to have done some runnin,' too."

Porter's ears perked at the name. He recognized it immediately, but he said, "What the hell, Jeffah!"

"No one heard a thing," he continued. "It happened sometime late at night. His wife, Mildred, had gone to bed. The poor woman found him the next morning sitting there in his chair, the mess, the gun at the side on the floor."

"Suicide?"

"Ha! That's what they're saying, the sheriff's report, anyway."

"What do you think?" asked Porter.

"I think he was murdered," Jeffah answered.

"Surely, Liam McO'Fayle isn't that numb."

"No—he's smart. Liam knows the score. 'Come and go in peace,' he says, 'for a small piece,' which is fine by me—it keeps him honest. He knows that the rum runnin' has kept all of Moose Harbor afloat. But mostly, he reckons, with six kids and a wife living and breathing there's a lot more at stake than one man who ain't."

"This is not supposed to happen here, Jeffah," said Porter, "Not violence like that—city violence. You sure it wasn't suicide?"

"Sure as shit!" he snapped. "Cripes! For starters, don't you think his wife would have heard the thing pop when it went off? But if you ask Liam, he'll tell you he did himself in, just read the damn report. It's all in there!"

"Hey, I'm just asking."

"I know, I don't mean to get short," Jeffah said. "Minard was shot at ten paces between the eyes. That's what you won't read in the report—and the bastard didn't even own a pistol, by Jesus!"

"Holy shit!" Porter exclaimed.

"There's more. I've made it a habit to scour the headlines—*Bangor Daily, Kennebec Journal, Portland Herald*—check all the papers, for a while now. Whenever I see a fisherman come belly up—accidental drowning, man fell overboard—I take note. I wanna know where it happened, circumstances, and, more importantly, when they lost him. A man goes belly up on an overnight run, you start to wonder. If the name's familiar, then I'll know for sure what went down."

"Like who or what?" asked Porter.

"Like Howard Bailey, who washed ashore over in Gouldsboro two weeks before Minard."

"Are you saying what I think you're saying, Jeffah?" Porter asked.

"And a week before that, another fisherman, Lawrence Philpot, his house burned to the ground—he and the house turned to ash overnight. A kerosene lamp, they say, fell over. Hell—it was thrown against the wall!"

Porter's head was spinning, and he wondered now how much Redfern knew and what he hadn't told him.

"It's like this, Porter. I believe the violence has always been around here, but low key, accidental. Minard was different for a reason, though."

"In what way?"

"A demonstration, a warning, a notice—I believe so."

"Yeah, but for who, Jeffah? What purpose?"

"I don't know, but I can tell you this. Wasn't that long ago that Minard, Howard and Lawrence made a rendezvous at Popham Island, made a drop at the Whale's Jaw." He pointed toward the islands in the bay.

"Wait—how do you know they even knew each other?" asked Porter, but he knew the answer before he finished the question.

"Because I was driving the boat," Jeffah sighed. He stopped and looked Porter directly in the eyes. "They worked for me."

The Custom House

The old Custom House was a landmark for Downeast Way and the entire Lost Kingdom of Moose Harbor. A triumph of perseverance and fortitude from the time the building was erected in 1776. Over the century and a half since its construction, the town folk had looked upon the Custom House as a grand symbol of the will of the people and American independence. The will of the people notwithstanding, the building came to be a year after the bombardment, burning and subsequent occupation of the town by the British. Spurred by the futile attack on Fort Norumbega by locals in late December of 1774, British warships arrived a month later and proceeded to set an example of the town for colonists far and wide. The wrath of His Majesty was unleashed in a furious cannonade that left fourteen dead and the town in flames. Two-thirds of the town, in total, was lost. Only a winter storm saved the remaining third. When the British came ashore, the will of the people faltered. They were no match for the Marines who occupied the Lost Kingdom for the next five years. When the British finally departed, quite voluntarily, in their wake, they left the town an architectural heritage, a quaint little seaport of newly-erected brick-and-mortar structures—late Georgian and early Federalist style row houses and buildings, shops and homes.

One building in particular, the Custom House, served as the focal point of commerce. It was there, from the top floor, beginning in 1851, the Huxley Empire grew. Textiles, real estate, lumber and mackerel were the source of the Huxley fortune through the remainder of the nineteenth century.

But there was more.

Because Maine had been a dry state for decades, Jonah had begun to dabble in the importation of spirits—gin, whiskey and Scotch—from Canada to Massachusetts. The profit margin was thin, the revenue lean at first, until the great boondoggle or boon—depending on which side of the aisle one was standing on—occurred on January 17, 1920. The imposition of the Eighteenth Amendment, the Age of Prohibition of alcohol consumption in the United States, altered the lives and fortunes of many a man and woman. It made many an honest man a criminal, and many a criminal a fortune. Somewhere, at some time between the fine lines, it did both for the Huxleys.

Sterling's hands were fidgeting in his pocket for his lighter when he noticed it on the desk. A cigar, a fat Corona, was protruding from his mouth, one from the last case he'd acquired in Miami Beach the previous winter. The vacation had been a much-needed respite with his wife, Florence. He lit the cigar and stoked peacefully, gazing out across the harbor. His view of the world had changed, but the view from the Custom House remained the same.

Prohibition had changed his life and his fortunes. Working the machine of fulfillment as independent parts, they, the Merchant House of Huxley, provided liquor to urban centers far and near. In the process, forming business associations and aligning themselves with a variety of good-natured hustlers, hungry mercenaries, willing or desperate fishermen, and a myriad of businessmen, who, with the advent of the Depression, became increasingly prone to deadly violence. Jonah, and Sterling especially, had accepted an uneasy coexistence with these alliances. Though Sterling had gone to law school, and applied the law in his business practices, he came to realize, much too late, that when any of your business practices takes you outside the law, there is no law to protect you. No sheriff, no courts, no cavalry to rescue you—there is no one, nothing! What comfort and security he had carried through the years of Prohibition had eroded these past few years, as the Depression wore on and bore into the heart and soul and psyche of every person on the planet. What little security he had was gained by aligning himself with the 'partners,' as he referred to them, in New York City.

It all coincided with the day they confided in Thompson Crowe. "We have but two choices," his father Jonah had said the day they were confronted with bringing the man into the business, "and neither is appealing to me. We need him, at the very least, for our banking, to let our funds dry. We have enough of a reserve for now, but if he cracks or makes a play, there'll be hell to pay and doom will follow." That was nearly three years ago, Sterling reckoned. Jonah had since died and Thompson Crowe was a reckless liability. In a business that demanded near invisibility, he had brought attention to himself in the most negative way. Pompous and arrogant, he foreclosed on his neighbors with sadistic delight, bullying people like Leo Caron or Jeff Grant or Porter Gibson, for what? On all days? The idiot sickened Sterling to no end. He tired of managing his erratic behavior, and came to know with increasing bitterness and frustration why Thompson's father, Wendell, had kept his son as far away from the business as possible. Jonah, ever looking for the advantage, had reminded Sterling often that, if anything, Thompson's well-earned reputation as an asshole served an unintended purpose. The focus was on him, not them. His behavior diverted the attention away from the Merchant House of Huxley. The afternoon's tirade was not atypical, but, even for Thompson, exaggerated. Why? Prohibition was coming to an end. That was certain. They would have to cash out. Was Thompson that numb? Not to see that something was afoot? Sharks were circling. Philpot was an eye opener. Bailey was a slap 'side the head. Severance was a punch in the face. How many more messages must be sent to shut the man up?

Prohibition will end with the election of the Democrat. Thankfully. The sordid business had pushed him to the brink. He longed for a sense of normality in his life. Not that anything would ever be the same again.

Sterling drew on his cigar, puffed gently, and heard the bell from the Queen's Chapel chime. Studying the trawlers in the harbor, watching them rise and fall, he thought, such is the fate of man and empires.

A Patient Man

"Need I remind you, Murton, what Mr. Walker said?" Hardy spoke quietly from the backseat of the car. The Packard was back in town, parked down the street from the Crowe Trust. "He was very clear. There are to be no loose ends."

"Another priest, Hardy?" Murton asked. "That's not good for one's reputation."

"First of all, he's a man, Murton, and not much of one. Secondly, a papist and, from his gait, a drunk," Hardy replied. "Thirdly, by the looks of the woman and child that passed us and entered the house—no doubt his concubine and bastard offspring—I would add fornicator to the list. He's anything but a priest, except in name only. One more example of the hypocrisy, corruption and incompetence of that whole damned, cursed religion."

"Granted," answered Murton. "I thought Mr. Walker also said to employ maximum discretion."

"I intend to, Murton." Hardy's frustration with Murton was growing, but he held his tone in check. "There's a fine line we tread upon here, and you, of all people, should know that. I believe this man knows too much—that woman just told him everything. I'm sure of it."

"Can you be that sure?" asked Murton.

Again, Hardy held his voice. "The Catholics have a ridiculous notion that they can be absolved of their sins through the mere act of admission— a confession to a priest—a *priest*—no matter what the transgression. Penance and contrition and prayer—and all are forgiven."

"Still, Hardy ..."

"I will not tolerate anyone questioning my authority," snapped Hardy. "Not when it comes to business, no matter the relationship. Do you understand?"

"I would never question you, Hardy," Murton replied, apologetically. "This could be high profile. That's all I meant."

Though a patient man, Hardy was confounded of late by Murton's inability to accept his role in the business at hand. In their Edinburgh days, he and Murton had run together—collections for a man named Mr. Browne. Hardy had landed Murton a situation when he'd arrived from Scotland in late '29 in search of a position. Murton was a qualified candidate, Hardy knew; enough of one to bring him in, with one condition. "It is delicate matters we attend to, Murton," Hardy had explained. "We resolve the most sensitive issues for the business. In our capacity, there are no questions. There are no answers. There is only ... *resolve*." Murton proved to be an able swingman for Hardy and kept a low profile.

All was fine with him until his return from Edinburgh the month before. Hardy sent Murton there to resolve an urgent matter. Settle a grievance. Locate a man named Burke, a man they both knew from the old days, and kill him. Murton was gone but a few weeks, yet, upon his return, he'd changed— taken to philosophy, Hardy figured—started asking questions. Maybe because Burke was his first. The man had been altered by the events that unfolded in the old city. "I tracked the bastard down, Hardy," Murton had reported upon his return. "He was dodgy, that one, Burke, but I caught him. I followed—right into Bell's Wynd. I think he knew what was coming, Burke did—expected it. No man can lead two lives without expectations of consequence. Sooner or later, one overtakes the other. Believe me, that night, in that place, I saw what consequence awaits us all."

That's what struck Hardy as queer, the idea of consequence. Murton, for everything he was in a man, was no philosopher or vicar. From that point on, Hardy began to question Murton's resolve. That he, Murton, had to talk through everything, question everything, seek answers—even in front of Mr. Calvin—was not suited to the business. It undermined the very fundamental nature of the situation. It fell upon Hardy to remind

Murton, time and again, to simply shut up. He was prepared to now, as they discussed the priest.

"I know what you meant, Murton," said Hardy from the backseat, leaning closely to Murton's ear. "We're not amateurs. Do you understand?"

"Yes," he said.

"A fallen angel is sure to be noteworthy, and draw attention," said Hardy. "But a full-fledged demon, maybe Beelzebub himself, come visit the priest—well, that's noteworthy, even newsworthy—and will make people think twice—the consequences—about dancin' with the devil. That may just be an option."

Murton had no reply, but thought of what he'd encountered at Bell's Wynd, what haunted him still. The red eyes, the thing that formed around them, that came from the deep darkness of the alleyway toward Burke, after he'd died. His body stilled, his blood spilling evenly onto the cobbled stones. The thought made him shudder, what he witnessed. He was a part of it, or it was a part of him. He couldn't shake it. Murton glanced at Mr. Calvin, who gripped the steering wheel of the Packard tightly, as he had at the church.

Hardy sighed and fell into quiet contemplation, studying the Dodge in the near distance, across the common, and then glanced up at the lighted, top floor windows of the old Custom House, wondering about Murton's resolve and the evening ahead. "Time to see the banker," he said, and the men got out.

A Matter of Trust

The knock at the door startled Sterling. "Come in," he called. The door opened to the lovely face of Abigail, his personal secretary.

"I'm back," Abigail smiled respectfully.

"So soon?" he answered. "Did church let out early for some reason?"

"No, no," she replied. "Today was confession. Tomorrow is mass, a holy day."

"I suppose I should know that by now," he smiled, "one of the holy days."

"Mr. Grant and his friend should arrive soon."

"I haven't forgotten, but when they do, let them wait five minutes before rousing me," he said, and held up his cigar. "I'm in the middle of something."

"I understand," she replied, and shut his office door.

"Abigail," Sterling thought, "what am I to do?" For ten years she had buffered him from the world. Her intelligence and professionalism was matched by her beauty. Miss Michaud's light brown hair and complexion, her bright blue eyes, proved a valuable asset for Sterling. The men he dealt with came from all walks of life, but all of them were hot-blooded. Each and every one of them who had entered his office had entered distracted and disengaged by the carnal energy that filtered through their minds at the sight of Abigail Michaud.

Miss Michaud had entered Sterling's world quite by chance. A first generation Franco-American, her family was part of the great migration of labor from Quebec into the mill towns and cities of New England during the last part of the nineteenth century onward. The story goes that Abigail's parents had settled in Lewiston, Maine, where she was born and where they worked—her mother in a boarding house near Bates College and her father in a mill. The memory she held of that man was dear, but distant. "The millworker is a prisoner to his own survival," her mother had explained to Abigail one day. The girl had returned from the mill, having brought her father his dinner. The heat of the summer was upon her, walking into the mill. The size of the machines frightened her in the dim light. The noise was deafening. Hundreds of people lined the machines in the cavernous brick tomb. She searched for a half hour, through floor after floor filled with dust, dirt, deafening thunder, and sweat and toil. She would shout out her father's name, to no avail. When she did find him, he yelled at her for being late. Later, he would apologize, but she would never go back again. "How could papá be so angry?" she asked her mother that day. "The machines, my dear," her mother replied. "They are the angry, savage beasts, not your father, but he is their prisoner."

That was Abigail's first experience of what the mill could do to a man. Her last occurred late one Friday afternoon when she was seventeen. The old man went to open a steam vat. The lock blew while releasing the pressure. The lid burst open, struck him squarely in the forehead and cracked his skull. Abigail's papá was dead before he hit the floor.

Sterling was not unfamiliar with industrial accidents. They were not uncommon to mill work. Most accident victims, or their families, were given token compensation for their suffering. If the accident was gruesome enough, or if there were more than one victim, a story in the local paper might be in order. Whether or not the working conditions placed the workers at risk was of secondary importance to the sensational angle of the accident. Could it sell papers? And how many? The day that Mr. Michaud had his bell dented was Good Friday. The accident, therefore, received considerable attention in the papers. *A Widow and Four Children—Easter Sunday—Tragedy at the Mill—Faulty, Aging Equipment Blamed*—all of that was bad enough and guaranteed front page fodder for weeks, if not for months. When Florence Huxley read the headline, *Black Friday at Huxley Mill*, she was deeply moved and appalled by the tragedy, and went into action immediately. She pushed her husband and father-in-law to improve the working conditions at the factories, institute routine inspections of machinery, and emphasize safety first with the workers. When at first Jonah balked, Flo reminded him of the adverse consequences a negative publicity campaign could have against Huxley Textiles by their competition at Hathaway. The year was 1917, America had entered the Great War, and Huxley Textiles had landed a greater contract with the War Department. American soldiers, sailors, and marines were wearing at least one article of clothing—be it socks, shirt, or skivvy—made by Huxley Textiles. Flo was a practical woman. She had learned and accepted her role in the family early on. She understood perfectly well the key to Sterling's mind was between her legs, and the key to Jonah's was his wallet. No matter what your politics, she realized, define your argument to Jonah as a financial advantage, and you'll win the day.

Improvements at the mill were one thing. The Michaud family was quite another. Where the former was a matter of practicality, the latter was an absolute necessity. There would be no perfunctory compensation to have the affair swept under the table. The family was offered a boarding house to run and eventually own. There was a modest pension for the widow, too. Quite remarkably, and on a lark, Sterling offered to send the oldest Michaud child, Abigail, to Bates College, where he was a trustee and Flo was an alumna. Sterling would later explain in an article in the *Lewiston Evening Journal* that he and his wife were motivated by a concern to set the right example for his three daughters. Truth be told, a fellow trustee of the college had made the suggestion to him. Women's Suffrage was beating down the door and was upon them. The image of the college *and* the Merchant House of Huxley would benefit immensely in the local community by such an act of generosity. Bates had always had a liberal tradition—it was founded on abolitionist principles in 1855. Its first female graduate, Mary Wheelwright Mitchell of Dover and Foxcroft, did so in 1869. Besides, Sterling rationalized, and as he explained to Jonah, sending the girl to college was a pittance in relation to public relations and the military contracts.

Sterling had never fancied himself a shepherd, nor Abigail a member of his flock. Still, she took the offer extended to her by him, and went to Bates, where she excelled in her studies and graduated with a degree in Math in three years. Soon after, again because of Flo's insistence, Abigail was offered a secretarial position at the Merchant House of Huxley. The post-war years were booming for the company. Abigail had not gone to college to become a secretary, but she had the good sense to know not to bite the hand that fed her and her family. The Michauds had been and were wholly dependent on the generosity of the Huxleys. She took the position offered and moved to Downeast Way. In the summer of 1921, she began her duties on the first floor of the Custom House. Two weeks on the job, and Sterling decided to use her stunning beauty to his advantage. A week later, she was on the top floor in the capacity as a general secretary for the executive pool. A year later, she assumed the position as Sterling's personal secretary upon the retirement of old Mrs. Dalrymple. In the years that followed, she gained firsthand knowledge of all the Huxleys's business ventures. By 1930, she was, de facto, the number three person in the organization under Sterling and Jonah. Then Jonah passed away. The textile business of the Merchant House sputtered. Real estate and lumber were at a crawl. However, they did provide the necessary front for the elaborate operation that had evolved. An operation that Abigail had become heavily vested in. By Sterling's reckoning, Abigail had, in her own right and her own sense of self, proved her worth—to her legacy, her family, and the fate that brought her into his life.

As Sterling sat at his desk, puffing his Corona, he heard the voices in the outer office. Five minutes passed and the knock came, the door opened. "Mr. Grant and Mr. Gibson have arrived, sir," she said.

His thoughts shifted from Abigail to the moment at hand. Great risk and peril were upon them all. The final move was at hand. Jeff and Abigail, and now Porter, were a part of it.

"By all means," Sterling finally said, "do send them in, Miss Michaud."

Casual Banking

A loud rap on the door and Hardy entered. Menace reeked from him. It always did, with each visit. "Come in," Thompson said. "Make yourself at home." He looked past Hardy. Ambrose stood in his wake at the door. He shrugged. "That will be all, Ambrose. Thank you for showing Hardy in."

"Do I detect sarcasm, Mr. Crowe?" said Hardy. He seated himself at a chair in front of Thompson's desk, removed his hat and placed it on his lap. "Neat," he said to Thompson, without a look his way, and Thompson obeyed. Hardy was tired of this man and ready to be done with him. He knew it from the first handshake. Knew the grip. A man of privilege. Their ilk, the *after* generation, never worked a day in their lives. Did not know a day's labor. Their means and fortune rested on a chance drop of sperm conceived in an act of mutually repulsive copulation. Their life unfolded in the aftermath. They believed that all gain, all advantage in their lifetime, was there to take, not earn; to pilfer, not pay for, without consequence.

Placing a full glass of Scotch before Hardy, Thompson moved around his desk and sat down. "I'm afraid it's not all good news—not all the properties have moved," he said. Thompson studied him for a reaction. Instead, he couldn't help noting that Hardy had not aged, or it seemed that way, since the first time he'd entered his office those years before.

"What is it you're getting at, Mr. Crowe?" asked Hardy.

"Sterling told me there are a couple more properties out there," answered Thompson, "that he hasn't moved."

Hardy did not blink an eye. "What, then, is there in the way of *good* news, Mr. Crowe?"

"I have your share, I mean Mr. Walker's share, from the properties Sterling has sold," he smiled weakly. Thompson reached into his bottom drawer and produced a small, black bag. Hardy opened it, thumbed the stacks of bills. "There's $185,455, from the sale of properties since your last visit. It's all accounted for. There's a list of the deeds in the bag, per usual. And per usual, we've subtracted the bank's fee, and that for the Merchant House of Huxley, your representing agent. Everything's in order."

"Very well," said Hardy. He took the measure of the man once again, as he had that first day, looking into the eyes of privilege, staring at Thompson. Above a whisper, barely audible, he calmly said, "I think it's time for the remaining properties to move."

"As far as I know, Sterling is making every effort to do just that. With the election coming up, it looks like the real estate market around here will dry up with it, for sure if Governor Roosevelt gets elected. There may not be a buyer."

"There's always a market for real estate, Mr. Crowe. Make no mistake," Hardy grinned. "There are always *buyers.* People like Mr. Walker are always looking for a safe place and a sure bet to invest their money. He's grown fond of the real estate market here." At those words, Hardy stood, and picked up the bag. "Need I remind you, there are as many ways to move property as there are ..." he paused, and added forcefully, "... other bankers."

Reservations

"Thank you, Abigail," Sterling nodded, and then drew on his cigar.

She nodded back, "Yes, sir," then turned and spoke courteously. "Gentlemen, Mr. Huxley will see you now," holding the door for them.

Jeffah, who had been staring at her legs when she turned, swallowed hard, and uttered, "Thank you, Abigail, and, again, my condolence about your mother. I was sorry to hear she'd passed."

"Thank you, Jeff," she said.

"Gentlemen!" Sterling stood and extended his hand, "Jeff—and Porter—always a pleasure."

"Mr. Huxley," Jeff said, nodding.

"Sterling," said Porter. "Good to see you, and congratulations about Enid and James. I saw Mrs. Harrington at the bookshop, and she told me the good news."

"Thank you, Porter," replied Sterling. "Mrs. Huxley and I are very pleased and excited about the coming union."

"I bet you are," thought Porter. Enid was born an angry, menopausal, controlling old lady—just like her grandmother was. You, sir, should receive the Distinguished Cross for having survived the years putting up with a daughter and mother of the same ilk. Granted, the old lady was a prize in her day—a Venus flytrap. That's what Porter wanted to say, but instead, he said, "Sterling, I'm very happy for you," and grasped his hand and shook it firmly.

Sterling smiled knowingly at Porter, and said, "I have two more daughters, yet, Porter, for Flo to find a match made in *heaven.*"

"That would count me out," Porter replied. "I'm one step ahead of the Devil and another ahead of the Angel of Death—or so I'm told."

"We don't have to tell Flo that, Porter," replied Sterling, smiling, and then adding thoughtfully, "I was real sorry to hear what happened to your teammate. Tell me, are things okay? Are you doing all right?"

Porter acknowledged the gesture with a nod. "I'm okay, Sterling. He was a good kid, a dear friend, and a great teammate."

"My intention was to pay my respects, not to bring you down," said Sterling. "I'd be remiss in not letting you know how sorry I am. Jeffah told me a few weeks back you'd be in town, and I wanted you to know how I feel, as do many in town. Those kinds of things can haunt a man—don't let it haunt you."

"Thank you, Sterling," replied Porter. "I'm genuinely touched by the sentiment."

Jeffah, who had been quietly reserved through much of the past several minutes, saw the slightest trace of water begin to well in Porter's right eye. "I got the *Catherine* filled and ready to go, Mr. Huxley," he said. "We'll be running with the tide in a few hours. I'm set to rendezvous with Williams around ten."

"Timing is everything," replied Sterling. "I know this isn't easy—it might be asking too much—to go out this soon, even though we've already canceled one rendezvous because of what happened."

"I'm not afraid," said Jeffah, "that much."

"Let's hope tonight's smooth sailing, Jeff," said Sterling. "I chose this night for a reason. There's no moon. I'm also hoping Hallowe'en will keep all the lurking demons busy," he added, with a glance toward Porter. "It's good to know there's someone we can trust with you, and you were able to find a recruit."

"I can't say I'm keen on going, but if he's going, I'm going," said Porter.

"That's admirable, Porter," said Sterling.

"No, it's insane, taking a hike into the Valley of Death. Yet I'm not gonna let Jeffah go alone, or with anybody else," said Porter. "But I would like to know why *now*? I mean, the intimidation and violence, after so many years?"

"That has perplexed me," Sterling admitted. "We're a remote wayside—working the margins of distribution. We make good on what we do because we can—the Maritimes are only a few hours away. We navigate the Gulf of Maine and the Bay of Fundy, and deliver." Sterling gave a heartfelt sigh, and looked at Jeffah. "I want you to know, I really do have reservations about tonight, Jeff," he said. "We've had a good run."

"Over a decade, Mr. Huxley," Jeffah replied. "Never thought it would come to this, never thought it could."

"I never thought it could or would, either," replied Sterling. "This business is winding down. Next year, Prohibition will surely be rolled back."

"An end of an *error*," Porter joked.

"Yes," Sterling smiled, "but one from which we've benefited immensely. We've succeeded for so long without notice, I guess I took it for granted that we were beyond any risk or danger."

"Life under the old mountain by the sea is not as safe or secluded as it once seemed," said Porter. A sense of danger struck him for the first time. It overwhelmed him—it overwhelmed all of them, he sensed. It resonated there in the room, out the door, on the street, and out on the sea. The pressure would continue to build up to the near point of suffocation, through the hours ahead and the night—being strangled by the unknown hand of Chance. The operation was at extreme risk. Deadly violence had entered the business—had made itself known here, on the fringe. Such was the grip of the invisible hands of the free market, good old laissez faire, pure capitalism. That, given enough rope and time, there was no eluding the eventuality, even here, that the free market would strangle itself by its own hand. The only people who did not know or grasp this were the American people themselves, who, even buried alive by a great depression and enormous debt, continued to cling to the vision that an unregulated marketplace with no public oversight is something as sacred as the Promised Land itself. Their 'betters' had bred that vision in them— the Captains of Industry and Bankers who had made their fortunes by regulating the marketplace—to their favor. That vision had proven time and again about as farsighted and secure as pulling up a deck chair on the *Titanic.* There are only so many dogs to a bone, reasoned Porter. Men are men. Greed is greed. It had made America a dark place. Was there anything more dangerous for the country than that?

Porter's mind raced. Fucking Redfern. Fuck him. Someday, someone will write a book about this.

"Hey," interrupted Jeffah, "nothing's gonna happen."

"Needless to say," said Sterling, "because there are only two of you, watch your backs. That's a big load tonight. Drop a couple dozen cases at the Whale's Jaw. Bring the rest of the load ashore to my dock and wait there. It's for Burke."

"That bootlegger's coming up from Portland tonight?" asked Jeff.

"After midnight," Sterling nodded. "Now, one more thing, you still carry that shotgun on the boat?" asked Sterling.

"Always," Jeff said.

"Good." Sterling opened the drawer and stared down. Porter glanced. Though his angle was obscured, he knew what lay there. Sterling reached in and pulled a pistol out, then placed it on the center of the desk. "It's a Smith and Wesson Model 10—been in the family for years. It's yours for tonight."

"Mr. Huxley," said Jeff. "I ..."

"I know—it was never supposed to come to this—never thought it would." He grabbed a small box of bullets from the drawer and placed it next to the gun. "You'll need these in order for that to work to your advantage, or be much use," Sterling added, forcing a smile.

"But, Mr. Huxley..." said Jeff.

Sterling raised his index finger to his lips and shushed. "Think of it as an extra hand."

Miss Giroux

"Mr. Grant, Father," said Miss Giroux. "Let *him* decide if he wants to tell Liam?"

For the better part of fifteen minutes, Father Durrell, between a shot of whiskey, and then another, had related the details of his last confession to Miss Giroux, who listened intently, before speaking. In the past year or so, she had learned to state what Father Durrell had difficulty articulating, be it a sermon, guidance or, of late, his crisis of faith. "When a man enters his forties, he'll muster a crisis out of his life," her mother had once said to her, "no matter what he's got or what he's done." Was she right? Had the time arrived for Father Durrell? Was it true? Had he mustered a crisis? And was it because of her and the child, Lucille?

"Yes, I think you're right, Miss Giroux," he said. "But I'm not too sure Jeff Grant will be at the Gaelic Hall tonight, which is where I must be shortly," he fretted. "I'm not really too sure how to go about contacting him with such a delicate matter—short of walking up to his front door and knocking."

"He needs to know," she said. "The matter is pressing, I would think?"

"Yes, yes," he said, confused.

"Perhaps you would have me go," she asked, "to Mr. Grant's? I'd be happy to."

Father Durrell entertained the thought for a moment. "I'm not sure that would be received well," he said. "No, I do not think it would, Miss Giroux."

"*You're* concerned what might be said?" she responded, amazed and puzzled. "At such a time? I could hand him a note sealed in an envelope, if it's a matter of discretion."

"No, no," he answered, raising his voice, firmly, but gently, "I believe there is the alternative."

"What is that?" she asked.

"Liam may wish to contact him," he replied.

He had wanted her advice on how to proceed with the warning, and she had offered it. Yet, he was still unsure what to do. Miss Giroux studied him, wondering why she had returned, or, at least, returned so soon. She and the child, Lucille, should have postponed their arrival from Auburn, even though the girl was quite anxious to see him. The child had rushed into the priest's arms when he walked in the door. "Father Durrell!" she affectionately called out, squeezing him tightly. "We saw hobgoblins today," she told him excitedly, "right in front of the Hall!" Before he could reply, she rushed off to play. "Miss Giroux," the priest had nodded to his housekeeper with a pleasant reserve, smiling and clasping her hands in his for a brief moment. Even though the years had passed since Miss Giroux had entered his life, and he, hers, there remained a formality in their rapport with each other, peaceful and caring, but distant, too.

In point of fact, the arrangement had worked favorably because of Miss Giroux's continued deference to Father Durrell as her employer, as her and Lucille's provider. The Church had turned a blind eye to the present arrangement, and she could only speculate why it was tolerated in Downeast Way as opposed to Auburn. They really didn't care, she concluded. They didn't want to hear her insistence of Father Durrell's innocence during the whole ordeal in Auburn. The day before he left, never to return, she was visited by a Father Cox and Brother Gilbert. The pair questioned her for two hours concerning the position she held at the rectory, how she arrived there, and the nature of her relationship with Father Durrell. To her credit, where a lesser man or woman may have collapsed under their unrelenting accusations, insinuations and questions, she did not waver before the Inquisition she was subjected to.

The next day, Father Cox and Brother Gilbert led Father Durrell away. Miss Giroux was promptly removed from her position, and went to live with her sister.

A month passed in quiet, though anxious distress, at her sister's, before the first letter arrived. Three weeks later, a second letter arrived, and two weeks after that, a third was received. The tone and substance of each were as formal as their relationship had always been, but filled with detail and description of his new flock, the rural community, and living on the seacoast. The fourth letter, when it came, expressed his need for a cook. His most recent servant had met with an unfortunate accident, it seems. The poor woman, well into her seventies, had slipped in the kitchen, fell hard to the floor, and broke her hip. There was only one person who had ever worked out, he had written her, and she was dearly missed.

The sentiment touched her deeply and, a few months after the baby was born, she and the child went to serve Father Durrell. Introduced to his parishioners as his recently widowed cousin, there, in obscurity and anonymity, she was welcomed into the flock of Saint Patrick's Church. The arrangement, their relationship, coexisted within the parish without much comment or gossip, and without any interference from the diocese. No, the diocese really didn't care. The parish was of no threat or concern to the ambition of the Bishop, as the substantial congregation in Auburn was.

Or maybe the Church simply knew, eventually, that she, a housekeeper, the likes of which had been dealt with a thousand times before, over a thousand years, whether viewed as an aberration or not, would go away.

Miss Giroux had gotten by raising the child in the Lost Kingdom these past few years, but Lucille was coming of age, growing and learning, and very cognizant of her small world—one where children talk and think and ask questions—and repeat the words spoken all around them. Was this the place for her? With a man they would know only as Father Durrell? A man in certain crisis? She had witnessed his spiritual decline firsthand, the erratic behavior—muddled and confused—along with his heavier drinking. What should she do about it? What could she do? How was she going to tell him good-bye? For now, she understood the priority of Father Durrell's dilemma, and how he needed her guidance.

"But will Liam be at the Hall tonight, Father?" asked Miss Giroux. She phrased it more as a statement than a question, to give him pause to think.

"Liam is as much of a drunk as the rest of them, Miss Giroux," he said, whilst he poured himself another short whiskey. "Hell—as much as us all, I suppose." He tipped the glass back and swallowed effortlessly. "I'll buttonhole him after I bless the drunks."

"Are we not all God's children, Father?" she asked, her frustration rising.

"I was joking, Miss Giroux," he said.

She studied him, unsure how to respond.

"For what it's worth, I count myself as one of them," he added, forcing a grin.

"Do not doubt yourself so, Father," she said, "or the parish. Tonight you are needed. You *must* act."

Father Durrell stared at her, confused, unsure how to reply, or what to do.

"With a little luck, then, maybe Mr. Grant will be at the Hall having a drink with Liam," she said, then called for Lucille. "If there's nothing else you need, Father, we are going to the children's Hallowe'en Social at Central Hall. You apparently have everything under control. We shan't be more than a couple hours, I think. When we return, we must speak."

Death Smiles Invitingly

"You don't have to go through with it," Porter said. He and Jeffah had exited the Custom House and were walking across the Common toward Market Square. Long shadows were upon them. The day was awash in twilight.

"You say it like I have a choice?" Jeffah responded.

"There's got to be a way out of this—there's always a choice. Sterling was all but giving you an out."

"What? Don't tell me you've lost your nerve!" Jeffah forced a grin.

Porter rolled his eyes and sighed, "My mind *and* nerves, a while ago, if you must know, but that's beside the point."

"Porter, you may think I have a choice, and Sterling acted like I had a choice, but the only person who has a choice over the matter is you. Believe me, I'm locked in."

"He flat out said you could back out, or whatever," Porter said.

"Porter, need I remind you, I have a wife and three kids—ages of eleven, seven, and four," Jeffah said. "It's more than their well-being—I'm

132

worried for them." Jeffah stopped short. They stood in the middle of the common. He looked Porter directly in the eye and said, "I know too much, Porter. Yet, I don't know what it is I know too much of. I do know this—my crew is dead. What's in store for me? I'll tell yah what! I'm worried sick for my family, that's what!" Jeffah shouted.

Porter rested his hand upon Jeffah's shoulder. "We're gonna get through this night somehow, and that will be it," said Porter. "Have Catherine take the kids and go to her mother's or sister's house for the night."

"Shit, Porter, I don't know if she'll do it."

"She doesn't know what's going on?"

"She doesn't know about Lawrence and Howie and Minard, the connection to me, anyway, what really happened to 'em and why. No, she has no idea they were my hands, and I plan on keepin' it that way."

"Well, you may have to tell her, come clean, or you're gonna have to think of something, 'cause she and the kids have to be out of the house tonight," Porter said. "Even if it's no questions asked. Let me tell you—if you're thinking it, Jeffah—that she and the kids are in peril—then you gotta follow your instincts."

"I don't know, Porter," said Jeffah, confused.

"Listen," Porter snapped. "Most people, when it comes to making a decision that could alter their lives, tend to think and re-think all the possibilities, good and bad. They hash it out in their heads—ruminate, ponder, argue all the pros and cons, over and over—then eventually do nothing and co-exist with the choice. Rather than act on their instincts, which, ninety-nine percent of the time, is what they should have done, they *do* fucking nothing!"

"What I'm hearing is, not to change the subject, but if you believe that—and there is truth in what you're saying—why the fuck are you still here and not heading for the hills? 'Cause I'm sure every instinct in that massive melon of yours is telling you to move on."

"God knows I got skeletons in my closet and demons knockin' at my door, Jeffah. Each and every one of them is telling me to get the fuck out of Dodge, 'cause they got plenty of haunting left in them before I take the big sleep. But I can't and I won't."

"Not so fucking easy, is it?" Jeffah poked at him.

"Listen, you fucking mackerel-head," Porter gripped his hand tighter on Jeffah's shoulder. "My instincts told me I needed to come back here—

for family and friends—and perhaps for my own peace of mind. I had been thinkin' about it for weeks. Then, after I got letters from you *and* my sister on successive days, I knew I had to come—for my sister, my aunt and uncle, and for you—and for that damned gypsy woman who's bored so far into my head I don't know what to believe, other than I'm supposed to be here. I've taken care of one, two and three. Right now—number four—it's to help you whatever way I can tonight."

In that moment, where, for any other two people on the planet, a bottomless chasm could have parted them, the bond between them clamped, as it always had, tighter. "All right, Porter," Jeffah mumbled. "I'll get Catherine and the kids out of the house tonight."

"Good," Porter said, releasing his hand from Jeffah's shoulder. "Now, when you turn, and we start walking, I want you to tell me what you see. I know it's getting dark, but make it real natural."

The men resumed walking across the common. Jeffah panned the opposite street ahead, fixed upon the silhouettes of two men. "You mean the pair in fedoras and long coats? Up by the bank?"

"Yeah," answered Porter. "Ever see them before?"

"Sure," Jeffah said. "Thompson's bank goons, they say. But I'm not sure who they answer to."

"Does Sterling know?"

"He knows something, but won't say much. He told me to stay away from 'em—'they're Crowe's problem,' he said. I asked him again the day they found Minard in his front parlor. Two of them arrived in town that afternoon."

"Sinister bunch," Porter said.

"I wouldn't expect any less from Thompson Crowe," said Jeffah, and spat on the ground after saying the name. "They show up every few months, but Sterling says they have nothing to do with us, and he wants to keep it that way."

"I saw a man dressed like that at a speako in Boston not too long ago. Turned out, he was a gangster and somebody shot him dead."

"No shit?"

"No shit. Horrific thing—wasn't too long after Scoop ..." Porter stopped short, hesitated, searching for the words, but could only say, "Ah shit, it just wasn't that long after."

"I'm sorry, Porter."

"Me, too, Jeffah," he said, and hung his head, "every-fucking-day."

A moment passed, Jeff reached over and patted his back. Porter raised his head, "Well, as I was saying, those goons look like gangsters."

"They fit the bill, all right. Once they leave the bank, they head over to the Silent Woman and brood. That's what Sally told me. She serves 'em—a teapot and slop, every time."

A third man exited the building, taller, with broad shoulders. Porter and Jeffah watched the three men glance down their way—long enough to know they were gawking at them—before they turned and began walking up the street. Porter and Jeffah followed, out-pacing them, intentionally or not, getting closer. They were close enough now that Porter could make out their features. When they crossed the street opposite the Silent Woman Tea Emporium, the big guy, the third man out, held the door open for the others to enter, and for him to take a good, hard look in their direction. The familiar swinging placard—a saucy, headless woman holding a pint in one hand with the other on her hip in defiance—rocked above his head. A lamp above the placard protruded like a high-hat from the side of the building that, in the dim light, cast an eerie glow over the scene.

"What about...?" Porter began to ask, but his question was sucked out of him, like he'd been punched in the stomach, by the shock at the sight before him.

"That's all I know, Porter, about them," Jeffah responded, without noticing Porter gasping for his breath. "They're not from around here—always come in that big Packard—usually two," he added, pointing to a dark motorcar halfway up the block. "They got that green registration plate from Massachusetts."

Porter never finished asking the question and never really heard what Jeffah said. Something mentioned about a big Packard. That was because, in the middle of the common, when Porter had asked Jeffah to turn and tell him what he saw, he'd found it odd that Jeffah did not mention *her*—the buxom blonde—dressed to the nines. She was stunning, standing long and lean in a black satin dress, hemmed just below the knees, black silk gloves and stockings, with black pumps. A black pillbox hat and veil covered her head and obscured her face. Porter was studying her all the while the two men had been studying them. He was certain they were not auditors from Morgan's bank. Somehow, he felt, they were related to all the trouble around here. His mind went to the earlier episode he'd had at the graveyard, of the big-chested blonde he'd encountered there. The moll with the gangsters looked every bit like the dame in the graveyard, except for the new look, the change of clothes, as though now she was heading for a funeral. He couldn't tell for sure if it was her, because of the veil. As the three men walked up the street, she walked with them, in unison, like she belonged to one of them—the big guy maybe. Yet, she kept glancing back at Porter and Jeffah as if to say, "Come on boys—follow me—what are you waiting for?" She was a vision of seduction. The way her hips were swaying—too familiar—similar to the object of desire at Fran's—the brilliant blonde hair flowing over her shoulders. Her impenetrable, veiled glances kept Porter off balance. His heart moved in the rhythm of her stride—magical and hypnotic—an overwhelming lust was rising in him. Porter was almost certain he picked up the scent of eau d' whatever—as at the graveyard, which startled him, made him grow anxious at the thought that this could actually be the same woman who appeared in front of him at the church. What was that all about—if that was her? Had she been following him? What was the possibility of that, and why?

Crossing the street ahead of Porter and Jeffah, Porter had almost asked Jeffah, then and there, if he'd ever seen the legs, but they were within earshot. The four of them were strolling gingerly across the street in silence, like they were bent on listening to the two of them. The last thing he wanted was a fight with these goons over a dame. Porter was busting at the seams, watching them fast approach the entrance to the Silent Woman. He was about to blurt out, "What about the moll?" but that's when the big guy with the thick moustache looked at them—at that moment—as he held the door open for his men and her. Right at that moment, right before she disappeared under the threshold, she raised a gloved hand and swept the veil aside. Half expecting her to blow a final kiss, half expecting the comely smile he had encountered earlier, Porter, instead, found himself struggling for a breath—words to express himself. "What about...?" he squeezed out, but could not speak further, from the horror of the spectacle. Exposed before him, beneath the veil, looking directly at them, was the bony, skeletal face of Death smiling invitingly.

The Forever Game

From the earliest days, there was never a time that Porter did not feel at home in a park. The park was rolling fields and manicured commons, winding wooded paths and pristine trails—an abundance of nature. But there was more—another kind—that was the baseball park. Each park had differed at every stage of his life. As a boy in Moose Harbor, the players had competed with the black flies the first half of the season, mosquitoes most of the season, and an occasional moose or deer or black bear throughout the season. The further defined Porter became as a ballplayer, the more grandiose the parks became. First, while playing at Dartmouth and the Eastern Schools, then when he joined the Brooklyn Base Ball Club, the Robins, out of college, which began the endless cycle of visiting the grandest parks in the country.

The park was his home—had been his home—he had to remind himself. No more. A wind had kicked up, was blowing hard, rearranging the order of things. The game had changed. He had changed. Every-damn-thing around him had changed. The whole frigging world was changing, wasn't it? Why not him? The Robins were not his team anymore. He'd lost the only manager he'd ever had. Old Wilbert Robinson, for whom the team was nicknamed for years, had retired the year before. The ballclub went ahead and renamed the team after its fans, a bunch of trolley dodgers from Brooklyn—at least, made it official, and put 'Dodgers' on the uniform. It had pushed Porter to think, brought him to the proverbial crossroad, and he had made his decision. Leave the game.

Then Redfern showed up. He wanted him, needed him to take a good look around the friendly environs of Moose Harbor. Could be something in it for him. Long-term. After all, the world was changing.

There was also the book.

The winter before, when he'd finished writing *The Deferential Continuum*, he was convinced he was heading in the right direction. The depression had got him thinking about the way people short themselves time and again—some, he reasoned, because they have shit for brains and others because their brains have turned to shit. The latter is what fascinated him. How can people stop thinking and let their brains turn to shit? Why do they allow it—stop thinking for themselves? Why do they defer to their 'betters' to make their decisions for them? Do the expectations they have of their leaders differ from what they have for themselves? Because it was quite evident that their leaders—their 'betters'—had turned everything to shit. Or do they just give up? It made him think.

He vowed he wasn't going to let his brain turn to shit.

The compulsion to travel overwhelmed him. Everywhere he went, he felt pressed. Urgency was upon him. Unable to relax or concentrate, whenever he stopped to think, *the* game came to him, playing and replaying in his head, over and over. Fate and chance and destiny, he thought, and now the buxom blonde again—the dame—the moll—the harbinger of death—the reaper—his guardian angel—*that fucking thing*—stalking him. She was there—in Boston—and, before that, in Brooklyn, in the stadium, at Ebbets Field, waiting and watching, there to collect him. His time had come, but for fate and chance and destiny, which stood in the way—his way.

Why?

How did Viola know? About that thing? About that day?

"Let's end it right here, old-timer," the kid had shouted out when Porter came to the plate. Scoop Comeau was on third base, dying to get home. They were playing the Reds and the score was tied at two a piece, with one out in the bottom of the ninth. Porter, who was nursing a sore elbow, was surprised when he heard his number called. "Pick up your lumber, 32," the manager, Max Carey, shouted. The pitcher was due and Porter was the last right-handed bat off the bench available to hit. "Porter makes contact," Carey would later say. "I needed a bat for a pinch in the nine hole. The game was on the line." A reporter from the Times *would drill Carey about his aggressive base running approach to the game—how that may have factored into the psychology of the play. The same reporter had eagerly anticipated an orgy of base stealing the previous fall, when Carey was brought in to replace Robinson. "The game's all about running and hustling, but it's also about situation and timing, knowing what your bench can do."*

There's a cliché in baseball among the bench players—keep your head in the game—that's what they say. It works for a few innings, but it's easy to drift, especially when you're on the road, it's the end of August, the team's long out of the race, or there's a hot speako everyone's heard about, or a dame everyone's heard about. It's even better if you got one at home—a speako and a dame. Porter was thinking of his when he heard his name called.

Walking from the dugout to the plate, Porter swung the bat a few times, stretched, and cleared his head, focused. That's when he noticed her. In the front row of the box seats, she stood. The shoulder length golden hair, curled locks, dressed entirely in black, with satin gloves and pillbox hat, a thin veil covering her eyes. A woman of angelic beauty,

Porter thought, innocent yet alluring—buxom, exotic, sensuous. He shook his head. His attention turned to the pitcher, Billy 'the Pumpkin Slayer' Hopkins. Lefty O'Doul had just popped out on a 2-0 breaking ball. "Son-of-a-bitch is not afraid to throw his junk on any pitch in the count today," O'Doul had said to Porter, as he walked past him to the dugout, disgusted. "The Pumpkin's location is on."

There was a good story behind Billy 'the Pumpkin Slayer,' how he'd earned his nom de guerre, down on the family farm in rural Iowa. Growing up, the southpaw would spend his fall days taking aim at innocent pumpkins with rocks the size of baseballs. Billy would collect dozens of pumpkins from the patch that covered the field behind the barn. Carefully stacking them one by one on a fence post, he'd start hurling the stones from thirty paces. "Can we afford it?" his mother would ask his father, "to lose that many gourds?" His father would answer thoughtfully, "Those gourds got nothing to fear and neither do you, Ma. He's not gonna put a dent in the crop." True, the story goes, literally and figuratively. Billy Hopkins whizzed and nicked many a pumpkin in his day, but rarely connected. The more he threw, the angrier he'd get, throwing harder and harder, until he did connect. The unlucky gourd that stood between Billy and an ever-expanding field of stones would pay dearly. When Billy did strike his target the pumpkin generally split open with a loud ka-thunk, depending on the thickness of the gourd's shell. Pumpkin guts and flesh and seeds splattered everywhere. The image of splattered pumpkin brains on an Iowa cornfield had earned Billy his nickname and a reputation throughout the league. 'The Pumpkin Slayer' threw hard, but wild. It was a reputation that Billy nurtured. No hitter would ever dig in on him without the thought of having his head split open like a pumpkin.

Porter understood the psychological edge a name like "Pumpkin Slayer" had over a hitter, particularly a rookie or younger player, but he would not buy into it. For, above all, Porter was a consummate bullshitter himself. Hopkins, he had found out on the sly, was from Pittsburgh, and the closest he ever came to splitting pumpkins was with a fork into a slice of pie. Nevertheless, Billy Hopkins threw harder than just about anyone in baseball. Porter could attest to that. Hopkins was also prone to spells of wildness. Porter could attest to that, too. He had received a bruised ass cheek the summer before, courtesy of Pumpkin Slayer's inability to find the strike zone for the three innings he'd lasted that day.

Porter stepped into the batter's box, letting thoughts of smashed pumpkins, bullshit, bruised cheeks and a sore elbow dissolve. The signal from the third base coach, Cilly Grabowski, came in. After, there would be talk among the scribes that a signal was missed, and who missed it. There's a tendency among the beat sports reporters to rehash and regurgitate every pitch of every missed opportunity on every player and play when the game goes against the hometown team. Porter was never quite sure what they had to say, if they really had anything to say, or if they were just that desperate to say anything that could possibly be construed as something that could sell the papers. These ilk of scribes were bantering over balls and strikes and a bum game, when half the city was unemployed, the country had gone to shit, and demagogues were preaching the end of the world. The Dodgers were playing an exhibition doubleheader against the clubs from the city, the Giants and Yankees, in a few weeks, a benefit to help the city's unemployed. No one was writing about that.

The Pumpkin Slayer's pitch was heat. The suicide squeeze was on, and the Reds catcher, Ernie Lombardi, knew it. There was nothing Porter could do but square and bunt. The ball was on top of him. No time to react. No time to think. So close he could count the stitches on it. That was because the pitch was coming high and straight for the middle of his face. Later, in Porter's mind, the fraction of seconds to impact would freeze frame, over and over. Every time he shut his eyes, there it was, the ball, closing in, inches from his face. But then he would open them—and suddenly, inexplicably, the ball dipped down and in. The bat cracked and the ball fouled off his left knee, which buckled from the contact. He followed the trajectory of the ball into the stands above the first base dugout. The ball went to her, a beatified vision of love and lust and longing. He absorbed her essence in that split second—the same instant he realized the bat had not cracked nor had he fouled the ball. His knee snapped back. He looked down at Scoop Comeau, unmoving, and then up. Ebbets had stilled. The entire field of players was rushing at him. But she was gone.

That Ol' Black Magic

"What's a matter, Porter?" said Jeffah. "You know that guy?" Jeffah had glimpsed at Porter, who stood there gawking with his mouth half open, trying to form words, as the big, moustached guy went inside the Silent Woman. "Porter—you okay?"

"Didn't you see her?" asked Porter, the horrific sight still lingering in his head. "The woman?"

"What woman?" replied Jeffah, confused. "You all right?"

"I'm not sure, Jeffah," answered Porter.

"Hey, I'm gonna go tell Catherine to spend the night at her mother's. We'll meet at the boat in a couple hours. Say, 'Hi,' to Stu and Effie for me."

Porter nodded silently. The sudden urge to tell Jeffah everything beset him. All about his decision to leave the game, his decision to hit the road—Redfern—all about fate and chance and destiny—that God-awful vision he'd just seen—the unending haunting by the thing—and how he really was convinced he *was* living on borrowed time. He wanted to tell him, but he couldn't, really didn't know where to begin … or end. When he did speak up, as the words formed on his tongue, in his mouth, all he could muster, all he could say, was all he knew Jeffah could relate to—"I really got to tell you, Jeffah, I think that gypsy woman put a spell on me."

A Macabre Play

Abigail stood at the window across the room from her desk. Below, she saw the bank auditors; the tall one carried a small bag, the other two watched him. *Serviced* money, Sterling called it. Her eyes fell upon Jeff and Porter. She watched them watch the auditors, curiously. A macabre play was unfolding. She knew where it was going, the final act, and she regretted her role in it. It had been a season of death. First, she knew of the men who worked for Jeff, Mr. Grant. Sterling seemed unperturbed by it, or steeled himself from the emotion. After the drowning, he had even pointed out the odd coincidence that the auditors were in town the same day. She then recalled they were in town the day before the house fire, too. She conveyed her worst fears to a man she loathed, but had no choice to confide, or she would lose everything. There was more than that, too, in this season of death. Her mother had succumbed to a cancer, withered away and passed weeks before. At the thought, she sighed the sigh of a weary heart.

"Abigail," Sterling called from his office.

"Yes, Sterling," she said.

He appeared in the doorway. "I wasn't sure if you had left."

She shook her head, no. "I was watching them," she tilted her head toward the window.

"Watching whom?" Sterling asked, walking over beside her. He looked down upon the street. "Oh," he said.

"I don't understand what's going on, or why," she said.

"There are some things you don't need to know, Abigail, for your own good."

"I fear for those two men."

"There's no need. They can handle themselves."

"You said the same thing about Mr. Severance, after Mr. Bailey drowned, following Mr. Philpot's death."

"I told Jeff to inform Minard of … possibilities," Sterling said. "I tried to warn him without frightening him into making any rash choices."

"Rash choices?" she snapped. "Dear God, Sterling! The man was shot dead!"

"Now, now, Abigail, as far as we know, maybe Minard really did pull the trigger on himself. Maybe the pressure *did* get to him. It's been a string of bizarre deaths, I'll grant you, but …"

"You can't really believe that, Sterling," she interrupted him. "That all of them died the way they did—that it was a coincidence?"

"I don't know what to believe anymore," he said. "That family over there," he pointed at the Crowe Trust, "has put us at risk for years. Wendell's death was a tragedy, but it was the right kind of tragedy."

"What *are* you saying, Sterling?" She looked into his eyes.

"That he did not know how to deal with those men over there," he pointed at Hardy and his men, who were entering the Silent Woman, "and neither does his son. I've had to clean up their mess time and again, to keep them at a safe distance."

She lowered her eyes, unsure what to think or say, and wondered if she had made a rash choice herself. One thing she was sure of now, certain, was the connection—the last three times that Packard was in town, death followed in its wake. Was she party to it? Only the night ahead, and what it held, would tell if it would happen again—if Jeffrey Grant would meet the same end as his shipmates—and she felt utterly helpless to stop it.

"Listen, I've always taken care of you, Abigail, and I always will. I promised your mother I would, a long, long time ago. Now, come here." He opened his arms and she fell into them. They embraced. He kissed her forehead, stroked her hair gently, like a child, and released her. "Later tonight, we're going to take that drive far away from here. Flo knows I'm leaving town—a business trip to Portland. When I call, you know what to do."

"I would like to say good-bye," she said.

"To whom? Mrs. Fontaine, your landlady?" he laughed.

"To everyone," she answered, but Sterling didn't hear her. He had already walked back into his office.

The Silent Woman

The tavern, if it could speak, could tell many stories. For the past sixty years, it had been referred to as a tea emporium, in name only, by necessity. Prohibition had been enacted in Maine many decades ago. Though it never could shake its original name around town, the King's Inn & Silent Woman Tavern, the word 'Emporium' had replaced 'Tavern' above the door. There were no presumptions. For the tavern to survive the years and decades of Prohibition, it meant adapting to a role, transparent as it was, of a tea parlor. Some might say that the building was too old for that. In fact, it was the first public building erected in town. The year was 1632. The codfish aristocracy had a place to meet and play. The tavern, with its famous swinging placard, greeted all those who dared to enter.

Hardy studied the room. The tavern had high-backed booths that lined the room. Dark, paneled walls, wide support beams and columns, dim lights and dimly lit—it offered little view of the people around him. A plump waitress, who had been flirting with a man in a nearby booth, looked and approached the men. Hardy briefly caught the man gazing at him in his sightline. He wondered what he was looking at, but his attention turned to the waitress.

"Good evening," she smiled. "Chowder's fresh, as is the bread and catch, mackerel. We also have a chicken stew and pot roast."

"How's the tea?" Hardy asked.

"Today—an Irish blend," she answered.

"We'll take a pot," he said, and slipped her a sawbuck, "and three stews." Mr. Calvin and Murton nodded. She walked off toward the kitchen and returned, balancing cups and saucers in one hand, and a small teapot in the other. She placed the cups down and poured the *tea* into Hardy's cup. He lifted it to his lips and downed it, then nodded his approval. She poured shots in the cups of all three men, then left for the kitchen. The pot was filled with Irish whiskey.

"The banker's gone soft. Drops Huxley's name all the time."

"What are you thinking?" asked Murton.

Hardy lifted his teacup. Sipped, and placed it down. "First things first—after supper, we need to visit the priest, find out what he knows. Squeeze it out of him if we have to."

Murton's stomach churned at the thought, but he said nothing. He did notice Mr. Calvin's mouth. How it cracked slightly, moved outward. A pretense of delight, or genuine? The waitress returned with the chicken stew and placed it down in front of them. Murton studied the mush of bird, dumplings, onion and carrots in a thick white sauce. Steam rose from the bowl. He picked up his spoon and stirred it.

Mr. Calvin said a prayer and broke the bread. A mockery, Murton thought, of all that *is* holy. The men ate in silence. Mr. Calvin shoveled the stew down between gulps of whiskey. He did not notice Murton's gaze. Devoured the slop and burped loudly. Murton found it repulsive, but he forced himself to spoon his own slowly.

Hardy noticed Murton's eyes at the mention of the priest, the pain and reluctance. He observed him studying Mr. Calvin. But mostly, he noticed his lack of appetite. Mr. Walker was right. Murton had lost his appetite— for everything. This was not how he wanted it to end for his old friend, but there would be no loose ends. Beside him sat Mr. Calvin, whose appetite— for anything—could not be satiated. He wondered if Murton had any sense at all as to why Mr. Calvin had really accompanied them. No. Murton trusted him. When they find the bodies in the morning it will be nothing more than a footnote in the rumrunner's war.

When he finished, Hardy placed his spoon down into the bowl and pushed it aside. "I suspect the priest will only confirm that which is known." He picked up his teacup, then downed the whiskey. With a sigh, he added, "And that is, the time has come to close out our accounts here. We've quietly taken care of three. Nothing has come back on us, but tonight, if it must be, we don't have the luxury of going quietly. Tonight, we must be firm in our resolve with each party and be done with it—one way or the other."

The men stood to exit. Whilst Murton and Mr. Calvin went ahead, Hardy glanced back. He saw the man in the booth looking in his general direction. He walked to his table, pulled a cigarette. "You have the time?" he asked.

The stranger eyed him for a moment, and answered, "I've lost track of time, if you must know."

Hardy cracked a smile, "How about a match, then?"

The stranger nodded, threw a box before him. "Keep 'em," he answered.

Hardy nodded, studied the man for a moment. He lit the cigarette, glanced to his left. A couple was sitting in the far corner, speaking softly to each other. There was another man in an opposite booth with his face in a bowl of chowder and a newspaper on the table. He looked back at the stranger, thanked him for the light, and left the Silent Woman.

Hobgoblins

Porter walked along Main Street, watching young children as they hurried in pairs or small packs, and dressed as an assortment of cowboys, devils, ghosts and witches. Parents followed casually, chatting with each other, making their way to Central Hall for the town's Hallowe'en Social. But he was lost in thought. His mind ached for a sense of normality. He couldn't get the Moll of Death out of his head. Was she coming for him? Was it all a slow tease? A macabre dance? It had been months of pain and self-pity, remorse and regret. Why Scoop instead of me? Never an answer. "Where art thou, Angel?" he spoke out in frustration. "Where the hell are you? Dammit all, show yourself."

A tiny hand touched Porter's. It was enough for him not to jump out of his shorts at the touch, let alone soil them. He looked down, stared in disbelief. Before him, a vision of innocence. "Have you seen the hobgoblins?" a little girl, dressed as an angel, asked him. He laughed out loud, and so did her mother.

"No, little angel, I haven't," he replied softly. "But I'm on the lookout for them. Maybe you could help."

"How?" she said.

"If you see any, could you tell me or your mother, and I'll get 'em.'"

Her mother, smiling, spoke gently to her, "No, dear, no hobgoblins. We are going to the Social, up to the hall ahead. Where all the other children are going, yes? Remember?" There was a hint of a French accent in her voice, he noticed, but her English was perfect. Looking at Porter, she said, apologetically, "Her first time and, truthfully, me too, this Hallowe'en affair."

Porter smiled back. "I think *she's* got the hang of it," he said, which drew a smile from the woman.

"But Mommy, I saw them today," she said, "in front of the church, in the motorcar, the three of them."

"Lucy, no," she sighed.

But Porter was intrigued. "You saw three hobgoblins today? In front of the church?" he asked.

The woman looked to Porter, and whispered, "It's nothing, her imagination, a story she heard from my sister once."

"You mean, about three men in front of a church?" he asked. "Because that sounds like the opening line of a joke I once heard."

"No, no," she laughed. "There *were* three men in front of the Gaelic Hall today, across from the church. They *were* in a motorcar, sitting in it, parked, when we passed them. She thought one of the men was a hobgoblin. The one in front, the driver. She can't get it out of her head."

"Ah, I see," he said. "How did you know," he asked Lucy, "that he was a hobgoblin?"

"His head was big and round and mean-looking. He was sitting in the big, black motorcar—as big as the car that comes to the cemetery on the hill—he wanted to hurt us. I could tell," she said. "I was scared of him and the motorcar."

"Lucy, *arête*—stop it!" she said firmly.

"That's okay, ma'am. I think I actually saw the same three earlier today myself—a bunch of ugly hobgoblin mugs if there ever was," he winked.

"You are kind," she smiled and took Lucy by the hand. "Come, Lucy, or we are going to miss the stunts and games and the bobbing for apples."

Porter watched them continue toward Central Hall for a moment, and then turned. Why had the three goons visited the Gaelic Hall today? What were they looking for? What were they after? Sitting there on a stakeout? He remembered what the priest had said, asking Jeffah if he was going to the party tonight at the Hall. Were they looking for Jeffah? Then it occurred to him that the woman he just spoke with, and the child, may have been the priest's. "It makes sense," he said aloud. Porter absently placed his hand in his pocket. It touched his lucky piece, a token. He pulled it out, studied it closely, as he often did when confronted by doubt, dilemma, or indecision. He took comfort in holding it, touching the bronze surface lightly, and then speaking to it. Large as a silver dollar, the ornamental coin was his father's—a relief of a guardian angel, its wings furled and arms spread, and set in a heart-shaped wreath. He laughed at the irony—another angel. Wherever Porter went, she was there, in his pocket. He thought to go ask the woman a few more questions about the men; like when she had seen them, the time; and were they there long, at the hall; but he glanced at his watch and realized he was running late for dinner with his Aunt and Uncle. They'd think he was up to mischief.

It was, after all, a night for mischief. He knew from his own youth. Hallowe'en meant mischief. The image of the three goons came into his head. What kind of mischief were those bastards up to? He wondered. Hobgoblins, she had said. A little angel would know such things.

The Friary in Kinsale

He stood under the swinging placard of the Silent Woman, buttoning his coat. Up the street, he watched the Packard turn a corner. He walked in the opposite direction, on his way to meet an old friend. A small town; streets winding and narrow in places, two-story and three-story brick buildings lined them. Some streets so narrow, buildings seemed to lurch over them. All the streets led out and led back to the center, a common. At any moment, he half expected the Packard to drive back onto the street from another corner.

He had just dined across from them, buried his face in the chowder when he thought he had been made. But, no. The big one they called Hardy thought it was the poor bogger at the other table. The one who was making a move on the waitress.

The night was dark and damp. Over his shoulder, the mountain named Agamenticus appeared as a shadow over the town. A metaphor, he thought, for the times. He turned up his coat collar, adjusted his hat. The people here, as in most places, had no grasp of the reality imposed on them. What was being taken from them, bled from them. He thought of his childhood friend, like a big brother, who had taken him in, made him read, made him think. He had told him to be *certain* in whatever it was he did, for the world, and the good Lord above, depended on it.

He was certain now. When his friend, Terence, Father Kelly, was at the friary in Kinsale, when the war was raging on, two men arrived at the town, an American and then a Canadian. Sent there to monitor the radio, it was said, for the Marconi Company. Kinsale had stumbled into the world's spotlight that spring, 1915, when the ocean liner, RMS *Lusitania,* ferrying close to 2,000 civilians from New York to Liverpool, had been torpedoed off its coast by a German U-boat. The bodies, and what survivors there were, were brought there. The American came shortly after, presumably, to listen and observe. America was not at war, then, but its interests were, and profiting greatly from it.

The American was a Catholic, and it was for that reason that Terence and he met one day after a service, and that the men eventually befriended each other. He taught Terence how to operate the radio, so they could always stay in touch. There were also sessions—fantastic tales over whiskey—that of Boston, where the man was from, or dangerous, radical talk of a course to free Ireland of the British. On one such night, cursing wildly, the American spoke of the fate of the *Lusitania*. The ship had four million rounds of American-made Remington .303 caliber bullets in its hold. The man had uncovered that in his investigation, and stated his findings in a report. They bet the lives of 2,000 people the Germans wouldn't dare, and if they did, all the better—the Americans would join the fight against them. A week after his report was submitted, he received a reply. Until further notice, he was to stay in Kinsale and speak to no one about his findings. The company was following up on his *allegations* and sending another man to further *assist* in the *inquiry.* That was the Canadian, a man named Pendleton, who, admittedly, was sent to keep the American silent. Except, he too discovered the truth—was shown the truth—crates of ammo had actually washed ashore—and it sickened him. But the men were ordered to be silent—you are part of a cover-up and deception—stay and live with the lie. "*Ordered?*" Terence asked them—the three were in a pub, with more than enough pints in each of them that their tongues had long turned to rubber when it came out. "I thought the two of you worked for Marconi?" "Ha!" the American laughed, before the Canadian blurted, "*Ostensibly.*" They all laughed. They were, as it turned out, naval intelligence for their respective countries. Terence helped them see through it, living with the cover-up, convinced them that their part in it was to find the truth, and then to do what they could to prevent any more innocents from dying. "Wherever the situation lands you, strive for the greater good, always," he told them. Terence always thought it more than a coincidence that the men should find their way *there*, to Kinsale—to the friary, which was, after all, a Carmelite Friary. The Carmelites were an old order, going back to the 12th century, and had long offered solace against the evil deeds of soldiers and men. How odd, but remarkable, that the pair would find solace there, too. After the war, they all vowed to stay in touch, and they did, because of the radio. In the end, it cost them dearly. The American, the same man he was on his way to meet now, Ambrose Hughes, carried a heavy weight because of it, and was eager for his, Malachi's, help.

That was all fine and good, helping them was helping himself and his employers, but then he approached the corner and, against his own instincts or maybe by the distraction of his thoughts, failed to look both ways. That's when the blow came, to the back of his head, like he had been struck by a concrete block. All went dark immediately, and Mr. Calvin and Murton tossed him in a narrow, dead end alley.

Dinner on Davis Street

From the street, on his left, Porter looked at the house he grew up in, and then to his right, at his Aunt and Uncle's house. Each two stories, side-by-side, a fence abutted the street, but the yards merged as one, four acres, like a compound, doors never locked. That was how he remembered it, and how it was, still. A small barn was at the rear of the property, between the two houses. As he approached the yard, an occasional squawk or cluck alerted him to chickens inside.

The dinner was a down east affair. Over chowder, baked bread, cucumbers, potatoes and sole, the talk ranged from the baseball season to the September elections, and what that foretold for the coming presidential race. Republican Maine had elected Democrats for Governor and two of its three House seats. "Governor Roosevelt was down in Portland tonight," Uncle Stu said. "First time a man running for president has stepped foot in the state since Bryan did, over thirty years ago." Porter had heard the last five minutes of the speech on the Majestic when he'd arrived.

Mainly, they spoke of the imminent arrival of Caroline and Gracie. Because of it, for the first time that day, Porter had felt at home. Uncle Stu had wired Gracie immediately after Porter left the shop, to let her know they'd spoken, and that her help was desperately needed. "It's too much for me, Porter," he said. "I was hoping you'd come back. Gracie? I thought she was married and happy. Though, to be honest, we never felt right about leaving Gracie with *him*," said Uncle Stu. "We only met him that one time—the day they married. Bernie was not the trusting kind—seemed distracted by his own wedding."

"No surprise. The man was a bookie," said Porter. The pair looked surprised.

"No, sah," said Uncle Stu. "I didn't know."

"When a bookie's in the money, they walk around stoned and cocky. When a long shot comes in—and it's against them and they gotta cover the bet—good luck finding 'em. They act nervous and suspicious. I'm guessing the day he married Gracie, he was looking over his shoulder."

"Wow! She told us he was in sales," said Uncle Stu, "so we supported her decision."

"Selling radios, she said," Aunt Effie added. "She sent us that Majestic for Christmas," and pointed toward the front room.

"Very convincing," Porter said. "Gracie thought the same thing." He told them the story of how he found Bernie in Saint Louis cheating on Gracie, though he had omitted a good part of the details about McInerney's Speako, the platinum blonde, him punching the bastard out, and the fate of Big Karl. Instead, he opted for a more sanitized version of how he bumped into Bernie at McInerney's Pharmacy, near the ball park, accompanied with another woman. That was enough. He also told them he would be out late with Jeffah, who needed help running a line of lobster traps that evening, which, by the looks on their faces, did not sit well with either of them. They knew what kind of traps Jeffrey Grant ran these days. But they did not press Porter about it.

"Ready for some blueberry pie, Porter?" asked Aunt Effie.

"Good God, Aunt Effie, I'm gonna blow at the seams if I eat any more," he said.

"Well, have some coffee and make some room," she said. "You'll need a full stomach to get you through the night."

Mr. Perkins, who had been stretched out peacefully in the corner of the kitchen, near the wood stove, sat up attentively and sniffed. The big pooch went to the back door and sniffed again, and then barked.

"What could that be?" said Aunt Effie.

"Easy, boy," said Uncle Stu, who stood and went to the door.

"Be careful, Stuart. Don't let him out," said Aunt Effie, "in case it's a skunk."

"Mr. Perkins knows all about skunks, Effie," said the old man. "He learned his lesson the hard way, if you recall, and so did we," but opened the door slowly just the same, holding the dog back with some effort, before he looked out through the screen.

Porter was at the window, but saw more of his own reflection within the lighted room than the backyard and adjacent street. It was too dark out. He stood and went to the door, took Mr. Perkins and held him, so

Uncle Stu could open it wide. Porter looked out over his Uncle's shoulder. Aunt Effie followed suit and squeezed in under Porter's arm. Mr. Perkins barked again. The three of them strained their eyes while the dog bounced around, wagging its tail as though someone were standing right in front of them. But they saw nothing unusual or out of place. A few wisps of fog, expanding and contracting and spinning counter-clockwise, drifted by. That was all. Mr. Perkins remained agitated. Porter pulled him firmly, but gently, "It's okay, buddy," said Porter, and they stepped back from the door.

"I don't know what to make of it," said Uncle Stu, as he shut the back door. "But they say dogs can sense—see and hear—things humans can't."

"Could be someone down the street," Aunt Effie said, but she seemed concerned nonetheless, "or a mile away, up on Celtic Hill."

"Well, I can find out what's bothering Mr. Perkins," said Porter. "I'll take him for a walk."

"Be careful," said Aunt Effie. "You better use the leash."

"Believe me, the last thing I want is a run in with a skunk, Aunt Effie," he said, "or any critter, for that matter."

"Let the boy be, Eff," said Uncle Stu. "The dog's probably got to do his business."

She smiled weakly, "I was just thinking out loud, that's all. I'll get the leash for you."

As she went down the hall, Uncle Stu leaned close to Porter. "You be careful tonight, nephew," he spoke in a low voice. "This doesn't sit well with me, and I can guess what's going through your aunt's head. They've shot more than one man over booze in these waters. Hell! They shot the Severance man in his front parlor!"

"Uncle Stu, I know." Porter sounded apologetic.

"Things aren't right here. People are talking. There's word of a G-Man of some kind." He gave a look over his shoulder. "Those men that come around in the Packard—they aren't bank auditors that visit Crowe's Trust." He nearly gagged at the words. "How could anyone trust a Crowe?"

"I know all about it. I don't want to go—*really*. But I can't let Jeffah go it alone, either. He wrote me. He asked me for help. What else can I do? Run?"

Uncle Stu sighed deeply. Shook his head slowly, and said, "No. You can't run."

"Thank you. Because I can't run."

"Just promise me this if things go south."

"Anything."

"Be sure to *duck*!" He said it emphatically, like it was the singular, most important kernel of parting knowledge he could share with him.

"I found the leash." Aunt Effie stood in the doorway, swinging it side to side, slowly.

"Oh, boy," muttered Uncle Stu.

"Oh, boy, what?" she asked.

"Nothing," he replied. "I was just saying to Porter, what's taking you so long."

"Stuart Gibson!" she growled.

Mr. Perkins barked suddenly and jumped at the door. Uncle Stu shrugged.

"Aunt Effie," Porter said. "If it's all right, I was just thinking I'd like to take Mr. Perkins with me tonight."

She looked at both of them. "So that's how it's gonna be." She handed Porter the leash. "Be careful, Porter." She looked at her husband. "He's an old man who easily jumps the gun. Be careful with Mr. Perkins, too. He's just as old and excitable. And please, dear boy—you be careful, too."

Porter nodded, slipped into his coat, then leashed Mr. Perkins. He kissed his aunt's cheek, hugged her and his uncle. Opening the back door, he spied the yard. "No skunks," he turned and chuckled. "Don't worry. I'll be back in a few hours," he shouted, stepping from the porch. The evening air was cool, but refreshing. Porter belched several times, tasting fish and cucumbers, while Mr. Perkins pulled. "What are you onto, Perkins?" he said, but let the dog lead him. It sniffed maniacally left and right and pulled forward. The dog whimpered anxiously, as though it were close to whatever had set it off, and then stopped, looked side to side, confused. Mr. Perkins started up but stopped again shortly, repeating the same frantic behavior and confusion. They went from the yard to the adjacent street, an old dirt and partly-cobbled lane that wound down to the harbor, past some of the older houses in town. Late eighteenth century farmhouses built on what then were large parcels of land. The surrounding meadows were carved from stone, the refuse of which were stacked neatly along the property lines as walls. He had argued the point once with a colleague at the university, challenged the traditional functional aesthetic of creating a wall of stone, by arguing the utilitarian necessity of making a stonewall. Case in point, Mr. Perkins pulled him hard to the left, lifted his leg and hosed the wall down.

He then pulled Porter back on the road, sniffed in the air, and whimpered again. "What the heck, Mr. Perkins—what's going on?" Porter asked the dog. "Where the bejeezus are we going, boy?" Almost immediately, the dog came to a halt and stopped sniffing and whimpering. He stared straight ahead, toward a patch of fog, which seemed to be rolling toward them, growing, taking form, into a life of its own.

The Cemetery

"I believe it's time, Mr. Calvin." He looked out from under the brim of his hat and nodded at Hardy, who glanced at his watch and said, "Go to the rectory. Make an assessment. See who's around. If the priest is there, make sure he's *alone*—no wench and girl. Am I clear on that? She was probably stopping by to make dinner for him. Not a live-in. But keep an eye for them." The three had returned to Celtic Hill. The Packard coasted in behind the church, rolled to a stop in the cemetery, where the car was out of sight from the street. "When you make your determination, return for us and we'll go in together." Mr. Calvin got out of the car and shut the door quietly. "One last thing," Hardy added. "I need to talk to that Priest. Discretion and restraint are in order." Mr. Calvin nodded and walked away, toward the church, and dissolved in the darkness.

Hardy said, "Better get behind the wheel, Murton, just in case."

Murton moved over and gripped the wheel, the size of a small wagon wheel. He began to peer into the inky blackness of the cemetery. Studied the shapes of the headstones, and how the fog or mist was rising and moving around them. Slowly, he relaxed, felt nothing, as he succumbed to a trance. Certain shapes were taking form around the granite tombs and headstones. There was movement, he was sure, around them. *Something* was there.

Hardy casually smoked a Chesterfield, keeping an eye for anyone who may wander by. From where they had parked, his sightline was limited. The Packard was out of sight from the street and surrounding neighborhood, parked on a dirt road, which cut through the side of a hill. The road wound its way through the cemetery, as necessitated, and dropped out of view of the street and surrounding neighborhood. The hill sloped sharply below the car, down to a meadow that bordered a tree line. That much, Hardy could see. He then scanned the top of the tree line for any signs of a break, to mark an unseen path, but it was too dark. He doubted anyone would stumble through this place after dark, go that way, if there was a path. The Irish were too superstitious. In front of him, he could see the back of the church and, beyond that, what looked like, in the dull, ambient light from the rectory or street, an old oak tree in the far corner of the backyard. He could barely make out Mr. Calvin when he stepped from the shadows and spied around the side of the church. There was nothing to his left or above him but uneven rows of tombstones, where the dead had been randomly planted. He lifted the Chesterfield to his lips. Inhaled deeply and released, saw that Mr. Calvin was gone. He didn't like being vulnerable, always anticipated trouble. When they had left the Tavern, he was certain the one who gave him the matchbox was watching them. He had Mr. Calvin clock him when he came out of the restaurant, whilst he drove the Packard around the block. The only problem was, he clocked the wrong guy. He realized now he should have sent Murton to the rectory, and was about to tell him to go get Mr. Calvin, but took notice of how Murton was breathing slowly and staring straight ahead, with a blank expression. This was not the man he had known. Murton sat, hands on the wheel, mesmerized like he was watching something just ahead of them, near an old tomb that was leaning on the hillside. The man was transfixed and Hardy wondered by what. The cigarette was but a stub. He tapped it out and, rather than throwing it out the window, he crushed it on the floor. An old lesson he'd learned years ago, more a habit now—if you leave a trail of breadcrumbs, rats will follow, and eventually find you. "Murton!" he spoke softly, but the tone was punctuated to get his attention.

Murton started. He dropped his gaze, shook the residue of thoughts from his head. "Yes?" he said.

"What are you looking at? You look lost."

Murton moved his lips. He was about to say, "Nothing," or something like that. But his mind was racing. He had slipped into the Edinburgh underworld. That place he had stumbled on, and roused a thing unseen and unknown to this world. A thing only dreamt of in the darkest nightmare. So, instead, he drew a sharp breath and answered, "The thing had two red eyes, Hardy, when it came after me, right after it got Burke." He swallowed hard. "I'd followed him, Burke, for some time. He was a man of habit, and I knew that he'd slip by Bell's Wynd nightly to make his way back from our man Browne's pub. I went there and waited that night, to be done with it. He came, and turned into the alley. I followed, but Burke had the jump on me, like he knew. Because he was ready, and swung at my head with a big bat of a club. I was ready, too, for anything, and moved just enough that he hit my shoulder before it clipped the side of my head. The blow staggered me. I was near collapsing, saw stars flash in my eyes. Burke laughed and called me a wanker, said I ought to have stayed in Boston. He began to pull a revolver out of his coat, laughing all the while. I was seeing lights pop, but I had enough sense in me to react. He was close enough, so I kicked him in the groin and, of all things, his gun went off."

"You mean he shot himself?" Hardy asked. "He killed himself?"

Murton moved his head slowly, up and down. "Clear through the gut." He paused, breathing quietly, and said, "That was it, I thought. I took a few steps back, leaning against the alley wall. The stars in my eyes were fading, and I'd found my balance, but I needed a minute. I pulled a fag from my pack, lit it. I couldn't believe my luck. I watched Burke's body go still, his blood bubbling up and leaking out of him ... And that's when *it* began. At first, I thought I was seeing the tip of my cigarette and seeing double, except it was in my hand, which was hanging loose at my side. No, I realized. Those were ... *eyes*. There was something there. It stepped from nowhere, from out of the wall—or somewhere. I just don't know. I saw it look at me and growl. Its eyes flared red. I heard a squeal of delight. It looked at me, then down at Burke, and back up at me. The thing snarled and pounced on Burke. It raped him, his soul, savagely. Burke, his spirit or soul, squirmed to get away, screamed in agony, but the thing clenched him tightly. My head cleared real quick, Hardy. I dropped the cigarette, and moved slowly, crept along the wall, away from it. I didn't make it, get away. It popped up, eyed me, and squealed out again. Like a rush of wind before a storm," his voice rose in intensity. "Before I could react in any way, it went through me. Right directly through me!" he cried out. "I doubled over as though I'd been punched by the likes of Jack Dempsey and fell to my knees. I couldn't breathe. I feebly gasped for air and, finally, when I caught my first breath, vomited a hideous-tasting bile. I remember, I crawled out of that alley on all fours. After that, I got up, staggered away. I don't know how, but the next thing I know, it's morning, and I'm in my room at Skelling House. I have no recollection of returning, or speaking to anyone. My head hurts and my stomach feels raw. It's like I was poisoned—hell—I am poisoned." He stopped, met Hardy's eyes. "That's what happened. I feel as though that thing is after me. That he got a taste and he ain't done with me, yet. So, Hardy, to answer your question, it's not so much what I'm looking *at*, but what I'm looking out *for*, in that tomb, right there." He pointed. "Forgive me for being adrift, but my limited interaction with the thing tells me that he or it is probably very comfortable in a haunt like this."

A silence passed between them. Murton didn't care. He'd said what he had to say. Hardy let it build. He pulled another Chesterfield without speaking, offered Murton one, who took it. He struck a match and lit both. Hardy smoked it slowly, letting the smoke curl up and out the window. He was half through it, when he said, "You've got to move beyond this, Murton. You had your bell rung, by your own admission, pretty hard. Most would say, because of that, your mind and eyes were playing tricks on you. But maybe that blow to your head offered you another sight. Opened another eye. Because, I believe you saw what you believe you saw. I'm not a religious man, but I have no doubts about hell, and finding it one day. For them, Burke and it—whatever you saw—it's the nature of the business at that juncture. Expected, I'd say. Once you fuck around with Judgment, no one is gonna grieve for you. I do believe there will be those who come for you, though—one way or the other—they will come." Hardy paused, and smoked the rest of the cigarette. He tapped it out and crushed it as before.

Murton did the same. When he'd finished, for no reason, he thought, other than to let Hardy know, he said, "Whatever happens, thanks for listening."

Hardy looked at him, and continued, "You said your piece, Murton. Now I'll say mine. We have work to do here. Business to take care of. This is where I want your head at. Not in a dark alley in Edinburgh. Do you understand?"

Murton nodded, and gripped the wheel. "I said my piece, Hardy. It's said and done with. I'm here."

"Good," Hardy said. He looked around, then said, "I wonder what's taking Mr. Calvin so ..." But he drifted off. Ahead of him, by the oak tree, he saw a small figure in white.

Murton sat upright. "What's that?" he asked.

"Good God, dammit all, why now? It's the woman and the girl!" Hardy whispered, barely containing himself. "Come on."

The Gaelic Hall

Father Durrell sat at the head table, alone, and stared blankly at the empty tea cup before him. In fact, other than old McAdoo, he would have been very much alone. He heard a dog bark in the far distance, a car backfire nearby. That was it. The dried mackerel, or maybe it was the turnip, was not sitting well with him. Either that or it wasn't sitting well with the whiskey. He should have left shortly after the benediction. Instead, he opted to stay and partake in the festivities. That was a distraction. Enough so that he was only now recalling what Miss Giroux had suggested—to speak to Liam about the mysterious confession and the threat to Jeff Grant. He rubbed his face with the palm of his hands, and concluded his life was a mess—that he was a mess.

McAdoo had been studying the priest out of the corner of his eye for the past fifteen minutes. He had cleared all the tables, but for one setting, and brought all the dishes into the kitchen for Mrs. Conley and her granddaughter to wash the next morning. That's what she had told him to do an hour earlier. Then she had left, complaining about her arthritis flaring up. Like hell! He'd had every intention of taking her for a roll right on the kitchen counter, like they'd done before, when they were alone, after everyone had left. But the drunk of a damned priest had stayed. For what? To spy on them? Was he on to them? The priest was looking a little pale now. McAdoo had finished sweeping the entire hall, but for under the head table. He'd cleared his throat several times. He'd stretched and yawned, but to no avail. Finally, he positioned himself with the broom before the head table, stopped, and leaned forward on the handle. "Hello, Father," he said. "Do you have the time?"

"What?" Father Durrell replied. "Oh, right. I can take a hint, McAdoo."

McAdoo doubted that, and raised a brow.

"I'll just finish my tea, man, and be on my way." He lifted the cup, and said, "Oh my, oh no! The cup appears to be already empty." He placed it to his lips and turned it nearly upside-down, savoring and licking the last drops with his tongue. "I thought there was more than that, McAdoo. I believe I have a piece of Mrs. Conley's sweet roll lodged here and I have nothing left to wash it down with," giving himself a rapping on the chest. "I must confess, I had one roll too many. That woman knows how to bake. She makes a sweet *roll*, eh, McAdoo?" He winked. "But I'm sure you know that. I daresay that woman knows her way around the kitchen better than most. Wouldn't you agree?"

Old McAdoo was flustered. He only wanted him to leave, not torment him. What did he want—a confession? It wasn't going to happen. "I can't argue with that, Father. She does her best work in the kitchen," and forced a smile.

"So, we're in agreement, then?" Father Durrell raised his cup. "I'm a well-connected man." McAdoo had a sudden urge to take the broom stick and connect it well to his ass. The priest, seeing his expression change, grinned. "What I mean, Mr. McAdoo, is that I know a lot of things about a lot of people. A lot of things I *need* to and *ought* to hear, but many more things I *have* to hear, if you follow me. It's the latter that makes the work of tending to a flock so bloody, damn difficult and trying."

McAdoo calmed at the words. Mainly because it was the first time in years anyone had addressed him as *mister*. Later, as he thought about the evening, he did not know why he said and did what he said and did next. First, he reached into the bib of his overalls and pulled a flask. He uncorked it and poured the priest two fingers. Father Durrell looked down at the contents of the tea cup. Grinning, he lifted the cup. McAdoo touched it with the flask. "*Sláinte mhaith*, Father," he cracked a grin, and both men drank. Then, as he let the burn run through him, asked, "Where does a man, a priest, go to confess? Where do you go to confess, Father Durrell?"

By the look on the priest's face, McAdoo thought he'd pried too deeply. Father Durrell's mood shifted abruptly. He looked at old McAdoo with the utmost seriousness, as though it was the first time he had ever been asked the question. In fact, it was. Truthfully, he asked himself—who did he confess to? He thought for a moment, began to speak, mumbled a few words, and then paused. Suddenly, he almost blurted Miss Giroux. He started to speak again, but only mumbled.

"Are you okay, Father?" McAdoo asked, concerned.

Father Durrell nodded slowly. The realization struck him like a flash of lightning at the height of a summer thunder storm. He felt the ghost of the sting from Miss Giroux's slap across his cheek. He reached and touched it, the spot where she'd connected. That was weeks before. The day she said she was leaving for Auburn, to live with her sister. She would no longer live a lie in the eyes of God, or her conscience. The shame overwhelmed him. For her and the girl—his daughter—their daughter. Why did it take so long for him to see that which was right in front of him?

"Father?" McAdoo interrupted his thoughts. "I didn't mean to pry."

"Actually, Mr. McAdoo, my name is Remy." He tugged at one side of his white collar and let it hang loose. For the first time in decades, he breathed freely. "To answer your question, honestly, I haven't been to confession since the diocese reassigned me here. You see, Mr. McAdoo, I was demoted, actually, for my relationship with Miss Giroux." McAdoo took a sharp breath. He tried to speak, to say something, but couldn't, because his jaw began to unhinge at the words. "The child, Lucille, my little Lucy, is our daughter. For once in my life, I'm gonna do the right thing and quit. Beginning right now!"

McAdoo's grip on the flask began to loosen. Remy, formerly known as Father Durrell, eyed the flask slipping. He leaned across the table and caught it at the moment it released. Remy handed it back to him. "Drink up, Mr. McAdoo. It's not every day you get to hear a priest's confession." He smiled, relaxed in the chair, and added, "Or, as of now, from this moment on, a former priest."

"Father—I—you ... please!" McAdoo tried to complete a thought, but couldn't. He had been a farm hand, a navvy for the railroad, then a mill worker, and now, at 63 years of age, a janitor. A widower, he shared his house with his daughter and her family. He could cipher and measure, read a little and write less than that. But he had never been prone to think or ponder.

"I'm serious, McAdoo. Call me Remy. I'm going to go tell Miss Giroux—Cecelia—now, my decision, and ask her to marry me."

With that, Remy Durrell finished his *tea* in one gulp and stood. He gave a nod to McAdoo, then pulled his collar off completely. Glancing at the thing, all he saw was a handcuff, and now he was free of it. He was tempted to toss it away. Eyeing McAdoo, he thought it better, if only because he would have to pick it up anyway, to hand it to him. "It's very starched and stiff, Mr. McAdoo. Be careful handling it. It's as sharp as a razor's edge and a very dangerous weapon in the wrong hands." Remy smiled. McAdoo stared blankly—at the collar and then at the man. He could not speak. Even when Remy Durrell walked away and out the door, McAdoo did not speak. Nothing when the sound of the front door slammed shut. He rolled the collar in his hand. Turned it over. Examined it closely. The edges were frayed. It was stained with sweat and specks of blood, and covered with lint. He folded it and placed it in his pocket. Then took one long, last swig from his flask and placed it back in his bib. He picked up Father Durrell's—Remy's—tea cup, went to the kitchen, and sunk it in the large slate sink with the rest of the dishes. He went to the light panel and threw the switch. In the darkness, he asked God and himself, "What have I done?" But there was no answer—from God or anyone. He was alone. Quietly, he went out the back door, and straight home. He would speak of this to no one. Even later, when news of the priest spread far and wide, he would never tell.

Mr. Calvin's Duty

Thoughts of Guy Fawkes and a papist effigy swinging freely in the cool evening air were in his head. The smile that came with the thought was thin. It barely cracked the veneer of his face as he drove the spade into the earth under the massive oak tree. But the thought pushed him. He wanted to see the effigy. It had been years since he'd actively participated in Bonfire Night, and this was the next best thing. With each scoop of earth, a burning desire for vengeance went through him. A blind rage came upon him, filled him. Catholics were whores. It was a whore of a religion. He glanced at the body, where he had thrown it. "Not a tragedy," he thought. Hardy stood silently with his hands behind his back. Murton was a short distance away, where he kept watch for anyone coming, hoping no one did.

Mr. Calvin grunted. When he had left the Packard in the cemetery, near a weathered tomb, he came up behind the church. There he paused, and stood. For some time, he'd watched the glutinous, drunken Mick swine stagger from their sty of a hall, yammering and belching. Finally, the hall fell silent. Minutes passed. Still, the priest had yet to come forth. Was the man in there? Licking the bottom of a tea cup? Drunk and stupid? He studied the house, a dim light in the kitchen. There was no movement from within. The rest of the house was black as coal. Maybe the priest was already in bed. He crept over toward the house, past a woodpile, a trash can, up the steps, and peered through the window of the kitchen door, looking for any sign or movement. He opened the screen door. His hand was on the doorknob, twisting slowly, when he heard the voice ask, "Can I help you?" Turning, he found the woman and child, the pair who had passed the car earlier that afternoon. The child, a girl, was in costume, a little angel, holding a small sack of some kind. "Where's the priest?" he asked the woman, adding, "Ah, I'm here for confession." She pointed across the street. "At the Gaelic Hall, but he holds confession at …" She stopped short, at the sight in his hand. Instinctively, she stepped in front of the child, lifted her, and began to run away, clutching her tightly. "It's the hobgoblin, mommy!" the girl shouted, suddenly aware. "Faster! Faster!" Only then, he realized his grip was no longer on the doorknob, but on his Webley Revolver, his weapon of choice. The first time he had killed with the model MK VI was during the War. That was 15 years earlier, in Belgium. He had picked it from the crumpled body of a British captain. An arrogant asshole from Mayfair who had killed more men through his incompetence than the Huns could execute in firing squads all day. He was admiring the weapon—the feel, the grip in his hand, the power—when the good Lord provided him with a charging Hun about to skewer him with a bayonet. He kept the revolver, rather than place it back in the dead captain's hand. He liked the size and the damage one shot in the middle of the chest had made. The gun was big—big enough that the British military no longer issued the MK VI. They had stopped doing so a few years after the war because the .455 caliber pistol and cartridge were too large for field work. Not so for Mr. Calvin. Without a thought, he pulled the trigger, just as the woman stumbled forward. He missed and cursed. He stepped forward, took aim again, but, as he did, his coat caught on the screen doorknob. She and the child ran into the bushes, and down a trail through the woods. There was a short, feeble squeak in the distance, and then silence. Mr. Calvin stared intently in blind rage. Walked toward them rapidly—began to pick up speed. He was at the edge of the lawn and fired his gun wildly into the brush, but hit nothing but the night. He suddenly remembered the priest, looked back at the house. He was not alone. There were also Hardy and Murton racing toward him.

The Personality of Fog

The fog, when it rolled in, had a personality of its own. Porter was sure of it, and so was Mr. Perkins, who sat calmly beside him. The mass was forty or fifty feet ahead of him, but moved toward him steadily, from up the lane. He studied its shape and density, how it was spinning, how it floated, whirled, and rotated. Was it mist? A patch of vapor? It was getting closer, the fog. He thought of Mount Agamenticus, its summit rising through a fog, and the time he, with Jeffah and Joe, made the climb to see the world above the *clouds*. Then, an image of a sloop went through his head, out on the bay, moving through a fog bank. It appeared and disappeared, quietly, sight unseen but for chance. Much like life at times—adrift, aimless, through countless vicissitudes and situations it throws at you. The transition between reality and the surreal is fine; a trance, hypnotic, lost in a fog, so much so, when you break through, you're not sure what side you've entered or are even on. A twilight world. Unable to fathom what has just happened—be it the skeletal face of death itself, guardian angels or even ... even hard sliders down and in.

Mr. Perkins stood, began to move anxiously, side-to-side, and whimper. Man and dog stared ahead. From the fog, a figure, a shadow of a man, appeared. Dimly, without recognition, it moved silently toward them. The mist and vapor clung to the man's ankles and calves, curling up around him like chains. The form—the man—slowed about twenty paces from them, and then completely stilled.

"Hello?" Porter asked more than said. Silence enveloped him. He studied the figure, frozen where he stood. Neither he nor it moved. Porter swallowed hard, felt a pull from inside his head. A sensation came over him, like he was moving toward it, or it was moving toward him. He couldn't determine one way or the other. Mr. Perkins had calmed and began to wag his tail playfully. That's what Porter noticed, the movement of the dog's tail, out of the corner of his eye. The flutter distracted him, enough, but not enough that, as he glanced at Mr. Perkins, the figure shifted from shadow to light to shadow. For an instant, Porter was sure he made out Scoop Comeau, standing in his Dodger uniform, dirty and sweaty, showing the side of his shattered and bleeding face, where the ball had struck him dead. And then the voice, "There are hobgoblins on the prowl—very dark matter." Porter heard it clearly speak. "*Listen* and be warned by a little angel."

The girl and her mother flashed through Porter's mind, the ones he had met on their way to the Hallowe'en Social. "How? Why? The child ..." It was all Porter could do not to scream when the light passed through shadow again and he saw Scoop standing there. He may have tried to scream, but the only sound he heard was Mr. Perkins's howl. As it was, he staggered, for he felt lightheaded and faint. Fear overwhelmed him in the end, and he spun around, quickly, found his legs, and the night beneath them. Running as far and fast as he could, he didn't slow until he'd reached Hancock Wharf. There, Jeff prepped the *Catherine*. Porter boarded without a word and sat. Only when he noticed Mr. Perkins rumbling down the dock did he pause to think what had happened. The big Newfie jumped on the boat, came up to him and licked his face, then stepped back, spun around slowly, wound himself down on the deck of the boat, lowered his head and slept.

Mad Dog

Hardy stood silently, enraged. He was in such a fury, he wavered momentarily. He needed to think, and decided to enter the house and wait for the priest there. "Come on, you fools," he snapped, and went into the house. He found a chair in the front parlor and sat. He was invested now. They all were. Murton knew better than to speak. He went and sat next to Hardy. Mr. Calvin stood near the door.

"I know what you're deliberating, Hardy," said Mr. Calvin. "But it's the fucking priest. If he had been home, or come home, rather than closing the place across the street, they wouldn't have seen me. We'd have come and gone."

"What is it you don't understand about the meaning cf discretion?" asked Hardy from his seat, "Meaning good sense and judgment, and not careless, thoughtless savagery."

"A priest with a wench and girl?" He spat.

"I asked you to keep an eye out for the wench and girl," Hardy said, "not to fire at them!"

"It's all hypocrisy," said Mr. Calvin.

"I didn't ask for your opinion," said Hardy.

"They got away, didn't they?"

"Now we have to deal with it. One more thing before we leave this cursed town—to find them—track them down. I ought to ..." He was about to add a few choice words, but then the front door opened, and there he, the priest, stood.

The Old Church

Remy lit a cigarette, watched the Gaelic Hall go dark from the middle of the road. He thought of the look on old McAdoo's face when he had heard *his* confession, and then laughed. He kicked a stone, started to whistle, some bar room ditty he'd heard long ago. The air was chilly, and he quickened his step. He fast approached the rectory, but stopped short. Something was not right. It was dark, too dark, and he wondered why Miss Giroux hadn't left a light on. "Maybe she went back to Auburn?" The thought struck him hard. He hesitated and looked up. His eye caught the silhouette of the steeple. He followed it to its peak, and to the cross above.

"You're an old church." Remy looked down, dejected, thinking—knowing—he'd waited too long to do the right thing. "You deserve better." God or Miss Giroux? He stood before the steps, looked into the rectory. Cold and dark within, he sighed, like a jilted heart. He thought about her, about Jeff Grant, about his miserable life. "God, what am I to do?" he shouted out. The first thought that came into his head was run—run away from here, you fool—all the way to Auburn. Run now. But he never had learned to listen—to God, to Miss Giroux—to himself.

He burped turnip and fish. Decided he'd leave, but wanted a drink first, to kill the taste, so he tossed the cigarette and went inside.

The shadow reached him before he reached the lamp. It pounced on him with a fury, grabbed his shirt collar and slapped him hard across the face. "That's for making me angry," a man, huge, with a thick neck and melon head, and grip like a bear trap, snapped angrily. He smacked him again on the other side of his face, harder. "That's for business." He tightened his grip. "Now, what did she tell you?" he demanded.

"*She*?" he responded, muddled. "Miss Giroux?"

"Easy, Mr. Calvin," a voice spoke from across the room. Remy looked over. There were two men sitting in chairs opposite him. The one who spoke had his legs crossed and a hat resting on his lap. The other man sat motionless, upright, hat on head. Remy was sure he could make out the outline of a revolver in the hand of the man who had spoken. How did he know these men? How did they know him?

"I want to know what the bitch told you," said Mr. Calvin.

Remy felt the grip tighten further. Mr. Calvin twisted his shirt collar like a tourniquet, choking him. He gasped. His face was turning a darker shade of puce. His windpipe was being crushed. He realized, all too late, how little he'd prepared for his own salvation. If he could speak, and he couldn't, he would tell him, any of them, anything. The man who spoke stood up, placed his hat on his head. Remy noticed the fedoras on all three men, thought of the Packard from hours before, and made the connection.

"Mr. Calvin," the voice said again, this time more forcefully. The look of menace and loathing staring out from under the wide brim at Remy grew fiercer as the grip began to recede. Remy took a breath and coughed. In a rare moment of clarity that had eluded him for years, decided then and there, when he could speak, he would lead them outside. It was Miss Giroux's and Lucy's only hope, if they were even here, to survive. The whiskey had made him dizzy and weak and indifferent to his fate. He held a hand up, forced a nod and the grip lessened. "I need air," he whispered, pointed to the back door.

Mr. Calvin looked at Hardy, who said, "A little air might be what we all need."

Mr. Calvin let go of Remy completely, whose legs immediately buckled and collapsed. Remy's stomach rumbled and bubbled. He started to rise, but stumbled. Mr. Calvin caught him, steadied him, and then released him with a slight push toward the kitchen. "Go, priest," he said. He fell again, and began to crawl through the kitchen, and breathed a low moan.

Hardy looked down on him, and asked, "What did that woman tell you this afternoon, priest? Or would you prefer Father?"

"I'm not a priest anymore. I quit."

Mr. Calvin began to laugh. "You never were one, you stupid bastard." He reached down and pulled Remy to his feet, and then Remy began to run for the door. He flung it opened, jumped the steps and tripped. "Agh!" Remy squealed, rolling on the ground, holding his ankle. Hardy, Murton and Mr. Calvin casually walked down the steps, surrounding Remy where he lay. Mr. Calvin jerked him to his feet again and held him by his throat.

Hardy, who *was* holding his revolver, took aim on Remy. "Last chance to speak, priest."

Remy shook his head slowly, completely muddled, lightheaded, slipping. He tried to speak, but only mumbled, "Bah, blah, ah."

"You think you're funny." Hardy pulled the hammer back.

"Wait," Remy found the words. "She said a man would die tonight. A good man."

Mr. Calvin squeezed him by the throat tighter and raised him up with one hand, so he stood on his tip toes. Remy thought he was about to be tossed, but Mr. Calvin said, "She mustn't been talking 'bout you." He began to squeeze tightly. "What else did she say?" The possibility to speak, to let him utter a fucking syllable, was lost upon him. The man was insane. Remy attempted to say something, tell him how fucking stupid he was. He really did, the words were being choked out of him, "Shtoop-ud fah-awk."

"Huh? What?" Mr. Calvin snarled. "Spit it out, you dumb bastard."

Hardy stepped forward. He had seen enough. "Mr. Calvin, let the man speak, for Christ's sake! Let him down!"

Instead, Mr. Calvin punched him in the stomach, smiling with pleasure at his work. When he did, it had an effect as though he had popped a boil. Remy vomited in projectile. Sprayed Mr. Calvin's arm, breast, hat and face with three quarters of a bottle of whiskey, and rancid, acidic, churned turnip, potato, apple, mackerel and pastry. Remy smiled, childlike, at the monster, who, stunned and in revulsion, crushed his vertebrae until his neck snapped. Remy's stupid smile froze. Mr. Calvin held him there enraged, watching his feet dangle and jerk spasmodically.

Remy's last conscious thought was the sensation he'd shit. But that was okay, for he was distracted now, by a light, a purple haze. It was expanding, all around, and consuming his being. He thought of Miss Giroux, and Lucy, a little angel. His angel. Was that them? There, across the yard, waving?

Mr. Calvin suddenly smelled shit. It was overwhelming him. As the jerking subsided, he saw the dampness had seeped down the priest's leg and onto his pant cuff and shoes. Finally stilled, Mr. Calvin tossed the body away, pulled a handkerchief from his breast pocket, and wiped his face.

"Well, that was helpful, Mr. Calvin," Hardy shouted. "I needed to question him—needed answers—and you put him down like a stray dog before he could tell us much of anything." Mr. Calvin began to speak, but Hardy held up his hand. He needed to think, and began to pace, and look around. How to ...? He first noticed a stack of wood neatly piled beside the back door ... Then, his eyes caught Murton's. The thought made him think of Bell's Wynd again and what he had said earlier about Beelzebub. A superstition—a dance with the devil. "Murton, go find one of the priest's vestments in the church," he said. "Mr. Calvin, you need to get the spade." Hardy walked toward the back door.

Within thirty minutes, a small fire blazed under the tree. The three men stood in a semi-circle around it. The dim, amber light cast an eerie glow across their faces. Above them, the priest swung freely from the tree. Beneath him, where the earth had been freshly turned, was the fire. Carefully laid out like the Cross of Saint Peter. When they found him, there would be only ashes and embers smoldering. A mystery for the superstitious to contend with. A mystery of a priest, the deal he'd made with Satan, and the night—All Hallows' Eve—it came due.

Murton raised his eyes, studied the motion of the priest, how his body rocked gently. The branches creaked. Dead weight. Murton returned his gaze to the flames. He thought of what lay ahead. He let a silent sigh. No demons, he thought, for now. Were heaven and hell united? Was all of this a part of some plan? Looking at Mr. Calvin, he wondered if there was—and if so—*why?* Was it all a matter of choice? Between the two? He wanted to say as much—he wanted out—to walk away into the night—but knew better and, instead, asked, "Could this be a sure thing, Hardy?"

Hardy, who had watched Murton's gaze rise and fall, caught something in Murton's tone. Doubt. More so, he caught wind of Mr. Calvin. He wondered seriously how mad the man was. He shook his head and said, softly, "No, Murton. I'm not sure. I am sure we'll have to track down the woman, both of them, if she hasn't gone to the police or to get help. But I don't think she has, or they would have arrived by now, someone would have. No, she's on the run. We'll backtrack down the hill, run the side streets, but we must leave here now. We'll stop by the train station for a look—it's the only way out of here this time of night. But then we must get down to the dock before our cargo arrives." Hardy was sure of one other thing, too—whenever and whoever found the priest—he'd be long gone.

All at Sea

"That should do it, Jeff," Williams said. He looked around. Some of his men had gone below, but there were two men beside him, ready to push off on his word. It had taken them less than an hour to transfer cargo. Jeff had pulled up beside the *Vivian*, more a floating warehouse than the sixty-foot schooner it was. Porter watched two more men wandering near the stern with shotguns strapped over their backs. Mr. Perkins sat beside him quietly, observing the world of men. When they rendezvoused, there was no effort to hide the shotguns. Williams had said a necessary precaution, but didn't say why. He didn't have to. The two of them hadn't moved that much—just stared into the blackness, scanned the horizon with binoculars—watching, listening carefully. Even when the other men were unloading the parcels and crates, they paid no attention.

"I really do appreciate you meeting me an hour out, Williams," Jeff said, "going so far off course tonight." He was holding an old flour sack and handed it to Williams. "You want to count it?" Jeff asked.

"Why start now?" Williams laughed. "I didn't mind coming here, it's on my way. Besides, I knew you were short. Happy you found another helping hand." He nodded to Porter and patted Mr. Perkins's head. The dog wagged his tail. "We heard what happened to your man a few weeks back. I'm really sorry. Never was supposed to be this way."

"No, it wasn't. It was about the adventure, eh, Williams?"

"The thrill, yes ... but oh, the money," he smiled, and held up the sack. "There's not enough mackerel in the Bay of Fundy to equal the catch we've hauled the last ten years."

"You got that right," Jeff smiled. "But it's all but over, I think, coming to an end."

"Old Henri Moraze thinks as much, too. He told me that before I left St. Pierre."

"Really?" Jeff asked.

Williams rested a hand on his hip, as though, like David, to ponder. With his other, he pulled a flask from his back pocket. Opened it, gave it to Jeff, who took a long pull. The burn warmed him. He returned the flask to Williams, who nodded and did the same and, then, thoughtfully, answered him. "He said it's over for men like us. The cow's gone dry."

Jeff let it sink in. The message was coming at him from every quarter. "Henri always knew what he was talking about," he replied.

"Cheer up, Jeff. He's going back to France—said he's gonna buy a castle in the country and a villa in the city—Paris—and learn to drink champagne all over again!"

Jeff smiled, was about to ask Williams the next question, to follow up. If Henri had heard anything, what he knew. But Williams seemed to know, and said, "He told me they had to roll back Prohibition, too much contempt for the law. Look what happened to the two men in Hyannis, gunned down in that warehouse. That's what it's come to. It has to come to an end." And then, as an afterthought, he added, "He said one more thing, too, to pass on. He's truly sorry it turned out this way for you. I want you to know, so am I, really am sorry."

"I don't blame you, Williams," Jeff said. "We did what you paid us to do."

"We've been running together for a long time."

"True, and it's been a good run."

"Nothing like this ever happened to anyone I've been associated with—the goons in Chicago, but not here. I don't know what's going on with anyone anymore. That's why I've got them with me." He jerked his thumb at the shotguns roaming the deck.

"Like I said, I don't blame you, Williams. We're straight between us."

Williams nodded, "I felt it was important to let you know, leave no doubt about Cape Cod. I can't figure it out."

"Neither can I, but I appreciate your concern, and all that you've done."

There was a momentary silence, then Williams thrust his hand out and Jeff took it firmly. "Farewell, Mr. Grant."

"Farewell, Mr. Williams."

Porter helped the two men pull the ropes and free the boats. The pair used push poles to shove off, and the *Vivian* slowly got under way.

Jeff and Porter watched the schooner drift off. "When I made my first run, there were only five agents covering the entire coast of Maine." Jeff studied the *Vivian*. It picked up speed. The silhouette of the schooner quickly faded into the darkness. He made his way to the helm, but waited. "I didn't even worry about getting caught and made no effort to hide. Think about it—the Maine coast has so many inlets, islands, peninsulas, bays and coves that if you walked it, tip to tip, from Eastport to Kittery, it'd be like you walked a straight shot from New York to California. The distance is that far." He listened. In the darkness, they heard the schooner cutting the waves. When he heard no more, Jeff started the engine and pushed the throttle. The *Catherine* was off. He opened it up, and shouted over the boat's two one-hundred horsepower engines, "Williams has always been honest—always on time," he said. "I'm gonna miss him."

"Seems like a good egg," Porter shouted back, and moved to the seat next to Jeff.

"He is."

"You trust him, then?" asked Porter.

"How much do you want to know?"

"I don't want to know anything, but since I'm out here riding shotgun," he paused and looked at the 12-gauge lying out on the seat next to him, "literally—thought I'd ask."

Jeff shook his head. "Williams hasn't changed. Years ago, when Sterling first approached me, he sent me to St. Pierre et Miquelon—a pair of small islands between Nova Scotia and Newfoundland—the last piece of France in North America. Did you know that?"

"No. Well, not 'til they passed the Volstead Act, I didn't."

"That's where I met him, Williams. He became our supplier. He's from Hebron near Yarmouth, but moved the whole operation to Lunenburg after Customs began to squeeze the running out of Yarmouth. Lunenburg's that much closer to St. Pierre, anyway, and the Americans haven't got their nose in Customs there. He was up in St. Pierre the day I arrived. I went up there with Minard and Howard, first time, to get the lay of the land, and Henri Moraze introduced me to Williams. We agreed, after that, we'd meet at Cape Sable. It's right on the way to Cape Cod or Montauk, or wherever the hell they go in Rum Row. Go off radio—they can't track you if you go off radio—then pick up a load, and return. From there, it's about 8 or 9 hours across the Bay of Fundy. We'd be gone about a day or so."

"Then what was that about, Jeffah? What did he mean by leaving, 'no doubt'?"

"That was about a job we did for him a few months back."

"You mean running a load?"

Jeff nodded. "This summer, we took a load for him down to the Cape."

"Let me guess—Hyannis?" Jeff could hear the frustration in Porter's voice grow.

"That would be it," Jeff said.

"Great! Are you gonna tell me what he meant by what he said, or are you gonna keep me out to pasture with the other heaping piles of bullshit?"

"Dammit, Porter!" Jeff snapped. "Can't you make up your mind? Just what is it you *want* to know? And how much of it?"

"I'll tell you what I want to know," Porter shouted. "Does it have anything to with what's been happening? Because the way Captain Williams was talking, I believe it does! Which means you've been holding out on me!"

Porter stared at Jeff, who was staring ahead into the blackness. The engine was loud, pushing the boat at top speed. Neither man moved nor spoke for minutes. Mr. Perkins, annoyed, raised his head and barked twice. He then lowered his head between his front paws, and kept his eyes on both of them.

"I think he's had enough," said Porter.

"Well, Mr. Perkins," said Jeff, "You think if I told this cocksucker what he didn't want to know or hear he'd stop asking questions?"

Mr. Perkins whimpered, and rubbed a paw across his snout.

"Yeah, I thought so, too. He'll never stop asking questions, either, always has to have answers."

Mr. Perkins stood, and lumbered over between the men and wagged his tail. Both men rubbed his giant head.

"Okay, Porter. A week after we made that delivery to the Cape, two men were shot dead in a robbery at a warehouse down there, a warehouse filled with booze. I read the story in the paper—how two men were killed in a gang-related hold-up, but I thought nothing of it, made no connection. Turns out, it was those two men who met us at sea at the coordinates that Williams gave me. They showed up in a boat too small for the load we had for 'em. I told them we couldn't wait there for them to get a bigger boat or to make two runs—it would be daylight by then and the Coast Guard could spot us. So they had us follow them into port. We pulled up to a dock at the crack of dawn. We unloaded the cargo right there on the spot and sailed off. We never even went ashore. Then, it wasn't but a couple weeks after the hold-up, my crew began to die off strangely, in succession. Philpot in the house fire, Bailey drowned, and Severance managed to shoot himself in the head from ten paces. Me and Sterling have talked it over every which way we can and have come up with nothing. That's why this is all coming to an end after tonight. I don't know what happened, but I know I'm through."

"Shit," Porter said. "I'm sorry."

"I should have told you," Jeff replied. "*I'm* sorry you found out the way you did."

"So, that's why—Williams wanted you to know he didn't finger you."

"Yes, Porter, and I never thought he did anyway."

"And the Frenchman out of St. Pierre et Miquelon? Henri Moraze?"

"Nope. He doesn't have to be in cahoots with anyone. St. Pierre's French territory—the Bureau, the Coast Guard, Customs—they can't touch old Henri. We, dear Uncle Sam, strong-armed the Canadians into an exchange of information treaty in '24. France would have nothing to do with it. That treaty made Henri a millionaire. Those islands are booming. It's like New Year's Eve every night of the week."

"What about those goons we saw today?"

"Likely candidates—capable no doubt. I'd guess they're a part of all this somehow."

Jeff began to cut the throttle. The boat slowed. On the far horizon, Porter could see dots of light ringing the entirety of Moose Harbor. Areas of concentration he knew to be Downeast Way. A smaller concentration to the south marked Bean's Point. Beyond that, he saw the beacon, Saint Mary's Lighthouse. Farther on, a light atop Fort Norumbega, an old colonial redoubt whose ancient walls staggered treacherously around the head of a peninsula but, somehow, held. "Hang on," Jeff said. Moose Harbor was suddenly eclipsed by a large shadow that thrust up out of the ocean, like a great whale rising from the depths and coming to rest on the surface. "We're here." He turned the bow and pointed it toward what looked like a natural quay, jutting perpendicular from a narrow cove. He gave a thrust, and then cut the engines completely.

"You ever do this before, Jeffah?" Porter asked, as the boat began to coast.

"Nah, but I've thought of doing it more than once." The boat was coming up on the quay rapidly, too fast, Porter thought, and braced himself for impact. But Jeff cut hard right, and the boat lulled and glided into something like a slip, a granite slip. "Tie us off, Porter—quickly, before we drift back," he hollered.

Jeff turned a beam of light on and aimed it along the quay. Porter scrambled to his feet and ran to the bow. Threw a line over a nearby branch, and pulled. He looked down and noticed rubber tires threaded through a rope that encircled massive chunks of granite that formed the slip. The *Catherine* rubbed against them gently. Somehow, Jeffah had pulled off something Porter thought improbable if not impossible—he had docked on the Atlantic side of Popham Island, on a spot reserved for Satan herself, the Devil's Cove.

The Whale's Jaw

"Rather cavernous, don't you think?" Jeff held an oil lantern above his head, moving it around, across the granite walls. "I can't imagine how big the storm was that threw these boulders here and left this hole for us to find ten thousand years later."

"It's not as big as I recall," said Porter. He looked down at the finely-crushed stone and pulverized shells. Cases of liquor were stacked high all around him. "But then again, maybe it's just all the booze." For the past forty minutes they had unloaded half the cargo they had received from Williams.

"This is the end of it. Sterling's gearing up for the holidays. By January, this place will be near empty."

Porter looked around, taking it all in.

"How long *has* it been?" asked Jeff.

"Huh?"

"Since you were here?"

"At least fifteen or sixteen years, I'd say."

"That long?"

"I think so. I think that was the last time, when we kidnapped cousin

Joe. We ran the dory like a sloop and made him hold the line most of the way blindfolded."

"I remember his look—shock, surprise, amazement—when the blindfold dropped."

"The same look we had when we found it, I imagine."

"The beauty about finding the long, lost hideout of a legendary pirate is, no one will ever believe you when you *do* tell 'em."

"Unless you show 'em, and we weren't about to show 'em."

"No. Never. Poor Joe, no one believed him. He tried to tell a few of his friends, but eventually gave up."

"The last time I saw him, before he left with the Expeditionary Force, we talked about that time. He wanted to know, so I told him."

"Told him?"

"Yeah, where it was. Here at the Devil's Cove. He was in Brooklyn, getting ready to ship out, and we met for dinner. It came up. When he came back, we were gonna come out here together. I promised him I'd hold the line, for a laugh. But …," Porter's voice crackled, "… he never came back."

"You know something—Minard knew him."

"Minard, your mate?"

"How many fucking Minard's do you know? Yes. Minard Severance—one of my men. He was in France. Fought with Joe in that battle in the village. He said it was a fight to the death. The Americans, they were all young kids from New England, were taken off guard. The way the Huns attacked, it was a horrific ambush."

"Why didn't you ever mention this before?"

"I only found out a short time ago—the details. I mean, Minard had said he knew Joe. They were the only two from the Lost Kingdom. But he never said much else until recently. It's like the battle was replaying in his head, he told me, and it was all he could do to stop thinking about it. Talking helped, he said, so I listened."

"And he told you about Joe?"

"Yes. He said Joe saved his life, actually. Shouted for him to duck when the first assault came, and he did, just before the volley sprayed the wall above him. He never had a chance to thank him."

Porter swallowed hard, thought of why Uncle Stu had told him, "Be sure to duck," before he left.

"Minard told Uncle Stu, a few years back, what Joe had done for him. That he owed him his life, and the lives of all the men who were near him.

Joe sounded the warning. He thanked your Uncle Stu for raising a hero among men."

The silence in the cave was whole, consuming. Porter felt the grief rise up in him, and a tear fell down his cheek, and then another, and another. He wiped them away, and said, "Uncle Stu never mentioned any of that to me."

Jeff shook his head. "I'm sure he's tried, and I'm sure he will one day. It took Minard eight years to tell your Uncle."

Porter's mouth went dry. "War is a racket," he mumbled. "Racketeers pull the strings—the high cabal. They play us for chumps and we rush in with open eyes, for what? They profit, we die. Dammit all ... poor Joe." He grabbed the nearest bottle, an Irish whiskey, from a case. Pulled the cork. He swallowed once, then again, then coughed and wheezed and spit. Jeffah took the bottle from him and hit it hard. He threw the bottle, with all he had against the granite wall. It exploded in a thousand pieces. Mr. Perkins barked loudly, then howled.

"Minard was a really good egg, Porter. Those bastards shot him in the head. They wanted something from him he didn't have. Hell, maybe this isn't about what happened in Hyannis. Maybe they wanted to know about this place."

Porter nodded, then hesitated, "Maybe, but maybe not."

"What do you mean?"

"Maybe it's a racket, too. Maybe Sterling knows something he's not talking about. Something he doesn't want you to know."

"Like what?"

"I'm not sure, but he should have warned you."

"Oh yeah, he did—remember? The fucker gave me some bullets."

"To run the gauntlet for him."

Huxley's Wharf

The dirt road wound its way through fields buffered on either side by stonewalls. On the northern side, where the edge of the field met the forest, the land rose sharply, forming a long ridge that surrounded the old, solitary mountain beyond it like a vast wall. Along the southern side of the road, the field sloped gently down to the sea, its view obscured by thin rows of trees, mostly pines, and some undergrowth, that stood like sentries over the rocky, rugged shoreline. Three miles out of town, the road forked, and the Packard went right for a few hundred yards. There, the motorcar made a hard right onto a narrow side road, more a cart path, that cut straight through the field. Despite the chill in the air, all the windows of the auto were down. Mr. Calvin reeked. Though he had changed, the stink of the priest was heavy on him. Murton's head leaned partly out the window. Hardy's gaze was fixed ahead, instructing Mr. Calvin when necessary. Shortly, the road intersected the trees. The auto passed through them and came out into a small clearing. They looked out upon an isolated peninsula, wide enough for the motorcar to turn on a dime. Ahead of them, nestled to their left, a dock stretched out into a cove, the opposite end of which was dimly lit by a pair of kerosene lamps hanging from posts on either side. The wharf was wide enough to accommodate a truck, and extended far enough out for a trawler to dock at low tide.

Mr. Calvin turned the motorcar around and parked it between the trees. Hardy and Murton jumped out before Mr. Calvin turned the engine off and walked to the clearing. Murton glanced to his left. There were large boulders, and a shoreline beyond, void of the large chunks of granite and small boulders that lined the coast throughout the region. A large mansion was set back, above, across a wide expanse of lawn, and another large house beyond that. They walked the length of the wharf. Murton noticed a very small dinghy tied off near the end. He then could make out the silhouette of a large sailboat moored at the edge of darkness.

Hardy glanced up at the lamps. "Two if by sea," he mumbled.

"Huh? What do you mean?" asked Murton.

"It means the cargo is still at sea," Hardy answered. "Despite Mr. Calvin's gross ineptitude and savagery, and our visit to the train station for naught, we are early." Hardy sensed Murton's confusion. "One lamp burning indicates delivery has been made. Two means it has not."

Murton nodded, "How original."

"Not really, but get your bearings, Murton," Hardy said. He turned up his collar, paced the width of the wharf and back. "It'll make our job easier."

Murton understood. "What now?"

"Now? Go down and blow out both lamps," Hardy said. "And then we wait, then we collect, and then we leave."

Realizations

"You never told me about the gypsy woman, Jeffah," Porter said. The boat approached the dock slowly. In the darkness, he could barely distinguish the shoreline. His only bearing was Huxley Manor in the distance. Pale light glimmered through a couple windows on the first floor.

But Jeff, as he had done so many times before, eased the *Catherine* toward the dock. The boat glided forward, past the silhouette of a sailboat to his right, through a veil of darkness, when he suddenly replied nonchalantly, "Oh, but I did," and he quieted. Maybe, Porter thought, to let his other senses take over. By now, he reckoned Jeffah could hear or could feel where it was he was going. The dock came up from nowhere. Porter made out a dinghy tied off ahead. Thought for sure they were going to ram it. But, with the slightest smack, Jeff guided the *Catherine* in, and kissed it gently and nestled the boat up next to rounded, thick wooden pilings. The dinghy bobbed a moment and stilled. "You just didn't listen, Porter."

"You never told me that you mentioned where I live—Brooklyn."

"Oh *that*. Does anybody admit to living in Brooklyn?" He thought about it for a second, then answered himself, "I suppose I just didn't want to embarrass you."

"Well, it's important to me. How much she knew about me before she supposedly read me like the proverbial book."

"Hey, it was nothing but in passing. Now that I think of it, when I mentioned it—Brooklyn—she shut down almost immediately," said Jeff. "*Okay*? There wasn't much after that. Except for the fact I lost the next forty-eight hours."

"I need to cover my bases."

"I would think you'd be more concerned about how your best friend misplaced a weekend after speaking with her."

"That's a mystery."

"No, that woman's a mystery," Jeff said. "I can't tell you much more than that. How and why she stopped here. What the hell is she even doing here in this country? Traveling around like that? Acting like she knew me—knew things before I could say them."

"About me?"

"You may find this hard to believe, but not everything is about you, Porter."

"All right, don't get sore. I didn't mean it that way."

"She was talking about me and my family, and then ..." he paused.

"And then what?"

"This is the thing. Just before my time lapse, she talked about you, and she talked about you like she knew you, or was looking—no—searching for you—said it would play out in the years ahead."

"*Huh*? I don't know what that means, Jeffah."

"And I *do*?"

They tied the boat off and jumped onto the dock. A chill struck Porter. Jeff cocked his head slightly like he could pick out something foul wafting their way. They took several steps, but stopped. Mr. Perkins let a low, barely-audible, growl, and then bolted silently down the dock.

"Burke? Is that you?" Jeff spoke out. There was no reply.

"This isn't right," Porter whispered. He lost sight of Mr. Perkins. Seconds passed. In the silence, the echo of a gallop could be felt on the dock.

Suddenly, a flash appeared ahead of them, out of the darkness, at the opposite end of the dock. Jeff jerked to his right and gasped. A burning pain erupted in his right shoulder. He fell to his knees, wincing. Porter leaned over him. Jeffah gave him a tug and pulled him to one knee. Later, he would say, it saved him. Because that's when the second flash came and, that time, each of them heard the bullet whiz over their heads. Next, a distant snarl, and a man cried out in shock.

"My shoulder," Jeff grimaced. "It's an ambush!"

"Jeffah, you okay?" whispered Porter.

"My arm is numb and my shoulder is on fire," he gasped. "If that's what you mean by okay."

They listened, stunned and frightened. Between them, they heard the sound of a savage mauling. A man screamed in agony.

"The shotgun?" Porter whispered.

Jeff gasped painfully, "What are you thinking?"

"I'm not sure ... You got the Smith and Wesson?"

Jeff nodded, took a breath to speak, but was interrupted by two loud pops, and then a screeching yelp.

"Ah, shit!" Porter shouted.

Jeff pulled the pistol from his pocket, stood. "Mr. Perkins!" he shouted. "You bastards!" He made it a few steps and began to stagger from the pain, fired off two shots, stumbled near the edge of the dock, as two rounds came back at him. The first went over his head. The second whizzed past his ear. He tried to steady himself momentarily, but then fell off.

"Jeffah!" Porter yelled. "No!" He rushed to where Jeff had fallen. There was no sound below. Porter peeled his jacket off, but a sharp blow to the back of his head left him staggering. There were stars and bells as he wobbled, before he keeled over on the dock.

Listen

"So, this is Moravia?" Porter stood halfway up a hillside, near the edge of a clearing. Below him, was a vast tract of forestland. Except for a narrow cart path that wound through it, he saw nothing but trees rolling across the far hills.

"Yes," Viola replied. "These are the foothills outside Brno."

He looked up and around, across the clearing. Atop the ridgeline, on a promontory, were ruins—walls partially collapsed between towers, and a castle within that had fallen into disrepair. It looked spooky and uninhabited. But then Porter noticed smoke rising from one of the buildings. Someone was there.

"When you come for me, it will be here," she said.

Porter looked back at the forest. "There is no undergrowth," he said. "It's a very clean forest."

"We like it that way."

"Fuel for fires," Porter said. "That makes more sense. Houses are heated, the forest will never burn."

"Mushrooms, too," Viola smiled. "The forest floor is covered with them."

Porter glanced around at all he could see and take in. It was twilight, a midsummer's eve. The air was fresh and clean. The scent of the forest cleared his head. "What do you mean—*come for you here*?"

"There is much to tell you," she replied. "In your own good time, you will know."

Porter was distracted by an unexpected whiff of smoke. He turned to the castle above. Suddenly, it was aflame, and the fire was spreading rapidly. It spilled over the ramparts, poured like a waterfall down the side, flowed like a stream onto the clearing. The meadow was blazing, and the fire was rolling right at him. The smoke burned his eyes, and he began to cough, struggled for air. "Viola!" he shouted in a panic. "Where are you?"

"Here! This way! Jump!" he heard a voice speak. "Porter? Do you hear me? You gotta jump!" Porter opened his eyes. The flames were all around him. He was disoriented and coughed hard. The *Catherine* was ablaze and he was in the midst of it. In the fire's glow, he could make out the wharf some thirty feet away. But that was not the direction the voice was coming from. "Dammit, Porter! Jump!" He recognized Jeffah's voice, and finally located him, in a dinghy, starboard from the *Catherine.*

Porter stood. He was dizzy. In the smoke and flames, he made out a black, shaggy lump to his far left, and a larger, blood-soaked carcass on his right. Its eyes unblinking. The hobgoblin. He vomited on it, and then leaped wildly from the boat into the water. Black ink consumed him in an icy grip. His struggle was immense. His limbs turned to concrete as he sank. A wave of panic overcame him. And *despair.* His lungs were burning. He needed air above. But which way was above? What was up? What was down? And that's when the voice whispered, *"Listen,* Porter.*"* And he did. He stopped flaying and let himself float. There was a tug and he began to rise. Another voice now, muffled, called his name. He let the sensation carry him. His lungs were set to implode, and they did, filling with air, as his head broke the surface.

He gasped loudly, breathed deeply and choked on the air, "I'm here, Jeffah." The dinghy was ten feet away, but Jeff's back was to him. He had somehow surfaced on the other side of the boat. The deck of the *Catherine* was fully engulfed in flames and drifting directly toward the dinghy. Jeff was looking in the direction of the flames, scanning the surface of the water. He turned to Porter when he heard his voice. The oar was like lead, but he extended it, wincing in pain as he did. "Grab it, Porter, quick." Porter did what he was told, and Jeff yanked him hard toward the boat. Porter gripped his icy fingers onto the edge of the boat. With his good arm, Jeff grabbed him and lifted. Porter pulled with all his strength, crawling over the side of the dinghy, as it nearly dipped into the water. He fell onto his back, gasping for air and shivering. Jeff wasted no time. He pulled the cord on the small outboard. The engine sputtered, choked, and revved, and he gunned the throttle. The dinghy lit off, away from the *Catherine.* Not far enough to miss the concussion when the gas tank exploded, but far enough to miss the debris as it rained down, just short of them, onto the water.

When Demons Rise

In the shadows, midway down the dock, Mr. Calvin made out the inky blots of two men. They had stood there—he, Hardy and Murton—watched the boat dock, watched them step onto the wharf. He raised his Webley and took aim. As he studied one of the blots, he realized, or so it seemed, that his hand was trembling—actually, his entire arm. He couldn't take proper aim, and dropped his arm. Nervous energy? Anxious? No. The dock was moving; wobbling and shaking—but by what? He remembered Mr. Hardy whisper, near silently, "What are you waiting for?" That was just before Mr. Hardy looked down, as did Murton, and actually saw the dock shaking. Mr. Calvin did, too, look down, and then looked up, leveled the Webley again, and fired unsteadily at the inky blots. He managed one more shot but, in retrospect, he thought, as he lay dying, he should have resolved the reason behind the dock shaking first, before firing. It made sense now. It was a fraction of a second after that last shot, the beast lunged for his throat. In the time in which his larynx was crushed and his trachea ripped apart, he became aware of a foul smell. He thought it was the beast. In a way, he was right. The horrific odor came the moment the black mass of a beast inflicted its fury and fangs upon Mr. Calvin's throat. Dark, short creatures appeared from out of the shadows. Many landed beside Hardy, less so Murton, but neither man noticed them. They, not the dog, he realized, smelled foul. They were hideous, impish things—oily, with eyes glowing—reddish, burning coals.

He had collapsed by then, stared into the darkness above. The animal, to the best of his recollection, had continued its assault, tearing into Murton or Hardy—he wasn't sure. There was a shot, and a brief yelp of pain, then a pause. "My fucking arm," he heard Murton or Hardy swear. He heard another round, maybe two, fired, but not much more. He took notice of a faint hue of violet light, which began to trickle out of the darkness in midair. The light grew in shape and size. Violet spilled out through spidery cracks in the ether, much like water would from the wall of a dyke moments before it ruptures. He had the sensation of moving or being moved. Yes, dragged along the dock, while Murton and Hardy spoke about the boat. They were dragging him to the boat. There was a gurgling sound near him, a moan. Was it the beast? No. It came from within. His ability to breath was blocked by the gush of his own blood in and out of his lungs. Murton and Hardy stood over him. They looked at him, each other, the boat, and nodded.

The air pressure dropped or compressed around him, just as the violet hue exploded all around him. From it, a winged creature emerged. Feminine, lithe, agile, beautiful—she, or it, held a scythe, its blade long and starlit. With one motion, she swung the blade and sliced through a half dozen of the imps that had gathered around him. They screeched out in agony and rage, as they dissolved back into the shadows and darkness. She continued on to the beast and picked it up in her arms, the spirit of the thing, brushed the animal's head and coat, and smiled affectionately. The dog's tail moved, jerked reflexively, and then fluttered like the wings of a moth. The dog's mouth opened, and it yawned like it had awakened from a long nap. When it shut, the dog's mouth, Mr. Calvin felt a sharp pain in his groin, like the dog's jaws were closing around his crotch. A thousand scalding-hot needles pierced his balls and ripped them apart. One of the oily, foul-smelling imps was at him, working its way through him. The pain was infinite. He was motionless and at the mercy of the thing gnawing and mutilating his crotch. Steadily, methodically, with razor-like precision, devouring him—his very being, his very soul.

Over and above the imp stood Hardy, who held a gun in his hand, called Mr. Calvin's name. Pointing it at him, he fired. He felt the white-hot trajectory of the bullet shred his heart and lungs. As the fire spread through his chest, the thing between his legs swelled up in size and stature, like a giant bear rising on its hind legs to unleash its fury. Grotesquely mutilated and deformed, an inhuman shape formed. Its jaws unhinged. Unleashed, the evil from within *him* spoke, and the depths of hell listened. For out of the jaws of the monster before him, those of its kind came forth, and savagely devoured Mr. Calvin in that moment and forever and eternity.

Keeping Afloat

"I knew she was gonna blow when the flame found its way to the reserve tank," Jeff said. He cut the engine and let the dinghy coast to the shore with a thud. Down the shoreline, the flames fizzled in the water, as the burned-out hull of the *Catherine* grounded on the beachhead.

"What the hell just happened, Jeffah?" Porter's teeth chattered. His head throbbed. He shivered, but forced himself up. He knew he had to move. Ahead of them was Huxley Manor. The air temperature was colder than the water.

"We were ambushed. I got shot! That's what happened."

"I thought you were dead, when you fell off the dock."

"I thought I was, too. But then I surfaced, heard voices on the dock, heard 'em say, "'Throw him in there.'"

"Me?"

"Yeah, you, and ... "

"... Mr. Perkins," Porter cried out, and began to sob quietly.

"Yes, Porter, they got Mr. Perkins." Jeff reached over and patted his shoulder. "They threw you and him into the boat."

"The dog was too fucking old." Porter fought the tears. "I should never have brought him."

Jeff stepped from the dinghy and pulled it up on shore with his good arm. "If he didn't charge them, we would have walked right into their arms and had our heads blown off."

"I can't believe this," Porter said, sniffling and wiping the tears and snot off with the back of his hand. "I saw you fall." He stepped out of the boat, regaining his balance and composure, on solid ground, "And your arm."

"It hurts like hell at the moment, but they only winged me, didn't hit bone. I just lost my balance."

"I was about to jump in to save you."

Jeff smiled. "When I came up, I swam for the dinghy. I could hear running on the wharf. Two of them came up behind you, two of Crowe's auditors."

Porter cupped his hand behind his head and winced. "They could have killed me."

"They tried, I'll give 'em that. I heard the shorter one say, 'Hardy, what are we gonna do?' The tall one answered right off, 'Save your bullets. We'll give 'em a Viking funeral. We'll make it look like this one and his dog did it.' He was pointing to you."

"The short one jumped in my boat. Smashed open cases of booze and tossed 'em all over the deck." Jeff paused and swallowed hard. "Shit. I almost went under, Porter. I had the dinghy between me and them. I was freezing, but couldn't move. If I did, it would have been the end for both of us ... But somehow ..." Jeff shivered at the thought.

"... Somehow, Jeffah," Porter repeated softly, "somehow."

"They got their big friend, dragged him down the dock. He was still alive—I could hear him moaning and choking, laying there."

"He was a mess," Porter said.

"What?" asked Jeff.

"His throat," Porter said in a hush. "I saw him before I jumped. It makes sense now. Mr. Perkins ..." he trailed off, unable to speak further.

"Yes, he got the fucker, Porter," said Jeff.

Both men quieted. Lucky to be alive, but for Mr. Perkins, they were.

Jeff cleared his throat and continued, "That's when one of them said,

'Mr. Calvin?' He moaned and made a gurgling sound. The taller one they called Hardy, leaned over him, studied him and said, 'Fucking mess.' Hardy asked the shorter one something and he handed him his coat. Without a second thought, he pulled a big gun from his pocket, wrapped the coat around it, and finished him."

"Holy shit," Porter said.

"There was nothing holy about it," Jeff replied. "But that was my chance. My extremities were all numb, but I pulled myself in the dinghy and pushed. Their backs were to me. They struggled trying to lift him, and could only roll him in my boat. They didn't even notice me. The big one tossed the lamp in the boat and the fire started. There was no fanfare in them. Once the flames took, they ran. Had to, I suppose."

"What do you mean?" Porter asked.

"The lights," he said. "They began to blink rapidly from up at Huxley Manor," he pointed across the wide, manicured lawn. Porter looked toward the mansion. Though he shouldn't have been surprised, he was startled when, at that moment, they heard the gunshot up at the house.

The Mess on the Waterfront

Sterling watched the flames from his study window. "Why not alert the entire coast, or better yet, simply radio the Coast Guard?" he asked. Hardy and Murton were behind him. "It's a mess, a fucking mess."

Hardy had just informed Sterling of the fate of the *Catherine's* crew, and the loss of his other man. "The whole evening has been a fucking mess," said Hardy. "They were ready for us on the dock."

"What do you mean, *ready?*" Sterling turned around. "All you had to do was let them come to you. Knock them silly, and sink them and the boat."

"We never had the chance to do it," Hardy fumed.

"A dog the size of a black bear attacked us," Murton shouted, and held up his bloodied hand.

"For the love of God," Sterling said, looking at the fleshy palm. "You're dripping blood on my *floor.* It stains, you know." He pulled a handkerchief from his pocket, and tossed it to him. "Take it outside."

Murton left the study. "That was rather rash," Hardy said, "and bad form."

"So is that boat burning out there," Sterling replied angrily.

"Better to burn the evidence," said Hardy. "It will add to the mystery and confusion when they find 'em."

"We were supposed to back out of the operation—*quietly*!" Sterling fumed. "*That*," he pointed at the burning boat, "was supposed to be an accident, like the other three."

"Runners' war takes a deadly turn," Hardy responded, "even better."

"Long after you're gone, I'll still be here explaining to the authorities about *it* and the bodies that wash ashore. On *my* shore! *My* property!"

"You also said it would be two men, not two men and a savage, fucking beast—a Hound of fucking Baskerville," Hardy said.

"You think this is funny?" Sterling shouted. "A game of chance?"

"Listen, you arrogant fuck," Hardy snapped. He then pulled his gun out of his vest holster and leveled it directly at Sterling's head. "I don't really care how you explain away your little problem," he nodded his head toward the window. "If one man shows up at Mr. Walker's office inquiring of the events of this evening," he shouted, "I will return." His eyes burrowed deeply into Sterling's. He held the gun there, controlling his rage. Then, pointing it at the ceiling, he fired. The explosion was deafening in the small room. "One by one, I'll pay your family a visit. Do you understand me?"

Sterling nodded his head slowly, and sat down at his desk.

"Good man," Hardy said. "We need to get out of here. Meet in thirty minutes in your office. We'll settle the last of the business when you get there. Do you understand that?"

Sterling nodded his head again, slowly.

Hardy holstered his gun. "Good! We'll make *that* look like an accident!" he said, then left the room. His rage was finally in check. Blowing Sterling's head off was tempting, but not an option. Not until he weaseled his way out of the mess on the waterfront.

Abigail's Warning

"The bank auditors called, Abigail," Sterling said. "I just got off the phone. I'm sorry, but this can't wait until tomorrow. Meet me in the office in forty-five minutes."

Abigail listened attentively, held the phone's receiver tightly against her ear. "What has happened?" she asked. "Is it serious?"

"No time for that now," he replied. "I'll explain everything when you get to the office—understand?"

She said she did, and he hung up. She waited, held the receiver to her head and heard a familiar click, then dropped it on the candlestick and placed the desk stand down. Mrs. Fontaine had listened to the conversation on the extension. Sterling had said nothing out of the ordinary. Yet, Abigail feared something was wrong. Maybe it was her, she thought. Was she calm, her voice? One glance at her hand, which was trembling, was enough to convince her. She had to suppress an urge to pace. It would give the landlady, Mrs. Fontaine, a concern, a pretext to come upstairs. The nervous energy was building. A thought rushed into her head—leave now and go straight to Lewiston, to her mother's boarding house. Get out! It would have to suffice.

She looked around her front room. But for her coat and hat, it was bare. Her bags were already in the car. She had moved them there when Mrs. Fontaine had gone out earlier. A part of her wanted to say good-bye to the old busybody. Thought it was right. But no, she had to leave like she would return soon—in a few hours. That was best.

That Damn Letter

"You alive, Sterling?" Sterling looked up, startled to see his wife in the doorway of the study.

"It's nothing, Flo," he said. "Go back to bed." Then he noticed the .38 Special. The old Colt he always kept in the back of the bottom drawer of his nightstand. The one which was now firmly in her hand and aimed directly at his head.

"*Nothing?*" she asked, and glanced at the ceiling and the splattered plaster on the floor.

"Whatever it was, Flo, it is done and over with," he said dismissively, as he focused on the instrument of death, the gun, and the realization it was the second one in minutes, in the hands of someone opposite him, leveled at his head.

"Is it, Sterling?" She held the gun tightly and took one step closer. "I was naïve enough to believe in you, but not anymore."

"Whoa, Flo," he said, "not now."

"*Not* now?" she shouted, incredulously. That's when *she* cocked the pistol.

"Why is this happening *again*?" he thought, but said, "You're sounding upset, a little too sinister, Flo," he said. "Please put the gun down."

She shook her head, no, and stepped toward him.

"What are you doing?" he asked, and stood up slowly.

"I'm protecting my family."

"If it goes off, you'll be destroying *our* family."

"I know what you did, Sterling. I know of the affair you had with that woman."

"*What* affair? *What* woman?" He stepped away from the desk.

"I know why you supported her after her husband was killed by one of your damned machines."

"For the love of God, Flo, what are you talking about? I have to leave."

"For years, I pondered why you brought that family into our lives." It was then Sterling noticed the envelope clenched tightly in her other hand. Mainly, because she held it up in a fist in the direction of his face, and shook it hard. "It wasn't out of compassion or concern. She was going to blackmail you into supporting her. But like a damn fool, I stepped in and supported her openly."

Sterling's stomach began to churn at the realization. His mouth began to dry. In spite of that, he said, "What the fuck are you talking about?"

"*Incredibly,*" Flo let out a mock laugh, "she was going to blackmail you, not because of the death of her husband, not that at all. It was *me*. She was going to tell *me* way back then. But she didn't have to. I did everything. I gave her everything—more than she could conceive." Flo let her mind go there, her thoughts. She'd been had. "Even *she* had enough sense to keep her mouth shut and keep the sham going ... which she did, up until I received this letter."

"Letter from *whom*?" he asked, deciding to play dumb, realizing the totality of her rage—that the bitch might actually pull the trigger before he could disarm her and get out of there. After all, there was the other bastard waiting to blow his brains out. What *was* his name? *Hardy?* "Let's not get too rash, now, Flo," he added. "And please stop pointing that gun at me, before it goes off," he added, with as much exasperation as he could summon.

"Don't fuck with me." She took another step closer, and then another. "I mean it, Sterling!"

"Flo," he whispered, and stepped toward her, then took another step, then rolled his eyes and grabbed the .38 from her hand.

"You fuck," she said.

"It just happened to happen," he replied, gave a shrug, and added with an air of nonchalance, "Be a dear and call the police in ten minutes. Tell them there's a boat on fire by our dock. I have that *meeting* to attend to down the coast." He feigned a smile, or so she thought, and said, "Oh, when the sheriff arrives, I was never here."

He tossed the gun over his shoulder and walked out of the house. Flo stared vacantly for a moment at the gun, where it landed in the corner, then went for it. She ran down the hall and out the front door, but, by then, all she saw was the taillights of Sterling's Buick. She raised the gun to fire, but the futility of it all—the night, the letter, her life, and the stark distance between her and that bastard—swept over her. She sank to the steps and dropped the gun between her legs in disgust. Her eyes followed the Buick until its lights disappeared around the bend. The night air was cool and damp. A chill came over her, and she lowered her head and wept.

The Return to Town

Murton had double-wrapped his hand with the handkerchief. The beast had bit him pretty good before Hardy got the shot off. He'd found himself kicking the thing after it went down. Then felt like shit for kicking a dog, let alone a dead dog. It stung, his hand, and throbbed, but he gripped the wheel of the Packard anyway, waiting. He didn't want Hardy to see him in pain, or bothered. He was unsure of Hardy. He knew him well enough to know that when the best laid plans went awry, he was prone to periods of rage, and anything could happen. He sure as hell would not discuss the fate of Mr. Calvin with him. Would not ask Hardy why he needed Murton's coat even as he wrapped Mr. Calvin's gun in it—his very own Webley—and finished him off. He, Murton, was fit to run wild into the chilly night, bloody hand and all. The thing arrived for Mr. Calvin just as they rolled him into the boat—right out of the ether—up through the dock, the demon came. Hardy saw nothing. He tossed Murton's coat into the boat. Murton watched it pass right through the demon, who looked up at Hardy and growled. Murton stepped back in terror. Hardy threw the lamp amidst the smashed bottles of whiskey. The flame spread quickly and grew. They pushed the boat off. The demon continued to ravage Mr. Calvin. Only the Huxley man's signal got him out of there, the both of them, before he outright bolted.

Alone, sitting there in the Packard, Murton was suddenly struck with fear. He glanced around, in hopes he had not been followed by the thing. His nerves were frayed and he thought to flee, run back to the house.

187

He would have, but Hardy rushed out of it. He paused, and took notice of the waterfront. "Are you all right? Can you drive?" he asked, climbing into the passenger seat. Murton simply nodded. "Good. Do not turn on the head lamps until I tell you. I gave Huxley 30 minutes to meet us. Now drive."

"Where to?" Murton asked.

"Town—we'll find a nice, quiet place to park and wait and talk about the future," he answered.

Murton put the car in gear, grimaced silently, and drove away from Huxley Manor, relieved. To their left, the flames fizzled out on the *Catherine*, as the tide pushed the smoldering hull on shore. There was another boat out there now, moving toward the *Catherine* rapidly. "Coast Guard, Hardy," Murton said, "I'd bet." Beads of sweat were dripping down his face. The panic subsided.

Hardy said nothing and did not take notice of Murton. He pointed ahead, as if to say, "Go," even though Murton had already accelerated. When the car cleared the field, he said, "You can turn the head lamps on now."

"They're a good fifteen minutes out, yet," Murton said, "and at least another fifteen minutes before they find what's left of Mr. Calvin and that other fella, if they haven't drifted off."

Again, Hardy said nothing, and the pair settled into silence. Murton focused on the pain in his hand, and his mind stayed there. Hardy brooded over the course of events for the past several hours. He was thinking of how to right the evening, at least in the eyes of Mr. Walker. Nothing had gone as planned, though the beast had done a great service for him. There was that much good out of it, but not much else. He glanced at Murton and sighed heavily. The car rolled into town through empty streets; not a soul was about. They drove past Crowe's Trust, around the Common, and up to the Custom House. As Murton slowed, Hardy said wearily, "Drive around back, Murton. I don't want anyone to see us."

Coincidence Is For Fools

"Coincidence is for fools," his father had told him as a boy. "But a meaningful coincidence?" he had said. "Therein lies a purpose for everything under heaven." He never gave it a second thought, until that Easter week, sixteen years earlier—in Dublin, with the Brotherhood, and the Rising, with all of them holed up in the General Post Office. He was half man, half boy of 17, then, and ready to die for the Republic. Hope lasted about one day. Hostages meant nothing to the Brits. That's how they reasoned. When the army brought in the artillery, they were doomed. But how to escape? The Post Office, and the Hotel Metropole next door, were on fire and besieged. Where was the leadership now? Connolly was tethered. His ankle was shattered by a bullet. Pearce, the schoolteacher and military *genius*, was tunneling out. It was The O'Rahilly, ever the gentleman, that volunteered and sallied forth to break the siege, shouting out, "It is madness, but it is glorious madness!" He was set, with a few others, to follow The O'Rahilly. At Moore Street, the machine gunner opened up on the sortie. The O'Rahilly took the first bullets there, and the rest of them in Sackville Lane, where he was left for a better part of a day before he died.

But he did not see any of that. He was with them at first, running down Moore toward Great Britain Street, alone on the left flank, when he heard it—his name—*Malachi*—spoken in his ear, as plainly and clearly as an actor speaks upon a stage. And then the word, "*Listen*!" A sudden flash in his periphery followed. It stopped him short and he tripped, as hard as if he had been pushed face first on the cobbled stone street. The others continued to rush forward. To this day, he wonders if they saw him fall and, if so, did they think he was hit? Why did they leave *him*? Did any of *them* call his name? He lay there, stunned—flat on the street—his forehead gashed and bleeding—his eyes seeing polka dots and stars—his heart pounding. He needed to move—precious moments were passing by—the army was bayoneting all who fell—dead or alive. But then he remembered the word, and thought, *listen* … but to …. *what*? And that's when the creaking sound came from his left. He lifted his head slowly and turned, looked, focused. A doorway, there, with its door opened an inch, and then another creak, and another inch. Inviting him in. The gunfire began ahead. Artillery and fire behind. He crawled inside. Rolled back on the door and lived.

When he awoke, he was quite alone. His head hurt. He touched his forehead and winced. The blood had dried. In the darkness, he made his escape, his head throbbing and on fire. Left the city and went south to Kinsale, where his old friend, Father Kelly, now served at the friary there. He took him in—at great danger to himself—and nursed him back to health. An American and a Canadian were there, too, under the auspices of the Marconi Company, and had become very good friends with Father Kelly. Many months passed, until, one morning, the military came to the friary looking for a person of interest—his name, Malachi's, was mentioned in connection with the Post Office in Dublin. In fact, he was made by a soldier who had been in Dublin during the uprising. That's when the American and Canadian came forward and said, "No!" He worked for them. It bought time, added to the confusion. He jumped a fishing trawler at dawn, on the Bandon River, that took him up to Cork. From there, he went to France, and managed to get caught up in the war. He learned to fight very well *and* learned to survive even better, skills he was able to parlay into what he was.

Above all, he promised himself, he would never be made again.

Or so he thought.

His attention was drawn to the scratching sensation on the tip of his nose. Next, was the scent of decay and rot, the thing's nasty breath in his face. He opened an eye, then another. In the darkness, he saw the creature, an alley cat, its paws extended, boxing his nose. He sat up. The cat hissed at the move. "You little shit!" he said, and gave it a quick backhand into a pile of nearby rubbish. The cat meowed and bolted into the night.

Malachi touched the back of his head. Tender to touch, it throbbed painfully. His thoughts were fragmented. He had not had that dream in years. He felt confused and lost. And then he remembered. Had he been made—again? "Fuck!" he cursed. How much time? He pulled his watch from his pocket and cursed again. He thought of Porter, and just as quickly, Father Kelly—of vengeance fulfilled. He stood. It took him a minute to find his center but, when he did, he steadied himself, which was a good thing. Because at that moment, the Packard drove by the alley and, for no other reason but the moment, he whispered, "Coincidence *is* for fools."

The Woes of Flo

"Hey, Flo!" Jeff yelled, as he and Porter came running up to the house. She was sitting on the front stairwell, under the portico, in a nightgown, sobbing. The door was open behind her. Dim light from the hallway cast a long shadow across the marble stairs. A pistol was on the stoop between her legs.

"I was going to shoot Sterling," she said, "the bastard. But I couldn't."

"I think you hit him," said Jeff. There were drops of blood on the steps leading inside and down the hallway.

"I was aiming between his eyes," she answered, then looked up at Jeff. "You're bleeding, Jeffrey."

"Seems you're not the only one who missed their target tonight, Flo," Jeff smiled weakly. "Thankfully, for me." He extended his good arm out to her, to help her up, but winced and had to steady himself from falling.

"I didn't miss, Jeffrey. I couldn't pull the trigger." She picked up the gun and stood. With her other hand, she wiped the tears from her face, and then wiped it clean on the back of her nightgown sleeve. "Come on in, Jeff. Let's clean that up."

"There was a gunshot, Flo," said Porter.

"Yes, there was," she said.

"Then what the hell's happening?" asked Porter.

"He—Sterling—is keeping company with gangsters," she said. "That's what's happening. One of them shot my ceiling."

"We gotta go after Sterling, Flo," Jeff said, stumbling. "The cocksucker tried to do us in and we're gonna find out why." He began to fall. Flo grabbed him, steadied him. Porter swung Jeffah's good arm around him and guided him inside, down the hall to the parlor, where Jeff sank into the sofa.

"You're not going anywhere, Jeffrey. We are going to clean that arm of yours and get you a doctor," Flo said.

"Mother!" The three jumped at the word. Behind them, backlit in the doorway, stood two girls in nightgowns.

"What's happened?" one asked.

"Mr. Grant hurt himself, Emma, that's what's happened," Flo answered her.

"There's a boat on fire down on the beach," the other said.

"Yes, Edith," she said. "There's been an accident. That's how Mr. Grant was hurt."

Months later, when Porter thought back on the night, and it was a long one, he would reconstruct the events of the evening, play them out in his head. Amidst all the savagery, mayhem and violence, there was but one moment to savor, a solitary fragment, and it was now. Jeffah, for his part, forgot the thousand nerve endings searing his flesh and felt no pain. Before them, Edith and Emma, maybe 16 and 15—Porter wasn't sure—

because they looked ten years older—stood there, radiant and innocent. Unlike their older sister, Enid, the pair was stunning. Porter would not have taken note of them, he would convince himself later, as would Jeffah, except for the way the light penetrated the sheer cotton fabric of their nightgowns, which rendered the cloth translucent. It bathed their silky smooth legs, bare asses and round breasts in an amber, coppery glow—revealing full-figured, nubile sirens—and leaving Porter and Jeffah thoroughly entranced.

"Emma," snapped Flo, which had the intended effect of rousing the men. "Go set the kettle on and bring me clean towels. Edith, get the operator. Call Liam and Dr. Bradbury and tell them to get out here right away." The girls went into action. "And for the love of God put on your robes before you blind these two men!" she shouted after them.

"Sah-sorry, Flo," Porter took a breath.

"I didn't mean to ..." Jeff mumbled.

"Forget it. I'm not numb, you two," Flo said. "Those girls are a handful and more, but need I remind either of you of the moment at hand? What the hell are we gonna do?"

"Shit, Flo," said Jeffah. "We gotta get going—find Sterling. Tell Liam I couldn't wait." He forced a smile and began to stand, but it was as though his feet couldn't locate the floor, and he keeled over onto the coffee table. Flo and Porter righted him back onto the sofa.

"Dammit, Jeffrey, you're not going anywhere," said Flo.

"I can go, Jeffah," said Porter. "You stay here and bring Flo up to speed. I'll find him. He's gonna answer for what he's done."

"Good luck finding him," she said. "He said something about Portland and business a few days ago. But if he had any sense at all, he'd keep driving all the way to Portsmouth, or even Boston, hop on a boat, and leave the country."

"You think he does?" asked Porter.

"What? Have enough sense?" She shook her head, no, and said, "Take my Nash. Try his office. He might be that bold, or truly that numb."

The Best Laid Plans

Thompson stood in his office window, arms folded, in the dark. He looked out on the town, empty streets under the faint glow of lampposts. He cleared his throat, was about to call for Ambrose to come and keep watch—they had been waiting on his friend, he was due hours ago—but then he was distracted by a light up the street. A car approached and passed. The Packard, but he only made out two shadows in the car as it passed under a street lamp. Interesting, he thought, and wondered about the other one. Dreadful business, these men are in. The car disappeared around the back of the Custom House. Instinctively, he patted his jacket pocket, felt the revolver there. If it came to it, he wasn't sure if he could use it. What madness would it be? But fear does that to you, blind rage and fear. He reached in his pocket and fondled the gun. Strange that he would be carrying such a thing around town, but this was *dreadful* business. He looked across the Common, eyeing Sterling's office window. Dim light bled out from the darkness.

Minutes passed and another car came into town. A Buick—Sterling was at the wheel. He slowed in front of the Custom House, but did not stop. Instead, he went up the street further, turned around, and parked there, toward the building. Thompson watched him, studied the shadow in the driver's seat. It sat for a minute or so, unmoving. Was the bastard actually losing his nerve? Having second thoughts? No. He opened the car door, but shut it quickly, lowered himself into the seat. What's this? A third car approached rapidly. It sped by his window—a Nash—dear God, it was Flo. A woman enraged. A complication. "Dammit!" Thompson cursed.

The car came to a skidding stop in front of the Custom House. The lights shut off abruptly and the car door swung open. The driver jumped out and stood momentarily, gazing up at the third floor. "What the hell?" Thompson couldn't believe his eyes. Porter Gibson passed under the lamppost, walked up to the door of the Custom House. He fumbled with a key momentarily, then pushed the door open and went inside.

Parting of Friends

"But I thought you were my friend—I thought we were good friends?" Murton pleaded. He was staring at Mr. Calvin's Webley, the barrel of which was pointed at him.

"Like a brother to me," said Hardy. "That's why this pains me more than you'll ever know."

"Why, Hardy? Why must you do this?"

"I have no choice." Hardy leaned back into the car door. He lowered the pistol, slightly, and began to speak with his hands. "There's no place in this business for philosophers."

"What?"

"I must save you from yourself, Murton."

"You're going to kill me to save me from myself? Because I'm a philosopher?"

"Earlier tonight, in the cemetery, you made it perfectly clear where your head is at. You can't stop thinking about it. You're haunted, Murton. Damaged. Mr. Walker was right. When a man takes to reflecting on the past, he has no future."

"I confided in you. I had to unburden myself. Do you understand?" Murton spoke haltingly, desperately. "What happened there in Edinburgh was not ordinary business."

"We've known each other far too long to give testimonials, Murton."

"It wasn't a testimonial, Hardy."

"No. It was the ranting of a madman."

"That's what my trust has earned? A death sentence?"

"Mr. Calvin *was* gonna do it, but, well, he never was man's best friend, was he?" Hardy laughed at the words.

"Not much of anyone's friend," said Murton.

"They'll find your coat when they find him," Hardy said. "They'll find his gun when they find you. Gangster wars and all that—they'll write it off."

"You've thought of everything."

"Improvised tonight," he replied. "Like I said, Mr. Calvin *was* gonna do it, then *he* was gonna be done with. Same ending, different order."

Murton sighed deeply. He looked at the gun, then Hardy, and said, "Funny, I always thought we'd have a future, no matter what."

"Yes—well, look at it this way—I'm doing this to preserve the future—to save the future. Your future."

"Save the future? *My* future? Ha! Killing me—your dear friend you love like a brother?"

"Yes, Murton. It pains me terribly. Truly. But the reality is, some time in the future, it *will* happen. You'll compromise our relationship and the whole operation. You'll get drunk—you'll confide in your brother—maybe a wife or child—your son or daughter. Because the weight you carry will not be your own. And when that comes, when you relieve yourself of the weight, then what have you done?"

"Yes? And what is that?"

"You will have transferred it—the weight—to an innocent person.

That's what you will have done." Hardy's voice rose in anger. "And then they, too, will have to be eliminated. Who will do that then? You? Kill your own wife? Your child? Brother, sister, mother?"

"You make a convincing argument." Murton leaned back.

Hardy shook his head, no. He regained his composure, and raised his pistol, and spoke coolly. "I tend to over-rationalize. But it helps me sleep," he said with a shrug.

"If I may," said Murton, raising one finger.

"Go on, then." Hardy nodded. "Just keep your hands still—keep 'em on the wheel."

Murton breathed in, and slowly placed his hands on the steering wheel. He clenched them, squeezed tightly, and released. His mauled hand did not even hurt, he realized. The end was fucking nigh. The pain had already released. Then a thought struck him, profound in its logic and simplicity. With a slight nod, he asked, "By eliminating me, you will save *my* future—*my* family and *all* my friends?"

"Yes, that is exactly right."

"Then what about *you*?"

Hardy paused, intrigued. In a world of endless possibilities, he wondered. For the first time in years, he wondered. A multitude of conflicted emotions welled up in him. The past, the present and the future rushed through him—the endless violence and an elusive peace—all that was, could have been and could be. He saw himself alone, standing on an abyss. He looked over the edge, and then looked up. Murton, who had sat there unblinking, a choice, could they run off? The money in the trunk? Drive away? Be done with it forever? He steadied the pistol, sighed, and then decided, there in the darkness, what had to be. "Ah shit, Murton," he cursed, with a tone of regret, and that was all.

The shot rang out. The bullet lodged into the center of his brain, and it was over with.

Foreclosing on Real Estate

Porter entered Sterling's office with caution, but no one was there. Maybe the cocksucker did head south, Porter thought. He went to the desk and turned on the lamp. He opened a drawer, and then another, but nothing. He opened a third drawer, and file folders were hanging neatly. Porter noticed a familiar name sticking out of a thick folder. He pulled the entire folder and spread it on the desk. In the dim light, he read the name, "Howard Bailey," on the corner tab of a file. He opened it, read part of it, and skimmed to the bottom of the page. A deed? Through the Crowe Trust? He was baffled. There wasn't much to read, excepting the fact that Bailey had recently purchased and sold a hundred acres over near Penobscot. Amazingly, a week after he had washed ashore. He placed the file down and picked up the next one. The name, Lawrence Philpot; the content was the same as Bailey's, except the acquisition and sale of his property was up on Duck's Head Pond. He continued through successive files, each of them deeds—the purchase and sale of property—and stopped when he came upon another familiar name, "Minard Severance." Porter opened it. He too had recently acquired and sold land, Dark's Cove. "But how? These men are dead," Porter said out loud, "and moving property ... somehow." Porter closed Minard's folder and placed it down. Hesitating, he picked up the last two files and looked at the names. He took a sharp breath. "Holy shit," he whispered. "All dead but Jeffah and ..."

"Porter!" the voice shouted out. "I must say, you're pretty fit for a dead man."

Startled, Porter turned. Sterling framed the doorway.

"Don't look so surprised. This is my office," he said as he walked into the room.

"You're brokering land through the Crowe Trust?"

"We have for a while. They are a bank. I am a lawyer, and *do* have my broker's license."

"For *dead* people?"

"Ironic, isn't it?" He went to the desk, stepped past Porter, picked up a file folder, "Tombstone deeds, very profitable. The dead don't haggle." Porter shook his head in disbelief. "Your house on Davis Street has sat there empty for so long, we actually joked of adding it to the portfolio."

"You've sold out your own kind, Sterling."

"Nonsense! They're dead."

"What about Lawrence Philpot, Howard Bailey and Minard Severance?"

"Like I said, they're dead."

"For Christ's sake, Sterling, they were family men trying to survive. They trusted you."

"Lawrence shouldn't have played with matches. Howard should have learned to swim, like every other fisherman in this mackerel hole of a town." He studied Porter for a moment, and added, with a grin, "Hell, by the looks of you, Porter, even you learned to swim. As for Minard, well, he wasn't much of a swimmer, but he hunted occasionally, though I heard he never was a good shot."

"That's coldblooded murder, you bastard."

"Not at all—I had nothing to do with it—never had a say. The discussions I had focused on the money. We needed a place to *put* the money, to have it come clean. The factories have all but ground to a halt. Jonah was approached with the idea—move property, literally, liquid and real, play the middleman and take a percentage, show your profit and your partner's profit that way. They called it servicing money. All we needed was a bank. Enter the Crowes, uncooperative partners, at best. Wendell turned a blind eye to it, but I'm not even sure how *aware* Thompson is, other than falling over that massive ego of his. Mr. Walker became quite the land baron in these parts over the last few years. He's moving property from Machias to Caribou to Kittery through dozens of corporations. We are but one cog in the wheel of fortune."

"You invited gangsters to Downeast Way? You let them enter our community?"

"Well, Mr. Walker's a partner, and I'll have you know he's not a gangster; only his henchmen are. And Wendell? Like any good banker, he held his nose and swallowed easily. It's worked over the years, rather nicely, very efficient. We've made millions of dollars, in the midst of a self-imposed blight that's afflicted the country, by simply giving the people what they want."

"It's not gonna work, Sterling. It's over."

"I'm afraid it already has worked, Porter," he replied. "Oh, and it's over, all right. For me, most of my funds have been moved into Mr. Walker's bank. Yes. Did I mention that? He's quite the financier, too. Wall Street investment house. Untouchable. Very profitable, even in these times. I have a nice trust set up for my daughters. They will be provided for while I'm away on *business*," he grinned. "As for you, in a moment, that big fellow will be walking through that door to finish what he started earlier this evening—sorry about everything—Jeffrey and even your dog, too. You should never have gotten involved, but you did, and now it's come to this."

Porter thought, to lunge at him or leave. One punch maybe, and go, would have been adequate, but the door from the outer office shut suddenly. He was trapped. "Ah, here he is now, Porter. Put on a good face. He'll be as surprised as I was to see you're still alive."

"Did you say Walker's bank?" Sterling and Porter turned toward the door, expecting Hardy. But Thompson Crowe stood there and entered the room.

"Oh, hi, Thompson, and yes, I did—sorry," said Sterling. "I meant to tell you."

"You had those goons pick up your money in my bank for what, then?"

"To keep you honest. Even your old man didn't trust you."

"We had our differences," Thompson said, "but not when it came to banking."

"We had our differences, too, your father and I. He began to sour on real estate. Sadly, that became an issue for the partners after a while."

"You mean … my father really didn't … fall …?"

"Oh, I believe he did, and rather hard," Sterling joked.

"You bastard!" Thompson stepped toward him.

"Wait a second," Sterling said firmly, and Thompson halted. "I was just as shocked as anyone. I only found out later, when the big one, Hardy, came by one afternoon to ask about you—if you could be trusted. I said, 'Of course.' And he replied, 'Good, then. Mr. Walker said it would be a shame if anyone else happened to lose their step and fall.'" Sterling shook his head, then smirked, "That Hardy, always has a way with words."

Porter noticed Thompson's vein suddenly bulge in his right temple, like it had in Leo's.

"Those bastards murdered my father! And you did nothing?" Thompson shouted.

"I protected you and yours," Sterling said calmly, "and me and mine. I think his words were clear. I didn't need an interpreter or have to form a committee. They apparently feared what your father might do, and so they did what they do to people they fear—they strike first. I really don't know what else I could have done at the time, short of leaping off of Parson's Drop or blowing *my* brains out?"

"So you dragged me into it?" Thompson began to fidget and pace in anger, cussing under his breath.

"Settle down, Thompson," Sterling said. "We're in the thick of it, but it is winding down."

"Was there anything else he said?"

Sterling shook his head, "What more needs to be said?"

"Off the top of my head, I'd say you're going to jail, Sterling," said Porter, "for starters."

"Ha! Porter! I almost forgot that you're still alive, let alone here."

"Ha! Sterling," he replied with sarcasm, "I was still deciding whether to rip off your arms and beat you over your head with them, or maybe just punch you in the face. But now I'm thinking jail time would be best."

"Really?" Sterling mocked him. "So tough—who's going to arrest me? Liam? He's on salary and he doesn't even know it. Who's going to prosecute me? The D.A.? He's also my attorney. This whole town has benefited from the rum trade by looking the other way. Hell—the entire country has! It's America—it's how America operates. It always has and it always will!"

"I have a friend or two who's waiting to hear a story, a story about what's happening up here. They're government men, with bright, shiny badges."

"How are you going to tell them your story? Even if you could, it's your word against ours." He pointed at Thompson, who was now, suddenly, his good friend. But Thompson shook his head no, and stepped away from him.

"They know most of it already, Sterling. The radio transmissions. That was a nice touch. Keeping your buyers informed before the bodies were even found. Absolutely brilliant!" Porter smiled, and added, "They've been listening for a while."

"Radio transmissions?" Sterling hesitated, genuinely befuddled. Then he remembered what Hardy had said to him on the dock, but had put the thought out of his mind the moment he had said it. He glanced at Thompson, who stared back with a blank expression, but then flinched. "You double-crossing, stupid bastard." Sterling slammed his hands flat on the desk. "Damn you, Thompson," and slammed his hands again. "I've got no one to blame but myself," he shouted. "Do you know why?"

"Please, do tell," Thompson smiled meekly.

"I've listened to your ranting and raving these past years since they tossed your old man away like the withered plant he was," Sterling yelled, "and long ago concluded you have nothing but shit for brains. You're a devious little prick—even your father despised you, like your own son does today. I see that now. Why he kept you out of the business."

"Are you done yet, Sterling?"

"You know, I can understand why you despise this man so," Sterling continued, pointing at Porter. "After all, he *did* fuck your wife."

199

Thompson snarled menacingly at Sterling. "You fuck!"

"Wait a second," Porter said. "It's not like that. It was ships passing in the night. He and Penny barely knew each other—hell," Porter looked at Thompson, "you weren't even married at the time."

"Well, they were when *I* fucked her, Porter!" Sterling said, and burst out laughing.

"Oh really, Sterling?" At the words, Thompson snapped. Veins bulged out of his temples and neck in rage. Porter would never forget the look— his eyes went loopy—the man was completely unhinged. "Let me tell you, the radio transmissions were merely an insurance policy, just as this is."

It happened so fast, Porter wasn't even sure it happened. He didn't have a second to respond to Thompson's move, not even flinch. Sterling didn't either, but he was also laughing like a crazy bastard. In fact, not only did Porter doubt Thompson had the move in him, it was so fast that if the move had been directed toward him, it would have been Porter, not Sterling, laying face down on his desk with a bullet through the side of his head. In a seamless motion, Thompson had pulled a revolver from his coat pocket, placed the barrel up to Sterling's temple, and pulled the trigger, while Sterling was still laughing like a lunatic.

There was also the added problem of the revolver and how it was now pointing in the direction of Porter.

Thompson let a deep sigh and smiled with a sense of satisfaction. "That was refreshing."

"I'd say he went out with a bang," added Porter.

"He deserved that, you know."

Porter nodded. "First the goon squad, then Flo, then you—strike three, as they say in the old ballgame—I'd say this was not Sterling's night—he was a wanted man."

"Oh, you're a funny man, Porter."

"It's kept me sane," he replied, "through the tribulations."

"Yes, the tribulations." Thompson waved the gun at him. "Now, what am I going to do with you, Porter?"

"We could have a talk, maybe, over a drink. Figure a way out of this mess."

"I'm thinking that maybe I'd like to figure it out on my own."

The gun was leveled on him now, and Porter had a sudden urge to shit himself.

"And I'm thinkin' I'll be pullin' this trigger," a voice interrupted them from behind, "if you don't drop that snub nose now." Both men turned to the doorway. The voice was Irish. Porter swallowed hard. He noticed the scar above the eyebrow immediately, the eyebrow on the forehead attached to the head and body of the gunman, the gunman from Fran's in Boston. He was standing there now, before him and Thompson, holding a very large gun. The bastard had actually tracked him down, Porter thought. What an unbelievable fucking night. If shit could repel a bullet, he was fit to let fly and try.

A Moment of Truth

Thompson studied the man for a moment, weighing his options, or so Porter thought, until Thompson lowered the gun, and asked, "Malachi?"

The man nodded, but waved his gun in the direction of Sterling. "Go stand beside him, by the chair," he said. Thompson looked confused, and hesitated. "Do it, man." He raised the gun at him, and added, "Do it *now*."

Thompson moved slowly, unsure. "It doesn't have to be this way, Malachi," he said, nervously.

Malachi rolled his eyes. "Drop that gun next to him," he said, "on the desk there, and then step away from it."

Thompson breathed a sigh of relief. "I thought ..."

"I know what you thought," he said. "If that were the case, I would have skipped the introduction all together."

"What about *him*?" asked Thompson, pointing at Sterling.

"'So are the ways of everyone who is greedy of gain,'" Malachi answered him. "'It takes away the life of its owners.'"

"Proverbs," said Porter thoughtfully.

"Chapter 1, verse 19," he answered. "Me best friend's a priest."

"He must be a wise man," said Porter.

"He *was* the bar-of-gold of our clan, if truth be told," he said, "until this bastard got him killed." He holstered his gun and walked over to Sterling. "A true toerag if there ever was." He looked over the body. "I'd spit on the langer, but we must keep up appearances."

"Appearances?" Thompson said.

"That the bastard did himself in, Thompson," said Malachi. "Are you daft? What else? In case you've forgotten, you just murdered a man. For your own sake, it's best you leave the scene with the air of self-explanation other than the actual murder you just committed." He picked up the gun from the desk, examined it, walked to the window and fired it into the night. Porter and Thompson jumped. Malachi laughed and walked back. "That will take care of another problem for Sterling," he said, and wiped the gun down with a handkerchief, fit Sterling's limp hand around it, then let the gun drop to the floor.

Thompson, unsure, looked at Porter, and said, "What about him?"

"What about *him*?" Malachi walked over to Porter, took the measure of him.

"It would *appear* he's a witness," said Thompson.

"It would appear so," Malachi answered Thompson, "but so am I." He continued to gaze at Porter, and said, "It's been my experience when a weapon is discharged in a small space, a room, filled with people, most duck or dive for cover in shock and fear." He paused, continuing to study Porter. "Of course, at that point, it's too late to duck. The bullet has already found its way along its intended path or some poor bastard's walked into it. But you didn't even blink that night at Fran's. You watched as though it were a moving picture on a big screen. You were the perfect witness to a heinous crime. Then outside, on the street, what I saw." He shook his head slowly in disbelief. "It was a moment of truth. And I've been thinking about it ever since. Now, I have to know. *How*—what happened—did you *survive*?"

Porter stared into the man's eyes. They were dark and as hard as coal, but there was a luster deep within, too. Shining and searching for an answer. Porter knew the look. He saw it every time he shaved, every time he combed his hair, brushed his teeth. Every morning, he looked in the mirror and wondered why—how *did* he survive? The tragedy and sorrow, the endless wandering, a journey without end, a life in search of an answer to its unfathomable fate, fortune and chance—Porter saw it in his own eyes and could see it in his. "It's not within my grasp, what happened then, or what's happened since," Porter said. "But nothing has, for so long, I can't remember."

"But what I saw happen outside of Fran's," he said. "Many years ago, it happened to me, something similar."

"Then you know," said Porter, his eyes widened. "You saw *her*—the burst of lightning."

He nodded, "Something of that sort, yes. You in the street, a brilliant flash, the car spin, its front end left smoldering, but I don't know what. I don't know how you survived."

Porter shrugged his shoulders slightly, unsure of what to say. Finally, he confessed, "Really, I don't know how I survived tonight, because that bastard was okay with seeing me dead," he pointed at Sterling, "And I'm pretty sure that bastard would like to see me dead—period." He pointed at Thompson.

"Such are those men," said Malachi. "But they are not one of us—those who live on borrowed time."

Delivered Again

The Dodge slowed when it approached the Buick, and stopped at the driver's window. "Sterling?" a woman's voice whispered. She studied the car another moment, as if to be certain what her own eyes saw were true. There really was no one inside it. She then drove around the Common and parked up the street. Murton saw and heard it all, because he was standing at the alley's edge, in the dark shadows, at the corner of the building, shaking, yet relieved. Miraculously, he had been delivered from the Angel of Death once again.

But why?

Hardy was fit to dispose of him, and he figured that was the main reason he had been brought along after all. The need for a patsy? To lay this all on him? Or, maybe, Hardy had simply lost faith in him and his will to do what the business demanded of him. Too much philosophy, too much of a conscience. Edinburgh had changed him. The dirty little job that he didn't even do. That they had tried to force him to do—murder. There was a consequence for that. He knew, and now Hardy did, too. For the thing had come for him, like the others. Leaving Murton in shock and horror again.

The man? Who was the man? The one Mr. Calvin had pummeled and left in the alley earlier that night?

Murton felt Hardy had showed some regret, at least he'd been willing to say his piece—why he had to do what he had to do. He had seen it in his eyes, in the dim light of a lamppost.

And then Murton had uttered those words, that stark question, "Then what about you?"

Hardy had paused, immersed in the logic, or the madness of it all. But he'd raised the gun anyway. Murton had gripped the wheel in anticipation, braced himself for the bullet, the end. His hand and mind had gone numb.

He'd felt nothing but acceptance. At peace and ready for deliverance into the hands of the monster.

Then *he* fired, the other man. Put the bullet right into Hardy's brain. He was just ... *there*. Out of nowhere, he was standing in the frame of the car window. "My friend was a wise man," he had said to Murton, who was gasping for his breath, overwhelmed and in shock, "too wise for a priest. He would often say that in every fallen man there is a spark of redemption waiting to ignite, deep within, if, somehow, someway, he is given a chance." Irish by the tone of his voice; from Dublin, Murton guessed. The Irishman had stepped back from the car window. Murton had glanced at the scar on his forehead and back at the revolver leveled at his head. Between them, Hardy shook involuntarily and finally calmed. "I heard enough to know whatever you meant to this man, and who he works for, it's over. You're not part of the plan, if you ever were. So in the name and memory of my dear late friend, Father Kelly, consider this your chance and be gone forever." Murton had begun to nod slowly, had tried to speak, but then the unspeakable happened. He caught the shadow in the corner of his eye and blinked at it. His eyes went back for Dublin, but he was gone, vanished. The monstrous thing had arrived for Hardy, just like he'd seen in Edinburgh and earlier that night for Mr. Calvin. It was all Murton could do to open the door of the Packard and run. He'd sprinted down the alley, unnerved, and stopped only when he saw the headlamps of the car approaching.

"*Why?*" he thought, breathing desperately. He could only wonder. "Why ... damn-well make sense of it all?" He recalled the name, Father Kelly. The priest Smith, Hardy and Mr. Calvin had visited. Murton got it. A determination struck him—an awareness. He would take the chance offered. From a stranger ... a hunter ... a man of vengeance. With a deep breath, he returned to the Packard. Hardy was dead. Limp and powerless now, small amounts of brain matter protruded like wilted cauliflower out of his head and across the front seat. Murton stared ... dragged to hell, the murderous bastard he was ... Hardy. But not him, not Murton. A spirit overwhelmed him—a positive surge—leaving him weightless. He studied the corpse. Reached into Hardy's breast pocket, felt for his billfold. Emptied it but for a few notes, then placed it back in his jacket. He thought of the bag in the trunk, the one Hardy left the bank with. He went for it. Opened the trunk and reached in. He picked up the bag and gawked with anticipation at the wads of cash. But just as suddenly, he dropped it.

His mind raced. It was too hot. Right now, he was presumed dead. His coat and papers were on the boat. If he took the bag, *they* would know otherwise. *He* would be hunted down just like Burke by someone just like Hardy, or worse, like Mr. Calvin. Instead, he settled on a couple wads of cash, stuffed them in his pocket. He closed the bag, but picked it up. There was another way. He shut the trunk and walked away with it in hand. Later, when he counted out the $1,722, from Hardy's wallet, he was stunned—couldn't believe the amount he was carrying. Wondered—did the bastard skim? All the better, he thought, if that's what Mr. Walker thought. The wads of cash equaled $10,000. With that and Hardy's money, he could buy a house or a life … anywhere!

Murton went back down the alley, and stopped at its edge. The night, all around him; a still, quietude … *No—someone is there.* He peeked around the wall and up the street. The woman was in her car. Her fingers tapped the wheel, but only for a moment longer. That was because the silence was shattered. A gun fired, a single shot, from the floors above him. She jumped from her car, panic-stricken, and raced down the street toward him. Then he heard another shot and really wondered what was happening above. Only when she had entered the building, did Murton walk up to the Buick. With nonchalance, he opened the trunk and placed the bag in. There was shouting above, commotion, and then a scream. He shut the trunk quietly, turned and walked up the street, away from the place. Leaving his past there with the sordid life he had always known.

Orphaned

She screamed, as people often do, in a moment of shock, horror, agony or pain—especially when all strike at once. Malachi knew the sound well, and what it signaled. The loss, the gaping hole, a sudden explosion in the middle of your soul. The pitch, the shrill sound, was deafening. In this moment, all four emotions were in play. She was losing it. It shook him.

He and Porter grabbed her by each arm, lifted and held her in free suspension. Her legs ran in place. She kicked and struggled. They carried her out of the office, all the way downstairs, and outside. They let her down gently. She wailed and screamed, threw a desperate tantrum into the night, in front of the building. The sorrow was painful to hear.

Malachi looked upon the creature before him. Porter was comforting her, and he turned away from the sight, and began to edge away. He noticed Thompson standing a short distance from them, glancing up the street. That was the direction the car came from, a sheriff's car, its single blue dome light flashing on its rooftop. Abigail stopped wailing, looked up at Thompson, and said, "You bastard."

"You really *were* sending the radio transmissions?" Porter asked Thompson.

He nodded and pointed at Abigail, "She told me what I needed to know."

"You blackmailed me," she snapped.

"I gave you a choice—public scandal or give me information. You chose wisely, Abigail. You protected your family." Abigail spat in his direction.

"You got about thirty seconds to level with me, Thompson, or my friends with shiny badges will be coming for *you* next," said Porter.

"Oh, really?"

"Really!"

Thompson looked back at the sheriff's car, bearing down on them. "I'll call your bluff, Porter, and tell you this much. I wanted nothing to do with the mess I inherited, and those thugs Sterling thrust upon me, having me hold his ill-gotten gains ... not my doing. Thank her landlady," he pointed at Abigail, "one of my good customers. Mrs. Fontaine set me straight about Abigail and Sterling, how deep their relationship went. A busybody she is, that woman. Has a habit of going through her tenant's mail when she's housecleaning."

As the car was pulling up, Abigail moaned, "You're gonna rot in hell."

"I saved your life, Abigail, from those beasts," Thompson shouted, "and from that son-of-a-bitch upstairs."

Porter held her tighter and whispered softly, "There's no time, and much depends on this fact—I'm not a party to this and neither are you, what happened upstairs. But if we speak out, *we* will own that which is not ours—you found Sterling that way—the way you *found* him—understand ... dear child? You know nothing about his dealings, none of us did—do you *understand?*"

Abigail sobbed uncontrollably, and squeezed Porter's hand. He soothed her as an orphan. Only later would he find out how true that was. Flo would tell him of a letter she received from Abigail's mother, recently deceased. A letter of forgiveness and hope—a hope for understanding and forgiveness for deception. It was not intended to be. It simply happened— lust. Flo dumped it on him after Sterling's funeral. The world had gone to shit by then, and was completely undone. Redfern continually pressed him for *truths*. Aunt Effie and Uncle Stu were crushed at the loss of Mr. Perkins but at the same time, overjoyed by Grace and Caroline's arrival. Jeffah had been arrested for smuggling. Considering the mess that was the body of a thug named Calvin—there was no other name found—in what remained of his boat, it was a blessing they had only charged him with smuggling. There was also the slug they carved out of Calvin. It was fired by the gun they'd found in the hand of a man lying across the front seat of a Packard, which was parked out behind the Custom House. The man, a big, hairy bastard with a thick moustache, lay there, across the front seat, because of a bullet lodged in his skull by the likes of Sterling Huxley. That's what was said. The man's identification read Finlay Tamhas Hardy and he, also, was a thug. There was a third man, too. A scalawag named Lewis Murton, presumed dead. A coat, singed and burned, was found washed ashore near the *Catherine*, with his wallet in the pocket. More than scorched, there was a bullet hole through it and bloodstains. All three men fit the description of the men Porter had seen that Hallowe'en day, walking from Crowe's Trust. The big, hairy one, the mean-looking bastard, was the one who held the door at the Silent Woman Tavern for the moll—the Angel of Death or his guardian angel? That mystery eluded Porter. Much like Malachi, who, upon hearing the words Abigail yelled at Thompson, disappeared. He was nowhere to be seen when the police arrived. Was he ever even there? No one would ever ask, because no one knew *to* ask. Porter wished he'd taken Malachi's cue and slipped away. But, instead, he held Abigail, comforted her, and protected her. She, the orphan.

Thompson and Porter had the sense to answer the questions directly when they were asked. They got out of Abigail what they could, or she just nodded.

That was because they found Sterling, Abigail's father, the way they did, upstairs. He had gone astray, and you'd know soon enough just how far, thank you, and rather than answer for it, he simply ended it.

A New Day

Near dawn, in the Catholic canon, All Saints' Day. An important one. Porter's hands were buried in his pocket. Before him was an empty space where the caravan had been parked, but was no more. After he had answered as many questions as they could throw at him, the police let him go, for now. He had been sitting there with Liam McO'Fayle, in his office, and a very serious man named Denton, Deputy Denton, from the Sheriff's Office, whose line of questioning was fast approaching an apoplectic seizure. He had a case. They were finding more bodies around town than there was room for in the morgue. Unfortunately, he didn't have a case against Porter, try as he might to connect the dots. Yet, somehow, in the Deputy's mind, Porter had everything to do with it. He knew all about him. He was a subversive, a radical Sacco-and-Vanzetti type—a finger-flicking, Commie bastard know-it-all. Well, he was a caged bird now, and he wasn't flying anywhere. Even though Porter had shown the credentials Lillian had given him, Deputy Denton continued to treat him as a prime suspect of some kind and continued to question him. There were no other suspects, certainly not the other two people with him outside of the Custom House. Neither the pillar of the community, Thompson Crowe, nor the grief-stricken young woman named Michaud, were suspect. There was a good possibility Porter would have still been sitting there now, listening to the Deputy's charges and accusations, or locked up, if not for the phone on Liam's desk ringing out suddenly, which had the remarkable effect of shutting the Deputy up. Liam, who had the sense to inquire of Porter's credentials, answered the phone and handed it to Deputy Denton, who said, "Yes, sir," cursed loudly, nodded, said, "Good-bye, sir," and hung up. "Don't leave town," he barked at Porter, and shooed him away. The directive came through the Coast Guard command to the Maine State Police to the County Sheriff's Office to Liam, to cooperate with Special Agent Porter Gibson in his investigation of illegal smuggling in the region, rather than interfere or detain him.

Porter went out to Flo's car and drove off. His intention was to return to Huxley Manor, to find Jeffah, and deliver the news about Sterling to Flo. But his thoughts were jumbled and his intentions became muddled. In his mind's eye, the past day slammed into him in shock waves, repeating, over and over. He must have thought to go back whence it began. Because, along the way, he had veered off the road to Huxley Manor, and headed toward her. The car rolled to a stop in the clearing and he stepped out. He wanted to speak to Viola, needed to. He had to let her know she was right about seeing him again, but so much more than that—the danger—and about *her*—his Guardian Angel of Death.

But Viola was gone.

Standing in the clearing, he turned completely around, slowly, looking and searching for something—anything—she may have left there for him. But there was nothing but a charred fire pit, shadows, and a mist— whirling, rising, dithering. "Where are you?" he shouted out. "Were you even here?" he sighed deeply. "Is *anyone* listening?"

The dog whimpered, right then. Porter heard it, but was certain that *it* was not real, or nothing was and would ever be again. It *had* to be his imagination. For if he did hear it, then reality, what it was meant to be, or the construct as represented and how he had always comprehended it, was, at best, a false narrative or even an illusion. Or—that really *was* Mr. Perkins.

The Way of Espionage

Just before midnight, the notion struck her to leave. That was soon followed by an overwhelming sense of danger—for herself. She would have stayed for him—to lead him out of there—take him with her—if he'd go. She was leaving the next morning, anyway. The journey through America was over, and she was returning home. Her father had made arrangements for her passage. A ship in New York was set to depart 14 November, for London and Hamburg. There was much to do before then, however. Now that her assessment of Fort Norumbega, Fort Knox, and the other coastal fortifications down east were completed, the next step was to make her way south along the coast of Maine to Bath. There, she would observe and photograph the Navy Yard, then on to Portsmouth, to do the same at that Navy Yard. That would finish her reconnoiter of coastal New England. Finally, she would assess the Navy Yard in Brooklyn. After that, she would meet with her late aunt's family—the Garrigues—from Brooklyn, where she would receive their condolences for the loss of *her* mother. Her stay with them would be short. She would meet the Czechoslovak chargé d' affaires and pick up diplomatic pouches to deliver to Prague. In London, she would meet with her cousin, Jan, the Ambassador to Great Britain for Czechoslovakia, and the son of the country's President, Tomaš Masaryk, her uncle and husband to her Aunt, Helen Garrigue. Their talk would be chit-chat at first, catching up on gossip and family news, before an in-depth discussion and briefing on the current state of international affairs, the economy and the depression worldwide. Upon her departure from London, she would set sail to Hamburg, where, upon her arrival, she would take careful note and many photographs of the harbor, port and its facilities. From there, she was to take the train to Prague, where she would meet with a secretary from the Foreign Ministry to deliver diplomatic pouches from Jan and the American chargé d' affaires, and to be debriefed on her stay in America. Next, she would visit her father at the British Embassy, where he served in the Foreign Office. They would make their way to the Café Louvre on the opposite bank of the Vltava River. They would sit in the corner table where they always do, drink pivo and dine on wild boar. She would discuss with him her travels in America, her many observations, and report her findings on the coastal fortifications and Navy Yards along the northeastern seaboard of America. "Nothing sinister," her father would say, "merely updating the catalog." She would then deliver her report and impressions on the Port of Hamburg. "Profoundly sinister, my dear," he would add, "a fine acquisition to the catalog, indeed." Madam Luna made no pretense of what she was. She had the gift of *sight* in so many ways. She had resolved early on to share what she knew with family first, before country—all three of them.

Viola had just rolled up the awning on the caravan, and was about to douse the fire, when she noticed a little girl dressed as an angel standing on the edge of the fire's light. There was a dark stain on her tunic and, as Viola approached her, she saw it was blood.

"Please help," the little angel shouted. "My Mommy, she's been hurt. A hobgoblin came after us and hurt her. She's bleeding." The girl turned and bolted. Viola followed her through a wooded path and, shortly, she came upon a woman on the ground, her back against a tree, bleeding down her forehead, across her face, and onto her chest.

"*Jesus Maria*," Viola whispered. "Can you hear me?"

The woman moved her head, and spoke, "Lucy?"

"Yes, Mommy?" the little angel said.

"My Lucy," she said, and raised her hand and touched the girl's cheek. "My little angel."

"Your angel brought me here," Viola said. "Where are you hurt? Can you tell me?"

"My head," she said. "It's on fire."

Viola tore a section of her own shirt off and used it to pat the woman's face gently. The blood was coming down through her scalp. "If you can stand, we'll walk to my caravan, and we'll take a good look at that wound."

"Wound, yes," the woman responded to the word. "We were shot at. I stumbled and tripped. It saved our life."

"I can see it did, dear," said Viola. "A millimeter lower and ... well ... tsk-tsk."

Viola pulled at her, and the woman, with effort, pushed up. On her feet, she staggered. Viola took her balance, placing her arm around her shoulder. They made their way back to the caravan, where Viola was able to clean and dress the wound. The bullet had grazed the top of her skull. It was deep, but not deep enough that she thought it would be a problem. The woman, who told Viola her name was Cecilia, explained what had happened behind the church, and how she picked up her daughter and ran for their lives. She begged Viola to leave. They needed to go to a place called Auburn, far from here. That she was certain the hobgoblin of a man was after them. Viola agreed, she could feel the danger. She poured Cecilia a heavy glass of slivovice and forced it on her. To Viola's surprise, she drank it, without a cough. She then laid Cecilia across the back seat of her car and put Lucy in the front with her. After thoroughly dousing the fire, the three of them, caravan in tow, drove off.

Parting Souls

Movement, there, in the shadows—or is it the mist? Is it getting heavier? A fog rising? No! His eyes were playing tricks? He rubbed them, and looked once more at the same spot. The dog whimpered again, he spun around, searching, saw only shadows and mist swirling. The darkest hour was still upon him, Porter thought. Dawn could not come fast enough. He shouted, "No!" Unbelieving, even when he saw him take form with his own eyes. Even when he stepped into full view, out of the shadows, wearing his dirty, stained baseball uniform; and Mr. Perkins, too, beside him, whimpering with joy and wagging his tail—Porter was in disbelief.

"Hello, Porter." Scoop Comeau smiled.

Porter gasped and nearly choked. Scoop's eyes were black and blue and purple. The front of his uniform was stained in dirt, grass, and ... blood around the collar. His skin was pale, nearly chalk. The side of his head was bruised and cracked. A trail of blood, out the side of his left ear, snaked down to his neck and spread like a delta. It was dry. That's how it dried that day. Porter remembered.

"Don't shit yourself, old-timer," Scoop said. "This isn't real. Just ask

Mr. Perkins here." He patted the big Newfie's head affectionately, and the dog returned the greeting with a yelp and flapped his paw, which left a smoky, sparkling trail in the ether. "Don't worry, Mr. Perkins. You're gonna be all right. I'll always be with you."

"I'm so sorry, Scoop," said Porter.

"Ah, don't be, Porter," he replied. "That blonde was hot. I'd a been gawkin' at her, too, if I'd a seen her."

"I missed the hit and run."

"She was an angel."

"But you died."

"It only hurt for a second, and then a stream of light came, a shade of purple. That set me straight, I'll tell you."

"I missed the sign because of her."

"You'd of missed the pitch, anyway. 98 mph spit ball—fucking, cheating Pumpkin Slayer."

"But you're dead."

"I know. My mother took it hard. I think it's gonna kill her. That or her cooking, one of the two, will be her end. It put my father in the ground—her cooking—turned his arteries to calcified bacon fat."

Porter laughed. "You bastard."

"Yeah, I'm guilty of that, too. But I'm a good bastard, a nice bastard. The Karl thing wasn't held against me."

Porter shook his head. "Wait. Is … is this real?"

"No, I just told ya, this isn't real. How can it be? Reality is too, well, relative." He rubbed Mr. Perkins's head and chin. "Ain't that right, big fella?" The dog whimpered excitedly and raised his paw again, which Scoop shook. "Boy, are we gonna have fun."

"A ghost, then?" asked Porter. "A phantom?"

Scoop laughed at the question. "It *is* Hallowe'en—the night the dead walk the earth."

"Wait! You said 'an angel,'" Porter blurted out. "A minute ago, you said she was an angel?"

"I'm disappointed, Porter. You're lagging in the conversation," he smiled.

"She *was* an angel?"

Scoop nodded yes.

"I saw her in the stands—that moment … before you …"

"Playful, isn't she? Showing herself in all those ways and places. You kept her pretty busy today. It's tough to get your attention, unless it's a sweet-looking dish."

"You *saw* her, *too?*"

"Not when I should of. Because if I had of, I would have stopped running like you stopped thinking, and you wouldn't be imagining this now."

Porter lowered his head. "I'm so sorry, Scoop. I lost my focus. I fucked up. I got you killed."

"You're not to apologize, Porter, again."

Porter raised his head, looked him over, and said, "Scoop, you're a fucking mess."

"Looks like you're the mess, Porter—a fucking mess." Scoop placed his hand on Porter's shoulder. Porter shut his eyes, braced himself. He expected to feel ice, to be stung—for the chill of the dead to pierce his soul. Take him aloft on a starry ride through an unending night. But no. Calm, instead, spread through him, over him—a warmth—soothing—cathartic. Scoop whispered, "No more," and lowered his hand.

Porter's head cleared. His spirit lifted. His eyes opened. He was awake and felt the world anew. There was Scoop, as he knew him. Handsome, young, square jaw, the ballplayer, in a clean uniform, eager to play the game he loved. No bruises, no blood, unscathed—happy and aglow with life. A single tear welled up in Porter's eye and rolled down his cheek. He smiled. Mr. Perkins wagged his tail like a puppy, leaving brilliant stardust tracers in the air. The Newfie leaned into Porter, nearly pushed him over, and whimpered with joy. Porter rubbed his head and neck. "So much love, my old friend."

The mist now had turned to a heavy fog, and began to rise up, in and around where Scoop stood. It formed around his ankles. At first, like wisps of smoke, then it crept slowly, heavier and thicker, over his calves and thighs, ever rising as he spoke. Scoop held up his hand. "There is no coincidence, Porter." The fog was now above his waist. "Once upon a time, many years ago, I was told that. Funny thing, though, I heard what the person said. The problem was, like most, I just didn't listen. People don't listen," he shrugged. " *Why?* When the heavens speak, when the universe talks to you—listen—it's not so complicated. You need to *listen*, Porter." The fog was now billowing around him, and had nearly consumed him. "Do you know who told me that, Porter?"

Porter shook his head. "Do I know her?"

"A gypsy woman," he smiled.

"I only met her last night."

"You've known her all along, Porter. She's been showing herself to you for some time, this one."

"I don't understand."

"You're on borrowed time, Porter ...," he hesitated, then whispered, "... Make the most of it, make a difference."

"The Angel of Death, Scoop?" Fog had enveloped him. "The gypsy woman? Do you hear me?"

"Listen, Porter," Scoop's voice faded. "Learn to *listen* ... There is no coincidence."

"Scoop ... Del ... I ... I," Porter shouted desperately, lunging through the fog and falling to the ground.

"Shush, Porter, you're talking to yourself. This isn't real."

"I ... miss you," Porter whispered, and rolled over on his back.

In the distance, a fog horn sounded and a car motored by. Mr. Perkins let one more playful yelp before he, too, faded into the shadows and fog. "Easy, boy," Porter whispered. Tears trailed down his cheek. Joy and sadness struck him. "That was just my imagination ... didn't happen ... isn't real."

All Saints' Day

Even for Liam McO'Fayle, the sight was gruesome. He had pulled fishermen out of water or picked them up on shore—some dead for weeks—bloated, greenish-gray and covered in piss clams, snails, crabs and strands of seaweed. He had gone into the forest to retrieve a hunter, casually mistaken for an eight-point buck, innards displayed like sausage at the butcher. But this was unholy, diabolical and profanely sacrilegious. On this All Saints' Day, at 7:30 in the morning, he found himself, with his two deputies, before an old oak tree behind the rectory of Saint Patrick's Church. They were waiting for the coroner and the County Sheriff. They were also looking up, bewildered and mortified. At their feet, autumn leaves whooshed and rustled around the ground in the cool, crisp air, unnoticed.

That was thirty minutes ago, and Liam was still searching for answers. He looked for evidence or clues, anything, but the imagery was too disturbing, and it distracted him. He had sent his deputies to turn back the growing crowd of gawkers out on the street, and they were failing miserably. One deputy, a man named Russ that everyone called Stumpy. The story goes, he had lost a portion of his left thumb in an incident trapping fox as a boy—'When collecting the pelt, it is always best to make sure the fox is dead first,' his father had warned him, to no avail. The other deputy was a portly, talkative sort named Harvey. Though slow afoot and wit, he was reliable and determined, and had the uncanny ability to make a first impression a lasting impression. The two of them were all he had at the moment, and neither had ever been tested like this.

A Sheriff's car arrived, then another. Two constables relieved Stumpy and Harvey, and the men accompanied Sheriff Maddox and a deputy to the oak tree. "Morning, Liam," he managed to say, before he was engrossed by the body swinging before him. A minute or so went by, and then he asked, "Who found him?"

"Altar boy," Liam answered, "an hour ago, around seven. Can't imagine he'll ever be the same."

"No," Sheriff Maddox sighed. "It's a terrible thing."

Finally, the ambulance, a '26 Cunningham, motored up the street. The constables pushed the crowd aside and the driver pulled in the dirt drive between the church and rectory. Doctor Bradbury, family practitioner and county coroner, jumped out of the passenger seat, and immediately shook his head in disgust. The driver followed, carrying a camera.

"Liam, Sheriff Maddox," Doctor Bradbury nodded. "Sorry I'm late," he said, walking up to the men. "I've had a busy night." He looked up from toe to head and back, breathing a soft, "tsk-tsk," and shaking his head again in disgust.

"I'm hoping this is the last one," said Liam.

"Anyone talk to his housekeeper?" Doctor Bradbury asked.

"She left weeks ago with the girl," Stumpy answered.

"Can't be," said Doctor Bradbury. He was circling the body, studying it. He pointed to the body with his hand like he was practicing karate chops. "This angle, Randall," he said to the driver. "And then here and here," he directed him. Randall lifted the camera and began to snap pictures. "And make sure you get that," he pointed to the ground.

"Why do you say, 'Can't be,' Doctor?" asked Liam.

"The missus told me she and her girl were at the Hallowe'en Social at Central Hall last night," he replied.

"We need to talk to her, then," said Sheriff Maddox, looking at the rectory. "She a live-in?"

Liam nodded. "No one's home, though, I've been through the house. The beds are made. The house is tidy. The kitchen is immaculate."

"She said they were going back north on the late train—leaving for good—live with her sister or something," Doctor Bradbury said. "I guess she really left."

"Well, this is no way to leave a man," Harvey said.

"I don't believe she left him this way, Harvey," Liam said.

"You think it's a suicide, then?" Harvey asked.

Stumpy laughed, "Hell—why would anyone kill themselves over a housekeeper, Harvey?"

Liam rolled his eyes.

"Four bodies in one night," Doctor Bradbury shook his head.

"Any more and you'd lose count, eh, Stumpy?" Harvey said.

"Harvey!" Liam snapped.

"Sorry, Chief," he answered him.

"Four bodies," Doctor Bradbury repeated. "I never thought I'd ever see something like this in these parts."

"You think they're connected?" Harvey asked.

"Like Siamese twins, Harvey," the Doctor answered, then added, "I've seen enough. You seen enough Sheriff—Liam?" The men looked again, one last time. Above them, the body of Father Durrell swung gently from a limb. The priest hung by his neck, entangled around a vestment. The body creaked when it moved, or was that the limb? Liam was unsure; so was Sheriff Maddox. The way the body dangled in the tree, it was as though Father Durrell had been climbing it, in his vestment, and slipped and fell. If it wasn't for the appearance of the priest—he was bruised and beaten, vomit was down the front of him, and, because Father Durrell's feet were eye-to-eye with the men, they could see and smell the shit all over his shoes—the notion of slipping and falling might have been plausible—at least to Harvey. Why the man, a priest, would be climbing a tree in the middle of the night with his vestments on was another question. There was also the bottom of his shoes, which were singed and sooty. That was a result of the fire that had been beneath him. Embers still smoldered on the ground. Most disturbing was the shape of the embers, in an inverted crucifix, the length and width as large as the man above it in the tree.

"Okay, then," said Doctor Bradbury, "Go ahead and take him down."

1933, Late Spring

New York City Observations

The first time he sensed he was being observed was late one afternoon in the Grand Central Terminal. He was in the main concourse, near a kiosk in the middle of the great hall. Sunlight flooded the vaulted main room through the arched windows high above. The room, as it always is, was crowded. Porter was transfixed by the sunbeams, like divine shafts of light that spanned the entire length of the concourse. When he dropped his gaze, he noticed a man a short distance away, near the ticket counter, wearing a long coat and fedora, peering over the top of a newspaper. His back was to a ticket window; his eyes were fixed directly on Porter. Thoughts of the goons he had encountered last fall rushed through his head. Porter took one step toward the man to confront him, but was overtaken by a rush of commuters. When the crowd passed, the man was gone.

The next occasion was outside the Imperial Theater, where he'd just seen the Gershwin musical, *Of Thee I Sing*, for the third time. He was humming one of the numbers, 'Wintergreen for President,' and wondering how *they*—the writers—got away with the biting political satire that would have landed him in jail back in 1918, but landed them the Pulitzer Prize in 1932. He was hailing a cab when, directly across the street, he saw the tell-tale fedora and long coat peering over a newspaper. A bus went by, and that was the end of him.

And then, just minutes ago, on his way to the Equitable Building to meet with Redfern about the trial, Porter saw the man again, on the opposite side of the street, hat on and eyes peering over a newspaper, but Porter was overrun and distracted by a bum with a sign board for a *Reverend John Chapman's Salvation Center*. When he looked back, the stranger was gone. He reckoned it was time to speak with Redfern about it. Somebody was watching him.

About Tesla

"Good afternoon, Porter," Lillian said. Her desk was stacked high with file folders, some an inch thick. Envelopes and newspaper clippings were scattered in the shadows beneath them.

"Greetings, Lillian," he replied. Among the clutter, Porter noticed her ashtray, which was conspicuously empty of butts and filled with apples and figs.

"Nick convinced me," she said.

"Huh?" said Porter.

"I quit smoking two months ago," she jerked her head at the ashtray. "I use it now as a fruit dish. Waste not, want not."

"I've been meaning to ask about Nick," said Porter.

"He said he quit smoking in his early twenties to save his sister's life. He did it and she lived. He told me that was my choice, too, if I wanted to see 1939."

"Interesting, but what I meant was ..."

"It made me think, I tell you. He told me it would take thirty days, but the last twenty-nine days of the month are the hardest," she smiled.

"I was just *wondering* ..."

"When it comes to Tesla, we *all* are, Porter."

"Anything else?"

"Mr. Redfern is waiting for you." Her eyes darted toward the inner office door. "Go on in."

A Bleak Interpretation

"Lick your wounds, Porter," said Redfern. He lifted his tumbler of single malt, and sipped. "You uncovered quite an operation up there."

"Me?" Porter sighed. He let the words sink in, held his glass up, and shook his head no. "The door was wide open and I just wandered right in." He took a sip of Scotch. It was near empty.

"Allow me," Redfern said, and refilled it.

"Whoa! That's enough, Red."

"Can't help it—you know I'm a heavy-handed bastard," he smiled.

"That would be Sterling."

"Huh!"

"What he did. He had everything," Porter said. "Yet, it wasn't enough."

"He wanted more," said Redfern. "Greed, power. It makes a man's dick hard. It happens, to some, anyway." Porter nodded. "I'm sorry about your friend, Jeffrey, too."

"Yeah, well, about him, we need to talk some more, Red," said Porter. "He's really a fisherman and family man, you know, trying to make a living."

"Porter, I'm working on it."

"He's been locked up for over six months. He was a victim, not the perpetrator."

"I read your report."

"The man's got a family to support."

"That I know."

"Prohibition is over."

"Yes, thankfully, but not officially. It has to be ratified first with another Amendment."

"What are you gonna do?"

"I'm trying to cut a deal."

"But he needs to be released."

"He's in deep! His boat, what was left of it, was found by the Sheriff's Office *and* Coast Guard on Sterling Huxley's shoreline at low tide. Do I have to remind you about the charred body amidst a deck load of Cutty Sark in the charred shell of your said friend Jeffrey's boat? The body had its throat ripped open and a bullet hole in its chest. I know why the Coast Guard got the call, because a boat was on fire. Like any blaze in the middle of the night, it attracts considerable attention. I also know why the Sheriff's Office was there, because of the said body with a bullet in it. Need I remind you, it would turn out the bullet was fired from a gun found literally in the hand of a gangster from Boston named Hardy."

"Sounds to me like you got your man, then," said Porter.

"Well, *they* did, the Sheriff and his merry men, and delivered him to the county morgue. He was found in the front seat of a Packard behind Huxley's office building with a bullet in his head."

"They said it was murder-suicide," Porter said, innocently. "Why can't we just put Jeffrey on probation and let him go home?"

"Well, you never quit, I'll give you that."

"Would you?"

"Need I further remind you, Jeffrey's employer, Sterling Huxley—the man who allegedly murdered Hardy for God knows how many reasons ..."

"Really!" Porter interrupted him. "From what I hear there was over 175,000 reasons—in hard currency—found in the trunk of Sterling's car parked right out in front of his office!"

"Yes, but he, Sterling, was found the same night, inside, steps away from his purported victim, Hardy, in the said building, upstairs in the said office, from a purported self-inflicted gunshot wound to his head. On his desk were files of enough phony real estate transactions to falsify the true source of his revenues, which was smuggling liquor into the United States, as it turned out, for well over a decade. Among those files on his desk was one with Jeffrey's name on it, which could lead one to believe he, too, may have been about to or was dabbling into false real estate transactions, possibly in league with Sterling."

"Or more likely he was about to become one of his victims," Porter replied, "considering everything that had happened."

"Come on, Porter," said Redfern. "Let's be honest. Why would someone like Sterling have his bags packed with that amount of cash in his car like he was on his way somewhere, but then walk into his office and blow his brains out instead?"

"Maybe Sterling had an epiphany—Hardy's dead, he's got all this money—but he realizes there is really is nowhere to go—no way out—no place he can run to where Hardy's people or the law can't find him! It's no wonder he took the cowardly way out ... purportedly," Porter smiled.

"*Seriously*, Porter?"

"Come on, Redfern!" Porter pleaded. "Nobody really knows what was in Sterling's head before that bullet entered it. But I can tell you this much—it's hard to see how Jeffrey was participating, had any knowledge of, or was even benefiting from Sterling's real estate racket. He had nothing to do with any of that! There is no connection. He was just driving a boat. For God's sake, Sterling was the one plotting and scheming and killing people, not Jeffrey!"

Redfern took a deep breath and released it slowly, frustrated.

"And you neglected to mention that Jeffrey was ambushed with me, and we barely escaped with our lives. It would seem to me that those files were also a list, and Jeffrey was one of the names on it. He was a marked man."

Redfern shrugged, but nodded, "Look, there's no argument here, but what I touched upon, that's the prosecution's case, the way they've framed it. He was a part of the operation. That's what we're up against."

Porter sighed, and then asked, "What about that investment banker— Mr. Walker—have you put the squeeze on him?"

"First of all, it's not me—I'm not a part of the prosecution—I'm with you. Secondly, you know how many investment bankers and captains of industry own property up in your neck of the woods, Porter?" he said, incredulously. "The Rockefellers, the J.P. Morgans, the Henry Fords—the list goes on and on. Mr. Walker is of *that* ilk. He has legitimate land dealings up and down the coast and up in the Woods of Maine. That he hired one bad agent in one small town cannot be held against him. He's already written a deposition. As far as the district prosecutor goes, there's no case against him."

"It looks like the bastards have thought of everything, Red," Porter said with disgust.

"You're a good friend, Porter," Redfern said. "However innocent Jeffrey is, or you believe he is, on circumstantial evidence alone, your friend's in deep shit. He has a lot of explaining."

"That's a rather bleak interpretation."

"That's a best case scenario. That's what I'm dealing with."

"What are his chances? What am I supposed to tell his wife? What am I supposed to say?" Porter asked, agitated.

"Settle down. The trial is coming up and your testimony will help. Though, you will just have to decide what it is you're willing to testify to—the truth, the whole truth, and all that. Think about that. I've given you their position—you have to decide what it is you're going to say."

"You told me when I got into this, Red, I wasn't being sent to spy on my neighbors."

"Porter, even I couldn't have predicted it would turn out the way it did. Hell! One of your neighbors tried to kill you *and* your best friend. Remember *that* when you're on the stand."

Porter took a deep breath and exhaled slowly. Lost in thought, frustrated, he finally said, "What about me? What we talked about earlier?"

"On that front? I will have someone look into it. We'll know soon enough if you're being watched."

"Soon enough?"

"Yes, soon enough. I'll be in touch—or send you a message."

The Messenger

Porter stared blankly at the brick wall, studying the aged masonry that held the building together. Mortar cracked here, bricks chipped there and there. Words were in his head, many of them, but the ability to put them on paper in an orderly, meaningful way was not working tonight. Brown wanted another book out of him. After several months of wavering, another chance, with one condition—write a novel. "Tell a story this time instead," he had told Porter. "Bury the facts in fiction. The truth is better served that way." Porter wondered if the old bastard was daft, but liked the idea. He said, "Sure," as if he could actually do it. With all that had happened, he reasoned, maybe he could—or maybe not. For the past several hours, he had attempted to write a narrative—piece together a story about gangsters and gin and gypsies and ghosts. How the hell was he going to pull the pieces together—Viola, Scoop, Jeffah, the Angel of Death notwithstanding—put it into words? He came across a journal entry he had written in December—"When the Ghost Becomes the Haunted"—and realized then how bleak his options really were. He didn't need Redfern to dredge it up and put it in perspective.

He picked up a postcard lying on the corner of his desk. Looked at the castle, the ruins familiar, picturesque and enchanting—flipped it over, studied her handwriting—as feminine and exquisite as she was. How did she find him?

Out the studio window, he heard a dog bark below. He thought about his dog. Mr. Perkins. Gone.

He felt like shit.

A creak on the landing outside his door caught Porter's ear. Silence followed, and he was about to call out, when he heard the soft knock on the door. "Yes?" he answered. Before he could utter another word, the door opened. A man stood there, familiar by the scar alone.

"Malachi," Porter whispered.

"Indeed, Mr. Gibson," Malachi said. "Or do you fancy yourself Mr. Digit these days?"

"Porter will ..." but the question Malachi posed registered—hard. "How ...?"

"Suffice it to say, we run in similar circles, you and I." He looked around the room, but hesitated at the door.

Uncertain of what to say or do, Porter said, "Come in, Malachi," and indicated a chair against the wall. "Grab a seat."

Malachi brought the chair to the desk and sat down across from Porter. Eye to eye, he studied Porter for a moment or two. Slowly, carefully, he reached into his breast pocket. Porter's eyes bugged out in fright. Malachi took notice and laughed quietly, only to pull out a large flask.

"You bastard!" Porter breathed in relief.

"'Tiz true," he replied. "But I'm a good bastard, so it's not held against me."

"Wha-*what* did you just say?" Porter asked in disbelief.

224

"I said I'm a good bastard so it's not held ..."

"... That's what I thought you said," Porter interrupted him and swallowed hard. "Pardon me, it's just an old friend said that to me once. I thought I'd never hear someone speak those words again."

"Ah, fancy *that* coincidence," he replied, and flashed a grin. Porter swallowed even harder. "I understand you're a whiskey man. I hope you're okay with an Irish blend. I've lost my taste for the Scots."

Porter mouthed a, "Yes," but stared curiously at the man across from him, unsure what was happening. He mumbled, "Glasses," and pulled out two from his bottom drawer and placed them onto the desk across from Malachi. The glasses were smudged. One had a residue. "My cleaning lady comes Thursday," Porter smiled weakly.

"No worries," said Malachi. "I'd drink this from a shoe." He poured two heavy shots, and pushed one at Porter. He raised his glass and said, "*Sláinte!*" The men toasted and drank. Malachi quickly filled the glasses again. "Most excellent." He lifted his glass, took another sip, and placed it down. "A dear friend had this stashed away. His 'reserve,' he called it."

Porter cleared his throat as though to speak, but Malachi kept talking, "I hear you're a radical of sorts, Porter. Gave meaning to the finger in our day and age. A known aggravator."

Porter smiled, "No, I see myself as a writer, really, who happens to see the world through the eyes of the position I play in the game of baseball—a catcher."

"I'm afraid I don't really understand your pastime well enough."

"I'm a wicket-keeper, if that helps."

"Ah, it does," Malachi nodded. "You see the whole field at once, and face all who are there to play on it."

"That's the gist of it," Porter replied. "And the finger, if you want to get heady about it, is more a symbol of our age and ages past—from the ancient obelisks of Egypt, to the monument in Washington that bears his name, to that behemoth of a building on Fifth Avenue, the Empire, or better yet, the one on Lexington Avenue, the Chrysler. Each and every one, a stark example of what the Captains of Industry and Banking have in store for you and I, and that is to give us the shaft!"

Malachi laughed loudly. "I never thought of it that way."

"Few do, but I have thought about it deeply, and found a way to express it in a simple hand gesture and in my writing. Because of it, I'm labeled a Communist, an Anarchist, or a radical, as you say. None of it is true." Porter took a sip of whiskey, and then added thoughtfully, "If people don't wake up, if they continue to ignore the past, see no evil in the present, then our future is doomed. There will be another war, and a war after that, and someone else is always to blame ... Malachi, if I'm guilty of anything, if I've come up short anywhere, it's a failure to connect and make people *aware*, help them beat down the misery."

"You would not be the first to come up short or fail to connect or seek blame," said Malachi. "Truth be told, it's a tough thing for an Irishman not to blame the Brits for our misery, or misery of any kind."

"It's a tough thing for anyone not to blame the Brits for everything that's gone to shit on this planet, Malachi," Porter replied, "until you meet a Wall Street banker and one of his lawyers."

Malachi laughed again and settled down, enough to take another sip from the glass. "Well, I expect you want to know why I'm here."

"To tell me you've been following me around the city, I hope?"

"If I was I would tell you so," Malachi shook his head, "but I have not."

"Then why are you here?"

"To help you clear your head," he replied. "I understand you're in a quandary and confused about what happened and what to do. It's natural to feel that way. Try as you might, you can't pull the pieces together."

"Suppose that's true."

"It 'tiz," he replied. "You can't deny it. But, so you know, you probably never will be able to pull the pieces together."

"That's encouraging," Porter said.

"Real comforting, I know, and I'm just warming up."

"That's why you're here?"

"I was sent by Mrs. Banks, our mutual friend."

"Our mutual *friend?*" Porter's eyes widened.

He nodded. "She speaks fondly of you and wanted you to know about me, said it was about time."

"About *time?*" Porter leaned forward in his chair.

"It was she who had me watch over you just in case, be your guardian angel."

"My guardian *angel?*" he shouted.

"Are you going to repeat everything I say?" Malachi smiled.

Porter settled back into his chair.

"Keep your head, man," Malachi said. "It was the right call. Think! I walked into that speako, Fran's, and arrived there just in the nick of time."

"But how did you know?"

"I was on your tail from the station, that's how. He was there, too, playing solo, to my advantage. Those bastards usually hunt in packs. I followed him as he followed you and your man who greeted you..."

"... That was Brown, from the publishing house," Porter interrupted.

"I didn't know who he was, but it was a good thing Brown was with you—to your hotel, to lunch, to the park, and then after—until you finally parted company, and were alone, that's when you were vulnerable for the first time."

"Brown offered me dinner, and then drinks. He wanted to go to a dive called Webster's. It's far from Braves Field, and even further from my hotel. I declined. The beer's flat and the booze is watered down. I was tired anyway, and planned to hit the fart sack early. Besides, I wanted to be alone in my retrospection."

"Yeah, well, you were almost retrospect'd into oblivion. He followed you right out of the park to Fran's. I had to do what I did to save you. He was going to kill you right then and there. Make it look like an innocent bystander, I suppose, maybe shoot the bartender first. The man was a murderous hooligan. I'd only find out later that he worked for Hardy—a trusted colleague of his by the name of Smith—and was in on the murder of a dear friend of mine, a priest over in South Boston."

Flustered, Porter asked, "Why me? What the hell did I do?"

"Relax," he said calmly. "I believe it was because of your friend, Grant. When he asked Sterling to approve you helping out on that final run, Sterling agreed, but ..."

"... But he was ready to write me off, too?" Porter interrupted. "Kill me?"

"Don't you see," replied Malachi, "if you went there, you would have seen too much, heard too much, and known too much. The plan was to have your friend killed after the run—remember the tombstone deeds? When you signed on to help him, you signed your death warrant, too. Your friend knew nothing of how Huxley profited off the phony real estate deals, or the size and scope of the operation. Your man Sterling knew you would have pried into it—exposed him and the whole scheme. So he decided to eliminate you beforehand—an accident maybe, or even suicide you, seeing as how distraught and depressed you were over the loss of your friend, that other ballplayer. But that fella Smith was too eager for blood, and apparently had other plans for your demise."

Porter let the words sink in. Troubled and confused, he said, "It just doesn't make sense—what happened to the man. Sterling betrayed his own."

"In the world of greed, betrayal is routine," said Malachi. "Sterling crossed over when a man named Burke approached him with a bag full of cash in return for an address."

"What address?" said Porter.

"The sort of address the man Burke could not find in any directory, and one he had been seeking for some time. The address for a warehouse filled with liquor and cash, down on Cape Cod, a small town named Hyannis. Burke was intent on seizing it for himself, steal it away from its owners," said Malachi. "Owners you know all too well."

"Wait! You mean the place where the drop was made last August by Jeffah and his crew? That's what this is all about?"

"Yes," Malachi said.

"Sterling sold them out for that?"

"He did," said Malachi. "Unbeknownst to your man Jeff, the exact location had long been a secret. He happened to mention the town, offhandedly, to your man Sterling, when he returned from the run. Sterling must have known its value, because he turned around and sold it to this Burke fellow."

"And then he turned around and framed the crew of the *Catherine*."

"Yes, to Hardy ..."

"That goon, Hardy," Porter sighed.

"The one and the same," said Malachi. "It was his warehouse—well, the warehouse he was charged with operating and managing—that Burke hit. Hardy was getting close, very close, to sorting the mystery of who or whom screwed him out of a small fortune and killed his men. He found the thief easy enough—the first rat to jump ship—Burke disappeared and turned up back in Edinburgh. I'm told he and Hardy worked for a man there named Browne at one time—a true den of thieves and thugs, if there ever was."

"How did Sterling do it, if Hardy was that good?"

"Hardy *was* that good. He knew his shippers and he backtracked every shipment that ended up in his warehouse in Hyannis—from St. Pierre et Miquelon to Yarmouth, down to Black's Harbour and St. Stephen's. How did it get there? Who delivered it and when? The only shipment out of the ordinary, a singular instance, was made by the *Catherine*."

"Yes, Jeffah told me they made the drop right in port, rather than at sea," said Porter. "So, Hardy came knocking on Sterling's door because of it?"

"He did. Sterling started feeding him bullshit, and then bits of information through his secretary, his daughter, that woman we carried out of his office."

"Abigail Michaud."

"She had been forced to *spy* on him, her father, by the muttonhead, Thompson, who was blackmailing her for information about Huxley Industries. Thompson wanted out of the real estate game, and was looking for an advantage. He found that advantage in her. Unfortunately, it was a deadly game played by ruthless men. Thompson was over his head, and so was the girl."

"How do you know all this, Malachi?"

"The priest I mentioned, he saved my ass over in Ireland once upon a time—in fact, befriended three wayward souls lost in war, uprisings and death. I lost him to the same goons who invaded your town. I'm not going to get into it with you—it's too long a story. But my friend, his name was Father Kelly, went to Boston after the war. There, he stayed in touch with me, and the other two, a man you know of—Ambrose Hughes—and another you don't—Sam Pendleton. Those two were radio men during the war, naval intelligence. Ambrose ended up in your hometown, working at the Crowe Trust and Pendleton down on the Cape, at the old Marconi station."

"He works for RCA?"

"Ostensibly," he grinned.

"Huh?"

"He really works for a man named Solomon."

"I'm not going to ask."

"Don't bother. All you need to know is Father Kelly was pretty adept with the radio by the end of the war and, when the trouble began up in your hometown, Ambrose began relaying what was happening to Father Kelly, who passed it on to Pendleton. They had worked it out, the three of them, to pass information that way. Make it look like an intercept—keep it under wraps. Pendleton would then forward the information to Solomon. They were building a case, slowly, 'til they found a man with a bullet in his head. Then, time to have a look-see."

"So he picked me?"

229

"I thought you weren't going to ask?"

"I was wondering out loud," Porter shrugged. "That's all. Go on."

"What Father Kelly ignored was the possibility that the goons have radio men, too, which they do, and they intercepted one message from him to Chatham about a fisherman named Bailey, and they … found him." Malachi paused. Searched for words, "They finally tracked down the goon's radio, well, Tesla did, after they murdered Father Kelly. By then, Hardy and his other henchmen were … *retired*."

"That was the connection," Porter said.

Malachi nodded.

"All the while, Sterling would feed Abigail some kernel of bullshit," said Porter. "She would run over to Thompson with it, who would give it to Ambrose, to send it to Father Kelly, in the belief that he was sending it off to someone who could prosecute Sterling."

"I suppose, in a simplified way, yes. Sterling knew she was informing Thompson—he could have told her anything plausible."

"How did he know she was informing Thompson?"

"Because she told her father Thompson was blackmailing her over their relationship."

"Incredible."

"It surely is, even more that Thompson truly believed he could frame Sterling."

"They were party to murder."

"No. The messages were mixed warnings; people were in danger, at great peril, yes. Not until the last one was found shot in the head did they all realize the gravity of the situation they were all in."

"In what way, Malachi?"

"A man dies in a house fire, another one drowns. Those are accidents, despite the coincidence. But a fake suicide? Ambrose contacted me then. He feared for Father Kelly, but it was too late. That's about the time you signed on, and about the time I became your guardian angel. Again, you can thank Mrs. Banks for that."

"Extraordinary," said Porter. "And Ambrose was sitting on all this information all along?"

"He was sitting on a great deal of it, Porter." He tipped the flask again and added to the glasses. "Truth be told, I had to make sure, so I tracked down the girl."

"Abigail! You found her?"

"Yes, and she was very chatty."

"Where in God's name did you find her?"

Malachi took a sip of whiskey. Moments passed in silence. He stood and went to the window, looked up and down the street. Finally, with a glance to Porter, he said, "Where she belongs."

Amends

The end of another academic year, the campus was near empty of students, all was good at Bates College. The trustees were satisfied with President Gray's report. Enrollments were up; endowments were inching up, ever so slightly. The college was in the black. Still, no one would dare say if they had weathered the storm. No one knew if the storm had passed. Though, the atmosphere in Washington had changed since the election of Roosevelt. The President was invested in the welfare of the nation, expressed it in his weekly chats on the radio. Nevertheless, the people in Maine still fretted because everyone knew how fast the sky could fall.

And no one knew that more than Florence Huxley. When the sky fell on her the previous fall, after Sterling blew his brains out—she scoffed at the thought—she persevered, scandal and all, and moved forward. Oddly, she felt no sense of loss, did not grieve, over Sterling's death. How could she? After Jeffrey told her what had happened down on the wharf—steps from their own front door; after the police, sheriff, and Coast Guard descended on the mess on the waterfront, and when Porter came back that dawn, shaken and reeling, informed her of how the man had made illegal money clean through something called tombstone deeds. Then, on top of all that, he told her the last two names on the deeds—Jeffrey Grant and, incredibly, Abigail Michaud—and what Sterling had planned to do to them. No, there was no sense of loss for him. *She* was at a loss over how she could have been so wrong about him. Wondered if she ever really knew him. She took no solace that the entire community was at a loss, too, as much as the community actually knew—more gossip than facts—that a perceived pillar of the community could have been that diabolical. Sterling's plan that night, after all, was to leave and never return—how remarkable that he did just that!

How remarkable, for whatever reason, that he managed one act of decency, or one his father Jonah forced upon him. In 1924, he had established a very sizable trust for her and their girls, not *his* girls. The courts could not touch that property, which included the two houses and considerable funds.

Poor Abigail. How to right a wrong? Flo had left the trustee meeting determined to do just that. She turned on Frye Street, and parked in front of the house, a large, three-story Queen Anne, with a big front yard and wraparound porch. On the lawn, a handsome wooden sign, ornately hand-carved, and mounted between two wooden posts, read: *Michaud House, Boarders and Students Welcome*.

A child, a young girl, was playing in the yard. Flo smiled and said, "Hello," when she passed. The little girl giggled and waved to her.

Flo paused at the door, took a deep breath, and then knocked. The door was opened by a plain-looking woman, thirty or so, with dark hair and eyes, who greeted her with a smile. The woman glanced over Flo's shoulder at the child and back again to Flo. "Miss Michaud," Flo began to say.

"No, I am not Miss Michaud," the woman interrupted her, "I am her housekeeper." Her English was pronounced, with a French accent, not uncommon in the Lewiston and Auburn area.

"Who is it, Miss Giroux?" Abigail entered the room. At the sight of Flo, she stopped abruptly in her tracks and gasped.

"An old friend," Flo answered, "come to make amends."

The Message

"There's one more thing," Malachi said. He looked one more time, up and down the street, before he returned to his chair.

"What is that?" Porter replied.

"I'm here to add to your quandary—tell you that you were correct in your observation—you are being followed," said Malachi.

"What!" Porter shouted in a panic. "By who or whom?"

"That doesn't matter—the less you know, the better."

"Someone's after me and you're saying it doesn't matter?"

"I didn't say someone was after to you, only that you're being followed."

"Am I at risk, *again*?"

"There you are, being daft," Malachi smiled. "No, you're not at risk, you're too high profile, now, Mr. Finger-flipping, baseball-playing writer. They put someone on you, and I'd wager he let you see him, let you know you were being watched, get inside your head."

"Kind of like what you're doing to me?"

"Similar, but I have no intention of making your life miserable if you don't heed my advice."

"I don't even know what you're talking about, Malachi."

"It's simple, Porter. Sterling Huxley needs to remain dead, and all his secrets buried with him. Your friend Grant will continue to serve time. He'll stay in the county jail, where he'll be treated right."

"Holy shit!" Porter exclaimed. "Those bastards want to buy my testimony?"

"You're finally tuning in. That's good, because, yes, they literally do. In return, Grant's wife and kids will be provided for. He's been approached, informed if you like, and has chosen the path of least resistance for kith and kin. He asks the same of you."

"What! Lie—perjure myself?" he shouted, incredulously.

"No—you're simply going to answer the questions asked of you, in mono-syllables, without fanciful observation and detail."

Porter's mind began to churn. He was about to speak, to say, "What if," or "Why," or "Blah, blah, blah." He was about to shout out at the indignity of it all.

Malachi laughed, watching him squirm, as if he knew what Porter was thinking. Truth be told, he did. "There is no, 'What if,' Porter. There are no, 'What are my choices,' either," he laughed. "In fact, there is no higher ground to climb to. You're on a very low hill to begin with, as far as hills go, and once you get up there to the top, there's really not much to see. Every single person involved with the debacle up there has met an end— just or worthy or not—for their part in it."

"And what about Crowe?" Porter asked.

"Especially him. He's on a clock, I'd chance to say, at the very least," replied Malachi. "But from another perspective, he really did one and all a big favor. The people Sterling betrayed are not very nice. They're doing business with the new chancellor of Germany—that man, Hitler—have you read *Mein Kampf*, Porter?" Malachi raised a brow. "Do that and you'll come to know—how easily they would have dealt with the likes of Sterling."

Porter buried his face in his hands, and then ran his hands through his hair. "Did Redfern send you here to tell me that?" he asked, wearily. "Mrs. Banks?"

Malachi shook his head, "No, they did not. It's implied, like everything in this business. They don't like it, but they understand how the game is played. It's a twilight world, Porter. There is no darkness and there's even less light. Every choice a Faustian bargain."

"A Faustian bargain?" Porter sat back and wondered. If true, what was his—and with whom? Was it death itself? Suddenly, in his mind's eye, the haunting, ghastly specter of Scoop Comeau appeared, but quickly dissolved into the man he had known. Was that part of the bargain? To be spared? How many times? The baseball could have killed him—the gangster in Boston was going to kill him—the motorcar should have killed him—Thompson and Sterling wanted to kill him—and he surely would have drowned, but for a gentle tug. He remembered the conversation with Jeffah that Hallowe'en day at Leo's—how they wondered where all the angels had gone? His eye fell on the postcard. He wanted her. Viola. Madam Luna. The gypsy woman. How right she was—Viola saw her there, hovering, watching over him, all along. But not to harm him, but save him … and at every turn protect him. On the Glebe Road, he heard her name in a breeze, a herald almost, in his head. He hears it still, and sees her there, standing across from him—a vision of seduction—of infinite wisdom and beauty—*Josefa*—his Guardian Angel of Death.

"Why? For what *end*, Malachi?" Porter finally whispered.

"Ha!" Malachi flashed a grin. "That's it, isn't it? Why? What deal was made and by whom? Who the hell made it? Who made that call?" Malachi picked up his whiskey, studied it in the light, and downed the last of it. "Yes, to *what* end, Porter." He set the glass on the desk gently. "That you and I are here—laughing and drinking and breathing—in spite of *everything*—living on borrowed time."

About the Author

John Derhak is a writer, storyteller, and historian. His general interests and inspirations include but are not limited to: P.T. Barnum as philosopher-king. History of plumbing. A new pen. The aurora borealis. Ursa Major. The Perseid meteor shower. Popular uprisings. Baseball. Fine red wine. Slow burning cigars. Sons. Generations. Family. Friends. Imagination. Astral projection. The Czech Republic. Common Sense. Mysterious forests. Moose. Prime numbers. Pooches. Czech Lagers. Gnarly Barley Ale. Aureoles. Mountains. Clean water. The Woods of Maine. Northern New England. The urban jungle. Florida winters. Guitar. moe., jazz, bluegrass, the standards, and rock 'n roll. Grilled asparagus. All the buzz about onomatopoeia. The Nutfield Derelict Association, aka, the NDA. The Center for Cultural Asylum on Little Averill Pond. Observations. The higher stages of the barbarian culture. Hope.

In addition to *The Guardian Angel of Death*, he is author of *The Bones of Lazarus* (2012), *Chill Your Cockles* (2009), and *Tales from the moe.Republic* (2007).

Acknowledgements

Truth be told, *The Guardian Angel of Death* was over a decade in the making. I first conceived it from a single line in "Requiem For the Bird Man," the story of Porter Gibson "Digit" that would end up as one of the longer tales in *Tales From the moe.Republic*. All about meeting a gypsy woman and living on borrowed time, that line steamrolled into a story before I finished *Tales*, and continued to roll as I wrote numerous other short stories, published and unpublished, and another novel. I was never in a rush, it seems, but I never did intend for it to go on this long, either. Ten years later, I'm happy to share another one of Porter Gibson "Digit's" tales.

There's a substantial body of work on: the Great Depression, Prohibition and the subsequent smuggling operations that ran from the French territory of Saint Pierre and Miquelon, through Canada and into the US, early 20th Century technology and communication, Czech industries, espionage, gangsters, the tragedy of the Lusitania, the 1916 Easter Rising, even what Halloween was like in the 1920s and 1930s, and so on and so forth. I used a variety of sources—journal articles, scholarly books, public documents, period newspapers, online libraries and museums, photographic archives, and documentaries, along with a few folk tales and anecdotal family yarns—to paint as accurate a picture of life in urban and rural northeast America of 1932 as I could conceive.

I couldn't have finished the book on my own. There was much help and inspiration along the way—from my family and many friends near and far—who have supported me in oh so many ways—to my years with moe.—many thanks to all. I thank Stephen King's Haven Foundation and the Carnegie Fund for Writers for their generous grants in my hour of need over the past couple years. I thank Signet Interational CEO Ernesto Letiziano for keeping the dream alive. To Joseph Vala, thank you for your long-time support. Thank you to my publisher, Jeffrey Zygmont, for putting this book out there and for his keen editorial eye and all his constructive feedback; and also Andrea Kolb for her feedback and editorial skills. This book is a better read because of them. Nevertheless, any lapses of premature senility, senseless blathering, and other such mistakes, are my own. Finally, to all of you who have kindly asked for more stories from me, I can't thank you enough for asking. This one is for you. I hope you enjoy it.

Other works
by
John Derhak

For more info about John or his books & stories, visit him anytime at moeRepublic.org

International Holdings, Inc.
Palm Beach, Florida

Advanced 3D
Visualization & Interaction
Technologies

Introducing a New Generation of Smart
Autostereoscopic Visualization Systems &
Smart Spatial Imaging Technology

Visionary, Cutting-Edge
Transdisciplinary R&D

At Signet, we start
from the future ...

www.SignetInternationalHoldings.com

www.ingramcontent.com/pod-product-compliance
Lightning Source LLC
Chambersburg PA
CBHW022157260626
47155CB00019B/3072